The Bomb Shelter

Books by Jon Talton

The David Mapstone Mysteries
Concrete Desert
Cactus Heart
Camelback Falls
Dry Heat
Arizona Dreams
South Phoenix Rules
The Night Detectives
High Country Nocturne
The Bomb Shelter

The Cincinnati Casebooks
The Pain Nurse
Powers of Arrest

Other Books
Deadline Man, a novel
A Brief History of Phoenix

The Bomb Shelter

A David Mapstone Mystery

Jon Talton

Poisoned Pen Press

Poisoned Pen
PRESS

First Edition 2018

10 9 8 7 6 5 4 3 2 1

Library of Congress Control Number: 2017946816

ISBN: 9781464209574 Hardcover
ISBN: 9781464209598 Trade Paperback
ISBN: 9781464209604 Ebook

Poisoned Pen Press
4014 N. Goldwater Blvd., #201
Scottsdale, AZ 85251
www.poisonedpenpress.com
info@poisonedpenpress.com

Printed in the United States of America

Once again, to Susan.
And to Jack August, Jr. (1954-2017),
gentleman, scholar, friend.

Chapter One

At 11:10 on the morning of Friday, June 2nd, 1978, Charles Page spun the platen knob of the Smith Corona Classic 12 typewriter on his desk at the Arizona State Capitol pressroom. It advanced a roll of gray newsprint that fed in from the back. He pecked out a short sentence and spun the nob again so the words were visible above the paper holder. They read:

Mark Reid, 11:30 a.m., Clarendon House.

Page slid a reporter's notebook in his back pocket, picked up his briefcase, and walked a block to his car. A mile away at the newspaper building, the presses were about to start their run, putting out his afternoon paper, the *Phoenix Gazette*. He didn't have a story in today's edition. The committee hearing he covered this morning hadn't produced news.

Outside, the temperature was already more than a hundred degrees, headed to a forecast high of 103. After stopping to make small talk with a state senator, he walked quickly across the plaza that separated the two chambers of the Legislature.

Page was a good-looking man, six-foot-two, still as slender at age forty-eight as he had been at twenty. His wavy hair was light brown, styled in an old-fashioned pompadour with more trendy sideburns. He favored leisure suits.

It couldn't have taken him more than five minutes to reach the parking lot, where his nine-year-old red GTO was parked in a space reserved for the press.

His mother and father called him Charlie. But when he flew for the Air Force in Korea, he gained the nickname Buzz. This had less to do with being a pilot of F-86 Saber fighter jets than the fact that his squadron already had two other men named Charlie. One stayed Charlie, the second became Chuck, and he was christened Buzz. Charlie and Chuck were later shot down in dogfights against Russian-piloted MiGs near the Yalu River, both killed. He survived fifty-six combat missions, came home, graduated with a journalism degree from the University of Missouri and, after working at some small papers, found his spot at the *Gazette*.

There he made a name writing stories on land fraud and organized crime. He regularly scooped the bigger morning paper, the *Arizona Republic*. Even though both newspapers were owned by the Pulliam family, each competed fiercely against the other. His success on the land-fraud beat and the other prominent stories he wrote earned him another nickname, "Front Page," from admiring colleagues. In recent years, he delved into RaceCo, a sports concession that ran the state's greyhound dog racing tracks and had connections to organized crime. And in 1975, he produced "Strangers Among Us," a five-day series of stories on the two hundred Mafia figures who had relocated to Phoenix in recent years. He named names, and how some were close to political leaders. It was a finalist for the Pulitzer Prize and enhanced Page's national standing among his peers.

He wore the acclaim lightly. Buzz was unassuming, a good listener who seemed shy outside his circle of friends who knew him for his loud laugh and practical jokes. This caused the targets of his investigations to underestimate him, which was an advantage. But the results he got made him enemies. All the years of going through documents and sitting at a typewriter also cost him his fighter pilot eyesight. As a result, he wore black, horn-rimmed glasses. Women liked him.

Then the bosses suddenly moved him to cover the Legislature. That had been a year ago. The demands of investigative reporting cost him his first marriage. People who didn't know him well believed he was happier to be out of the pressure cooker and the regular threatening phone calls and letters that came with his old beat. He stopped his ritual of putting scotch tape where the GTO's hood met the fender—if the tape was broken, someone might have tampered with the engine, even placed a bomb there. Or that was what he told his friends and colleagues.

In fact, he hated the change. He was mostly bored. Nor did the capitol job keep him out of controversy. When the governor named the wealthy rancher Freeman Burke, Sr., to the state Racing Commission in 1977, Page wrote several stories on Burke's unsavory past and how he had been the biggest contributor to the governor's campaign. The Legislature refused to approve Burke for the board that regulated, among other things, dog racing.

I would learn later that "Front Page" was quietly working on a project that would get him back as the *Gazette*'s top investigative reporter. The week before, he had run into a colleague at a grocery store. He told her he was wrapping up "the story that will bring it all together, blow the lid off this town, finally." Page was not given to bragging or superlatives. I would also learn that he was keeping a sheaf of sensitive material, too hot to keep in his desk at the capitol bureau or in the *Gazette* newsroom, much less unattended in his apartment. He moved it around, to hiding places only he knew.

He was on his way to meet a source at the Clarendon House Hotel in Midtown Phoenix, a couple of blocks north of Park Central shopping center. Buzz Page didn't know what to make of Mark Reid. He was cautious. Reid was an enforcer for his old nemesis, Ned Warren. Page's stories helped put Warren in prison on multiple counts of land fraud and bribery. This after years of well-documented crimes and foot-dragging by the County Attorney. Another red flag was that Reid hung out at the dog tracks. Page was convinced that pressure and threats from RaceCo had forced his bosses to send him to the Siberia of the capitol bureau.

On the other hand, Reid promised Page a piece of information that was critical to his big story. If he never talked to riffraff, he wouldn't have half as many sources.

Their relationship went back two weeks, when a source of Page's at the courts connected him with Reid. They met at The Islands, a bar on Seventh Street in Uptown. Reid said he had evidence that would connect organized crime and RaceCo to prominent local leaders: Congressman Sam Steiger, Senator Barry Goldwater, and Harry Rosenzweig, a long-time Republican boss and businessman. Page was skeptical. Steiger had been a good source on his land-fraud stories. Goldwater had always been friendly.

But his gut told him to see what Reid had to say. That meeting provided little. Reid said he needed time. He would contact the reporter when a man from Los Angeles visited. The mystery man had the details Reid had dangled.

More than that, Reid seemed clued in when Page asked vague questions about his current story. Not enough to show his hand, but to elicit more information from Reid than the reporter gave away. The strand seemed promising.

The call came that morning. "Meet me at the Clarendon."

Page probably avoided the straight shot north. That held too many bad memories. Not long before, his girlfriend Cindy had been killed by a train at the railroad crossing west of the six-points of Grand Avenue, Nineteenth Avenue, and McDowell Road. Friends said he stayed away from that intersection as if it were radioactive. They didn't know how he continued to work, he was so grief stricken over her death.

Instead, he went east to downtown, ran a quick errand, and then, back in the car, drove north on Third Avenue. It was a little more than a mile and a half to the Clarendon, through the old residential neighborhoods that were declining—at some point the Papago Freeway was coming through. Midtown, with its new high-rises along Central Avenue and busy Park Central mall, was vibrant, the place to be. Sometimes Page went to the Playboy Club, drank bourbon on the rocks and looked out at the lights of the city. More often, he had lunch at the Phoenix Press Club. Unless it was necessary to meet a source, he tended to stay away from the nearby bars where the mobsters and lawyers drank.

Around 11:30 a.m., Page swung the GTO into the second line of spaces behind the hotel and parked. It was an unshaded surface lot like most of those in Phoenix, no tree to keep the car cool as with his capitol parking spot, but nothing could be done. The asphalt lagoon was empty of people and only about one-third full of cars. No sign of Reid. The lunch crowd had yet to arrive.

Reid wasn't inside, either.

Page waited inside the lobby for fifteen minutes and then heard his name being called from the front desk. He picked up the white courtesy phone and heard Mark Reid's voice.

"The meeting's off for today," Reid said. "The guy from LA chickened out. Maybe I can talk him into it later."

"Well, thanks for calling at least. Let me know if he changes his mind."

Page put the phone down and walked back out into the heat. There was time to have lunch at the Press Club. He slid into the GTO, started the car, and backed out. The car rolled fifteen feet in reverse when the explosion came. It ripped upward, slightly ahead of the driver's seat, blowing out the glass of the driver's side window.

The sharp sound could be heard a mile away. The explosion shattered all the windows on the Clarendon that faced the parking lot. Hubcaps and other auto parts were strewn across the asphalt, while a blue haze hung over the area. Witnesses recalled the blood, so much blood, a man calling, "Help me, help me!" and a hunk of bloodied flesh the size of a baseball lying twenty feet from the car.

Within ten minutes, fire trucks arrived, then an ambulance. Page was still conscious as they pulled him out and carefully placed him on a stretcher. His body below the waist was a mangle of burns and smashed bones in a soup of blood. His left arm was barely attached to his shoulder. His face was gray with ash and shock. His eyes were wide and unfocused. The EMTs and firefighters applied large trauma dressings and tried to stanch the bleeding.

St. Joseph's Hospital was less than a half-mile away. As the they laid him flat, trying to keep his limbs together, he screamed in pain. But words came, too, through clenched teeth. He fought to get every syllable out.

"They finally got me," he gasped. Then louder: "Reid, Mafia, RaceCo! Find Mark Reid..."

Then he passed out. But even unconscious, he twitched and moaned.

Later, a veteran Phoenix detective would say he had never seen a human being who suffered so much.

They finally got me. Reid, Mafia, RaceCo! Find Mark Reid.

Those were the last words he spoke.

Chapter Two

The weather is strange and a second lock is being installed on my office door.

"Give me an hour, at least," the maintenance guy said. "County's very picky about these doors, everything in the building, see? It's historic. Plus, there's other stuff...."

I asked him why I needed another lock. What was the "other stuff"?

"Work order." He waved a piece of paper at me, as if that explained anything. When I didn't take it, he turned to his tools, stored in a rolling rig like a suitcase.

I did feel proprietary about my space, even though the taxpayers owned it. My office in the 1929 Maricopa County Courthouse was not the expansive room I had taken over when I first came back to the Sheriff's Office. In those days, the building was largely empty, and I rather liked it that way, communing with the ghosts of old Phoenix a floor below the former jail. Among the former inmates: Ernesto Miranda.

When the county began an extensive remodeling a few years ago, the building was reclaimed and my old office became a courtroom. The replacement was decent, a fourth-floor room at the end of long mahogany hallway lit by hanging period lamps. It offered spacious ceilings and tall windows overlooking First Avenue. The door was crowned with a transom. I furnished it with a desk and swivel chair, two straight-backed chairs in front, and a six-foot-long lawyer's table, all in dark cherry wood fitting the period. I added bookshelves, file cabinets, a small refrigerator, and a Bose speaker. The furniture was aged and dinged, scrounged from county storage, but it fit and I liked it. On one wall, I had a large combination cork-board and white board. And I had brought back my photograph of Sheriff Carl Hayden from 1909, placing it squarely behind my desk. I could turn and look at him when I needed inspiration. Outside the door was a placard that read:

DEPUTY DAVID MAPSTONE
Sheriff's Office Historian
Mike Peralta, Sheriff

Now I left the workman to his work order and singing drill. The hall opened onto the atrium and I took the curving staircase down, appreciating the Spanish tile, chandeliers, and carved ceilings, polished and restored to their original grandeur. That was when Phoenix had a population of forty-eight thousand, and this was one of the most impressive results from a decade of building—a combination county courthouse and Phoenix City Hall. The staircase, like its companion on the opposite side of the tall atrium, rose against the walls like a necklace. When I reached the second floor, looking down into the ornate lobby, I saw a man with horns waiting to go through the metal detectors. Yes, horns. He was red. Red sleeveless T-shirt, reddish tint to his tan.

It wasn't supposed to be this obvious. I remembered *Broadcast News*. The devil would be attractive, nice, and helpful, dress well like William Hurt. Great movie, sad scene. And Baudelaire said the greatest trick the devil ever pulled was convincing the world he doesn't exist. But subtlety didn't play in Phoenix.

I studied the man. The horns protruded from beneath his shaved scalp, one on each side. Maybe they were a birth defect or perhaps they had been implanted from the same artist who had inked his muscled-up right arm. Another elaborate tat snaked up from inside the shirt onto his neck. Maybe he was the chief executive for a tech startup or maybe he was a defendant who had somehow made bail. One never knew today. I didn't think he was an over-enthusiastic Sun Devils fan.

But the sight made me stop and tense. He was third in a line of eight people, waiting to go through the metal detectors. Bouncing on the balls of his feet, he kept nervously looking around. But he didn't think to look up, so he didn't see me.

Courthouse shootings were well established on the menu of national mayhem and I wondered if it was about to be our time. He wasn't wearing a trench coat concealing a shotgun or an assault rifle, nothing that obvious. But would we be the mass shooting of the week? The deputies at the security checkpoint were watching him, too. I couldn't see his left arm and hand. He seemed to be deliberately keeping them at his side, out of the deputies' sight. Or he might have a gun tucked behind him in his waistband. If things went sideways, I could probably get a good aim point. But the black, wrought-iron railing provided no cover. I would get one chance to drop him. I slowed my breathing but could feel my heart thudding and my mouth was dry.

Cops under stress were always in danger of tunnel vision, only seeing the threat immediately in front of them. He might have been a distraction. I scanned the lobby inside the front doors and the people waiting in line to get in the building. The woman behind him looked iffy, torn jeans and a zip-up hoodie. She swung down a backpack and reached inside. I was about to crouch and reach for my weapon when her hand came out and it only held an ID card on a lanyard, which she slipped over her hoodie. A county employee.

A deputy stepped forward and stopped the reddish man before he went through the metal detector. He ran a wand over each horn. The nervous head finally looked up and gave me a prison-yard glare. A dyed blond scraggly goatee hung from his chin like a tumbleweed. I stared back.

These days, I looked like the freak. No ink-slinger had touched my skin. I was wearing a navy pinstripe suit, starched white dress shirt, and the Ben Silver Old Albanians regimental tie, that one a gift from Lindsey this past Christmas. I was a living anachronism. Virginia Woolf said that "on or about December 1910, human character changed." I couldn't pinpoint a date. Maybe it was September 11th, 2001, or the presidential election of 2016, or when smartphones ate an entire generation's brain, when the joylessness of post-modern American life locked into place. But I felt the same, despite my historian training that nothing was new under the sun. Human character had changed, at least for Americans.

The suitcoat was cut roomy, so he couldn't see my semi-automatic pistol. I had reluctantly put my Colt Python .357 magnum revolver in storage at home. It was too damned heavy. The new gun, a Springfield Armory XD, was small enough to fit in my hand or pocket, although I kept it in a Galco Summer Comfort holster on my belt. A gift from the demand generated by the "concealed-carry movement." I had abandoned my fear of a semi-auto jamming at the wrong moment. Chambered for .45 caliber, the new pistol had as much stopping power as the big Colt plus more ammo: nine rounds in the magazine and one in the chamber. He also couldn't detect the Smith & Wesson Airweight .38 revolver, strapped in an ankle holster, my backup gun. The suitcoat concealed the gold deputy's star on my belt, too. Accessories make the man, but to anyone looking up, I appeared to be an overly formal lawyer

The horned man stepped through the metal detector without incident. The devil was in the building. I took the last flight of stairs and walked through the lobby.

Outside, it was in the high seventies. In Phoenix. The first week of June. If this was climate change, count me in. Unfortunately, the weather forecast was for an unseasonably warm 110 degrees or hotter later in the week.

I enjoyed being outside while I could, sitting on the ledge of the Jack Swilling fountain and listening to the trickle of water. I had a stack of unsolved homicides on my desk, each case compiled in the binders called murder books. I could have brought one. Instead, I unfolded the *Arizona Republic* and scanned the newspaper. There was less and less to it, short articles, reporters with millennial first names, journalists that I didn't know. Things were so crazy in the nation and world, it was painful to read the paper now. Things in Phoenix seemed normal.

Over in Maryvale, seven killings were linked to the same perpetrator. Phoenix PD was reluctant to say they had another serial killer. A couple in the San Tan area, southeast of Phoenix, had been arrested for abandoning their baby while they played Pokemon Go. An angry husband in Glendale burned down his house, with his wife and baby inside.

Another day in paradise.

Next I read a story about an event last night to commemorate the fortieth anniversary of the car-bombing death of *Phoenix Gazette* reporter Charles Page. This made me feel old. I couldn't believe it had been forty years. The *Gazette* was the afternoon newspaper with a focus on the city. Page was a famous investigative reporter. The assassination briefly exposed the city's extensive underworld. Then life went on. Millions more people came from the Midwest and probably few had heard of the Page murder.

I wondered if the case were still open.

Chapter Three

Walking across Washington Street and going a block east, I caught a northbound light-rail train. I turned the *Republic* inside and read more about the Page anniversary. Nobody else on the train was reading a newspaper. On our block, Lindsey and I were one of only two families that subscribed. Every morning, the local paper and the *New York Times* arrived on our doorstep. We were dinosaurs in the "post-fact" age. Most people got their "news" from social media, or so I had read. Even the Sheriff's Office had Facebook and Twitter accounts.

The calling that Charles Page had given his life for was in deep trouble. Pick your causes: Craig's List taking advertising, a dumbed-down society, management chasing the flavor of the week. His own paper, *The Phoenix Gazette*, had closed in 1997. But when Page was alive and for years afterward, newspapers were more than media. They were powerful forces in every city. This was one reason the Page bombing was so shocking at the time. It was an attack on the public. That was then. Now it was hard to even find a *Republic* newsrack.

A quick mile-and-a-half later, I stepped off at the Encanto station. Another two blocks and I was home for lunch with Lindsey in our oasis, the Spanish colonial revival house built in 1924 with its shady canopy of mature palm trees, Texas mesquites, and ficus.

We ate chicken Caesar salads and talked about neighborhood gossip she had picked up on her morning walk with three friends who lived on Cypress and Holly streets. She updated me on her gardens. Soon the heat would overwhelm them. But she was tending the last of the tomatoes, as well as lantana, plumbago, and Mexican bird of paradise in the shady interior courtyard. We talked about some of the articles she had read from publications on what we dubbed our Sanity Table: *Tin House*, the *Paris Review*, and the *New York Review of Books*. She had a *New York Times* science section folded open to a story with the headline, "Dark Matter's Deep Reach" and a pen atop a Moleskine notebook.

I momentarily envied her time at home to read anything she wished, but I knew it was a good thing. It was also deeply, satisfyingly subversive that my love, the computer nerd, enjoyed reading on paper. As a child, her mother would scold her, "Get your nose out of that book and go outside and play." These months when she had read ever more fiction, poetry, criticism, and even some of my five-pound "history porn," had only deepened her knowledge. I was so proud of her. I had definitely married up.

My reading time was extensive, but during the day it almost always involved violent death, people at their worst—and it wasn't fiction. I didn't tell her about the locksmith or the devil. I don't know why.

"Sharon Peralta brought me a flat of zinnias from Whitfill's," she said. "I still miss Baker's. That was my favorite nursery."

"Another peace offering?" I finished a can of Diet Coke.

"There's no need, Dave," Lindsey said. "I don't remember anything. I'm doing fine. She shouldn't feel guilty. She said she and Mike were binge-watching the Poirot series on Apple TV. We should do that."

The "anything" she didn't remember was being shot and nearly killed.

When I didn't respond, she said, "You look very dapper. How's the return going?"

"It's almost as if I never left."

"Has *El Jefe* loaded you down with cases, History Shamus?" *El Jefe* was her private nickname for Sheriff Peralta.

I nodded. Twenty-five open-unsolved. The oldest was from 1938 and the newest happened in 1969. This seemed to please her and I knew why. They were musty and forgotten.

"That should keep you busy but safe." Then she straightened her shoulders and lowered her voice to a growl. "Mapstone, progress! Why the hell do you ride the trolley, Mapstone?"

I laughed. It was a good impersonation.

I said, "Be careful. Say his name and he will appear."

Chapter Four

A little more than an hour later, I returned to the courthouse. The maintenance man had left an envelope with my name on it at the downstairs security desk. Inside was one key, only one. I slipped it on my keyring, thought about walking up to the fourth floor, and took the elevator instead.

I still didn't understand the need for the deadbolt lock. The building was already very secure. And half of the mahogany door was frosted, pebbled glass. Anyone who really wanted in could simply break the glass.

The door was unlocked.

Inside, the office looked different. Several cardboard file boxes that hadn't been there this morning sat in a neat row on the lawyer's table. A small white electronic device was installed in the upper right corner of the wall. And Sheriff Mike Peralta was sitting behind my desk, impatiently swinging his bulk back and forth in my chair. He wore his dress uniform, unusual because he usually preferred an expensive suit and a Hermès tie. The uniform was black, not the venerable tan-and-brown—a holdover of the change from made by his short-lived predecessor. Four gold stars gleamed on each collar. His handsome face seemed barely changed by the years. The only indication time had passed were two vertical furrows above and between his eyes that turned into deep defiles when he frowned, as he now did.

His voice rumbled. "Drinking at Bitter and Twisted?"

I studied his face as I eased into one of the straight-backed chairs in front of the desk. Aside from the frown lines, his features were impassive as usual. You could never tell if he was serious.

"Lunch with Lindsey."

"How is she?"

I said she was fine.

"Sharon was going to stop by this morning."

"So I heard."

He said, "We need to get her back here."

I didn't take the bait. "What brings you here from your Starship?"

"I like the new headquarters," he said. "Even though you keep saying it looks like..."

"An alien spaceship mated with a strip mall. So very Arizona."

He raised his right index finger. "We held an architectural competition..."

"You should have picked Will Bruder's design."

He shrugged. "Everybody's a critic. Well, as long as it's not an *illegal*-alien starship. Then I'll be in trouble again."

The right edge of his lips came up an eighth of an inch, an expression of raucous mirth for Mike Peralta.

He stopped swinging and aimed his head at me, but looked into the far beyond. "Who do you think murdered Charles Page?"

"The courts said it was Mark Wayne Reid," I said. "He planted the bomb, dynamite, under Page's car. Then he made a deal and implicated his co-conspirators. Dick Kemperton, who detonated the device. And Darren Howard paid them to do it."

"Very good." Now his eyes focused on me. "But who really killed him?"

"Who ordered the hit? The conventional wisdom was Freeman Burke."

"Richest man in the Valley," he interposed.

"Right. But they could never prove it. There were sleazy lawyers, too. The land-fraud and dog-track connections. Behind all that, organized crime. Lots of open questions."

He nodded. "Exactly. So *why* was Charles Page killed?"

I shrugged. "The frontier justice theory held that it was revenge for the articles he wrote that got Freeman Burke kicked off the Racing Commission. Burke either ordered the killing or one of his minions took the hint. Maybe Howard did it as a favor. Burke helped him get his start as a developer. Another theory is payback for something Page wrote about RaceCo or the mob." I thought about it. "None of them makes perfect sense. It used to be the made men never killed journalists or cops. Old-man Burke was so rich, why would he risk it? Darren Howard was a successful builder. He claimed he was innocent until the day he died."

"So, you don't know why Charles Page was murdered."

I sighed. "Does anybody? Are you on your way to give a fortieth anniversary speech?"

"I did that last night." He leaned forward. "It's interesting to me that you never asked to investigate this case. The only murder of an American journalist in the United States in modern times. Seems like it's your kind of case. Somebody knows the why."

I shifted in the chair. "It's a closed case and a Phoenix PD case."

"It was everybody's case. FBI, ATF, PPD. AG's Office. Still technically open."

His curiosity made me uneasy, gave me a feeling like the way the sky changes color before a bad dust storm.

I said it would be a tall order. The Page killing was the Cecil B. DeMille of homicide cases, with its colorful cast of dozens if not thousands. If anything, too much had already been written about it. In addition to the initial investigation came years of discovery during the appeals. Investigative Reporters and Editors, a journalism group, assembled a team of reporters from around the country that produced "The Phoenix Project," a series of articles that ran in newspapers nationwide. The *Gazette* and *Republic* and *New Times*, the alternative weekly, published plenty, too, not only in the immediate aftermath but for years after. I didn't know how I could bring something new to the story.

"You're a historian," Peralta said. "For years, you've been bitching about coming back to the Sheriff's Office, threatening to go to a university again." He snorted. "Good luck with that. Giving students 'trigger warnings' about offensive material—everything's offensive now. Giving them safe spaces. You'd last about a week before the complaints started coming in, too much Western Civ from Professor Mapstone and his white male privilege. Whitesplaining! If you cooked fajitas, you'd be guilty of appropriating my culture. Face it, you're a walking micro-aggression."

I kept quiet. He wasn't here to discuss academic freedom.

He held out his arms expansively. "Instead, you found the right home here. Using the historian's techniques to solve cold cases. You closed more than a hundred."

"One-hundred-seventeen."

"There you go." He stood and walked to the lawyer's table, running his large hand across the file boxes. "You have a chance to look into the most notorious crime in Arizona history as a serious historian. Hell, you might get a best-selling book out of this and you can blow this taco stand if you want."

I leaned around to study the five boxes. They were legal sized with removable lids on top, not new. Each bore red evidence seals on two sides where the lids connected to the boxes.

"Those are the case files?"

"Some of them. Copies, unfortunately. I've been collecting material over the years."

I asked him why, considering the Sheriff's Office wasn't involved.

"Hobby."

Now red alert was sounding in my brain. "You don't have hobbies."

I pushed it. I told him if this was really going to be approached as serious history, I would need to hire a research assistant, maybe two, grad students or post-docs at ASU. It would be fun pushing them around...er, mentoring them.

He shook his head. "Nobody else can know about this."

I took a shallow breath. "Why?"

"Because. I need an answer in three weeks. Who killed Buzz Page? And why?"

I almost leaped out of the chair. I wanted out of this conversation, out of this room. But Peralta stood between me and the door. I walked to the high widows. Outside, the lunch crowds at CityScape were thinning out. The streets and sidewalks, car rooftops and tops of baldheaded men glared brilliantly from the sunlight. The scene melted my anger enough to speak.

Quietly, I said, "Are you out of your fucking mind? How does a year sound? Nobody goes to Robert Caro and demands the next LBJ volume in three weeks!"

To be sure, I was no Robert Caro.

He walked over and stood beside me, draping a long arm around my shoulder. "I think you're intimidated." He was trying to get inside my head, something he was often very adept at doing.

"I'm not intimidated." Well, maybe I was. I said, "Let's set aside the timetable. Are you sure you really want to go there? Digging into this goes into the old Phoenix power structure and it could make enemies from the people you cozied up with to become sheriff again."

He turned and poked me in the shoulder, hard enough to set me back a step. "I didn't cozy up to anybody."

"Sure. I'm only saying they might not like what I find."

"If you want to be liked, become a firefighter. Otherwise, follow the evidence where it leads."

"But why? Why this case?"

His arm returned and tightened its grip on me. "It's so big and forty years later we still don't know all the answers. We don't know some of the most important ones. You think three scuzzballs did this with no help, no orders from someone higher? Who really ordered the hit? Freeman Burke, Sr.? Somebody else?"

"Burke's name is on buildings all over the state," I said. "He's still got friends alive who would want to protect his memory."

"Tough luck. Let the chips fall where they may."

When I didn't respond, he said, "So it's settled. You'll report only to me, as usual. Nobody else in the chain of command. I want daily updates."

He let the big-brother arm fall and headed for the door.

"Your hobby won't be enough," I said. "The Attorney General took over the case from the County Attorney. I need to see the entire thing. Where is it?"

"The official files are at the Arizona State Archives."

"I need to go there."

He adjusted his black-leather duty belt and leaned against the door. "Negative, Mapstone."

I asked him why not.

"There are three levels of classification over there for the Page case. Even for the lowest, the public files, the staff gives a courtesy call to DPS when somebody wants to examine them."

"I thought you and Milstead were friends?" Colonel Frank Milstead was director of the Arizona Department of Public Safety, the state troopers.

"We are. But this is off the grid, discreet, read me?"

I absently nodded. "What are the other two levels?"

"One requires a court order. And the last batch is sealed for fifty years from the conclusion of the last appeal."

"Fifty years? I've never heard of such a thing. How many other cases are under this degree of security?"

"Only this."

I took it all in. I didn't like it.

"Some detectives and lawyers involved are still alive. Reporters, too. I need to interview them before they die off. How do you want me to pull that off?"

"Very carefully. I want to know who you're going to talk to in advance. Then, go as a historian, not a deputy sheriff. You haven't been in the media since we came back. That's an advantage."

Again, he turned and got his hand on the doorknob.

"What aren't you telling me?"

His shoulders tensed and I went on.

"Remember, after the diamond heist went bad and Lindsey was shot? You know, that my-wife-almost-died whoopsie?" I heard the heat in my voice, the macro-aggression, and dialed it down. Rage, however justified, never got results from him. "After we went back to work? You agreed, no more secrets. No more hidden agendas."

"Goddamn you!" He swung around. "I've handed you a deal any other historian would jump at, and you think I have an agenda. Why?"

I folded my arms and said nothing. The silence gathered for several minutes. He glared at me a long time before returning to the desk chair and plopping down. He swung to face me.

"Last night was the fortieth anniversary event at the Clarendon." He spoke quietly, fiddling with his iPhone. It was strange to see this old-school lawman with an electronic device. "I was on the program to give a speech and I did. When it came time for questions, a reporter asked why I didn't reopen the case. I told her it was still open. She came back at me. Why didn't I do something to find the truth?"

"And you said you would."

"I should have kept my mouth shut." He sighed. "Anyway, an hour later, I received this text."

He handed me his phone. I read the message:

Leave the dead reporter case alone if you love your family. Your daughters and grandchildren will suffer for a long time before I kill them. Be smart. The sins of the past are unforgiven.

It was followed by a devil's head emoticon. The bubble was attached to a dialogue box labeled "unknown." The time was 9:45 p.m. yesterday.

"You checked on them?" His daughters lived in San Francisco.

"Of course." He took the phone back. "They started a month-long family vacation in Canada, so they'll be fine. They wanted Sharon and me to go."

"You should have done it. What about your digital forensic people? Can they trace this?"

He shook his head in frustration, not a strand of thick black hair moving. I wondered if he dyed it now. It had worked for Reagan.

"No way," he said. "I wouldn't know who to trust."

"We could message back. 'What are you afraid of?' Something to bring them out."

"Too risky."

I asked him how many people had this phone number. Given his tendency to showboat with the press and be available to a who's-who of judges, lawyers, and high-ranking cops—too many.

"Did this get in the media, or did only the people in the room hear it?"

"I didn't see it anywhere." After a pause, he laid it on me as a casual afterthought: "Lindsey could trace it."

"She hasn't even opened her computer for more than a year."

"You could ask. You're so stubborn. What does she do?"

"She gardens and cooks and reads."

"Sharon says she seems healthy."

"Is that her professional opinion?" I said. "Is she diagnosing when she visits?"

"Don't get so touchy. How can Lindsey be content with that?"

I worked to keep the anger out of my voice. "Lindsey is taking time for herself and the arrangement works well for both of us. We have a good life."

He shook his head, slid the iPhone into his pocket, and spread his hands. "Well, now you have it. No secrets, like we agreed. But I need your help. Forty years later, something is so explosive..."

"Pun intended?"

He looked momentarily befuddled, an uncharacteristic expression. Then, "Slip of the tongue."

"Does Sharon know?"

He shook his head.

"You're going to have to tell her."

Peralta grunted.

"What about your security detail? Where are they?"

"Nothing's going to keep me from walking around my downtown."

"Right, Peralta is the law."

"Not at all." His voice was mild. Two beats later: "I'm the law west of the Mazatzal Divide."

"Well, you'd better use that security detail. This isn't history. This is now. You said something that caused somebody to worry now, forty years later. Why?"

"That's what I want you to find out," he said. "Remember what Hemingway said, 'The past is never dead. It's not even past.'"

"Faulkner."

"What?"

"William Faulkner said that, not Hemingway."

He studied me with shrewd, sensitive eyes. "Don't pout, Mapstone. It's not becoming."

"It's not becoming to do a bait-and-switch. First, you play on my desire to write real history. Then it turns out you're in danger and the clock is ticking. Go look in a mirror and talk to me about what's becoming."

A vein throbbed on the side of his forehead and I knew

I was in perilous territory. Peralta ran the Sheriff's Office with a combination of charisma, an encyclopedic knowledge of law enforcement, and skillfully timed outbursts of temper. His deputies and civilian employees loved him. And they feared him. Even though he and I had been friends for many years, I stepped back and shut up. He had power over my paycheck and my and Lindsey's health insurance.

His forehead smoothed out and he said, "Did it ever occur to you that I was trying to protect you?"

When I didn't answer, he opened the door and was almost out when I said, "You had to do this?"

He turned. "This?"

"Yeah, the whole damned thing. Shutting down our PI business, going back to being sheriff, bringing me with you, all of it."

"Yes," he said, "I did. Make sure you lock up and use the alarm system every day. The instruction book is on the desk."

The door closed. The sound of his footsteps floated down the hall and then there was only silence. Until I heard my voice say, "Three weeks."

He had to do it.

We had a good thing going with the PI practice. Even though I was shocked that he lost the election amidst the anti-illegal immigrant fever, lost only because of his last name and unwillingness to play U.S. Border Patrol, I was more shocked that he seemed at peace, happy to be a private detective. His successor was young, good-looking, and Anglo. A former FBI agent from the Heartland named Chris Melton.

Yet it didn't take long for Melton to earn the nickname "Crisis Meltdown" and the Sheriff's Office went to hell. Melton did immigrant sweeps. But he also allowed response times to suffer, a slew of sex crimes to go un-investigated, and several prisoners to die in the Fourth Avenue Jail. Lawsuits cost the county millions of dollars. The feds went after him for racial profiling and civil rights violations. He tried to take on a federal judge. He lost and was held in criminal contempt. The Justice Department placed an independent monitor over the department. Then they found the child porn on Melton's office computer. He was forced to resign that day.

I should have known Peralta had a hidden agenda when we helped the Goldwater Institute, the most powerful right-wing advocacy outfit in the state, get out of an embarrassing blackmail jam involving one of its high-profile fellows. As PIs, we did other cases for the powerful, collecting, I now realized, favors. Peralta went back on the rubber-chicken circuit, focusing on Republican groups in the suburban areas around the county. Places with the well-off Anglos who voted.

With Melton out, Peralta announced he would run in the next election. Peralta was contrite in his speeches in places like Sun City, Peoria, and Chandler, saying he had been wrong not to take a hard line against illegal immigration. He promised that as sheriff his top priority would be protecting the border. He traveled to Salt Lake City to renew his dialogue with grandees of the Mormon Church, a critical force in the East Valley.

In the previous election, the party abandoned him, labeling him a RINO—"Republican In Name Only." His opponent's surrogates called him the "beaner sheriff," and that was the nicest of the epithets. "River nigger," "taco jockey," and of course "spic" were generously applied on social media, the intellectual STD of our time.

This election, the party welcomed him back. For one thing, the boosters thought it would be good for the state's battered national image to have a Mexican-American GOP elected official.

For the first time, he used his war record in his media campaign. Television ads showed him as an Army Ranger in Vietnam, his Bronze Star and two Purple Hearts. It played into his campaign slogan: "Battle Tested American."

The spectacle almost made me ill. He won the election with nearly seventy percent of the Anglo vote. All had been forgiven.

And me? I could have soldiered on as a solo PI at our office on Grand Avenue, with the restored neon sign from its days as a motel. But the big clients came our way because of Peralta. At my age, not too many other employment options were open. It had been years since I had been on a university faculty and in the time since, I had published almost nothing. The world was awash in history PhDs. An adjunct gig at ASU would have qualified us for food stamps. I wondered if I could sell my knowledge of mayhem to real-estate agents. That house five blocks away on Coronado Road was the site of an infamous 1961 murder. Dream on, Mapstone.

Our house was free-and-clear, but our savings were modest. Lindsey received several offers from tech companies in the Bay Area and Seattle: come work for us to strengthen our security. She was one of the most capable hackers in America. But she didn't want to do it. Hers was a profession where average programmers "aged-out" at thirty-five. To me, she was far from average, but this was her fear. She visited Amazon in Seattle where she was interviewed by a boss who was ten years younger and condescending. "She doesn't know what she doesn't know," Lindsey said. All her potential "teammates" were even younger. Lindsey held the special antipathy of a Gen Xer for millennials. I tried not to generalize about generations, but I was getting sick of being "oldsplained" to by millennials myself. And neither of us could bear to part with the home that had been passed down from my grandparents.

So I went back to the Sheriff's Office like a bad habit.

Chapter Five

That afternoon, I put Sinatra on the Bose speaker and started by pulling the yellowed *Phoenix Project* book from the shelf. It was a compilation of the newspaper stories published from 1978 and 1979 and I began to re-read it. If this were serious historical research, I was starting with a survey of the material already written.

Using the Internet, something that wasn't available to history majors when I was in graduate school, I searched for more, bookmarking a dozen of the most promising news articles. There were so many, but it was a start.

After an hour, when "In the Wee Small Hours" came around, my eyelids were getting heavy so I put the *Phoenix Project* in my briefcase to bring home. I would have to set aside my latest history porn—this was Lindsey's playful term for my favorite genre of pleasure reading—Sven Berckert's *Empire of Cotton*.

Next, I slit open the evidence seals on the first box, sneezing from the dust it released. The files were a mess. Nothing was in order. No index. It would take me a day at least to sort and catalogue the material in this box alone.

One large transcript caught my attention and I paged through it. The state gave bomber Mark Reid a deal: flip on your co-conspirators and avoid the gas chamber. So he did, in a long interview with Phoenix Detective Tom Goldstein. I was still reading when my desk phone trilled and I jumped. Solid, frosty David Mapstone.

It was a deputy downstairs. My four o'clock appointment, which I had forgotten about, was there waiting. The man needed clearance to come to my floor, and I said to send him up. The transcript went back into the box and I quickly put the top on and shut Frank off.

The man who walked in was young, African-American, amazingly free from tattoos, with a posture that conveyed authority. He was handsome, with high cheekbones and close-cropped hair, skin the color of rich dark chocolate. I put him in his early thirties.

During the pause in our private investigator practice, while Lindsey was healing from her gunshot wound, I had written a brief history of Phoenix for the Arcadia Press. It was probably a mistake. Too much work gathering photos and too little space for the narrative needed to even break the surface of Phoenix's fascinating past. It brought hardly any money and didn't open any doors to write further. But Malik Jones found me through this channel. We exchanged pleasantries and sat in the chairs in front of the desk. From a backpack, he produced an iPad and placed a small tape recorder on the desk.

"Do you mind if I tape the interview?

I didn't mind.

Aside from the visitor's badge, he wore a quarter-sized button on an otherwise snow white t-shirt, black background with white letters. It contained so much type—and I wanted to maintain eye contact—that only gradually did I take it in.

"Like I told you in the e-mail, I'm a doctoral student at

ASU," he said. "I'm pitching a dissertation entitled 'Race, Gender, and Crime in World War II-Era Phoenix.'"

I nodded as he praised my little book, one not worth praising, but there it was. Moments such as these were an enjoyable break from cold cases. I genuinely missed teaching and enjoyed helping any students and amateur historians who came calling.

"People here say Phoenix has no history, so I was amazed by your book," he said.

People are always amazed by Phoenix history. I suggested he read Phil VanderMeer's longer *Desert Visions and the Making of Phoenix*, but he'd come to interview me.

"So you're a deputy and a history PhD?"

"Perfectly trained for the New Economy," I said. "My undergrad minor was music."

He snort-laughed. "Tell me about it."

"Maybe we can open a history shop on Mill Avenue. Anyway, my specialty was the American Progressive era and the Great Depression."

"I'm not sure that's even taught most places nowadays," he said. "Like political history or military history. If I had my way, I would have specialized in military history. I deployed twice to Iraq. But my parents are here, getting older, so there was no way. I have to focus on gender and race at ASU. It doesn't help that I'm sis."

I left that last line alone as he continued.

"I did read your earlier book, *Rocky Hard Times*. How the Depression impacted the intermountain West. Impressive stuff."

Now I had it. The button said "Black lives matter," but was surrounded by other phrases: "Hands up, don't shoot," "I can't breathe." That was as much as I could put together between glances. So our conversation was fraught beneath the surface. I could read the tickertape running across his eyes: racist. No matter the academic niceties, he was a black man and I was a white cop. It didn't give me points that the only people I had ever shot were white.

I thanked him for the kind words about the Depression book. "That was my thesis. Defending it was about like getting a root canal without anesthesia." I was talking, but my brain was pulled back to the threatening text sent to Peralta.

Still, I spent the next hour talking to him about crime and segregation in old Phoenix. The red-light district in the black areas, rackets run by white criminals or city commissioners and overseen by some detectives. Payoffs also going to the city treasury. The Thanksgiving Day race riot during World War II. The infamous but little known killing of a black patrolman by a white detective and the patrolman's partner killing the man in revenge. Phoenix as a back office for the Mafia in Las Vegas. I suggested some archives and gave him a file to borrow that I had put together on the subject.

He taped our talk but also made notes on an iPad sitting on his lap.

"It seems as if Jews were prominent in Phoenix organized crime," he said. "Gus Greenbaum..."

"He was sent here by the Chicago Outfit to run their gambling wire. Then he was moved to Las Vegas to clean up one casino after another. 'Clean up' meaning ensuring the mob got its tax-free skim from the profits. When he skimmed too much for himself, they killed him." The murder happened only a few blocks from my house. "But there were plenty of Italian Mafiosi here, too.

"What about Barry Goldwater and Harry Rosenzweig?"

I told him this was speculation. The senator enjoyed

the company of an eclectic group, including mobsters. Rosenzweig, one of the downtown merchant princes and the head of the local Republican Party, might have been involved with the mob but nothing was ever proved.

I said, "The two ran as reformers on city council after the war. When Harry laid out the anti-vice platform, Barry supposedly said, 'It's all the things we like!' But they were elected and city government was cleaned up, at least on the surface."

He laughed but his face quickly turned serious. "Goldwater opposed the Civil Rights Act."

"He did. Later he said he regretted that."

"Do you believe him?"

"I suppose."

Jones' voice fell into a lower register. "By then it didn't matter, right? Goldwater opposed civil rights when the vote counted, when his support was needed. Now he's considered a statesman."

"Good point." Nothing more I could say would make it right.

"And Freeman Burke, Sr.? Was he involved in organized crime?"

I smoothly avoided looking at the file boxes on the lawyer's table. "Probably," I said. "But I don't know how much he would inform your dissertation. It might be worth chasing, though. Maybe his papers are available."

"According to my research, he owned a building in a black neighborhood used for prostitution," Malik Jones said. "I've heard he owned others."

"It wouldn't surprise me."

"When a complaint was made about the whorehouse, the Phoenix Police backed off. Didn't follow up."

"Because Burke put on some pressure?"

"That's my sense," he said. "Do you think he ordered the killing of Buzz Page, the newspaper reporter?"

I steadied every muscle to keep from showing how his question jolted me. I studied him anew. Did he have another agenda? Did anybody walk into my office with only one?

"It was never confirmed," I said.

Chapter Six

That night, after martinis and dinner, we sat in the living room looking out the big picture window onto Cypress Street. I told Lindsey about my afternoon, beginning with Malik Jones.

She said, "And you were pleased that someone born after 1984 was interested in history."

I nodded. "He said he was sis. This came out of nowhere. It doesn't matter to me. I didn't think it was politically correct to call yourself a sissy."

"It's C-I-S, Dave." She laughed into the high ceiling. "As in, cisgender. So he identifies with the equipment he was born with. As opposed to, say, transgender."

I felt my face warm. I felt like an idiot. "Who knows how many years these terms incubated in academia before they broke into the mainstream?"

"You come from a different century, Dave."

"A different millennium."

"Me, too. Nobody cares about us Gen Xers now, and everything is the fault of you baby boomers."

"Hey, the boomers Peralta's age got drugs, sex, and rock 'n' roll, secure jobs, and pensions. My group got disco and 401(k)s and 'gigs' instead of jobs."

After we laughed, I told her about being assigned the Page case.

She is younger than me so she didn't know about the killing until she read the anniversary story in the *Arizona Republic*. It sounded interesting, she said. At first, I kept my misgivings to myself, but she read me, as she always did. I told her about the text message Peralta had received after his off-hand comment on reopening the case.

"Had he traced it?"

I shook my head. "He's afraid to try. Maybe he's being paranoid."

"Just because you're paranoid doesn't mean somebody's not out to get you. That it mentioned his family is creepy." She slowly shook her head. Then, "I could do it."

"I know, and he wants you back." I stroked her straight dark hair. "I want you safe. I never want you to be hurt again."

She nodded slowly. No one knew the difficulty of her long recovery after the shooting more than she.

"He's such a son of a bitch," I said.

That familiar ironic smile played across her face. "You're only now reaching this conclusion, Dave?"

She took my hand and led me to the bedroom as we dropped a trail of clothes.

Not for the first time since she came home from the hospital, she said, "You're not going to hurt me, Dave." So we had fun. Skin on skin. Breath on skin. Somehow we had solved the riddle of romance and made a good marriage, if not without mistakes. Somehow we had kept the lust. Yet I had the luck to marry my best friend. I didn't take any of it for granted.

Afterward, as she lay sleeping, the room was bathed in bluish light from the streetlamp mid-block on Cypress.

I lightly touched her back and listened to the old house breathing.

Peralta was right when he said I was intimidated. Why had I never asked to look into the Page case? The truth was, I had more and more approached my open-unsolved cases as a detective, not as a historian. I was rustier in the academic skills than I cared to admit.

Now I regretted that I wouldn't have enough time to delve deeply into an American crime story that had enormous notoriety in its day—and retell it for today's audience, with new resonance. I could do this. Our knowledge of the past was being expanded, revised, and argued every day. Historians were even giving Genghis Khan a pleasing facelift.

Cops and historians shared similarities but they were also divided by important differences. Both investigated and assembled facts. Too often cops followed the most promising avenue—a majority of people were killed by those they knew, show me a dead woman and I'll immediately suspect her boyfriend or husband and try to make the case. This could carry risk—that tunnel vision. Often the obvious suspect really was guilty. Sometimes crime surprised.

Science had revolutionized detective work, especially with DNA and advances in evaluating trace evidence such as fibers and the chemical composition of, say, a bomb. None of this had been around when Charles Page was killed. Still, forensic science had its limits. The accuracy of so-called feature comparison, such as matching bite marks, was the subject of fierce scientific debate.

Then the facts had to stand the test of being evidence that could convince a jury beyond a reasonable doubt. Sometimes this failed. When the actor Bob Crane was murdered in Scottsdale in 1978, it seemed a mystery to the public. But the cops had a suspect almost immediately plus a kinky sex story. Yet they could never make a successful case, even though it finally went to trial.

Historians were allowed to employ more open minds than most detectives, or so I told myself. Many detectives followed the first clues, the obvious, to build a case toward arrest and conviction. Case clearance was everything. Historians thrived on the discovery of new material and fresh angles, uncovering a past their predecessors had missed. These attributes had helped me clear some cases that had kept others at dead ends for years. I told myself that one, too. Peralta hadn't kept me on merely out of friendship or pity or because I was simply a decent investigator, had he? Such were the self-doubts of blue-lit rooms, even with a leggy beauty lying naked beside me.

The best historians, serious scholars, enjoyed the luxury of time—no boss was on your back to solve the case—and of perspective, not merely the first leads and clues. Time lets things gel. If you were lucky, archives were opened, letters and diaries and documents discovered. You didn't have to convince a jury, only weather peer review. But in the history business, you also needed citations. Primary sources, vetted for their biases. As my doctoral adviser said, if you didn't have "the cites," something might as well never have happened.

Historians were judge, jury, and executioner. Three weeks allowed no time for any of this.

When I was awarded my PhD, I looked forward to a very different life than this, one of teaching and serious scholarship. I dreamed of writing best-sellers that would break important new ground. I lingered in bookstores and thought about the reviews I might get in the *New York*

Times: "A compelling and extraordinary story, beautifully researched, and elegantly told." Unfortunately, while I was a very good teacher and lecturer, I wrote almost nothing. My panic attacks—for years, I didn't even realize that was what they were—made it difficult to sit alone and write for hours. And without publishing, I perished before the tenure committee.

A car drove down Cypress without slowing.

The intrusion redirected my thoughts to the troubling three levels of access to the real case files at the state archives. I could understand the first two. A courtesy call to DPS would weed out serious researchers from sensationalists. And the second level likely covered such materials as privileged conversations between lawyers and clients, thus the need for a court order.

But the deepest? Sealed for fifty years after 1993 when the last appeal was handed down. It wasn't as if we were dealing with national security issues. British intelligence kept Ultra, the famous top-secret code-breaking operation, sealed for twenty-nine years after World War II. Here, we were looking at a half century. What was in those files that was considered so dangerous that it had to be kept out of the public realm so long?

This was not an academic issue. Peralta had received an actionable threat.

I knew he got menacing correspondence all the time. In his earlier terms as sheriff, he would get a letter once a week from a woman in Laveen, several pages, all different sizes and stocks of paper, tiny handwriting on every millimeter of empty space. She wrote of conspiracies and space abductions and how Peralta was really part of the one-world government, how voices told her to kill him. She was eventually committed to the state hospital.

She was relatively mild by comparison to some correspondents, especially as the anti-Hispanic fervor came blasting out in the late 2000s. E-mail, comments on the newspaper website, and social media had freed many people of any constraints. And, of course, there were always the courtroom outbursts promising revenge, and even a few threats that came from released convicts. But the latest seemed different, more sinister, and not merely because it had come via text message to his personal phone.

I decided to use more than the historian's craft. Before leaving the courthouse that day, I had called the Hotel Clarendon, asked for a list of attendees at the fortieth anniversary, and was promised an e-mail of names tomorrow. I would run the names through the system, see if any had records, warrants, or histories of their own with the sheriff. Peralta didn't need to know about this, so I told them to send it to my Gmail address. I understood his demand for discretion. But I also didn't want to miss a low-hanging fruit that might lead us to the source of potential danger quickly.

After an hour of brooding, I finally stiffened my spine to the work ahead. "Dave." Lindsey whispered it, in case I was asleep.

"I'm here."

"I want to help. Have Peralta bring the phone by tomorrow afternoon, so I can have a look."

I started to speak, but she put a slender finger on my lips. "I'll be fine. Don't worry."

Chapter Seven

The next morning, I settled into a chair in the living room and continued reading the *Phoenix Project*. Lindsey bivouacked at the desk in the study, put on her sexy oval tortoise-shell glasses, and downloaded a year's worth of updates to her souped-up MacBook Pro. Every few minutes, she let loose with a profanity.

The book was a compilation of the stories written by forty reporters and editors from twenty-three newspapers around the country. They descended on the city after the Page murder and, from rooms at the Hotel Adams downtown, proceeded to give Arizona a journalistic colonoscopy.

I hadn't read this material in many years. It reminded me that the primary mission was to send a message: If you attack one of us, you attack us all and we will get payback. This was back in the day when owning a newspaper was a license to print money. Investigative journalism was at the height of its glamour after Woodward and Bernstein brought down a corrupt president.

The stories delved into the city's and state's many dark crevices, including organized crime, land fraud, and their connection to the local power structure. Some wandered into other seamy terrain. For example, a long story detailed the illegal immigrants living in squalid conditions working on the vast citrus operation called Arrowhead Ranch. Barry Goldwater's brother Robert and the Martori family owned it.

Other articles examined land-fraud king Ned Warren, who evaded prison for years, and the whiff of the mob that trailed leading citizens, such as the Goldwater brothers, developer Del Webb, Harry Rosenzweig, and, especially, Freeman Burke, Sr.

The reporting exposed a Phoenix much at odds with the chamber of commerce image of a new, sparkling city of resorts, golf courses, and good honest Westerners. But much of this had long been known locally and even previously reported by the *Republic* and *Gazette*, including by Buzz Page. Some of the sourcing seemed sketchy—it wouldn't pass muster with a grand jury or even for a master's thesis at a reputable university. This was perhaps why the Pulliam newspapers refused to run it, although more malevolent theories existed for their spiking the stories. *New Times* and the Tucson paper did run them.

The biggest frustration was that the reporters didn't close the deal. They didn't prove conclusively who ordered the bombing of Buzz Page or why.

Peralta arrived at 12:01, "the afternoon," almost on the dot, wearing a summer suit and a blue tie with turquoise swans on it. He stomped across the front path, his torso tilted slightly forward in that bull-ready-to-charge posture. Through the picture window, I also saw a black SUV with two plainclothes deputies inside.

The sheriff carried a bag full of Mexican food from Carolina's in the barrio. He gave Lindsey a long hug.

"You look fabulous," he said. "The other night when

Sharon and I were watching an old *Law and Order*, I said, 'Lindsey looks exactly like Jill Hennessy, only better!'"

There was a resemblance, now that I thought about it, although Lindsey had blue eyes. I thought she looked more like the bad girl on the third season of TV's *Fargo*. What was her name? Mary Elizabeth Winstead? But Peralta wasn't tossing idle compliments. He was "on" because he wanted something.

Lindsey thanked him and we went into the kitchen where we gorged ourselves and each finished a Negra Modelo.

Afterwards, Lindsey asked for his cell phone and his password.

"Do you have a warrant?" she asked, already knowing the answer.

He shook his head.

"You know anything I find can't be admitted as evidence, right?"

"I know, I know. You're the only person I can trust on this."

She was sucked in, nodded, and took the phone, disappearing into the study again. I stayed with him in the kitchen. The thermometer outside the window, in the shade near the hummingbird feeder, registered 109 degrees. The air conditioning was running nonstop.

I asked him if he had gotten any more texts from "unknown." He shook his head.

I said, "Have you ever received a threat by text before?"

"This is the first."

I asked who else texted him? Sharon and his daughters.

Then, "What was your role in the Page bombing?"

He seemed surprised by the question. "I didn't have one. Back then I had made senior deputy. I was working patrol and serving warrants."

"What about your buddies?"

He rubbed his jaw. "The Sheriff's Office didn't take part in the investigation, as far as I know. Tom Goldstein was the lead investigator for PPD. Always wore a black Stetson. He was a good detective. I knew him to say hello, but to him I was a nobody deputy. I got to know the investigators better years later. What have you found in the files?"

"It's going to take time."

"That's the one thing we don't have." He stood and gathered up the trash and plates, tidying up the kitchen.

My back was turned to him when I spoke again. "I've never seen you so spooked about a case."

I braced for a potential eruption but I only heard dishes and silverware being placed in the dishwasher. He returned to the table, sat down, and leveled his gaze on me.

"Crisis Meltdown had three years to screw up the Sheriff's Office, put people in jobs where they didn't belong, demote some of the best, hire some unqualified place-holders, disband my organized crime and cybercrime units. I don't know who to trust besides you and Lindsey. If I make the investigation into the threat widely known, who knows what might happen? That's why it's important for you to get the most out of those files I gave you."

I said, "If the official files are under lock and key at the state archives, is it even legal for us to have these copies?"

He shrugged. "I'm not going to ask."

•●⬤●•

An hour later, Lindsey called us into the study. Peralta claimed Grandfather's comfy leather chair, as always.

"You and the person who sent the text both use AT&T," she said. "That made it easier, although it's still not legal. Does the name Rudy Jarvis mean anything to you?"

Peralta stared at his hands. "Never heard of him."

She said, "His phone sent the text. He's a white male, thirty-nine years old, Arizona driver's license, address in Scottsdale, no criminal record. He runs a company that installs swimming pools, high-end stuff for custom homes. His call records look pretty normal. His most recent call was to a pool supply store this morning, so it doesn't look as if the phone has been stolen."

"And you're sure he sent the threat?" Peralta said.

Lindsey nodded.

"I sent him a text..." she started.

"No!" Peralta vaulted out of the chair.

"Calm down, Mike," she said, a rare use of his first name. She adjusted her glasses. It sat him back into the chair.

"He won't know the text is from you. I hacked into an Israeli cyberarms firm."

"Cyberarms?" I asked.

"Big money to be had," she said. "They do stuff for Mossad, NSA, other governments and corporations. I used one of their malware programs to embed a link into the text. The usual installation fee starts at half a million dollars."

"You stole it?" Peralta made a face.

"Asks the man without the warrant." Lindsey made a dozen more keystrokes before continuing. "When he clicks on the link, we'll be able to download everything on the phone: contacts, photos, e-mails, everything. We can track what he types in real time. And we'll be able to track him."

I shifted my weight, "Is the Mossad going to come after you?" I said it with a smile, but that smile didn't extend to my insides, where lunch was starting to creep acid into my throat. I already missed the Sanity Table and the gardens.

She put a reassuring hand on my arm. "They'll never know I was there, Dave. Neither will the NSA, despite its latest effort to trap-door me with my software upgrades."

"I don't want you to go to prison," I said.

"Don't worry. Anyway, Rudy Jarvis will think the text is coming from one of his suppliers—I found their number among his calls—and it has a link to an important new product upgrade. When he clicks on the link, we're in. It'll never leave a trace."

Peralta laughed and blew out a long breath. "You are dangerous, Lindsey. Remind me never to piss you off."

She looked up from the screen with a sweet smile. "Don't ever piss me off."

Chapter Eight

"He went for it." Lindsey met me with a satisfied look. "We're in and he's on the move."

"I want to see him."

It was an hour later and Peralta was gone. I scooped up the car keys. "Can you vector me to him?"

She stood and grabbed her iPad. "I can take us right to him."

Then she opened a desk drawer and slid her baby Glock 26 into the back of her black jeans and an extra magazine in her pocket. Seeing my expression, she held out a cautioning hand. "You worry too much, Dave. Be prepared, right?"

Outside, the blast furnace hit me in the face the second I opened the door. The difference between 101 degrees and 109 was profound. At 101, you could still be somewhat comfortable in the shade. Above 105, there was no place to hide from the wrecking ball of summer. It's a good thing Lindsey remembered to grab a frozen bottle of water. I cranked up our trusty old Honda Prelude, headed out to Third Avenue, and turned north.

Lindsey opened her iPad and kept it low, out of the sun. The screen was a Google street map with a flashing red dot. "He's westbound on Camelback coming out of Scottsdale. We ought to be able to intercept him. He's driving a red Ferrari 488 GTB."

"Geez, why didn't I become a swimming pool contractor? Even plumbers make more than me."

"You do have a nice butt crack, Dave."

"Do I have a big butt?"

"No."

We left the quaint houses and shade of Willo at Thomas Road and passed the hulking white buildings of St. Joseph's Medical Center. They had saved Lindsey's life after the renegade female Mountie shot her, the bullet passing within an inch of her heart. Still, I didn't like to look at the place now.

"Should we notify *El Jefe*?"

I thought about it and shook my head. "Let's wait and see what happens."

"He'll be angry."

She was right of course. A half mile later, we caught a green light at Osborn and continued north toward Indian School Road. The Hotel Clarendon was a block to our left, apparently thriving after an expensive redo a few years ago. I also appraised the cluster of skyscrapers to the east facing Central at Indianola. They had once been called the Rosenzweig Center, developed by Harry and his brother Newton in the early 1960s. It was the site of the pioneering family's homestead. They helped pull offices out of downtown before other real-estate booms pulled them farther into east Phoenix and finally north Scottsdale. Hardly anyone knew the once-powerful name now.

"He's at Twenty-fourth and Camelback." Lindsey touched the map on her screen. "Making good time. Still westbound on Camelback."

With two vents blowing cold air in my face, I drove north.

Third Avenue didn't cross the Grand Canal, so I made a right on Indian School and drove toward Seventh Street. The economy was finally digging out of the recession, so traffic was busy. A red light stopped us at Central while a light-rail train came through, heading south. We were on an interception course.

"He's at Seventh Street." She turned up the air conditioning. "Now making a turn north."

I punched it across Central, went half a mile, and turned left on Seventh Street by the stark white, scandal-ridden VA Hospital. Camelback Road was a mile away, so I revved us up to sixty, swinging in and out of clotted traffic.

"Don't worry, History Shamus," she said. "As long as he has the phone, we can track him. He doesn't have to be in sight." She opened the water, which was already melting, and had a sip.

I let the car slow. A trick to driving Phoenix streets was that the traffic lights were timed. In most cases, if you went the speed limit you would hit almost every green.

That's the way it played out, past Camelback, Missouri, and Bethany Home. At Rose Lane, I caught sight of the sleek red machine. He was driving faster, so the light at Glendale Avenue stopped him. It was the typical Phoenix intersection: six-lane avenues coming together, concrete and asphalt everywhere, a Chase bank branch on one corner surrounded by gravel radiating enough heat to kill the yucca and other plants they had installed, a cheap shopping strip across the street with a few spindly palo verde trees that provided no shade. This had once been a paradise of groves and graceful haciendas. You could drive a couple of blocks west and still find the shady, deep-water-irrigation properties of North Central Phoenix, but the historic oasis was contracting fast. The temperature has gone up more than ten degrees in my lifetime.

The Ferrari stood in the fast lane, firetruck red, seemingly in motion even when stopped. I pulled behind an old Chevy pickup one car back.

"Subtle." She punched me in the shoulder.

"I'm only looking." But I couldn't see much. Like most Arizona cars, including ours, the Ferrari had dark tinted windows. The only thing I could make out was the silhouette of the driver. He was alone. The car looked new, the red paint gleaming hot in the sun. Why had this guy texted a threat to Peralta about a forty-year-old murder?

After the light turned green, I let him race ahead, remaining first a quarter mile, then a half mile behind, passing the huge chain drug stores and gas stations that claimed prime corners. Lindsey had him on the map, at least as long as he carried his cell phone. And with no clouds in the sky, the width of the Phoenix avenue, and the red Italian icon-on-wheels, I could still make him out.

I drank cold water and drummed my fingers on the wheel. "Where the hell is he going?"

Lindsey flipped back and forth between screens on the iPad. "I don't know. He hasn't made or received a call or text since he left. At least on this phone. He might have another one. Or a burner. Wait. He's turning left on Bell Road and stopping."

I made up the distance quickly. A man was standing on the corner with a sign advertising tile and carpeting. I didn't know how he avoided heat stroke. We got the green left-turn arrow and went west. The Ferrari was parked in the asphalt lagoon of a one-story shopping center. If the occupant had stepped out, I couldn't see him. When the median allowed it, I turned left again and crossed Bell Road into the lot of a Sprint store.

We slid into a parking spot facing across the wide avenue toward the Ferrari. In a city full of the working poor's junker cars, it stood out. As I slid the transmission into Park, my phone rang, the "old-fashioned" ring. The readout said, "Peralta."

Lindsey looked at me. I shrugged and answered.

"Where are you?" His voice was so loud that I held the phone a few inches from my ear. "I stopped by your office and it was locked."

"Don't break in. There's an alarm."

"Smart ass. Report."

Lindsey stifled a laugh.

"We're following Rudy Jarvis."

When he didn't say anything, I went on. "He activated the malware link, so we've been following him. He drives a new Ferrari. Right now, he's at Seventh Street and Bell, just sitting here."

"Has he made you?"

"Of course not."

"You're a real asshole, Mapstone." He clicked off.

"He thinks I'm an..."

"I heard," she said. Then, "Check it out."

A late-model blue sedan pulled beside the Ferrari, driver's door to driver's door. Maybe it was a Toyota. They all looked alike. I retrieved the binoculars from the console and had a look. The Ferrari's passenger side was facing me. The sedan window came down and I caught the briefest glance of a Hispanic male, shaved head, then he was shielded by the sports car.

Lindsey anticipated me. "This is very strange. Maybe the guy works for him."

"Maybe."

A conversation or a package could have passed between the two cars but four minutes later the Ferrari swung out and powered onto Bell barely ahead of an SUV. Two seconds more and a weaker engine less and they would have collided. The SUV honked. The Ferrari sped west.

"I have him on the screen," Lindsey said. "See if you can cross over and get a license tag on the blue car."

I cursed the traffic engineers with their berms and medians, which ate extra time merely getting to the other side of a street. By the time I was in the north-side parking lot, the blue car was moving. I came close enough to get a make, Nissan, and a tag number, which I called out to Lindsey. Then I headed west on Bell.

We hit all the green lights doing the speed limit. He was gunning it up to fifty or sixty and hitting all the red lights. By the time he turned south on Nineteenth Avenue, we were only a few blocks behind. We went through Greenway and Thunderbird, curved around the hard edge of Shaw Butte, and in a few more miles passed back over the Arizona Canal again. I was glad we had a full tank of gasoline. The vicious sun cooked the cars.

When Lindsey assured me she still had him on her iPad, I let the line play out. No need to worry about keeping Jarvis in sight. Entrances to subdivisions, apartments, and long rows of low-rent storefronts flashed past in stucco sameness.

"He's past Christown," she said. "Now he's turning in a couple of blocks south."

Christown, at Bethany Home Road, was one of the oldest malls in Phoenix. It was built on land from a farmer named Chris Harri and middle-class housing had grown up around it. Bobby Kennedy had made a campaign appearance at the mall in 1968. Over the years, the place had deteriorated and then been reinvented as a "power center" with a Super Walmart. But, as in most of the west side, the old Anglo middle class had fled, replaced by poorer Hispanics.

"He's stopped at Seventeenth Avenue and Denton Lane, south of the mall."

In five minutes, I turned from Nineteenth Avenue onto Montebello, near the light-rail station and south of the mall. We had the good luck to be behind another old white Honda, which obligingly turned south on Seventeenth. Ours was the most forgettable of cars and having a lookalike in front was even better.

Seventeenth was two lanes wide with a fair amount of old shade and citrus trees flanking 1960s-era two-story apartments. Someone had tossed a pair of shoes up on a power line crossing the street—how long did it take him to do that? The Ferrari was pulled behind one of the buildings on the west side, parked under a long old-style carport for residents. These used to be common in Phoenix—I parked under one when I got my first apartment. The Ferrari's door was open and a dark-haired Anglo was standing, looking around. He wore a purple, short-sleeved pullover shirt. I went past at a normal speed.

"He didn't notice," she said. "He was looking south at something."

"Maybe another meet?" I continued a couple of blocks down to Colter, turned right and jumped over to Nineteenth, a clockwise turn, to make a second pass. "Was that him?"

"Based on the driver's license photo, yes. I haven't had time to download the data on his phone, much less dig into it."

We went a block and she checked her screen. "He's still there. No calls or texts."

By this time, we had driven far enough to cross a New England state and learned nothing about the man who promised to kill Peralta's family if he looked into the Page case. I was frustrated that we couldn't take him down and put a stop to this now. But what probable cause? Nothing legal on our part. And yet I was having fun for the first time since I had come back to the Sheriff's Office. Lindsey's presence helped. So did the adrenaline of the chase. I almost didn't feel the brutish heat radiating through the window. The water bottle was entirely melted and I took one last swig of cold water before passing it to Lindsey to finish off.

I signaled for a right to make a circle back around. At Nineteenth, a southbound train was pulling into the station, where a couple of dozen people were standing on the platform.

"This is not right," Lindsey said. "He's got to have a second phone."

"Or he's waiting for somebody."

I checked the rear-view on the chance that someone was following us. Nobody was, or it was a very sophisticated tail.

By this time, I was turning on Seventeenth again and in another few seconds pulled off to street parking, a little north of Denton. It had a battered neighborhood sign above the street sign, "Metro Manor." Most of these were made up in a hopeless attempt to give an identity to cookie-cutter subdivisions. The Ferrari was still parked beneath the long, shaded carport. It was about thirty yards away across the street, past a wooden utility pole and palm tree, and behind the closest apartments. The man had disappeared. No other cars were parked nearby.

Lindsey said she was going to download the information on his phone. Then I saw brake lights on the car and he started backing out.

I said, "He's on the..."

Suddenly an orange flash erupted and a millisecond later came a sharp boom. I instinctively pushed Lindsey down and huddled on top of her as the initial blast turned to a roar and the shockwave wiggled the Prelude. When I rose up—fire and black smoke, then gray smoke rising. Somehow the fifty-year-old parking cover was still there. The Ferrari wasn't. Parts were blown across the asphalt and into Denton Lane. Some of them looked human.

Lindsey started for the door handle.

I stopped her.

"No."

"Dave, he's in there!" She struggled against me. My ears were ringing from the blast and I could barely hear her. But I knew...

"We can't..."

At that second, people ran across the street. Four of them, two men and two women, in street clothes but carrying guns out, tucked against their legs, and with Phoenix Police badges on their belts. All wore sunglasses. They never even looked at us. They holstered their weapons, stood there, and watched Rudy Jarvis burn. One cop rested his hands on his hips.

Lindsey slumped in the seat, staring. I started the Prelude and drove on. At Nineteenth Avenue and Camelback, I pulled over for three fire engines. I slid into yet another parking lot and took Lindsey in my arms. She was shaking and quietly crying. I wasn't in much better shape.

Chapter Nine

In a few minutes, we were sitting inside a spacious Starbucks at Seventh Avenue and Missouri. It was blessedly dimly lit. I was drinking an iced mocha and Lindsey was twirling an iced coffee with a green straw. Merely crossing the asphalt lot from the car to the door had my shirt sticking to my back from sweat. The air conditioning gradually evaporated it.

Four young Anglo women were gossiping and laughing at a table near the front windows as Bob Weir sang "Only a River" on the sound system and several marked Phoenix Police SUVs ran north with lights and sirens. After the noise faded from outside, "Til Kingdom Come" came on, but I could never remember the singer.

Lindsey gave me a searching look. "History Shamus, am I responsible for that?"

"Of course not."

"I put the malware in his phone. What if…?" She let the thought dangle and then shook her head. "It's impossible. If it had been beaconing, I would have known it."

I didn't know what beaconing was, but I had no doubt Lindsey would have known if it were in play.

Twenty minutes later the women walked out the door,

nearly colliding with the Maricopa County Sheriff. They looked back as if they should know him.

The place was empty now. Peralta brought over a hot coffee. He was wearing a suit and showing no effects from the blast furnace of a day. His two bodyguards stood by the door looking as inconspicuous as a pair of Abrams main battle tanks in a grocery store aisle. Outside was Peralta's gray SUV, two cornrows of short antennas on the roof.

"So you had a blast." He arched an eyebrow.

"We watched a man die." Lindsey looked at him in horror. "This wasn't supposed to happen!"

"Well, it did." Peralta shot me an angry glare. "You and I will talk about this later, Mapstone."

"Don't be a jerk, Mike." Lindsey's expression was full of steel. Any doubts of a few moments ago were gone. "I suggested that we follow the car. You can blame me."

Peralta, surprised, held up a big paw. "Nobody's blaming. I only want to understand."

I suppressed a snort. The Law West of the Mazatzal Divide suddenly *wanted to understand*. Doctor Sharon had taught him a few moves.

His eyes moved from her to me. "Well?"

I ran through it with him: intercepting the Ferrari on Seventh Street, following it on the long, circuitous route over the mountains and into far north Phoenix, the meet in the strip-center parking lot, then the journey back to the apartment south of Christown.

He took the notepad where Lindsey had written the license tag for the Nissan, pulled his phone, dialed, and spat out some orders. Less than five minutes later, his phone rang—the ringtone was the theme for *Dragnet*. He answered and wrote on his own yellow legal pad, making grunting sounds as he took in the information.

He looked up. "Jarvis didn't have a sheet but he was running with some bad people. The car you saw on Bell Road is registered to one Hector Morales, arrests for drug possession, assault, auto theft, and yet he's out on the street. I love our criminal justice system. He's a member of the Wedgewood Chicanos."

"One of the westside gangs," I said.

"One of many." Peralta ticked off them off until he ran out of fingers. "Happy Homes, Brown Town, WetBack Power, Los Crazy Mexicans, Coffelt Jets, WS City, plain old Maryvale, Maryvale Park, Cashion Park, West Side Chicanos, Tre 5 moving in. All of them doing narcotics business with the cartels. Heroin is back, black tar, to be exact. Very popular and profitable. Dangerous as hell. Wedgewood Chicanos traffics it. Our fair city."

I asked Peralta what he knew about the explosion. He shrugged. "Big response to Seventeenth Avenue and Denton Lane. Phoenix PD, Phoenix Fire, ATF. It's too early for me to butt in. I'll call the chief later."

I was tempted to quote Stalin, "No man, no problem." As in, Rudy Jarvis, who sent the threatening text to Peralta, was gone, so perhaps the problem was gone, too. Remembering Lindsey's upset, I kept it to myself.

"Maybe that's why he drove the Ferrari," she said. "Drug dealers make way more than swimming-pool contractors. It also would explain why the cops were right there after the bomb exploded."

"Were they following him—or you?" The vertical canyons on Peralta's forehead deepened.

She shook her head. "We came close to him three times, but the tracking grid allowed us to stay miles back if we wanted. I never saw a tail on us."

"What about whatever it was you did to his phone?

Could that be traced back to you? Somebody knew you were following him and decided to put on a show."

"That's not possible." She stared back. "The expertise you would need to reverse that malware and beacon me, know we were following him, you're talking about something only a nation-state possesses the expertise to do."

Peralta relaxed a notch. "I don't think Putin cares about us. So, a coincidence you were there. Maybe the cops were narcs, staking out the building from another apartment across the street. I still can't believe they didn't stop you."

I thought about it again: cops and tunnel vision.

"We look like every other car west of Central," I said. "They were totally focused on the Ferrari and the parking lot. They never even looked as we drove off."

Lindsey leaned toward Peralta. "It still doesn't explain why he texted you. Did you have a history with this man? Did he have a grudge against the Sheriff's Office? Maybe the text was a red herring."

"Maybe." Peralta looked over the legal pad. "Looks like all of Morales' busts were done by Phoenix PD. And, no, I had never heard of Rudy Jarvis. What else can you tell me?"

She slapped closed the cover of her iPad in frustration and ran her hand through her hair, which fell back perfectly into place on her shoulder-length bob. "Not much. I didn't think to download the data in his phone while we were following him." She took a deep breath. "I thought we'd have time."

"Who else did he talk to?"

"He didn't make or receive a single call or text on that number while I was tracking him," she told him. "Maybe somebody else used his phone to send the threat."

"Maybe." Peralta slid a file across the table. "But maybe not."

I opened it and examined the single sheet of paper. It was an Arizona birth certificate.

"I had that pulled this morning," he said.

The baby's name was Rudolph Anthony Jarvis, born August 27, 1977, 11:04 p.m., Maricopa County, Phoenix. I scanned down. Mother: Kathleen Jarvis. Father: Mark Wayne Reid.

"Holy crap," I said, and passed it to Lindsey.

"His father was the Buzz Page bomber."

Peralta said, "Well, technically, he was the one who made and planted the bomb under the driver's side of Page's car while Page was inside the Clarendon. Dick Kemperton pushed the button that set it off. But, yeah, close enough."

Now the store was playing tunes I didn't know at all. I sipped my iced mocha until I froze my upper palate. After it warmed enough, I managed: "Why would this give Rudy Jarvis a motive to worry about you investigating the case? It's not as if you would do further damage to his father's reputation."

"Who understands fathers and sons?" mused Peralta, whose own father wanted him to become a lawyer, not a cop.

"I didn't even know that Mark Reid had children," I said.

"Looks like he didn't want them," Peralta said. "Rudy took his mother's last name. She probably raised him alone. Maybe he got to know his father when he was in prison. Maybe his father had more to hide than we know. And the son either didn't want that to come out or he thought dad was framed and wanted revenge."

"I don't buy it," said Lindsey.

Neither did I.

The door opened with a whoosh and a Hispanic boy stepped in. The bodyguards watched him as he saw Peralta and approached shyly.

"Sheriff?" he said, still six feet away.

Peralta smiled broadly, switching into politician mode. Outside the spotlight, even a small one like now, he never smiled like this. When he smiled like this the power use spiked at Arizona Public Service. "Come over here, *chiquito*."

"My parents are happy you're back," he said. "Could I get your autograph?"

"What's your name?"

"Jesús Ortega."

Peralta produced a four-by-five leather holder from his suit pocket and pulled out a sheet with his name and badge at the top. He scribbled and handed it to the happy child.

"Thank you, Sheriff." He read the inscription and carefully folded the paper. Then he pulled something from his pocket and the move made me uneasy. I didn't reach for my weapon but I was glad to feel it against my waist.

It was an ordinary Number Ten envelope, white.

"This is for me?" Peralta was still smiling.

He opened the envelope and a black USB flash drive fell to the table. Peralta unfolded a sheet of white paper and read it. His smile went away.

"Where did you get this, Jesús?"

The boy looked down and fidgeted. "A man gave it to me across the street and told me to bring it to you. He said you needed to see it. He gave me twenty dollars. I'm not in trouble, am I?"

Peralta paused. "No, not at all. What did this man look like?"

Jesús licked his lips. "He was Anglo. My dad's age. Dark hair. Sunglasses. He was in a black car, one of those bad-looking Dodges."

"Very good, Jesús," Peralta said. He pulled out his own envelope and handed it to the child. "I'm going to make you a Junior Deputy Sheriff."

"Really?" Jesús' eyes went wide as he pulled out a plastic star. One of Peralta's many marketing tools. He made the little boy raise his hand and swore him in. Lindsey discreetly rolled her eyes at me.

"Now this is very serious, Deputy," Peralta said. "Is the man still over there?"

"No, sir. He drove away after he gave me the envelope."

Peralta eyed the parking lots across the intersection. "I want you to give your address and phone number to those men by the door, in case we need you. And I want you to call 9-1-1 if you ever see this man again, but don't approach him. You tell the dispatcher he's wanted by the Sheriff's Office."

Even in the age of video gadgets and electronic overstimulation, this caused the boy's dark eyes to gleam in excitement. "Yes, sir!"

The boy went away and Peralta produced latex gloves from his pocket of treasures. He perused the letter again for a long five minutes. Then he turned it around so we could read it. The envelope had his name printed in the center. Below that and to the left was "personal" and to the right "important evidence."

Dear Sheriff Peralta:

I know you. You gave my text message to your Cybercrimes people to run down. It's too bad you lost your technie brainiac to the feds. The pretty one with the dark hair and blue eyes and short skirts. Looking at her was like watching poetry. Lindsey could catch me.

By the time you read this, you'll learn your trick didn't work out. LOL History doesn't repeat itself but it rymes.

Are you going to waste time chasing a ghost? Or will you solve the case? Are you up to it? To revenge his most foul and unnatural murder? If you can't, I will. All you can do is watch and be surprised. How does it feel being helpless?

Here's a tip: You did exactly what I expected. This little gift will give you some clues about what happens next. But you'll always be a step behind. All their sins will be remembered. More surprises are coming.

You can call me Sly

P.S.: Maybe you should have stayed in retirement.

Chapter Ten

Peralta folded the letter and returned it to the envelope.

"I'm going to run this for fingerprints, everything."

He wouldn't find any. The letter was on ordinary paper that could have been purchased anywhere. The typeface was Helvetica, printed on a laser printer. It wasn't like a typewriter that could be identified by distinct keystrokes. This thought formed only a passing backbeat to what was building in my mind.

He tapped the correspondence. "Impressions?"

"He knows about Lindsey. He knows her *name*!" I tried to keep my voice calm but it was no use. "We're going down the same goddamned road! No! She's not going to get hurt again. If this son of a bitch even tries to hurt her, I swear to God I'll stake him naked under the sun in the desert and watch him die. Two hours, two days, I don't care, I'll have the time. Then I'm coming for *you*."

The words were out before I even realized it. Peralta's expression was like nothing I had ever seen before. He opened his mouth and closed it. He looked suddenly old.

After a hideous slow ten beats, he said, "I believe you."

I felt Lindsey's hand on my leg and regret washed over me. Something terrible had just passed between me and the sheriff. But I didn't apologize.

Instead, I put my shoulder to the task. I said the writing indicated that "Sly" planned the bombing to coincide with delivery of the note. Sly had followed Peralta. He was probably surprised when the sheriff pulled into Starbucks instead of going to Seventeenth Avenue. I didn't know how he planned to get the note to him on a scene surrounded by cops. Maybe impersonate an officer or a reporter and ask someone to take it to Peralta.

"He thinks he's clever," I said. "Maybe young, with the LOLs. Yet older, with the salutation, 'Dear Sheriff Peralta.' He has distinctive misspellings. If we get a suspect we could have him write 'rhymes' and 'techie,' see if they match what's on this letter."

Lindsey asked why he didn't use spellcheck.

"Maybe he's arrogant," I said. "Or in a hurry."

"Or trying to throw us off," she said. I waited for her to say more, but she only stared down at the iPad.

I said that he'd probably researched the Page case carefully, had a stake in it. He knew that Rudy Jarvis was Mark Reid's son. Perhaps he knew Jarvis personally somehow—friend, employee, schoolmate. The cops should check all that and not be thrown off by the drug connection. There was a chance Jarvis was set up, told to meet Hector Morales under false pretenses.

Peralta said, "Male or female?"

"I bet male," I said.

Lindsey shrugged.

Peralta swirled a finger around the top on his coffee. "What's with the 'murder most foul line'?"

"Trying to be cute?" I speculated. "It's a line from Shakespeare, where the ghost is talking to Hamlet. He reveals that Hamlet's father was murdered. It's the most famous revenge play in the English language."

"Round up all the actors," he said.

I forced a chuckle. "What do you think?"

He bolted down the boiling coffee as if it were iced tea. "He's a risk taker. Why else send that text? Why get the kid to come over here with the letter when there was a chance we might catch him? The kid might take the twenty bucks and scoot right on past, not want to deal with Five-O. Somehow he had the balls to plant the bomb in the Ferrari, maybe make it himself. Or he has an accomplice trained in explosives."

I said the bomb had to be on the Ferrari before we ever saw it. The killer couldn't have planted it under the carport—Jarvis never left it, as far as we could tell on our circles of the scene. And the police stakeout would have seen it.

We both wound down and looked at Lindsey.

"This person's technological expertise is unclear." She spoke slowly, eying the flash drive on the table. "Not as smart as he thinks he is. By the way, I'm using 'he' as a neuter pronoun, as unfashionable as that is today. It could be a woman we're dealing with. He believes I'm still in D.C., unless somebody else in Cybercrimes who looks like me also went to work for the feds."

Peralta shook his head. "The unit was almost completely disbanded while I was out of office. Only one tech and one deputy left, both overweight males." He looked at me. "I will pull records on anyone working there when Lindsey was a deputy. She might recognize someone who hit on her."

Lindsey said, "Sly doesn't ring any bells. Any woman who's not four-hundred pounds and scowling is going to get hit on if she works for a police agency." A smile. "You hit on me, Dave."

She cocked her head. "Sly's information is out of date, although he or she's seen me before in the department. Seen me close up. Don't discount a disgruntled former deputy or other cop. Also check females—they might be attracted to another woman, too. A computer genius? If this person was really good, he or she would have detected the malware I inserted and have to brag. The entire letter reads that way. Too smart by half. That's his vulnerability."

Using one finger, she traced invisible loops on the cover of the iPad. "Like I said, if my back door into the phone had been detected, it would have alerted me. What's more likely is that he already planned to kill Jarvis. He sent you the threat text from Jarvis' phone, knowing you wouldn't let it alone. Anybody in the state of Arizona knows that about you. Us being there when the bomb detonated happened by accident."

I hoped she was right about all this.

Peralta said, "At least I haven't gotten any more threatening texts."

"I know," Lindsey said.

He tilted his chin up.

"I embedded software in your phone." She smiled. "I'll know if anyone is trying to hack your calls or texts, or the location from where any new text was sent. It's for our safety, too. We don't want Sly to know you're in touch with us or that I'm back in Phoenix. You probably shouldn't come to the house again until we catch him or her."

Peralta gave an admiring nod and tapped the little USB flash drive. "I want to see what the hell is on this."

"Wait." Lindsey said it in a tone of voice I had rarely heard her use. Peralta set it back on the table.

"I said he wasn't a computer genius, but I don't want to bet the city on it. Maybe he knows a computer genius.

Maybe...I don't know. But do not plug that drive into anything. It could be a weapon."

"As in, it blows up?" Peralta said.

"Worse," she said.

We both leaned in and she spoke barely above a whisper.

"You've read about Stuxnet, right?"

We answered simultaneously.

"A little," I said.

"What?" Peralta said.

"It was the thing that crippled the Iranian nuclear program a few years ago," I said. "A computer bug that the U.S. and Israelis sent into the uranium enrichment lab at Natanz. Set the program back at least a couple of years and kept the Israelis from starting a war."

"Technically a worm," she said. "Aimed at PCs running Windows. Super advanced for its era." She sounded as if this was decades ago. "The worm secretly infiltrated their computers and caused the centrifuges involved in uranium enrichment to blow up. The Iranians didn't have a clue. They thought it was human error. They fired people. So far, so brilliant, right?"

We nodded.

"But Stuxnet got loose. It started infecting other systems, including a nuclear plant in Russia. Think of a pandemic. A security firm in Belarus finally ran it down. When I was in Washington, I spent a lot of time at Fort Meade trying to protect us from our own rogue cyberweapon. Even though we still deny it was ours. We have much more dangerous weapons now, offensive and defensive capabilities..."

Peralta interrupted. "Fort Meade is the NSA, Lindsey."

"That's correct," she said. "And headquarters of the

U.S. Cyber Command. Almost all of what I told you has been reported in the media by now. If I tell you more, Dave's worries about me going to federal prison might come true."

I continued to learn about her secret life while she was on the other side of the country, supposedly working for the Department of Homeland Security, and we were estranged. Peralta fidgeted and reached for the thumb drive. Lindsey slapped his hand, hard.

"You don't get it. The Iranian enrichment lab was off the grid. They thought they were safe. But somebody brought Stuxnet into the building in one of these." She pointed to the little plastic memory stick. "All it took was plugging it into a computer and the worm was loose."

"It could shut down the Sheriff's Office," Peralta said.

"Or the Palo Verde Nuclear Generating Station during high summer," she said. "It could also be ransomware."

When we looked clueless, she continued.

"That's a malware that locks up all your data and the hacker demands a ransom. If you pay it, maybe he gives you your data back and maybe not."

The music had stopped and it was quiet except for a barrista grinding coffee. Then, silence.

"Let me take this home," she said. "I'll see what we're dealing with. My Mac has firewalls that even the government can't penetrate. I hope."

Peralta produced an evidence envelope and slid the drive inside, then sealed and signed it. Lindsey reflexively started to sign it, too. This preserved the chain of custody if—when—the case went to court.

Peralta stopped her. "You're not a deputy again, yet." He emphasized the last word and she didn't argue about it. "Mapstone?"

I signed and added my badge number, the date, and time.

The outside door opened and a couple entered, walking to the counter to place their order.

"History doesn't repeat itself but sometimes it rhymes." I almost chanted it to myself. "Mark Twain."

Peralta shot an annoyed look, familiar, *don't be such an intellectual, Mapstone*. It was a relief to see.

I said, "We saw this go down. And it looked like a replay of the Page murder."

"Oh, come on," Peralta started to stand.

"Listen to me."

He sat on the edge of the chair.

"Rudy Jarvis was supposed to meet someone behind those apartments. That individual never showed up. Jarvis was outside the car waiting. But the meet never happened. Sound familiar? The only difference is there wasn't an air-conditioned hotel lobby for Jarvis to walk inside while he waited to be stood up. Then he climbed in his car, like Buzz Page did forty years ago, started it and backed out ten feet, like Page, and the bomb went off."

Peralta stood and his face took a harder cast. "If you're right, it will be a dynamite bomb. And if someone is taking us down memory lane, we've got a world of trouble."

He pulled out his phone and fiddled with it for a moment before handing it to me.

It was a photo: his two daughters, Jennifer with a baby on her hip, Jamie holding the hand of a four-year-boy, the two husbands. A beautiful group. They were on a walking trail, trees on one side, water on the other, a towering suspension bridge in the background.

"Vancouver," he said. "Next they're going to take the train through the Rockies and then rent a car for the trip to Banff National Park."

I handed it back to him. "Your family is probably safe."

He cocked an eyebrow.

"The note isn't completely clear," I said, "but I think he wants you to investigate the Buzz Page bombing."

"Why the hell didn't he say so?"

"He's a manipulator." This from Lindsey. "You ought to call a press conference and announce that you're reopening the Page case."

Peralta's expression was non-committal.

She said, "He might have a hit list of people associated with the Page case, potential victims if you don't move forward."

Peralta fiddled with the knot in his tie. It was already perfect. "First I'm supposed to do nothing. Now I'm supposed to protect the offspring of a forty-year-old case. I'm not a short-order cook for psychos." He assessed us for a moment. "I'll think about it."

I started to walk with him toward the door when I heard my name.

"David."

Lindsey almost never called me anything but "Dave." It immediately stopped me. She was still at the table.

"Sit with me."

I did.

Peralta and his security team walked across asphalt nearing its melting temperature and climbed into the SUV. Two more minutes and they were gone.

"He—or she—may be watching," she said.

I felt like an idiot. I could have blamed it on the concussion of the car bomb or the heat or my worry that this killer somehow knew my wife.

I sat back to finish off the iced mocha. "I hope this won't make you stop wearing short skirts."

She flashed a saucy smile.

Back in the Honda, we retraced our path trailing Rudy Jarvis. I doubted we would learn anything new, but both of us were still keyed up. We started back in the historic districts, jogged over to Seventh Street, and once again aimed north to Bell, twelve miles straight north.

Phoenix, Arizona. Four million people in a skillet. Almost three hundred sunny days a year. Five-hundred-eighteen square miles in the city limits alone. Add in supersized suburbs and you had an urban area five or six times that large. A totally manmade environment and on days like today, ominously vulnerable to power outages, gasoline pipelines rupturing, the extensive waterworks that slaked its thirst breaking down. The largest nuclear power generating station in North America was sitting a few miles upwind.

Phoenix was never a Wild West town. Instead, it was once the center of an agricultural empire, reborn on what had been the most advanced irrigation society in the pre-Columbian Americas. The settlers cleaned out the old Hohokam canals, dug more, built dams, and by the middle of the twentieth century, boasted more than half-a-million acres under cultivation. Promoters, with some truth, called it "American Eden." Even when I was a boy, you could drive through miles of citrus groves and farms. Those were gone now. Use it up, throw it away, move farther out.

When Phoenix became a big city, the street grid was built on the old farm plats and irrigation laterals. A major street such as Camelback every mile, a feeder arterial such as Osborn every half mile. Except where the city had sprawled into and across the mountains of the Salt

River Valley, this was the predictable layout. The Phoenix Mountains, Piestewa Peak, and Camelback Mountain to the north, South Mountains and Estrellas to the south, White Tanks to the west, and Superstitions, McDowells, Four Peaks, and others to the east. When it wasn't too smoggy, you could see them all. Unlike, say, in an older river city back east, it was hard to get lost in Phoenix. This was a place built in a hurry and for the automobile to speed quickly from place to place, real-estate enterprises connected by wide highways called "city streets." Few believed me when I said it used to be beautiful.

Once again, we crossed the Arizona Canal into Sunnyslope. We left behind the lush footprint of the Salt River Project and climbed into the desert district. North Mountain stood before us, rocky and bare. Sunnyslope was probably the only part of Phoenix that could have been its own city. It started as a ramshackle settlement of "health seekers" early in the twentieth century. After World War II, it attracted more upscale housing. But residents voted down several measures to incorporate, so Phoenix swallowed it in the 1950s. Still, it kept its special vibe, a desert town with bikers and eccentrics, "Slopers," or at least that's the way it used to be. When Lindsey and I started dating, she had an apartment here. I wondered if her old building were still standing.

At the huge five-point intersection where Cave Creek Road split off northeast from Dunlap and Seventh Street, Jarvis had kept northbound, past Hatcher, Mountain View, and Cheryl Drive with the National Guard Armory on the left. In the 1980s, the city punched Seventh over the bare hills on the east side of North Mountain Park to serve the new Pointe Resort at Tapatio Cliffs. The Ferrari had climbed effortlessly and the Prelude didn't do badly. In a few minutes, we again descended back down to more of the monotonous single-story shopping strips and commercial buildings and, behind them, fathomless subdivisions.

The shopping strip at Bell looked unchanged, as did the roads and surroundings all the way back to Christown and the site of the bombing. We did our part on greenhouse gas emissions, but nothing to answer all the questions the day had dropped on us.

Chapter Eleven

I had witnessed a serious crime, but Peralta told me to keep it to myself. We were in dangerous territory now. I didn't like it.

Of course, telling Phoenix PD would lead to questions about why we were at Seventeenth Avenue and Denton Lane, a location its detectives had staked out. Why we were following Rudy Jarvis. We had been in dangerous territory from the start, when Peralta received the threat and insisted on handling it his way. What were another few steps off the trail?

Sure enough, the next day the newspaper reported the bombing in the briefest of terms, with a photo and a video on its website of the aftermath. No curiosity by the reporter on the identity of the victim. No identification of the victim. "Police suspect it was gang-related," she wrote, copying the police press release. Not even a mention of potential domestic terrorism. Move along, nothing to see here.

Peralta elided the truth when he contacted his friend, the police chief, on Saturday. A friendly call, could he offer any help? Sure enough, Jarvis was blown to pieces by a dynamite bomb. The device was very old school, the chief said, in an era when bomb-makers preferred plastic explosives such as C-4 or the ammonium nitrate used by Timothy McVeigh in Oklahoma City. The cops and ATF were trying to trace where the dynamite had been procured.

My opinion was that Peralta should announce we were reopening the Page case and assign his best detectives. He again brushed this aside. "I need to think about it."

Lindsey spent Saturday at her MacBook Pro with the USB stick. I watched her insert it into a port. The house didn't explode. Even the air conditioner kept going, fighting against the 110-degree heat outside. I left the room but heard her say, "Holy shit" and "wow" more than once. Plus, "You are Sly, but so am I." I let her alone and went downtown, beginning the process of putting the files in order, spending four hours each on Saturday and Sunday.

I also had the e-mail from the Clarendon, a list of attendees at the fortieth anniversary event. It consisted of sixty-two names. Most I could easily sort into categories: cops and retired cops, journalists and retired journalists, and active politicians. Over the next few days, I ran a few names at a time through NCIC and the Sheriff's Office database. I took my time while Peralta was in silent mode. Maybe nobody would notice. Probably not. But a big dump of sixty-two names at once might get people in the Sheriff's Office talking, speculating, gossiping. Nobody loved gossip more than cops. Peralta still didn't know I had done this. And there was a further hitch: about half the names had "and guest" attached. But no names of the guests.

Saturday night, Lindsey and I committed cultural appropriation and cooked chicken enchiladas. I am very proud of my chicken enchiladas. Over dinner, she told me what she had found.

"This person has expertise." Her voice contained no Gen-X irony. She was impressed. "You open the flash drive and it has a file of *New Times* articles from the 1990s on the Page bombing."

I told her that I had those bookmarked but hadn't made the time to read them.

She held a fork of enchilada suspended in midair. "And that's all a mere mortal would see. But the drive contains a version of what's called PoisonTap, something devised by a hacker named Samy Kamkar. Hard to find, almost impossible to fight. I'll spare you the nerdy details but it would provide a very subtle backdoor into any PC and its network, including the intranet."

"As in, Peralta's computer and the Sheriff's Office internal network."

After she finished chewing: "Exactly."

"So what do we do?"

"I need to think about it. Maybe I can build something that makes the device think it's in the network. We could even feed the person false information. Or..."

She let the thought hang as I let the cheese and onions make love to my palate. I said, "You're still not ready to say him or her."

"Nope. Or assume an age. Could be twenty. But Bill Gates and Satya Nadella are your age, History Shamus."

I studied her face. It had been days since she had read from the Sanity Table.

"I'm okay, Dave," she said, reading my thoughts. "It's fun to be back in the game. Don't worry."

Then she asked the most obvious question from the previous day. "Why was Rudy Jarvis using surface streets?

If you were going to meet someone at Seventh Street and Bell and you were coming from Jarvis' house, you'd hit the freeway system."

"But he didn't."

Her eyes darkened. "I was so careless not to be downloading the data from that phone while we were tailing him. Because I bet he received a text before he activated my worm. I bet it told him to take that specific route, meet someone in the parking lot on Bell, then take surface streets down to the apartment on Seventeenth Avenue and wait. It probably threatened him and his family, like the text to Peralta. And it warned him that he was being watched."

"A candy-apple red Ferrari does stick out. But the guy—or woman—had the Sheriff's Office garage staked out, to see Peralta leaving."

"Sure, and Rudy Jarvis was afraid, had been told not to contact the police, that they were watching him and monitoring all his phones and computer."

"Unless he was running heroin for the gangsters."

"Bullshit."

She was right, of course. I retrieved two cold Modelo Especials from the refrigerator and sat back down.

"You could hack his texts."

She shook her head. "This is a homicide investigation. I'm not going to do something illegal that could get tossed out in court. They could get texts older than 180 days with a simple court order. But for newer ones, they'll need a subpoena, and that will require probable cause. If Peralta announces he's reopening the case, then we can move forward."

She was indeed back in the game.

Chapter Twelve

Starting Monday, I spent almost four solitary days behind the deadbolt lock and presided over by the alarm system. No panic attacks. I allowed myself a lunch break but that was it. I slowly made sense of the contents of the boxes: copies of formal detective notes and copies of scribblings, incident reports, news clippings, intelligence reports, ATF analysis of the explosion, the long confession that Mark Reid gave PPD Detective Tom Goldstein, and court transcripts. It was hundreds of pages. Yet it was far from complete or definitive.

By Wednesday, I was using the white board to begin organizing, taping things up, making notes and drawing lines with a marker.

I put up the timeline I had written on my laptop. It began with the bombing, followed by sometimes hour-by-hour events in the immediate days after the killing. Then time stretched out—all the way to the eventual deaths of the three convicted conspirators, the last one happening after the turn of the century. By Thursday, I would replace it with three updates, gleaned from the files. It was three feet long. I used a ruler to separate months, then years, with lines from a highlighter. I hoped having this as physical paper let me see events, context, and patterns that keeping it trapped on the computer screen wouldn't.

Next, I taped up some of the crime-scene photos. Closeups of the GTO from the driver's side. The car appeared surprisingly intact, with only the left door blown wide open. The driver's seat was shredded and the floor partly missing. In the black-and-white photos, the blood was dark and abundant. Another shot was wider, showing a Phoenix Fire Department ladder truck parked nearby. I was reminded that all the cops wore helmets back in those days, a legacy of the civil disturbances of the sixties. Small pieces of debris were scattered across the scarred asphalt. The glass in the car's windows had been blown out, the hood was slightly up and bent in the middle, yet the windshield was still in place. Perversely, so were the windshield wipers. A cop kept bystanders at a distance. A firefighter atop the aerial ladder, although it was sitting in place horizontal to the truck, looking down on the scene. It was still midday, judging from the narrow shadows thrown.

Then I started writing names on Post-it notes and placing them on the board. In the center, I placed the three individuals convicted of the crime.

Mark Reid. Like many criminal monsters—Lee Harvey Oswald, John Wayne Gacy—he was invariably identified in newspaper accounts with his middle name, "Mark Wayne Reid." In real life, he didn't use it. He was thirty-three years old at the time of the Page murder. Rudy Jarvis' father.

He was a small-time hood in the Midtown bar scene and at Phoenix Greyhound Park. He made his legitimate money as a parking-lot enforcer who would attach cinderblocks to offending vehicles. Want the block off your car? Pay up. I taped up an eight-by-ten photo of a flat-faced, dark-haired man in aviator sunglasses and sideburns, a nose that had been broken, probably more than once.

Dick Kemperton. A struggling roofing contractor nicknamed "Dick the Roofer" by the newspapers, he was also thirty-three. From a distance of four-hundred feet, Kemperton watched Page get in his car and pushed the button on an electronic box to detonate the bomb. At first, the device, designed to send a signal via an extendable antenna, didn't work. That accounts for Page being able to start his car and begin backing out before the bomb went off.

Darren Howard. Reid told the cops that Howard, age thirty-four, hired him to kill Page.

With Kemperton and Howard, I had to settle for mug shots. The former was nearly bald and the latter had prematurely graying hair combed back. Both showed expressions of mild surprise as if they had rolled out of bed and into the booking room. It made me wonder who had taken the more candid photo of Mark Reid and why.

The big three. The obvious three. One, two, three.

Except very few people believed that rolled up the case.

Kemperton always maintained his innocence. He won a new trial. Reid refused to testify against him again. As a result, the charges were dismissed and two further attempts to prosecute him failed. The feds put him away for five years for attempting to have Reid killed. Kemperton died a free man in 2013.

Howard's first-degree murder conviction was overturned, too. But the state persisted and he died in prison in 2009. He never wavered from claiming innocence, saying he had been framed, including by the Phoenix Police.

Reid served twenty years and got out, dying in obscurity. He made the sweetest deal with prosecutors, implicating Kemperton and Howard in exchange for avoiding the gas chamber. Yet he seemed the guiltiest of the three. Page had specifically named him. He made the bomb and set up the meeting at the Clarendon House. None of these facts were in dispute. I didn't get it.

Reid was more articulate than I expected when I read his 223-page statement given to Phoenix homicide detective Goldstein a month after the bombing. The statement had been taped and transcribed. He spoke in complete sentences and used the Queen's English, something rare today from criminals or even law-abiding citizens. It appeared as if this statement, in its specifics, was the roadmap used by the cops and prosecutors.

Specifics such as preparing for the assassination. Reid went to the *Republic* and *Gazette* parking lot to scope out Buzz Page's car. Then he visited a Pontiac dealership. He had to settle for the used-car lot because Pontiac stopped making the GTO in 1974. But according to Reid's statement, he sat in a GTO and measured the location of the driver's seat, so he could precisely plant the bomb, with magnets. The trouble was that Reid was five-foot-nine and Page was six-two. So the placement was off enough that Page wasn't killed outright.

Peralta was fond of saying, "Thank God for stupid criminals." But Reid's stupidity had contributed to the suffering of Buzz Page.

The detonator? Reid purchased it from a hobby shop in San Diego the month before the bombing.

The statement was full of these convincing details.

He told Goldstein that Page wasn't killed for anything he wrote, but for *something he was about to write*. Out loud, I said, "What the hell?" Something he was about to write. Everything I had read in the news clippings and the *Phoenix Project* said Page was off the investigative beat and happy to be on the more routine stories covering the dull state Legislature. Maybe Detective Goldstein didn't press it. I sure would have. What was Page going to write that caused his murder? But the transcript moved on to other things.

The three conspirators knew each other from North High School, the second high school built in Phoenix. Located on Thomas Road on the edge of the city at the time, it was funded thanks to the New Deal and opened in 1939. When I was young, it had a beautiful leafy campus. Now it had been taken over by parking lots, was in the central core, and considered an inner-city school. But when Reid, Kemperton, and Howard attended, North was a solid middle-class institution.

Howard was the outlier of this trio, even in high school. He was a star athlete, A-student, and senior-class president. The other two were nobodies. Howard went on to become a respected and successful general contractor. When he was arrested for the bombing, many people couldn't believe it. But he had the means to pay Reid fifty-eight-hundred dollars to kill Buzz Page. The motive was unclear unless...

Unless you went to the one who got away with it: Freeman Burke, Sr. The old man's patronage had launched Howard in business as a contractor. He probably built some of the dreary landscape of tract houses Lindsey and I had driven through while following Rudy Jarvis. And, according to Reid, Howard paid for the Page hit because of stories the reporter had written about Burke's organized-crime connections, accounts that cost Burke a seat on the state Racing Commission.

I wrote out Freeman Burke, Sr., on another yellow Post-it and placed it on the white board.

Burke was one of the richest, if not the richest, men in the state. He was seventy years old at the time of the bombing. Much of his wealth came from extensive land holdings. Someone of Burke's stature would typically pick up the telephone and call the *Gazette* publisher if he had a beef with a reporter.

But I knew enough Phoenix history to understand Burke's dark past. In the 1930s, he organized farm owners to arrange for gangs that beat union organizers and drove them from the Valley. When Prohibition ended, he won the most lucrative liquor distributorship in the state, one with ties to the Capone organization in Chicago. As Malik, Jones, the doctoral student, had said, Burke supposedly owned brothels in town and paid the police to leave them alone.

Did Burke really order the killing? Did he merely do a version of "Who will rid me of this troublesome priest" about Buzz Page and a grateful Darren Howard took the hint? Or was the list something Reid made up? Nothing was ever proved. Burke was never charged and even won a libel suit against Investigative Reporters and Editors. The Phoenix Art Museum had a Freeman Burke Gallery, one of many pieces of his philanthropy. But Burke had a motive to kill the reporter and aficionados of the Page case called it the "frontier justice" theory.

Other theories existed: Page mentioned the company RaceCo, which ran greyhound racing in the state and had been implicated with organized crime in a Nevada case. Page had written about RaceCo. The reporter had made enemies in writing about land fraud, too. And he had also said, as he lay ripped apart, "Mafia."

As with RaceCo, no convincing Mafia evidence was found—or at least pursued by the police and, later, the state Attorney General's chief investigator Rusty Clevenger. Reid claimed that the bomb was constructed with three sticks of dynamite. But the ATF investigation indicated it only had two sticks—another reason Page survived at first. One anonymous detective's scribbling came from an interview with an Italian made man, who scoffed at the idea that they were involved. "If it had been a Mafia bomb, Page would have been blown to bits...We do it right. Also don't kill reporters or clean cops. Part of the code. Bad for business."

Still, I put up lines of Post-it notes with names of people close to the case: mobsters, lawyers, and politicians. I still had one last file box to go but the white board contained forty-six names.

I was perilously close to the rabbit hole, where I could go in a hundred directions, and I was no closer to getting the necessary answer. Who had threatened Peralta in the here and now? Who had murdered Rudy Jarvis?

As I had warned him, this was a case with too many players and too many theories. About the only thing everyone agreed on was that Buzz Page had died from a bomb planted under his car.

The days passed without panic attacks, which was strange because I was working alone in silence, the perfect setting for my malady. I didn't know why. Maybe it was because I had real anxiety.

I needed a short cut. One that would identify the bad guy, discover his motive, and bring a SWAT team to his house. But history didn't offer short cuts, not reliable ones.

Chapter Thirteen

By Wednesday afternoon, I was lying on the lawyer's table next to the file boxes, looking at the white board for inspiration. It didn't come. Then I sat in a chair across the room and bounced a tennis ball against the far wall, catching it perfectly after a few practice misses. Pop! Pop! Pop! The only risk was shattering an expensive period light fixture or window. I tossed the ball, waiting for the clues to gel. Only they didn't.

All week I labored as a scholar. Peralta didn't so much as call. It made me suspicious.

Outside, the temperature stayed hellish or above. The overnight lows were in the nineties as the concrete and asphalt exhaled the heat they had been absorbing during the day. For years now, the summers had been getting hotter and staying that way longer than normal. The rich were at their houses on the California coast, the San Juan Islands, and Hawaii. The resorts promoted cut-rate prices.

It would stay bad for months, past Halloween even to Thanksgiving. Phoenix used to cool down in September. As a grade schooler, I sat in classrooms without air conditioning. That would be impossible now. Those rising overnight lows were "local warming" because of paving over the citrus groves and farms, cutting down shade trees to widen roads. Now things were changing for the worse. These few days had been much hotter than a normal June. And yet the media usually displayed a curious lack of curiosity about climate change. Every day the fire department was dispatched to rescue one or more fools who had attempted to climb Camelback Mountain. Even with my frozen water bottles, the walk to and from light rail left me in a constant state of low-grade heat exhaustion. Lindsey's flowers died. She and her girlfriends canceled their morning walks until the fall.

On Wednesday night, Lindsey enlivened cocktails with a miniskirt and a 1970s playlist coming from the Bose speakers. Here, convenience and funding—the ease of compiling music on iTunes and our lack of a turntable and vinyl records—outweighed her year-long retreat into the analog. She was a disco fan, for its kitsch factor. So we listened to "Get Down Tonight," "Disco Inferno," and other crap that I had hated at the time. But the collection was curated with a sweep of those years. She even had the Ramones and the once-famous Phoenix Concerts by the folk singer John Stewart. Luckily for me, she also included Linda Ronstadt, Joni Mitchell, and the Eagles. The songs brought back memories, not all of them good. We switched over to our summer favorite, gin and tonic, made with Beefeater, Jack Rudy tonic mix, and fizzy water.

"Tell me about the city then," she said.

Where to begin? "It was smaller. More beautiful. So much was landscaped—you didn't see all the gravel they throw down now. Downtown's old bones hadn't been swept away, although it was beginning. The Fox Theater was torn down. The city was still surrounded by miles of citrus groves. Bell Road had been two lanes in the desert."

"No way."

"Yes. In high school, my friends and I would shoot off our model rockets near Scottsdale Road and Bell. We went target shooting around Pinnacle Peak. It was nothing but empty desert. There was only one freeway, Black Canyon, which bent to become the Maricopa. Then by the mid-seventies, they opened a few miles of the Superstition Freeway, two lanes each way. You could drive for miles and never leave the orange and lemon and grapefruit groves."

She made a sad face. "No wonder you get cranky when we go driving now."

"I don't want to sugar-coat. The smog was getting worse. You could see a yellow-brown cloud over the city most days. There were no business signs in Spanish then. It was a very Anglo city. Arizona had plenty of lurid crime. Gary Tison broke out of prison, went on a rampage with his sons, and killed six people. Still, there was cruising on Central, especially Friday and Saturday night. The teenagers stopped for burgers and shakes at Bob's Big Boy at Thomas. People bowled, and not as some retro thing. Bowling alleys were all over town. Downtown was dying but the action was only two miles north in Midtown."

"Which plenty of people call 'downtown' today and drive you crazy, Dave."

"Know the difference!" I held up a finger. "People move here, don't care about the history, and think they can redraw the city's geography. Anyway, Park Central was a real mall with stores. Central Avenue was busy and lined with businesses. Greyhound's headquarters was at the Rosenzweig Center." It was a startling contrast to the deflated Midtown of today, where so much action had decamped for Twenty-fourth and Camelback or Scottsdale. "You didn't have to drive five miles or more to shop. Lots of bars in Midtown, too, including a Playboy Club. I went once."

"Bad boy. These were the bars where the bombers hatched their plot, right?"

"That's the story."

"You doubt?"

"The historian doubts everything." I tried my most pompous academic voice.

She demurely attempted to pull down her skirt. Slowly. "What are your office hours, Dr. Mapstone?"

"Anytime for you. Extra credit. But I want it on my desk as soon as possible."

I told her that despite my one-time Playboy Club visit, I experienced almost nothing of the Midtown bars. My grandparents were teetotalers and I started my drinking at dives near the university campus, Coors beer. Anything I knew about Midtown's dark side was what I read. How guys like Mark Reid and mobsters mixed with lawyers and businessmen.

She said, "Most people wouldn't associate Phoenix with the mob. I thought Tucson was the Mafia town with Joe Bonnano."

"Phoenix was new and clean, the city of the future," I said. "That was the image. The reality was different. The Chicago Outfit had been here since the 1920s."

"Which makes me think Phoenix was never really clean."

"Definitely not," I said. "I heard Phoenix was an open town for gangsters, not ruled by any one family. Phoenix was a back office for Vegas, too. Most important, there was a very large gray area where the made men and local leaders mingled. Barry liked to run with a fast crowd. He wasn't the tightass conservative portrayed in the eastern press, at least not in person. Harry Rosenzweig, Del Webb..."

"Who's who."

"But nobody's ever proved they were mobbed up."

"Did they know Buzz Page was going to be killed? Did one or more of them order it?"

I sipped the cold gin and thought about it.

"People have speculated about that for forty years. Bombings weren't unheard-of here. Back in the 1950s, Willie Bioff was relocated to the Valley under an assumed name. He'd testified against major Mafia figures, including Frank Nitti. They caught up with him and planted a bomb under his pickup truck in 1955. Another man who had turned state's evidence in Illinois against the Outfit was killed by a bomb in Tempe in 1975. So, it's possible the mob was involved in Page's murder. The files I have don't show anything conclusive. Bombings were big in the seventies, especially with student radicals. I read there were a thousand in that decade."

"But back to Page. One of the last things he said. 'Mafia.'"

I told her that a few years before he was killed, Page did a series for the *Gazette* called "Strangers Among Us," about the growing Mafia influence. He was fearless.

"What about my Dave? Am I driving you crazy with these questions?"

"No, not at all. I'm glad to be pulled out of the files and actually think about times I lived through. In the seventies..." I stared through the glass and a sudden sadness overtook me. This was my least-favorite decade. "I had a scholarship to Stanford..."

"You never told me that."

I nodded. "Never went. Grandfather died my senior year in high school, and Grandmother wasn't that well. So, I stayed and went to ASU. With a start at Stanford—and credentials do matter—I might have been a contender. As long as I could have still met you."

She smiled but I couldn't tell what was behind it.

I said, "I was very grown up in some ways, book-learning ways, and very backward in other ways. Social skills. The ability to flirt."

"You caught up," she said. "Anyway, you had a girlfriend."

"One. She left me for a rich older man." I thought about how that was the same year, 1979, when I lost Grandmother. How I joined the Sheriff's Office as a deputy while I was in college, a youthful adventure, hell, maybe I'd use it for novel material. But I met Peralta and the rest was...history. How I hated the seventies. Bad clothes. Bad economy. Hemlines fell. And so much loss. I was so alone and lonely.

"What?"

"Nothing." I lied. "Anyway, I'll never forget how lovely that Phoenix was then. And even though the population was about six-hundred-thousand, it felt like a small town. At least down here."

"Still does," she said. "And all the important people know each other, and look out for each other."

As the Eagles kicked into "Peaceful Easy Feeling," a song I had always loved, I asked about her progress.

She squeezed her lime into the drink. "Peralta should plug that drive into his PC."

I stared at her in silence.

"I've debugged it," she said. "It can't do any damage, I

hope. I gave him a patch to send out to everyone on the Sheriff's Office intranet. It will protect them. But don't you use it, Dave. The hacker will have a special interest in you and I want them to think their back door is working. Once Peralta plugs it in, we can see where they go in the system, what they're after. If it works, we can find them."

I noticed the pronoun she used.

"They're probably suspicious that Peralta hasn't used it already. I don't know if that gives us the advantage. It might tempt them to do something else to get attention. If you have a better idea, Dave?"

I didn't.

Chapter Fourteen

On Thursday morning, my phone rang and it was someone from Cronkite News. These were journalism students at ASU's downtown campus, but their stuff appeared in the *Republic* and elsewhere. It had the extra benefit of being free.

He identified himself as Luc Iverson, making sure I knew how to spell his first name, a pleasant young voice. I wondered how many tattoos he had.

"Now that Jack August has passed away, you're my next historian on the list."

Maybe I should open that history shop.

"You know they're working on that mixed-use project downtown with a Fry's supermarket."

"Block Twenty-Three in the original townsite," I said. "It was intended as a public plaza and had city hall for awhile. Then it was the site of the Fox Theater, our grandest movie palace. Torn down, of course."

I couldn't tell if I was being helpful or boring, so I stopped.

He said, "The construction people have found a bomb shelter there."

Growing up in the Cold War, I coped by learning

everything I could about apocalypse. From the throw-weight of nuclear missiles to the difference between counterweight and countervalue targeting, I knew it all. Every Saturday at noon, they would test the air-raid sirens and the sound put an icy spike in my stomach as I imagined the coming flash, heat wave, and blast from a one megaton warhead that would obliterate Phoenix, even though Tucson, with its Titan II missiles, was a first-strike target. Phoenix would be a second-strike, to hit the two Air Force bases and the Cold War industries like Motorola. Such a strange little boy I was.

One thing I was sure of: It wasn't a bomb shelter, which implied it was hardened against blast. They had probably discovered an old fallout shelter. These were meant to protect only against radioactive fallout and had been set up in basements all over downtown. There were never enough to shelter the city's population.

I could hear him typing as I talked. So I also told him about the bunker built into a small butte on the military reservation at Papago Park, meant as the emergency operations center during a crisis. It was still there.

"I suspect they found old federal civil defense supplies," I said. "Water, food, geiger counters."

"Interesting, very interesting," he said as he typed. "This was in the old J.C. Penney building, or where it used to be."

That didn't surprise me. By the seventies, it was the last department store left in downtown Phoenix, built in the fifties when the others, such as Goldwater's, were preparing to leave for Park Central in Midtown.

"Thanks," he said. "This is a big help."

"I'm not the definitive source. You might also contact the city's preservation office."

"Don't sell yourself short."

I thought that was a peculiar comment from someone so young, but he had probably spent his life learning self-esteem.

"While I have you, I was wondering if you were looking into the murder of the reporter, Charles Page?"

Suddenly, my personal NORAD went on full alert.

"No."

"Mmmm. It's the fortieth anniversary. There are so many unanswered questions and you are the Sheriff's Office historian."

Nonchalance took me a moment. "I don't know there's anything that can be found. Anyway, my cold cases are back in the 1940s and before. I have plenty to do and a sheriff who wants results on them."

"Oh, well. Thanks for your time."

And he hung up before I could even get his phone number.

I was probably being paranoid, but I made a mental note to look for his story.

Next I called Peralta.

Chapter Fifteen

Kathleen Jarvis wasn't hard to run down. I had her full name and date of birth from Rudy's birth certificate. Using the AutoTrack database, I found her Social Security and driver's license numbers, a marriage in 1980 and divorce in 1983, her active license as a registered nurse, a worker's comp claim in 2011, as well as several addresses she had used over the years. Like her son, she had no criminal record.

She was still also in Phoenix, notable for a city with so many comings and goings. Hell, I wouldn't still be here if I hadn't failed to get tenure in San Diego and ended up cleaning up open-unsolved cases for Mike Peralta. She worked as a nurse at the county hospital. I wrote down her most recent address and headed out in the Prelude Thursday afternoon. The temp had gone down to a more normal 106.

It hadn't been easy to talk Peralta into letting me out of my historian's cell. But the files weren't getting us anywhere. One box was left unopened, but I wasn't hopeful. This seemed like a prudent next step. It was unlikely "Sly" even knew about Rudy Jarvis' mother, much less expected us to contact her. He was expecting Peralta to plug in that

USB drive. In the meantime, the sheriff consented to me doing some old-fashioned police work—or being a historian seeking out a primary source. I had no idea what I might find.

The address went to a house on East Flower Street near Thirty-Sixth. Like most of its siblings on this block, it was a ranch house built around the late 1940s, but with a fresh coat of paint that was a mixture of olive and taupe. The floor plans of these houses were all alike. Master bedroom facing the street with two wide windows, living room set in under a small porch, a driveway, and carport. In Jarvis' case, an old Buick Century sat out of the sun. Her son hadn't bought her any Ferrari. The white front door was slightly ajar. That looked promising for catching her at home.

I drove past. A majority of the houses still had mature trees, but in most cases the once well-tended lawns had gone patchy. There were no flowers on Flower Street anymore. The curbs were rounded and had no sidewalks. A couple of pickups sat in driveways but otherwise the street was deserted. A lonely blue recycling hamper sat out in front of one house, three down from Kathleen Jarvis' property. I swung around and parked one house away, climbed out into the sun's glare, and walked toward the olive-taupe ranch. It was two p.m.

I heard the woman's screams even before the dead grass scrunched under my feet.

Things slowed down. I felt suddenly cooler.

The screams were not sexual or anything happy. Someone was in trouble. Then I heard a sharp concussion and the screaming stopped. I walked slowly to the small concrete slab of a porch. I didn't want to be out of breath or have my heart rate jacked up when I entered. Another look around showed no cars on the street except mine. The small XD semi-automatic was in my hand, my finger resting along the perfect ergonomic frame but ready to move to the trigger. It still amazed me how light it was compared with the Colt Python. The new sidearm was deadly but it was as if I were carrying nothing heavier than an overloaded wallet.

Close up, I saw the door was slightly open because it had been kicked in. The frame was wrecked by the torn-away lock and naked wood splinters were hanging out of the white paint.

"Police! I'm coming in armed!"

I crossed an unoccupied living room with five long strides and found a motionless woman facedown on the floor of the kitchen. She was wearing light-blue scrubs. The back door was open and a man was running. I went after him. He was tall, young, Anglo, brown hair in a man-bun and a small black backpack. Black jeans, short-sleeved black shirt hanging out, tanned muscular arms. He was also wearing what looked like black tactical gloves. That was as much as I saw before he effortlessly vaulted the unpainted wood of the back fence without looking back. I thought about going after him but the barrier was at least eight feet tall and I wasn't in that kind of shape.

I came back to the kitchen and knelt down to check a pulse. The woman suddenly rolled around and started fighting. It surprised me enough that she got a scratch down my cheek. Fortunately, her attempt to kick me in the balls went awry. I held her down until she stopped struggling. Wild eyes stared at me, then at the gun.

"Deputy sheriff!" I managed my most commanding voice. "Is anyone else in the house?"

I had to repeat the question until she took a breath and said, "No." I holstered the gun and helped her up.

That was when I saw the plastic flex cuffs on the floor. Two sets, along with a roll of duct tape. God knows what was in his backpack. He had bad plans for her. Given the tactical gloves, we had no likelihood of getting fingerprints.

Chapter Sixteen

"We should call 911," I said.

"No!"

We were in the living room. She sat on a burgundy sofa. I pulled in a straight-back from the dining table, so I could sit closer. The front curtains were drawn.

"Why not?"

She looked into her lap. "I have cocaine in the house, okay? A small amount, personal use. Are you going to bust me?"

I shook my head.

"It's a bad habit. Here's another." She pulled out a Camel and lit it, taking a long drag. "I don't recommend either. I don't want to lose my license. I don't want to go to jail."

I told her nobody was going to take her in. She asked if I was a real deputy and I handed over my six-pointed star and credentials, which she took time examining.

As she did, I examined her. She was about my age, with short auburn hair disheveled by the fight. Her eyes were large and the color of strong coffee in a pleasant face set off by a wide mouth. The cruel sun had cut lines around her eyes and into her forehead. It made me grateful again for Lindsey's Ivory Soap Girl fair skin. But Lindsey stayed out of the sun all she could, and wore the most protective sunscreen when she couldn't. She gardened wearing a floppy hat. Still, it wasn't difficult to imagine that forty years ago Kathy must have been what was then called a fox.

I brought ice in a dishtowel and she held it against the left side of her face. Her neck still showed the finger-sized red marks from where the man had tried to choke her. As for me, my cheek stung from her scratch but I didn't detect any blood. She told me to call her Kathy. She said she was sorry she scratched me.

"Who was he?" I nodded toward the kitchen.

"I have no idea. I worked a twelve-hour overnight shift, stopped off at a girlfriend's house to help her pick out paint—my exciting life—and had just gotten home. Came inside and went to the kitchen to grab a bite when I heard…it sounded like an explosion…."

She snuffed the cig in a clean ashtray and lit another.

"It took time to realize it was the front door being kicked down. Before I could decide between grabbing a butcher knife and running, he was there. Grabbed my hair, pulled me back and slapped me, rammed me against the wall, and started choking me."

It made me wonder if he meant to catch her at night, the way he was dressed. All that black stood out in the daytime. But he had to wait, either on the street or follow her home from the hospital.

"He was talking crazy things."

I asked what he said.

"It was something about me being a nymph and, uh, and sins over and over, something like that."

"Nymph, in thy orisons, be all my sins remembered?"

"That's it! Except he said, 'your sins.' Meaning me. I'm sure of that."

"It's Shakespeare. *Hamlet*. Mangled, though. Hamlet is talking to Ophelia and says, 'be all my sins remembered.'"

Hamlet is asking her to pray for him and I'm sure it has deeper meanings. But here the man had turned the lines into a threat. The words echoed the note delivered to Peralta. The suspect had fled with a young actor's physical grace. But he also either had training in taking someone down, or he had done this before. In my mind, I went back to those black clothes.

I whispered. "Nay, then, let the devil wear black, for I'll have a suit of sables."

"What?"

I told her I was only talking to myself.

She said, "He had his hands around my neck and I was about to pass out. I managed to scream. Then he, like, threw me against the wall and I was on the floor."

"Have you seen him before?"

"Never."

She described him as being in his late twenties or early thirties, narrow face, scary eyes. Maybe she could pick him out of a photo array, but that could wait.

Besides the sofa, the living room consisted of mismatching armchairs, side tables, cheap art prints bought from a mall, big ashtray on the coffee table, and a hutch with photos of a young man in his graduation cap and gown, and another with the same man older, smiling. Her son. My body taught me the truth behind the expression "my heart sank."

I asked her about any threatening phone calls or e-mails. Any enemies she had made? Any sense someone was following her? Each time, she shook her head.

"What about scoring coke?"

"I get that from a doctor friend. Not a prescription, and he's not going to send someone to kill me." After a minute of silence, she continued. "When I heard the door, I thought it was a burglary. We've had break-ins in the neighborhood. The street has gone downhill since the porn studio moved in."

I raised an eyebrow.

She said, "LA passed an ordinance requiring adult films to use condoms, so they've moved a lot of production here from the San Fernando Valley. They're probably all over Phoenix. Two or three times a week, I'll see half a dozen cars parked outside the house two doors down. They're filming porn videos or whatever the technology is now. Beautiful women with fake tits go in and out. You can tell the studs by the way they hang in their pants, right or left, if you know what I mean."

I took a deep breath and not over her description of the studs.

"Tell me about Mark Reid."

Her head came up and her eyes were wide.

"Is that what this is about?"

I told her I didn't know. And we sat in silence for a good five minutes. I had propped a magazine stand against the busted front door to keep it closed and the air conditioning was doing its job.

"We dated for less than two years," she finally said. "I was eighteen. I met him at the dog track in 1976. My boss took me there, thinking he could get in my pants. I was working part-time as a secretary while trying to go through school. Anyway, my boss got shitfaced and Mark moved in and, what would you call it, rescued me?"

"That doesn't sound like the small-time hood I've read about."

"He was way more than that." Her voice grew stronger. "The newspapers, like, never understood. He owned dogs and raced them. Mark was smart, not only street smart but intelligent. He always had plenty of money, a real wad. I found out why pretty soon. Do you know the name Ned Warren?"

I did, indeed.

The King of Land Fraud in Arizona, real name Nathan Waxman. His crimes in the 1960s and 1970s were legendary, taking hundreds of millions of dollars from gullible easterners. They thought they were buying a piece of the wide-open West. In reality, they were buying land that didn't exist, or had been resold many times, or property to which Warren and his shell companies held no title. Arizona was wide open, all right—to all manner of criminality, and Warren was one of the most notorious criminals of the era.

In one infamous play, promising land near Prescott, Warren got Harry Rosenzweig to persuade Barry Goldwater and Congressman Sam Steiger to write letters of recommendation. Each deal left the would-be buyers with nothing. And each time, he avoided prosecution. Buzz Page wrote extensively about Ned Warren and land fraud. Those stories made his name as an investigative reporter.

Kathy said, "Ned was in jail in 1978."

"That time, they would finally put him away for life."

She nodded. "But you don't get it. Mark was second in command, so he took over Ned's, like, crew of enforcers. The newspapers always portrayed Mark as a low-level thug, some nobody. That's not the truth. He was the most dangerous gangster in Phoenix for those months before..." Her throat caught.

"Before the bombing."

She became teary. It looked sincere. "I didn't know anything about that!"

I tried my best reassuring look.

After a minute, I said, "Why did you stay with him?"

She shrugged. "I was young and stupid and I always went for the bad boys." She shook her head. "I got way more than I bargained for."

When she went quiet and smoked, I let it lie for awhile with only the kissing sound of the air conditioning. She finally filled in the empty space.

"Mark was very magnetic. I knew I wasn't his only girlfriend, but I was attractive and had a body to die for back then. He liked showing me off at the bars and restaurants. His friends were jealous, I could tell."

"How did he take that?"

She looked at me full-on, the brown eyes clear and young again. "Mark didn't take shit. One time one of his friends touched my shoulder and Mark beat him bloody, beat him unconscious. And we're in, like, a very fancy bar. Nobody acted like they even noticed, much less called the cops. He told me he worked for the cops."

Reid a confidential informant? That might explain his sweet deal to avoid the death penalty. It might explain more.

"Did you ever see him talk to a police officer?"

She knocked some ash off her cigarette and thought. "Yeah, once in the Ivanhoe. This guy came in, leaned against the wall near the back until Mark saw him, and they left for maybe twenty minutes. Maybe they went into the parking lot for privacy. He was wearing a gun in a shoulder holster inside his suit jacket. I could see it when he raised his hand up against the wall. It made an impression."

"Any chance he could have been a mobster?"

"He didn't dress that well. Of course, Mark didn't tell me what it was all about."

"How did all this make you feel?" I felt like Dr. Sharon Peralta asking that, but I wanted to keep the memories coming.

She took her time to choose her words. "Like I was with somebody important in a very glamorous and dangerous world. Check this out. When we were at a bar, he'd leave me at our table and go talk to businessmen but also to guys like out of some mob movie. Huddled in close. Smoking of course, everybody did." She blew smoke off to the side. "He'd go over to the pay phones and make calls, give orders. I don't know what about. Guys came to him, tough-looking guys and he'd, like, leave for a few minutes, get in these real intense conversations at the end of the bar. He'd be pointing his finger. They'd go away to do God-knows-what. Sometimes they handed him thick envelopes."

She studied the Camel and tapped off some ash. "Some days, when I was thinking clearly, I knew I had to get away or something like that, the beating, would eventually happen to me. He'd already slapped me twice, hard. I don't even remember what for. But he gave me expensive presents, drugs, and we went to the track several nights a week. The dog track was a big deal then. 'There goes the rabbit, rabbit, rabbit.'" She laughed. "He paid my tuition. Why would I want some broke boyfriend my age? Being with him was...thrilling."

"And he gave you a son."

Her expression hardened. "I was five months pregnant when he was arrested. I already knew where I stood. His Number One girlfriend came first. She was older than me, prettier. I called her The Bitch, to myself, at least. Sometimes he'd disappear and I wouldn't hear from him for days." She sighed. "That February, when I told him I'd missed my period, he said he'd give me three hundred dollars for an abortion but I said no. So he dropped me like a hot rock on a summer day. The Bitch went with him when he went to Lake Havasu City to lay low after the reporter was bombed, you know?"

I was about to reflexively say I was sorry, but that was a foolish comeback. The sequence of events might have saved her from far worse. Until, perhaps, now, based on possible motives of the man who had broken open her door and was waiting for her, likely the same man who had murdered her son.

"Did you ever see him with Dick Kemperton or Darren Howard?"

"Kemperton, yes. He was a regular at the Ivanhoe, Durant's, the Playboy Club. He and Mark had gone to high school together. But I never saw him with that other man. I only read about him in the papers. Same with Freeman Burke. Mark never mentioned him, not that he ever told me about his business."

"What about the time before the bombing. Was anything different?"

"Interesting you ask," she said. "He dumped me in February but came back for a couple of weeks in May. I wasn't showing yet and I had this stupid idea that he might do the right thing. No chance of that. But he was more jacked than normal. I got the sense he was expecting something really big. Mark was spending money like crazy, telling me 'there's a whole lot more coming, Kat.' He called me Kat..." The reverie lasted only a second. "That was probably why I was never called in by the police after he was arrested. His buddies only knew me as Kat, one of his girlfriends. Do you think what happened today had to do with Mark?"

I slowly nodded.

"I need to call my son, let him know. He'll help me. He's a good man, nothing like his father. Unfortunately, I don't see him as often as I'd like. His new wife dislikes me and I feel the same way about her. So it's put some distance between us."

My stomach got a strong acid bath. I couldn't believe the carelessness of the police.

After few seconds, I said, "I have some terrible news, Kathy."

Chapter Seventeen

Kathy Jarvis would stay with her sister and brother-in-law in Mesa. It took them about half an hour to arrive. The woman looked nothing like Kathy and the man was a big boy with a giant Dodge truck. While they loaded her things, I wandered into the carport and surveyed Kathy's ancient dark-blue Buick Century. It was cool and out of the sun. The carport had room for two vehicles and was bracketed by two doors, one to a storage room and the other that led into the kitchen. The car had recently been washed but that couldn't help the rust eating at the bottom of the body.

It couldn't possibly…

But one never knew.

I got on my knees and peered under the chassis. Instead of a pack of dynamite sticks, I found an envelope taped to the underside, directly beneath the driver's seat. Retrieving some latex gloves from the Prelude, I returned and cautiously pulled off the envelope. A printer had written: SHERIFF MIKE PERALTA and PERSONAL.

By this time, the brother-in-law had hammered shut the front door and they were ready to leave. I gave Kathy my card and watched her back out in the Buick without incident and follow the pickup truck east on Flower and back to Mesa.

I wondered if she had taken her cocaine with her.

In the Prelude again, I let the engine run with the windows open, then pulled out my phone. Peralta answered as if we were in mid-conversation. "If you remember, I didn't want to plug in that flash drive. It could have a virus on it. But I did, and now the entire Sheriff's Office is offline and shut down. Nobody can do anything. I warned you…"

"What are you talking about?" I sat on the street in the Prelude with the windows down, waiting for the air conditioning to stop blowing hot air. "When we were at Starbucks, you were ready to see what was on the drive. Lindsey stopped you."

"Mmmm. I don't remember it that way."

"Of course not. Did you tell Lindsey what happened?"

"Yeah. She said she had to let it shut down our intranet so Sly would think he had gotten into the system. Now she says we have to leave it down for two hours. Goddamn. I was playing solitaire on my computer. Thank God it didn't hit the 911 system."

"So things are going as she intended."

"All right, all right. Did you find this Jarvis woman?"

I filled him in for ten minutes and he listened without interrupting.

"Sounds like he was going to take her off and probably kill her."

"Not probably," I said. "We're going to need to put her under twenty-four-hour protection."

"Crud. That's overtime."

"Quit whining. It's going to get worse. Sly is out to kill people associated with the Page case and we've got to get ahead of him."

I heard him impatiently tapping the keys on his dead computer and cursing.

"There's something else."

He sighed heavily but quit the theatrics when I told him about the envelope taped under Kathy Jarvis' car.

"Do you mind if I open your mail?"

"Read it," he said.

I gingerly unsealed the envelope, holding it outside the window in case it contained a little extra, such as anthrax. Inside was only an eight-and-a-half by eleven sheet of white paper, printed in Helvetica type, like the one delivered to us in Starbucks. I read it aloud:

Dear Sheriff Peralta:

No, it's not a bomb. That would set what you people call 'a pattern,' which would make it easier to catch me. You're not going to catch me. LOL. By now, the whore is with me. I plan to take my time with her. When I am finished, you can have what's left.

She's not the last. This isn't going to stop until you and I set things right. This bodes some strange eruption to our state. And then it started as a guilty thing upon a fearful summons.

Get moving.

Sly

More of *Hamlet* interspersed in the note. After a long silence, I said, "It's time."

More dead air. Thank goodness the car was starting to cool down. I closed the windows.

I tried again. "You've got to call a press conference for tomorrow morning. Announce that you're reopening the Page case. That's what he wants. That's the only thing that will at least put him on pause so we can find him. If you keep quiet, he's going to kill again and soon."

Peralta sighed heavily. "Then you're going to be there with me."

He cut me off when I tried to protest. "Lindsey will be fine. She's working from home and he thinks she's in D.C. You're the Sheriff's Office Historian. If you're not there, the media are going to ask why."

I sank into the driver's seat and accepted the logic of his reasoning. I had been the lead in every other historic case.

"We're going to have to be careful," I said. "We'll have to decide whether to mention the Rudy Jarvis bombing. If not, have an answer in case a reporter brings it up. And you've got to tell the other jurisdictions..."

"Mapstone. I didn't wander up from Mexico this morning looking for work on a framing crew."

The car keys glinted from the angle of the sun and I suddenly felt a chill up my neck.

"Call you back," I said and clicked off without waiting for his benediction.

The family of anti-personnel explosives was a large one. I was working a case in San Diego when I came upon a Claymore mine in a darkened apartment. I didn't realize what it was until I saw the helpful lettering, FRONT TOWARD ENEMY, pointing two feet away from me. Only a fast sprint out the door and jump across the second-floor outside railing into the swimming pool saved my life when it detonated seconds later. I was underwater by that time and barely avoided a sizeable cinderblock that fell into the pool, too. A large, unhappy family. Tolstoy didn't know the half of it. Another member uses a pressure plate. The unwitting soldier steps on it and arms the mine. When he steps off, it explodes. I had carelessly started the car without incident, but what if Sly had installed a pressure plate on the driver's seat while I was inside with Kathy? And this wasn't even counting a remotely detonated device of the kind that had killed Buzz Page and, apparently, Rudy Jarvis.

Was I being paranoid? I reasoned with myself: Why kill me, when I had the letter? Only maybe he didn't count on me. When I showed up it made him change his plans. Plenty of time elapsed while I was inside the house. What if he didn't know I had the letter and was, therefore, expendable in another spectacular stunt?

The pavement in Phoenix summers can cause first- or even second-degree burns on unprotected skin. Only my forearms and hands were exposed.

I said a prayer and pulled on the door lever. The door popped open as it should and I was still there. The sound of my breathing was now a very prominent part of my senses. Next I rolled quickly onto the pavement and kept going until I felt the gentle slope of the curb and dead grass and dirt under me. Nothing exploded. I opened my eyes and stood up fast, feeling the singe of heat on my arms and hands. I studied the car. Everything looked normal. The street was still as I had found it when I had arrived.

Back at the Prelude's side, I pulled out the floor mat and placed it on the pavement as insulation against the heat. Then I knelt down and studied the underside, especially beneath the driver's seat. Nothing. Still not satisfied, I walked around the hood, looking for what? Fingerprints in the dust, maybe. Nothing again. Finally, I popped the hood—eyes closed and head down—and examined the engine. It was unmolested.

I climbed back in, shut the door, and took a long pull on what had been a frozen bottle of water in the console of the Prelude. It tasted like deliverance.

•••••

Although I also policed the Prelude for a tracking device, I took a long, circuitous route back to Willo, mindful of cars that stayed with me. None did. Even so, I pulled into a driveway on Holly Street and watched for any followers. There were none. Back at home, Lindsey was in the study with her laptop open.

She gave me a smile but her eyes quickly went back to the screen. "I've never heard *El Jefe* panicked before."

"You interrupted his solitaire game when the computer system shut down," I said. "He also tried to rewrite history, said he hadn't wanted to plug in the drive."

She laughed but didn't look up. "Had to make it look realistic, Dave. I'm sure it's driving the county IT people crazy. They'll be even more baffled when I bring it back up, as I am doing…now." She looked me over. "Why is your shirt dirty? Your arms are scuffed. Are you okay?"

I sat beside her and told her about the attack on Kathy Jarvis, what I had learned about the much greater importance of Mark Reid, and finally my bomb scare. Pretty soon, I would be like Buzz Page and start putting Scotch tape on the hood of the car.

"Hold that thought," she said. "Somebody without authorization is in the Sheriff's Office computer system."

"Sly?"

She nodded.

I stood and walked to the picture window, surveying the empty street with satisfaction.

"Can you tell where he is?"

"Nope. He's pretty good. The IP address says he's in Romania."

She sat back and her expression changed. The color drained out of her face.

"I think he knows exactly what he's after," she said.

I turned toward her. "What's he looking at?"

"He's looking at you, History Shamus." She did some ferocious typing. "In your personnel jacket. I changed your address to a house on Susie's Circle, right off Campbell. The house is unoccupied."

After ten minutes, she spoke again. "Is your MacBook plugged into the county T-1 line?"

I nodded.

"Well, he's in it, going through the case files on your hard drive. Right now, he's in a Word document called Timeline."

I cursed. Everything about Page had been done on paper, except this one thing. It was the timeline I had made of the Page assassination and its aftermath, then printed out and taped to the white board.

Chapter Eighteen

An hour after the press conference, I was back at my office in the old Courthouse.

It had gone well. Peralta reminded the reporters that the Page case had never been officially closed. But he was making it an active investigation by the Sheriff's Office. He talked about the Rudy Jarvis bombing coming forty years to the month after the assassination of Buzz Page and the likelihood of it being a copycat crime. How "certain other information" pertinent to the 1978 crime had recently emerged.

I couldn't hear reporters scribbling furiously, as in old movies. From the podium of the Starship media briefing room, with its klieg lights in my face, I could only see heads and the lenses and lights of video cameras. Of course, Peralta held back critical information: the attack on Kathy, the texted threats and computer hacking, and, most important, that Rudy was Mark Reid's son. The point was to show activity, indulge "Sly" before we could catch him.

My phone rang right on time and I said to send up the visitor.

Five minutes later a tap came on my door and Malik Jones stepped inside. He didn't even say hello because his eyes caught the white board's expansive array of Post-it notes and Magic Marker scribbling. The board had been empty the first time he was here. He walked over and studied it a long time in silence. I let him do it.

He tilted his head my way. "Damn, Dr. Mapstone. I knew you couldn't stay away from this one."

"David is fine," I said, but I was momentarily gripped by doubt. He had asked about the Page case the first time we met. This, even though I had checked him out. He had arrests from protests the past year, charges dismissed, but was also a West Point graduate who won a Silver Star and Purple Heart in Iraq. He rose to the rank of captain before leaving the Army five years ago. His back was still to me. "Are you a Shakespeare fan?"

"No," he said without hesitation. Such a serious young man. He reminded me of myself.

I decided to take the leap. It hadn't been easy to get here. Getting here had required a serious fight with Peralta, with him doing a thermonuclear temper tantrum. For a few minutes, I didn't know if I was going to be fired or if he was going to have a stroke. Dr. Sharon had explained these eruptions before: *He's afraid or anxious about change, so he reacts with anger.* Whatever. It never made it easier.

But I won. Now Peralta was under even greater pressure elsewhere. He was still beholden to the federal monitor who had been placed by the District Court over the Sheriff's Office because of Crisis Meltdown's many infractions. Peralta was on his way for a regular checkup at that moment. And he had thrown down against "Sly" in public, although he didn't use the name. Not only did he say he was reopening a forty-year-old notorious case, but it was connected to the bombing near Christown.

Unorthodox methods would be required.

"Mark Wayne Reid," Jones said, resting a finger on the yellow note. "Bomb maker. Made a deal with the state to implicate his co-conspirators. Dick Kemperton set it off. Darren Howard paid for it. What's new?"

I told him a few things I had learned: Reid as a capo to the King of Land Fraud, maybe a police informant. How Buzz Page was assassinated because of something he was *going to write*, not as revenge for something he had written. And then I told him about history's long, implacable reach: the threat against Peralta, the bombing of Rudy Jarvis, and the attempted abduction of his mother.

"These five boxes contain material squirreled away by the Sheriff. I've been through these four." I ran my hands across them.

By this time, Jones was sitting at the lawyer's table. I sat beside him. He wore a white T-shirt with black lettering: HANDS UP! DON'T SHOOT!

He leaned forward and pulled the top off the fifth box. He thumbed through more files. Those could wait. My brain was researched-out for the week.

"What's this?"

He twirled a key with a faded orange plastic tag attached. A black number was stamped on it.

"I have no idea," I said. "But you're curious. Do you want a piece of this case?"

He cocked his head.

"You mean help the Man?"

"Exactly. I don't know if you're doing any teaching this summer, but I can offer you a thousand dollars for fifty hours of research. I need a historian's eyes on this."

"That's a pretty big ask," he said. "Considering the crimes against people of color by the Sheriff's Office and all the shootings of unarmed black men by police in the Valley."

I could no more fix that situation than go back and undo 1619, the year when the first Africans were first brought to Virginia, two-and-a-half centuries of slavery, another hundred years of Jim Crow, and the seeming impossibility of reconciliation. If I told him about recently re-reading James Baldwin, including the essay "The Devil Finds Work," he would dismiss me as another guilty-minded, privileged white intellectual.

I had forebears who fought in the Union Army, true. But, then, on my mother's side, were the ones who fought for the Stars and Bars. Arizona Territory was first created by the Confederacy, carved out of New Mexico Territory. Arizona sent a delegate to the Confederate Congress every year. Phoenix practiced segregation for decades before the 1960s and Arizona was a national embarrassment in the 1980s with a governor opposing a Martin Luther King, Jr., holiday. How much had changed? Much, I hoped. Yet I recalled the intense, visceral hatred many white Arizonans held toward Obama. We were so not in a post-racial America.

I rested my hands on the tops of my thighs. "The bad sheriff is gone. The rest, I can't claim to be able to change. Good cops are trying. I can't deny there are bad cops." I left out the fact that people of all races, who lived an oppositional lifestyle, refused to stop and show their hands when a police officer told them to do so. Or tried to take the weapon away from a poorly trained officer who panicked and fired.

And there was another backbeat here. Blacks were once a substantial minority in Phoenix. In the sixties, when Dr. King marched in south Phoenix with blacks and liberal whites, including our senior minister at Central Methodist, it was a very big deal. The black ministers themselves were a force, and an African-American on City Council was a given. Elijah Muhammad, the Black Muslim leader, had a home in Phoenix, too. Now African-Americans were much diminished by the great Hispanic migrations north.

Jones said, "What does Mike Peralta say?"

"He wants you." That was not exactly the truth, but what the hell.

"My father thinks I'm foolish to study history," he said. "History is just one damned thing after another, he said."

Of course, Jones knew the quote originated with the great historian Arnold Toynbee but I let that lie. If Toynbee had actually believed this, he wouldn't have spent his life on a twelve-volume set on the study of history.

"We search for the truth." I heard myself lecturing and toned way down. "It's true that most historians are a disposable commodity. Our work is often destined to be set aside or forgotten. New scholarship comes along. Tastes change..."

"But we have to try, right?" His eyes brightened. "Plutarch, Thucydides. Their work is still relevant."

"Plus, 'Who controls the past controls the future. Who controls the present controls the past.'"

"George Orwell. My dad says I'm a quote machine."

"Orwell also said, 'In a time of universal deceit, telling the truth is a revolutionary act.'"

"I think about that a lot these days."

I tried to seal the deal. "Think of this as enhanced post-grad work. In history and crime, somewhere, somebody's digging for the truth. Anyway, real lives are at stake at the moment. It is a big ask. But there it is."

He sighed and looked for answers in the high ceiling.

"Who was Ida Wells?"

"A journalist," I said. "The first who documented

lynchings in the United States. One of the co-founders of the NAACP. A Republican in a very different Republican Party."

He clapped his hands. "Very good. What's the plan?"

"We need to go backward and forward."

He nodded. "Backward to find out what really happened in 1978, who ordered the killing, and why he got away with it. Forward to get ahead of this dude 'Sly' and protect his next victims. What are you guys doing to get at his computer?"

Again, that little catch of doubt hit me. I pushed it aside. "Deputies from the Cybercrimes Bureau are working on it."

"Are they any good, Dr. Mapstone?"

"I think so. And I'm David."

He laughed. "No, if we're going to do this the right way, I'm Mr. Jones and you are Dr. Mapstone, or Professor Mapstone, your choice. I'm sure as hell going to use the honorific when I get my PhD. How about Chief Mapstone?"

"Mr. Jones," I said, "are you on board?"

"See, I'm played by Sidney Poitier as *Mister* Tibbs. Down here in redneckville to save your white supremacist asses. You don't look like Rod Steiger but you'll have to do as Chief Bill Gillespie. And when we solve the crime, a smidgen of brotherhood and understanding will sneak in the door of American racism. Until the next unarmed black man is murdered by the police."

His eyes were part playful, part mournful, and I couldn't tell if he was playing me.

He said, "I'm on board. What do you want me to do?"

"Go to the State Archives." I explained the occult classified nature of the Page files. Peralta would arrange for him to have access to the first level until we could get a court order for the next, more sensitive material.

Mister Jones blinked at me. "Is it too late for you to put me on that train headed back north, Chief?"

"It's too late."

Chapter Nineteen

On Sunday, a week and two days after the Rudy Jarvis bombing, I grabbed two frozen water bottles, filled up the Prelude with gas, and took Interstate 17 north out of town.

The I-17, the Black Canyon Freeway, vaulted nearly a mile in altitude to Flagstaff, 145 miles away. This had once been a stagecoach road through rugged country to the mines. The highway became an Interstate in the 1960s, but it was built to rural specifications, two lanes in each direction. This wasn't a problem when the entire state's population was a little more than a million. Now, at seven million, the road was often clogged with traffic, like today. Arizona was decades behind in its infrastructure.

About twenty miles north of central Phoenix, beyond the abortion of Anthem's suburban pods, Black Canyon City sat among jagged, saguaro-studded hills beyond the New River Mountains. It was not close to Black Canyon, which sat farther north. It was never much of a city, either.

If you drove south from Flagstaff, the Interstate rolled downhill from the high grassy plateau of Sunset Point. Black Canyon City suddenly appeared off to the right, below the highway, which hugged the side of an ancient lava flow. The dry Agua Fria River cut through on its way south to Lake Pleasant. Coming north, Black Canyon City was less of a surprise, only 900 feet higher than Phoenix. Most of my life it had been a little outpost for the most hardened desert rats and a stop for motorists. That was back in the days when the climb caused cars to overheat and conk out on the side of the highway. Now it was fast becoming a Phoenix bedroom community, complete with subdivisions of faux Tuscan-Spanish schlock tract houses.

Tom Goldstein's address was separated from this shoddy modernity, a faded double-wide trailer on Nasty Ridge Trail, backstopped by a craggy ridge, and, beyond that, the majestic purple-blue Bradshaw Mountains rising almost eight-thousand feet to the northwest, full of played-out mines, pine forests, and legends. I came unannounced, but was happy to see a dusty Chevy pickup parked outside. He was home. So were several skins of rattlesnakes, heads and rattles attached, hanging from the wooden railing that made an L-shape leading to the front entrance. The snake eyes were glassy in the sunlight. It was a "not-welcome" mat. I stepped up anyway and knocked, but was careful to stand aside of the door. You never knew if someone would fire a shotgun through the entrance to make a point about unannounced visitors.

The man who answered the door looked every bit of eighty. In the old photos, Goldstein was powerfully built, always wearing a black cowboy hat. Now I surveyed a much slimmer version, not much more than skin on bones, but still wearing the hat. Underneath the headgear was a long face riven by so many wrinkles that it resembled the contour lines of mountainous land. His jaw was square and the tip of his nose looked as if a cat had chewed it. Goldstein waved away the identification card and star I held out and stepped back.

"I was wondering how long before you showed up." His back was to me and he gesticulated. "Peralta can't stay away from the television cameras. Never could. Better than that joke who played sheriff for awhile."

I pulled off my sunglasses and let my eyes adjust to the dim interior light. Every window was covered by a shade. My attention instantly went to a model railroad layout that took up the entire length of the living room. It was built on narrow wooden "benchwork," as the modelers called it, maybe sixteen inches wide, but at least ten feet long. I had been working on my own HO-scale layout in the garage for years, but life and lack of money kept intruding. I hadn't touched it since Lindsey was shot. Goldstein had already built my vision: Phoenix Union Station, circa 1950. The scene was wonderfully detailed, from the long Mission-style depot right down to baggage wagons and little model men loading sacks of mail and express boxes onto a Southern Pacific baggage car. He had taken time to smudge the car so it looked realistically road-worn. One of the main tracks was occupied by a long passenger train, the cars silver with a red stripe, the diesel locomotives in SP Daylight colors. The station looked built from scratch, not from a kit, and a perfect reproduction of the old depot. So were the surrounding buildings. At the back was a photo panorama of the city's skyline from the same era. The tallest building was the Hotel Westward Ho, sixteen stories and the fanciest hostelry in town. Now it's Section Eight housing.

"I love this," I said. "Beautiful work."

"Keeps me busy."

I wanted to linger. My grandmother would take me to Union Station when I was a boy to see the trains. Now Phoenix was the largest city in the country with no intercity passenger trains. Unfortunately, I had work to do.

He indicated that I should sit on the sofa. I sank down, causing a plume of dust to erupt. It smelled vaguely of Lysol. The room was welcomingly cool, though. I could hear an air-conditioning unit laboring somewhere outside. The walls were empty of any art except for a framed map of the world from the Age of Exploration or maybe even Medieval times. It was an odd contrast to the railroad layout. A plasma screen television sat at one end of the living room, turned to a cooking channel but muted. Paperback books—mostly mysteries—filled one floor-to-ceiling set of shelves.

"Water?" He pulled a cold plastic bottle from the refrigerator, walked over, and handed it to me. "Can't drink the local stuff. Arsenic. The water company says they treat it, but I don't trust 'em. Sorry I can't offer you a real drink, but I had to give it up. People tell me I'm not much fun anymore." He opened a bottle for himself and sat slowly, as if the movement hurt. Prominent below his weathered jeans were expensive tooled cowboy boots. "This is a waste of time. Peralta is making a big mistake."

I asked him why.

"It just is."

I cracked open the bottle.

He said, "*L'chaim.*"

I raised my bottle and put my throat into my voice. "*L'chaim.*"

He gave a grudging smile. "Very good. We'll make you an honorary member of the tribe." Then he retreated into silence. I stretched an arm out on the sofa and looked at him. I had all day.

Finally: "I am absolutely confident we got the right guys. Reid, Kemperton, and Howard. They did it."

I said, "No doubts after all these years? Howard said he was framed."

"None. Howard made the payment to Reid a week before Page was killed."

I thought about the incomplete court records I had skimmed about Howard's appeal. "He said he was passing along the money as a favor."

"I know, I know. But Howard lost twice in court." He shook his head. "Why he chose that idiot Mark Reid is beyond me."

Kathy Jarvis would have differed about her boyfriend's intelligence. "Reid was running Ned Warren's crew that summer. He couldn't have been too big an idiot."

"He was," Goldstein said. "That only made him more dangerous. Warren wasn't a psycho. Mark Reid was. Anyway, Warren was spent by that time anyway. We finally got him good, although the trial took a long time. There wasn't a whole lot left for Reid to run for Warren in Phoenix by 1978."

"No chance Warren didn't order the hit on Page from prison as revenge?"

Goldstein shook his head. "No chance, like you said. Warren was sick. The feds had his assets. His mob friends had abandoned him. Anyway, the mob didn't kill reporters. It was Reid, Kemperton, and Howard."

I pulled out a pen and notebook. "Why would somebody like Darren Howard get mixed up in this? He was a successful businessman, respectable."

"What did respectable mean in Phoenix back then? Barry Goldwater was dirty. So was Harry Rosenzweig and the bunch of them. Reid said that Howard wanted to get revenge on Charles Page for the stories he wrote that got Freeman Burke kicked off the Racing Commission.

Howard owed his start to old man Burke. He wanted to repay him or maybe he was trying to curry favor. Howard hung out in the same bars as Reid: the Ivanhoe, the Phone Booth, Smuggler's Inn, the Clown's Den, Chauncey's, Mister Fat Fingers, the Velvet Hammer, Kemo Sabe, the Garnet Lounge, Durant's, Navarre's, the Islands, Chez Nous. Phoenix had real bars back then. We had witnesses who saw Darren Howard talking to Mark Reid two weeks before the bombing."

"What if Burke ordered the hit himself?"

He removed the hat and set it, crown down, on the table beside his chair. The top of his head was a nest of wispy white hair. "We could never make a case. Did he order the bombing? I'm agnostic."

"You interviewed Burke?"

"We did. He denied everything. The old man was still full of piss and vinegar. When we got back downtown, he had already called Chief Wetzel and threatened to sue us for harassment."

I was undeterred. "So after the threat to the chief, you backed off."

He shot a gnarled fist at me. "We didn't back off anything. We couldn't connect Burke with enough evidence to make a case. Let me tell you how it went down, young man."

It was nice somebody thought I was young.

He continued: "I was at the scene of the bombing within twenty minutes, then I went to St. Joe's. Reid was on our radar screen immediately. Page named him. His appointment was typed on his typewriter at the Capitol press room. Then we had a tip and we were watching him. But we waited for Page to die so we could arrest him for murder." He sighed and stared past me. "He lingered for ten days. They amputated one arm and both legs, trying to save him. My God, I never saw a man who suffered so much. When he died, we arrested Mark Reid for murder. Then he rolled on the other two."

"You arrested him on June 13th?"

He scratched his chin. "You know that. You've read the reports. If I didn't know better, Deputy, I'd think you were interviewing me instead of asking for a professional courtesy."

"Not at all." Of course, I was doing that. I need corroboration of everything in this case: dates, times, people. I ran through the timeline, asking more questions in a pleasant voice.

"Who first told you that Reid was the suspect?"

"I can't disclose that."

"Why?"

"It's time for you to leave, kid." His voice was angry. "I was solving homicides when you were still in grade school. Remember the 'Harpoon Killer,' 1964? I broke that case, and a hell of a lot more."

He stood. I didn't. But I knew I needed to take a different tack.

"You're right. I'm a kid. I wasn't even a deputy sheriff when Page was killed. But I have a demanding boss and I want to get it right."

After a minute, he shook his head in disgust and sat down. I told him that I had read the confession. I asked why Reid avoided the gas chamber and received a relatively light sentence, only twenty years.

"Because he was willing to testify against the other two," he said. "We rolled up the conspiracy. Period, the end. Add in Howard's history with Freeman Burke, Page's negative articles about Burke, and you have the core theory of the prosecution. Pulling other mob stuff into it only clouds the base facts and sends you off chasing the minutiae."

He took a deep breath and stared at the floor. "I always believed that Freeman Burke did the bombing or it was done for him. But we couldn't make the case. And thanks to forty years of the Freeman Burke, Sr., Foundation endowing projects all over the state—even putting his name on a college at the University of Arizona...It's strange how time changes everything."

He made so much sense, for about ten seconds. Then I felt anger as a hotspot in the middle of my chest. He was blowing off "the kid." As camouflage for my reaction, I admired the model railroad for a moment. A to-scale Phoenix Police car was parked beside the dark-green Railway Express Agency trucks at Union Station. I wondered if Goldstein imagined himself in that car, a young man forever.

I said, "It was interesting that Reid said Buzz Page was killed for something he was going to write, not for something he had written."

"So that undermines the 'frontier justice' theory against old man Burke, having him killed for the stories about the Racing Commission. You see how this merry-go-round works. Defense attorneys make their money off seeding reasonable doubt. Prosecutors don't want to take a case forward when they think they'll lose before a jury."

I pressed. "But what was he going to write?"

Goldstein opened his mouth, breaking strings of saliva, and then closed it. He tapped his forehead, looked into his lap and didn't speak for several minutes.

Then he raised his chin high. "You know what they called me? Detective Yid. The Homicide Hebrew. I didn't mind. Took it as a badge of honor. My partner and I introduced ourselves as Detective Yid and Detective Goy until the commander found out and got pissed. I cleared more murder cases than anybody on the homicide squad before I finally put in my papers and took my pension. You ought to show more respect, kid."

Now the hotspot threatened to spread up into my face. I drank more cold water.

"Nobody is questioning your work, Detective. My job is historic cold cases. That doesn't automatically imply that the original investigators screwed up. New information arrives."

"Yeah, yeah, Dr. David Mapstone, the history professor who's a sworn deputy. I know. You did okay on the Yarnell twins case. You're an eminence in the intellectual culture of Phoenix."

He was good with the insult. It was like being called the surfing champion of Tempe Town Lake or the second-best sports columnist in San Diego.

"That was a long time ago," I said. "What was Page working on that got him killed?"

He told me they never found out. None of his *Gazette* colleagues knew. A couple of them said Page had told them he was busy on a big story that would get him back on the investigative beat. But after examining his files, they could never find what Page was doing.

"And you got all his files?"

"And notebooks. I went through it all personally."

"Did anything seem missing?"

He spread bony hands. "How would I know that? Page was a good reporter. Trustworthy. Did you know he was a fighter pilot in Korea? Most people didn't. He didn't talk about it. I knew him, gave him some background when he was working on some stories."

"Which ones?"

"About Warren's land fraud and organized crime. Probably others that I can't recall. Anyway, he wasn't a file clerk. His stuff was disorganized. I couldn't tell you if anything was missing."

I asked him what he found. He said notes and court records about land fraud, the dog tracks, RaceCo, and the Mafia. All of it for stories he had written, including his series on mobsters in Phoenix.

"Nothing about an upcoming story?"

"Not a thing. He was covering the Legislature lately. Most of his files about that were dull as dirt."

"What about his car? Any files there?"

He shook his head. "None. His reporter's notebook was sitting on the front passenger seat, spattered with blood. It was completely empty except for the first page. It had 'Mark Reid' written at the top. I suppose this was in anticipation of interviewing him at the Clarendon, if Reid would've shown."

"Any idea what Reid wanted to talk about?"

"You read the transcript. Reid wanted to introduce Page to a made man from Los Angeles who might have some OC information." Organized crime.

"And you never found this individual," I said.

Goldstein shrugged and finished his water.

"I heard Reid was a CI."

Goldstein's head snapped up. "Where'd you get that?"

"I can't disclose that information. It's an ongoing investigation. You know how it goes."

Goldstein glared at me. After a long pause: "He might have been. You need to understand there were two Phoenix Police Departments. One, professional and honest, reformed by Chief Charlie Thomas in the fifties. The other was lazy and dirty, penetrated by the Chicago

Outfit. Thomas never completely rooted it out. Neither did Chief Wetzel. If Reid was a confidential informant, he was working for one of those bad cops."

"Such as?"

"I never found out." He sighed. "You know, Reid did another bombing, up on the Navajo Reservation, the year before?"

I didn't know.

"This wasn't in the confession. Goldwater was in a battle with the tribal chairman. The senator wanted him out, said he was corrupt and he was, but so were the whites involved in some of the deals involving the tribe. So Barry needed to show things were out of control on the rez. One of Barry's aides, who was assigned to keep an eye on the Navajos, supposedly contacted Reid to plant a bomb at the tribal headquarters in Window Rock. That's what Reid told us, at least. He rigged up a bomb with three sticks of dynamite and hit the road. Only he chickened out on the way and dropped it in a dumpster. If what Reid told us is correct, he was perfecting his bomb-making before Page."

"Could Goldwater have ordered the Page hit?"

His eyes fixed on me. "Makes you wonder, doesn't it?"

My circle of wonder kept widening. "Is that why the case files are sealed for fifty years?"

Goldstein crushed the plastic water bottle and put on the cap. "That was from the Attorney General's office. They took the case away from the County Attorney. You'd have to ask them. I think Rusty Clevenger, the chief investigator, is still alive. Look, there are transcripts of phone taps in those case files, including on the mob. If it became public, it could get people killed, even now."

"You're saying there was a Mafia connection?"

He shrugged. "We chased dozens of leads. Was Reid a made man? Maybe. There's no question the mob was very active in Phoenix then. RaceCo, the whole dog-track empire, was wrapped up with organized crime."

"Page specifically said 'Mafia' and "RaceCo' before he passed out."

"He was in shock. We never got a chance to interview him. But we never connected them to the bombing. I talked to a wise guy a few weeks after that and he said if it was a Mafia job, it would have been done right and Page would have been left in pieces all over that parking lot."

The note I found in the files to that effect had been written by Goldstein.

He pointed a gnarled hand at me. "If I had my way, Reid would have been sniffing cyanide at Florence. The AG made the deal in exchange for his testimony against the other two. Courts tried to impose the death sentence on him twice, including when the little schmuck wouldn't testify again against Kemperton and Howard when their convictions were initially overturned. Lucky guy."

"Were you at the fortieth anniversary event?" I asked.

He nodded. "It was fun to see the old gang."

"Anything strange?"

"Well, a woman at the bar asked me if I wanted to go up to her room. That doesn't happen anymore. Back in the seventies, now those was good times. Page was in that scene, too, you know. His steady girlfriend had been killed in a nine-sixty-three..." radio code for an auto accident with fatalities..."and he was pretty broke up about it. But even that didn't stop him from stepping out, if you know what I mean. Those were fun days."

I steered him back to the anniversary event, the bar, the woman.

"She was blond, forties, good looking. I told her I didn't go up to hotel rooms with females I didn't know and that was the end of it. Never got her name."

I persisted. "If all this is wrapped up with a bow on it, why did somebody threaten Sheriff Peralta, blow up Mark Reid's son in a copycat bombing, and attack his mother at her home?" I told him about the Kathy Jarvis incident, which hadn't been in the media.

He shifted bony shoulders.

"I didn't know Reid had a son." He bit his lower lip. "Crazy person. Lot of 'em out there."

"Not someone out to settle a score?"

He stood, again with care but then attained his authoritative bearing. "There's nothing unsettled about this case. Anybody who could settle it is living with underground furniture now." And his face shut down.

At the door, I told him we were concerned about people close to the incident being targeted and asked if he wanted protection.

"I'm well-armed up here. Ask those unwanted visitors." He indicated the rattlers. In the distance came the sound of a semi rig downshifting on the Interstate.

Then I heard his voice as I walked to the car.

"You have a good day, Deputy. Sounds like you're the one who needs to take care."

I opened the door and faced him. He was holding one of the rattlesnakes by the head. Its mouth was frozen open, fangs out.

"Did you see that map on my wall? Out on the edges, the unexplored and dangerous places, the cartographers wrote 'here be monsters.' You think about that, kid. You're sticking your nose in places that were buried a long time ago."

I was about to ask him what he meant but the door was already shut.

Chapter Twenty

Five minutes later I was parked near the Rock Springs Café, sitting under the shade of a big cottonwood, with the air conditioning turned on high. The temperature gauge on the Prelude was sitting at the safe seven o'clock position so I stayed put, parked beside several Harleys. I avoided the temptation to go inside for famous pie. It might have taken some of the edge off my frustration.

Goldstein was the lead homicide detective on the Page case, yet he gave me next to nothing. He showed no curiosity about the new developments. Most investigators had cases that bothered them for their entire careers and into retirement. What could be more of an un-scratchable itch than the Page murder, a case nearly everybody thought was never resolved? He was holding back. I also envied his fine work on that HO-scale railroad.

I pulled out my cell, attached my earbuds, and dialed a number in New Jersey from my list of contacts. I didn't know if it was still an active line. A woman answered on the first ring.

"David Mapstone. You never write. You never call. You must want something."

"I'm sorry, Lorie. I'm a crappy correspondent."

"Yeah. Are you still married to Mimsy?"

"Lindsey," I said. "And yes."

Lorie Pope knew my wife's name was Lindsey. She liked to pull my chain. She was an expert flirt, a skill I didn't master until I was in my thirties. But she was a grand master in her twenties, when she was a cops reporter for the *Arizona Republic* and I was a rookie deputy sheriff. Our relationship progressed into something more than a romp or a fling, but never reached the status of a love affair.

We remained friends. She won a Pulitzer at the *Republic* while I was away from Phoenix trying, and failing, to get on the tenure track as a professor. We renewed our friendship, minus the sex, after I came back and went to work for Peralta. It had always involved sharing information. But like so many of the most experienced reporters and editors, she had been run out in the years after Gannett bought the newspaper. The veterans cost too much and didn't cotton to seeing one of the largest dailies in the country run like the *Shreveport Times*.

"Tell me how you are?"

"I'm loving the gig economy," she said. "A freelance article pays me five-hundred dollars, if I'm lucky. My adjunct professor job at Montclair State is thirteen-hundred a semester hour. Add it up and I'm probably making what I did when I was twenty-seven. Living with my mom, trying to help her out."

"How is she?"

"Not good."

The line was empty for a long few seconds before I filled it. "We're investigating the Charles Page killing again."

"Holy crap, David." Her voice thrummed with concern. "Is that a good idea?"

"Why do you say that?"

"Because there are still plenty of toes to step on. Arizona doesn't like boat-rockers."

"Tell me about it. This is the fortieth anniversary and someone pulled off a copycat bombing on Mark Reid's son."

I heard a gasp on the other end. "Dead?"

"Yes. And then somebody went after his mother, but I got there in time."

"My David, always the tarnished knight." I hoped I heard some fondness. Then her voice changed. "I can't believe you're still in that hellhole of Phoenix and still at the Sheriff's Office playing cop after all these years."

"Seems like yesterday when I came back without a job and Peralta gave me some old cases to clear up. I intended to sell the house on Cypress and move on."

Lorie filled in the rest. "And you stayed. David, you worked so hard to get your master's and your PhD. I assumed you would be long gone and would be teaching again."

"Starbucks employs plenty of barristas with PhDs in history."

"They're not smart like you. I don't get it. You're not a power freak, not badge-heavy. All I can guess is you're an adrenaline junkie and this job feeds that. What a loss at a time when people need to learn history more than ever."

"Jeez." I felt taken down more than a couple of notches.

She sighed. "I'm sorry. Because I'm bitter about my career doesn't give me the right to judge the choices you made. Half the country doesn't believe in facts. The president called journalists 'enemies of the people.'"

It was past time to move on. I said, "Can you tell me anything that might be helpful?"

"'Front Page' was killed my first day in the *Republic*

newsroom. When the word came that a reporter had been bombed in the parking lot of the Clarendon, the city editor yelled, 'Where's Al Sitter?' He was one of our top investigative reporters and for a while everyone assumed he'd been the target. Maybe forty-five minutes later, we learned it was 'Front Page' from the *Gazette*."

"And?"

"And, it was all hands on deck, at both newspapers, for days, months. One of ours had been killed, we took it personally, and we were going to get the bastards." She let out a long breath. "But we never really did. Freeman Burke got away with it."

"You're sure it was Burke?"

"I was only a cub reporter. But I worked like hell to help. Later, I was the lead writer in a twenty-year retrospective. We dug into the case again, bottom to top."

"And?"

"And it's a hall of mirrors. You know that. Dozens of cops, gangsters, lawyers, sleazebags. Gangland killings. Corruption. Compromised politicians. Nothing is what it seems. It goes back generations in Phoenix—makes Jersey seem clean by comparison—but it really came to a head in the seventies."

I asked her what the retrospective conclusions were. I hadn't read the stories.

"Nothing could be proved beyond the three who went to prison, and even with their convictions there were holes you could drive a truck through. Beyond that, the Burke theory was still the most compelling. Another was that Page was killed by the Chicago Outfit or as revenge for helping take down Ned Warren, the land-fraud guy, remember? And then there was RaceCo, which operated the dog tracks. The Cameron family owned it. Mobbed up to the eyeballs."

"That sounds promising."

"Page had written plenty on the organized crime connections to RaceCo, and Sitter worked an angle that Joey Cameron, the son and heir apparent, had put a contract on Page. He was crazy enough to do it. The mob typically didn't kill cops or reporters. It broke their code and brought down more scrutiny. But Joey, maybe. Freeman Burke, more than maybe. We had to be careful what we printed. Potential for libel was everywhere. The editors were afraid about getting sued by Burke's family. Burke himself won a libel suit years before against IRE for the *Phoenix Project*."

"Was the police investigation handled well?"

"God, no," she said. "The Attorney General took it out of the hands of the County Attorney. And there were the missing files."

I asked about that.

"Phoenix Police records. The infamous 851 files."

I asked if that was a type of report. I had never heard of it.

"No, it was the file number, supposedly containing multiple folders. Somebody took it, a cop I mean, and also took the card catalogue card referring to the file. Did it have inconvenient information on the bombing? I'd bet it did."

"What about Goldwater?"

She laughed. "Talk about off limits. He was an icon. But I looked anyway. Barry had every reason to fear Buzz. But my sources said he was surprised to hear about the bombing. He was upset and angry about it."

I knew better than to ask a journalist about her sources. "What about Page's files? Were they preserved?"

"That was the *Gazette*, remember? Our competitors.

There was an urban legend that Page's files disappeared after the bombing but it didn't happen. My friends over there confirmed that. The cops took them. Tom Goldstein."

"I finished visiting with him a few minutes ago."

"My Lord, is he still alive?"

"Very. In a double-wide out in Black Canyon City."

"I'm not surprised. Still wearing that black Stetson?"

"Yep."

Lorie paused. Then: "I never really knew Page except by reputation. But one of my boyfriends, who worked at the *Gazette*—sorry, David, you weren't my first—was close to him. He was his editor. I say that because you asked about files. This guy told me that Page never kept his most sensitive stuff in the newsroom, much less in his desk out at the Capitol press room. He carried it around with him in a briefcase. I saw him once when he was leaving. He checked me out, a long undressing with his eyes. Didn't bother me, but today it would go to HR as a firing offense. Anyway, I noticed he had a classic soft leather briefcase with straps that closed it. Most reporters didn't carry them and the ones that did had hard-sided attaché cases back then. It stood out. Looked like he probably had it for years."

"Goldstein didn't say anything about finding a briefcase."

"Really?" Her voice sounded like the old Lorie, her curiosity piqued. "My friend told me Page never let the briefcase out of his sight. He was paranoid, and for good reason. He wouldn't have left it in his car, even locked in the trunk. He would have taken it inside the Clarendon and brought it back outside."

"Yet Goldstein said the only thing in the car was a reporter's notebook on the front seat, nothing in it but Reid's name written on the first page."

"Somebody stole the briefcase," she said. She made a clicking with her mouth. "Unless he accidentally left it behind in the hotel, unlikely, considering how careful he was, and if he had, they would have found it and given it to the police. Maybe Page stashed it somewhere."

"What else did your fabulous lover tell you?"

"David Mapstone, you're jealous and territorial after all these years. I like that. You were my fabulous lover." She purred the words but I didn't believe them. "Anyway, he said Page was working on a big story when he died. Something that would 'tie it all together.' That's how he put it."

"What did that mean?"

"Nobody ever found out."

"He was Page's editor. He must have known something."

"He refused to tell me. Said I was safer if I didn't know. People were really afraid after that bombing. But it still pissed me off that he wouldn't tell me what he knew. By the time I wrote the retrospective, well... I never found out."

"There's a lot of that going around. Goldstein gave me nothing. He's got dead rattlesnakes hanging on his front porch. I expected more help from the man who solved, quote-unquote, the most notorious crime in Phoenix history."

"It was more complicated than that," Lorie said. "Tony Peterson and J.C. 'Jack' Wesley from the Organized Crime Bureau ran down the tip on Mark Reid and handed the case to Homicide on a silver platter. If they're still alive, you need to find them."

I wrote down the names and asked for the former boyfriend's contact information.

"He's dead." Her throat caught. "He put a .45 to his

temple, parked out on Shea Boulevard outside Fountain Hills, 1979. He never even owned a gun."

"Did they investigate?"

"Your Sheriff's Office. The medical examiner declared it a suicide."

"But you don't believe it."

She sighed. "No."

I asked her if she received any threats while she was working on the twenty-year retrospective. Aside from the usual nuts who wrote reporters, she had not.

"So why now?" I said. "It's been forty years. Why is someone out for revenge now."

She considered the question as the hum from Interstate 17 filled my ears. "Maybe somebody got out of prison," she said. "But I can't think who it would be, it was so long ago. Otherwise, it was some kind of trigger."

"The killer likes to quote *Hamlet*."

She snorted. "Something is rotten in the state of Arizona."

"Lorie, this new bombing was an exact copycat of how Page was killed. Do we need to be worried that a journalist might be next?"

"I doubt that. Newspapers hardly cover crime and the TV stations only want quick visuals. Did you know forty percent of journalists have been laid off since 2007?"

I didn't.

She said, "The old cops reporters, people like me, were deeply imbedded with law enforcement. We had sources. Now, the local media have twelve-year-olds who take dictation, put out the police press releases verbatim. That's not a threat to the bad guys or anybody in power. The old guard, like 'Front Page,' are all gone outside of New York, D.C., maybe Chicago and L.A. Maybe John

Dougherty's still around. But this is the era of fake news, otherwise known as lies. But half the country believes it. There's no place for someone like me. Or you, David. We're dinosaurs."

We talked on for several more minutes and I thanked her, promising to keep in touch.

She said, "If you ever dump Mimsy, come visit me. Hell, come visit me anyway. We can pretend we're kids again."

Chapter Twenty-one

After I clicked off from my call to Lorie, I noticed the black Dodge sedan sitting at the end of the parking lot facing me, a silver sunscreen in the front window. I swear it wasn't there when I first drove in. No one had walked into the restaurant while I was on the phone, either. If somebody was inside the car, he was making a rookie mistake. As a private investigator with Peralta, I had learned to park faced-away from the vehicle under surveillance and use the rearview mirror. The car was also close enough to the one described by the little boy who delivered the message to Peralta in Starbucks from Sly.

My attention was diverted by movement behind me. A marked Yavapai County Sheriff's cruiser swung in. Two minutes later a uniformed deputy was approaching the car.

I could say, it was a good thing I was white. I had no experience with what Malik Jones likely faced with every driving-while-black traffic stop. On the other hand, a woman impersonating a state trooper pulled me over on the road to Payson a year ago. She took me behind the car—Sharon Peralta was sitting in the passenger seat, unaware—and the "trooper" unholstered her sidearm and pointed it at my crotch. Only the surprise appearance of another car stopped her. She went on to shoot Lindsey a block from our house on Cypress Street. Eventually I shot her on a snowy night at the foot of the Mogollon Rim. She was now in a federal prison. This gave me an entirely new perspective of being on the other end of a traffic stop. My heart rate was already jacked up when he tapped on my window.

I kept one hand on top of the steering wheel and used the other to lower the window, then placed it on the wheel, too.

"May I see your license and registration, sir?" He was young, tall, tanned, with a high-and-tight military cut.

"I'm on the job," I said. "Maricopa County deputy."

He was standing slightly behind the door, proper procedure so a driver couldn't pull a gun and easily shoot him. "Then," he said, "you won't mind showing me your ID and badge. And I'd appreciate if you'd do it slowly."

Slowly, you bet. I slid my right hand into the front pocket of my slacks, pulled out my badge case with care, and handed it out. He took his time looking it over.

"Mind me asking what you're doing in Yavapai County, Deputy Mapton?"

"Mapstone," I said. "I was visiting with a retired cop. Tom Goldstein."

"Oh, yeah." His voice relaxed. "I love that railroad he has."

"Me, too. I'm on my way back to the city."

I was tempted to ask him why he had dealings with Goldstein. I also came close to requesting that he check out the Dodge. But I let it be. He handed back my badge case, walked to his cruiser, and spun out of the lot.

I rolled up the window and called Goldstein. He

sounded even less happy to hear from me than half an hour ago.

"Page carried sensitive files in an old briefcase," I said. "Did you ever find it?"

"I heard the same thing. But, no."

The line went dead.

In a moment, I shifted into drive and entered the freeway going south.

The black Dodge came, too.

It could be a coincidence. I was very capable of paranoia. I even used to own an old black Coach briefcase that my first wife, Patty, had given me. Eventually, Lindsey tired of it and bought me a new Coach briefcase, disposing of Patty's memory at the thrift shop of Hospice of the Valley. But just because you're paranoid doesn't mean someone's not out to get you. We had a dead man from a dynamite bomb. His mother almost kidnapped. The Sheriff's Office computer system was infiltrated and someone was snooping after me there.

Now the black Dodge stayed one or two cars behind as the highway sloped into the valley. I sped up to eighty-five and swerved between some other cars and a semi. The Dodge followed. Past the 101 freeway loop, where Black Canyon widened into multiple lanes, I took the slow lane and let the Prelude drop to fifty-five. The Dodge did the same. The driver was alone, looked Anglo, but otherwise I couldn't make out a face.

Not for the first time, I hated this cheapskate state for only having license plates on the back. The front below the grille was bare. I couldn't get a tag number. His white-on-rice following made it impossible for me to get behind him. I had paid careful attention on my drive up to see Tom Goldstein. He hadn't been on my tail then—unless he really wasn't an amateur and only now wanted me to know he was here. And if so, things might get very dicey, very soon. As it was, I decided he had staked out Goldstein and noticed me.

I called home and Lindsey answered on the first ring.

"Are you all right, Dave?"

"I think."

"Is that Mapstone?" Peralta's voice rumbled in the background. Suddenly he was on the speakerphone.

"Where the hell have you been?"

"Black Canyon City, interviewing Tom Goldstein, like I told you."

"And he gave you nothing."

"He's holding back," I said

"You missed all the fun," Peralta said. "A maid discovered what looked like a bomb and guess where it was?"

He didn't give me a chance to guess.

"The Hotel Clarendon. Scene of the original crime. In a room on the second floor. Phoenix PD went in with a SWAT team. They ran a scope under the door and the room was empty except for the shoebox sitting on the floor."

"That's not good," I said.

"They evacuated the hotel and called the bomb squad. A robot went in and found the shoebox contained three road flares taped together and attached to an alarm clock. It was made to look like a dynamite bomb."

"The shoebox was fake?" I said.

"Yes," Peralta said. "It had another note that said, 'You're looking in all the wrong places. Revenge his foul and most unnatural murder.' It was signed by 'Sly' and addressed 'Dear Sheriff Peralta and…"

"Tell him," Lindsey said.

"'Dear Sheriff Peralta and Deputy Mapstone.'"

"Great. Any luck tracing the computer user who gave Peralta the data stick, Lindsey?"

"None," she said. "This person is good. Maybe better than me."

Peralta cut in, "Nobody is better than you, Lindsey."

There was no way I was going to lead the driver of the Dodge back to Willo. I took the Camelback Road exit, turned left, and drove east through the bedraggled westside commercial strips, past liquor stores, title loan outfits, yerberias, and plenty of for-lease signs. I explained my problem to Peralta. At Nineteenth Avenue, the light-rail line joined us in the middle of the street, and then crossed to go south before Central. I stayed on Camelback, doing the speed limit, the sun thankfully at my back. I made all the lights. So did the black Dodge.

"You could have Phoenix PD pull him over," I said.

He huffed. "For what? Following a historian? Give him the slip."

"Our guy is right here." I could hear the heat in my voice. "We can see if there's any PC in the vehicle, show his photo to Jesús Ortega and Kathy Jarvis. It's Sunday evening, so we can lose him in the Fourth Avenue Jail at least until tomorrow morning."

Peralta still didn't sound convinced. "Or he could make bail and be gone. Why don't you go to the fake address Lindsey gave you? See what he does?"

"There's no way I'm getting trapped in a cul-de-sac," I said.

I could hear the scoff in Peralta's voice. "You and cul-de-sacs…"

"If he or some gangsters hem me in and open up with automatic weapons, it's going to be a problem."

"You have too big an imagination."

"You taught me all this shit!"

"Stop it!" Lindsey said. "You two squabble like brothers."

Peralta let out a long sigh. "That's what Sharon says."

"She's right," Lindsey said. "We need to solve the problem."

Peralta said, "I'll make a call. Give me your twenty and your license tag."

I told him my location was crossing Sixteenth Street. The real estate began improving. Camelback Mountain was straight ahead of me, the Phoenix Mountain Preserve and Piestawa Peak off to my ten o'clock, shimmering in the heated smog.

The red light at the freeway made us stop. The Dodge was three cars behind me.

Suddenly, I turned off the air conditioning. I had the chills.

"Wait a damned minute…"

Peralta snapped, "Do you want me to call or not?"

"I want you to call but I want you to listen." I tried to keep my voice steady. "All these crimes have been canonical."

"Can-what?"

"True to the canon of the Page murder, or at least the lore of Phoenix organized crime. Rudy Jarvis was blown up by dynamite, right?"

"Right. They did more damage because the Ferrari is made of composite materials, not steel like Page's car."

"And the dude with the man-bun wasn't going to kidnap Kathy Jarvis," I said. "He was going to prop her on the sofa and cut her throat, like Gus Greenbaum's wife in 1958."

I could hear Peralta in the background talking to Phoenix Police.

Lindsey cut in. "What, Dave?"

"What if there's a bomb under me in this car and the guy behind me has a detonation device, like with Page? It would be true to the canon. Willie Bioff, mob enforcer, knocked off by a bomb in 1955. "Louie the Baker," who testified against the Outfit, bombed in 1975. Whoever is doing this has really studied this case and the Phoenix underworld."

The light turned green and we were moving again.

"Dave, stop the damned car and run like hell."

I said, "It's tempting, but he might press the button before I shifted into park."

Peralta said, "Why would he kill the Sheriff's Office historical case expert if he wants the Page case solved?"

"Maybe he's crazy. That's what Goldstein said." I left out my conversation with Lorie.

I didn't know what to do.

At Thirty-Second Street, I turned right, continuing to feed Peralta my location, continuing toward the address in Susie's Circle. But now I floored it, watching the speedometer shoot up to seventy. The Dodge fell behind. At Campbell, I turned left, accelerated again, and was beginning to worry when I saw a police cruiser pull in behind the Dodge and light him up. He went maybe a block before pulling over and by that time a second unit had arrived.

I drove on more slowly, checking the rearview mirror. The three vehicles remained stationary. No gunfire erupted. The cops would use the PA system to order the driver to show his hands and throw out his keys. By this time a marked police SUV sped past me going west, hemming in the Dodge from the front.

After a circuitous route home, I hoped we were making the right decision. Those doubts were erased when I was about to pull into the carport on Cypress and saw the sun glint off something where the hood met the right fender.

I already knew what it was before I parked and stepped out: a three-inch strip of Scotch tape.

Buzz Page had used tape to protect himself when he was an investigative reporter. If the tape had been broken, he might have a bomb in the engine. I spent fifteen minutes checking the underside of the car and then opening the hood. Nothing amiss. I knew there was no point in having the tape dusted for fingerprints. He was too careful. This time, I hoped he had stumbled.

Chapter Twenty-two

The first thing I heard was Lindsey say, "oh, shit!" and she was out of bed by the time I opened my eyes. I checked the time: three a.m. A beeping was coming from the study. In a minute, Lindsey walked back into the bedroom, holding up her MacBook Pro, the screen lighting her face. Note to Apple: Want to sell more computers? Run an ad with my lovely naked wife carrying your products.

"What's up?"

She slid back into bed, propped up, studying the MacBook's screen.

"Something's wrong. How can he be in jail and infiltrating the Sheriff's Office computer system at the same time?"

"Maybe Peralta gave the inmates free WiFi to atone for the Tent Jail."

"This is serious, Dave."

After a few minutes of silence: "Fuck me!" I wished she meant it literally.

"What?"

"Do you have the SO phone directory?"

"Somewhere," I said. I climbed out of bed, went to the desk in the study, and opened drawers. I finally found a directory that was at least four years old.

"Call the jail," she said. "There's a prisoner escaping."

"Our guy?"

She nodded.

The number I dialed went to voice mail. I dialed another, same result. Then I called 911, gave my star number, and waited while they sent me through three different layers of law-enforcement bureaucracy on an early Monday morning. I finally reached a human being at the Fourth Avenue Jail. And I realized I didn't even have the prisoner's name.

"He would have been booked in around six p.m. maybe, suspicion of murder or attempted murder, the bombing a week ago, direct orders of Sheriff Peralta."

This got the correction officer's attention. I heard her typing quickly.

She gave me a name. "He's in his cell asleep. Nothing's happening."

"When was the last time you did a bed check?"

"One a.m.," she said. "We're short-staffed tonight. But I can see him on my screen right now. He's in his bed, lying on his side. My other screens show the entire bloc quiet, the whole jail. I can see it all. It's the middle of the night." She sounded offended.

I conveyed this information to Lindsey, who grabbed the phone.

"You're watching a loop that was inserted into your system. It's probably from an hour ago, only rerunning, not real time."

She repeated this in greater detail and greater frustration twice more.

"Me? My name is Lindsey. I'm watching this on my computer. A worm has gotten into the Sheriff's Office computer system and is causing this. It's allowing an escape. Lock things down now!"

She handed me back the phone and the corrections officer still didn't sound convinced. She asked for my badge number and name again, as if this were a prank. She wanted me to spell my name. I did.

I covered the phone. "Can you do anything from here?"

Lindsey shook her head in frustration. "It's one step ahead of me. He's probably already gone."

The officer put me on hold. I climbed out of bed as if ants were crawling over me. At the window, I pulled down a blind but the street was empty.

I looked back at Lindsey. "Call Peralta."

She didn't even look up. She was typing furiously. "Can't, Dave. I've got to kill this malware now."

I was the one who had to wake him.

Chapter Twenty-three

A little after six, we were sitting in the shaded corner of the patio of First Watch, a breakfast place at Park Central—Peralta, Lindsey, and me. We took stock over omelets, huevos rancheros, fried potatoes, and bacon, drinks from Starbucks next door.

Peralta was calm and focused. That meant it was a serious crisis, no time for theatrics.

Contrary to his media image, the job of an Arizona sheriff is often dull: executing warrants, serving processes and notices issued by judges, and, especially, running the jails. Transporting and housing prisoners, attending to their medical needs (or not, in the case of Meltdown), monitoring the visits of family and lawyers. We had patrol contracts with several suburbs, such as Guadalupe, Litchfield Park, Sun City, and Fountain Hills. That brought with it a full range of cop work, from detectives to choppers, a SWAT team, Peralta's famous posse. We had statewide jurisdiction and backed up local law enforcement. But the Sheriff's Office wasn't the same as a city police department, particularly because of its responsibility for four large jails and thousands of prisoners. Someone had walked out of the maximum-security Fourth Avenue Jail downtown three hours ago.

Lindsey walked us through how the escape had happened. The malware carried on the USB stick Peralta received at Starbucks had infected his computer—then penetrated the entire system. She had tried to wall it off with the patch, but had obviously been unsuccessful.

The result was to allow an outside hacker to run fake footage on the jail cameras and open every door, from the cell to the three secure exits leading to the outside.

Peralta took it surprisingly well. I thought about what Lorie told me about the media. It was so denuded by layoffs and lack of veteran reporters that the incident wouldn't be known unless he himself announced it. That would also involve telling how the overnight Sunday-Monday shift was minimal, relying more on cameras than guards, because of the legal expenses necessary to comply with the federal oversight of the department.

"I'm not going to do it," he announced. "No reason to give this asshole a reason to crow."

Who was the asshole? We didn't know yet. His driver's license was a well-done fake, his Social Security number traced to a boy who died at age fourteen in Indiana, fingerprints not in the system. He was booked into the jail and not interviewed by detectives—that was supposed to happen this morning before his initial appearance before a judge. His vehicle, however, held some interesting clues: plastic flex cuffs, duct tape, tactical gloves, cell phone, and a folding combat knife. I studied his mug shot: dark hair, stubble, angry eyes, man-bun. In the side shot, his hair was done up with exquisite care. I'd bet he was the guy who vaulted the fence at Kathy Jarvis' house. Soon enough we'd show her the photo and find out.

Lindsey said, "I don't understand why the patch didn't work."

Peralta shrugged. "We had a saying in the Army: 'There's always some S.O.B. who doesn't get the word.' The Fourth Avenue Jail supervisor was on vacation and didn't install your patch. His second-in-command didn't, either."

Lindsey opened her computer and showed us silent footage of Madison Street outside the jail, captured by two surveillance cameras, in the moments after she had detected the escape. The first showed a male corrections officer walking out a side entrance.

"That's him." The camera was close to the door and his hair was down, but I recognized his face from the mug shot and the uniform didn't fit. He walked past the lens.

She said, "Now, here, from another camera." This angle was across the street, showed him stepping to the curb, and a dark sedan, maybe a Chevy, sliding up. He climbed in and the car disappeared from view. No license tag visible.

Peralta said, "He's got help."

"And I bet it's a woman." Lindsey closed her laptop and slid it into her backpack. "She's the computer braino."

"You always suspected this," I said.

"The bug in that flash drive was…" She trailed off and reached for my mocha, taking a sip. "How do you drink this, Dave? Anyway, she codes like a girl. I mean that as a compliment. Sometime when you have insomnia, I'll explain why I thought that."

She tapped the plastic container of sugar packets, meant to deter the birds from stealing them. "I thought I had built a wall around the malware. But PoisonTap is very sophisticated and she put it on steroids. It exploits every back door. So, last night—this morning—after the jail break, I had to shut the whole thing down and purge it from the Sheriff's Office system."

"Good," Peralta said.

"There's downsides." Lindsey went back to her cup of French roast, washing away the chocolate taste of my mocha. "First, I can't track her back, not that I was having any success. Second, she'll know I killed her malware baby and this might provoke her to something new. Something worse."

Peralta noshed and spoke. "That was a cold-blooded operation. Walk out of a large jail. How could…?"

"Nothing is safe now," Lindsey said. "Russia hacked the 2016 presidential election. We're living in an era of information warfare. In the digital age, the battlefield is everywhere. As for the jailbreak, they planned this in advance. They probably had floor plans, watched the Sunday-night shift on camera. He memorized the best way out. Thanks to the hack, at every step a door opened for him, and the guards watching on camera were blinded."

Peralta's forehead canyon deepened. "What about your theory, Mapstone? How was the escape canonical, as you say?"

I didn't have to think long. "When Detective Frenchy Navarre gunned down Officer 'Star' Johnson in 1944, he was bailed out by the mob. Made men lined up at the jail to spring him, even though he was charged with murder…"

Peralta started to wiggle like the bored student of history he was. I spoke faster.

"Being the wiseguy to pay his bail was considered a point of honor. It was paid in a suitcase of cash, no questions asked. Another example is a detective who told me about being a young patrolman in the 1960s. He arrested a man with a suitcase of cash, took him into police headquarters. The man couldn't explain where the money came from. After a few minutes, his superior told him to release the man and give him his money back. The cop speculated it was receipts from a gambling operation with police protection. So, yes, in its way this is canonical."

They ate and looked at me, so I continued. This case had been an example of misdirection from the start. A threat to Peralta because he had mentioned reopening the Page murder. Only the people who made the threat actually wanted him to do exactly that. The bombing of Rudy Jarvis at a known drug site, sending investigators to think he was involved with a gang. The snippets of *Hamlet*. Then the man following me so close it was as if they wanted us to arrest him so they could show how helpless we were.

"I don't like being helpless." Peralta stabbed his huevos rancheros angrily. "We did pick up Hector Morales of the Wedgewood Chicanos. Sweated him for a few hours, threatened to put word on the street he was an informant, before he told us a woman had paid him a hundred dollars to meet Rudy Jarvis out on Bell. Morales told Jarvis he'd kill his family if he didn't drive to that address on Seventeenth Avenue and wait for a further phone call. It had the effect of distracting us, making us suspect Jarvis was involved in drugs."

"We've got two crimes," Lindsey said. "The assassination of Charles Page forty years ago. And now the killing of the assassin's son and the attempted abduction or murder of his mother. Kathy Jarvis had nothing to do with the original crime. They bleed together, but how? Why her? Why her son?"

"And who's next?" I said.

Peralta folded his napkin. "I don't get why they want us to solve the Page case. But I'll tell you this, we can't protect everyone."

Freeman Burke died in 1990. He had three grandchildren, all living elsewhere, like so many offspring of

Phoenix gentry. One was in Boston, another in New York City, and the third in London. The local police contacted all of them and none reported anything amiss.

Dick Kemperton, the triggerman on the bomb, had a daughter. She was living in a nursing home in Fresno after suffering a stroke. The cops there said she was unable to speak. She had children but detectives hadn't yet contacted them.

Darren Howard, convicted of paying for the hit, always maintained his innocence, said he was framed. He had a son, living here, who had an alibi for both the night of the anniversary party and the day Rudy Jarvis was murdered. Howard also had a daughter, living in Thailand and working for the State Department.

Buzz Page had two children from his first marriage. They had motive for revenge if anyone did—but both lived in other states and had alibis for the date of the Jarvis bombing.

The dog tracks were closed. The old-time Mafia was virtually nonexistent in Phoenix now. The offspring of the gangsters had long since gone legit in real-estate development and speculation. Today's organized crime was the gangs that ran drugs and protection. Matters hadn't been helped by Sheriff Crisis Meltdown disbanding Peralta's Organized Crime Bureau, so he could put more resources into running illegal immigrants into the shadows.

And nobody connected to the Page killing had recently been released from prison.

"We have bupkis," Peralta said. "Any of the offspring could be potential victims. But any of them could be suspects if the motive is revenge."

Lindsey said, "Maybe there is no motive that connects with forty years ago. We have new killers with an obsession about Phoenix's underworld, who have latched onto this. They're thrill killers and the anniversary is only an excuse."

It was enough to make us all finish our breakfast in silence. By then, even with the umbrella shading us, it was too hot to stay outside.

Chapter Twenty-four

On Tuesday, I awoke alone in bed. Indirect sun was coming into the living room as I padded in wearing shorts and a T-shirt. Lindsey was reading a short story from the Sanity Table, pausing to scribble in her black Moleskine notebook. I kissed her good morning, glad she was taking a break.

For the first time in weeks, I went to the gym in the basement of the Central Park Square building three blocks away. I took the second Stairmaster. An older, distinguished Hispanic man, who I usually saw in suits, occupied the first one. He nodded and I nodded back. Alfredo Gutierrez had spent years as the Democratic leader of the Arizona State Senate, in a very different state. He had started out as a student activist at ASU. Now he was an elder statesman. Such was the slipstream of time.

"So, David, I see that your boss has reopened the Buzz Page case." His voice was gravelly as usual, and even though he was moving at twice my pace, it showed no signs of stress from the workout. I was already sore.

"He has. Did you know Page, Senator?" Even though he called me David, I had a hard time calling him "Alfredo." Part of my upbringing, I suppose.

"I did," Gutierrez said. "A good man. I saw him the day the bomb exploded, you know."

He stepped off the machine and ran a towel over his face, although I didn't detect a drop of sweat.

"He was leaving the Capitol and we talked for a minute, then he walked on. It was a hot day. A couple of hours later, I heard about the bombing. Peralta is poking a hornet's nest."

Here be monsters.

I asked him why.

He put his hands on the front of my Stairmaster.

"Lots of secrets, David. Things Arizona wanted shelved away and buried."

"Freeman Burke?"

Gutierrez nodded. "That's the tip of the iceberg, as I'm sure you are finding out."

He turned and started to go.

"Senator."

He flipped the towel over his shoulder and faced me again.

"Did Buzz Page have a briefcase when you saw him?"

Gutierrez closed his eyes for a moment. Then: "He did. It was the one he usually carried with him."

Out in the garage, I checked out the Prelude. I had pried off the Scotch tape and no one had replaced it. Lindsey said it was virtually impossible to detect explosives in a car, sometimes even with sniffer dogs. She had installed a device that would indicate if a tracking device had been placed on the Prelude, did the same for Peralta's SUV. As for a potential bomb, I depended on the gathering dust on the paint—it was now weeks since I had washed it. No new finger scuffs. Opening the door, I pulled out a DIY underside inspector, a mirror attached to a push-broom stick. All looked normal beneath the car. I started it without incident.

•●⬤●•

A stiff wind came in from the west and blew all day. The flags stood out straight and the smog headed to eastern Arizona and New Mexico. Yet higher up, ghostly wisps of clouds lingered in the light blue sky. After a morning in my office, paging through forty-year-old files, I crossed the street to Sticklers—still missing my old standby Tom's Tavern—and ordered a sandwich and Diet Coke. Unfolding the *Arizona Republic*, I saw a story about the new Fry's grocery coming to Block Twenty-Three. It would be the first grocery store downtown in decades. But construction was held up by the discovery of the "bomb shelter" where the old J.C. Penney's once stood, as well as prehistoric artifacts.

I had forgotten about my conversation with the journalism student from the university. Luc Iverson. A *Republic* staff reporter, not one of the Cronkite School students, wrote this story. It made me pull out my iPhone and go to the Cronkite News website. It had nothing on the fallout shelter, and nothing by someone named Luc Iverson, either.

I filed that away for follow-up and ate fast. Peralta wanted to see me at one p.m.

The temperature had settled on the normal June broiler, around 106 degrees. That was in the shade at Sky Harbor. On the sidewalk, the temp was much hotter. The wind provided no relief. It merely blew the flaming blast in your face. Was it better than 110? You bet. So, armed with my bottle of melting frozen water, I walked a few blocks to

550 W. Jackson Street, Peralta's Starship. Out front, in jarring contrast to the modernity of the building, was a horse sculpture honoring fallen deputies. For a second, I looked longingly south, at the edge of Union Station, the real thing, wishing for passenger trains that would never come back.

Inside the Sheriff's Office Headquarters, the air conditioning was on high and took the edge off my impending heat exhaustion. Employees were coming back from lunch so it took me a few minutes to be waved around the metal detectors. I rode the elevator up to the command-staff floor and walked toward Peralta's office suite. As I started down a hallway, twenty feet ahead was a woman wearing a white blouse and dark blue short skirt, swinging saucily against very pretty legs. Her dark hair bounced perfectly slightly below her neck and against her shoulders. Five-feet-seven, I'd guess, and about five feet of it legs.

Hey, I'm married but can still appreciate.

Then I closed the distance.

"Lindsey?"

She turned and smiled. "History Shamus. Imagine seeing you here."

Seeing my expression, she walked toward me and placed her hand on my chest. "You're overheated, parking-lot man." It was one of our jokes, that I absorbed heat like a Phoenix parking lot and then radiated it back for a long time after exposure to the sun. When I didn't smile, she continued: "We can fight about this later. But I needed to come down here. I'm tired of being played by this person. Maybe I can force her hand."

Maybe you can get killed, I thought, but only sighed.

"Are you going to *El Jefe*, too?"

I nodded and we walked together.

"What have you got for me, Mapstone?" he demanded before I even had my butt in the chair before his enormous desk.

I told him about the missing briefcase. He wasn't impressed.

"Well, I have something for you two," he said. "Our boy came back with a positive ID from the FBI."

"Criminal?" I said.

"Military," Peralta said. "He served in the Army, three deployments to Afghanistan. Get this: He was an explosives ordnance specialist. Honorable discharge. No priors. His real name is Ryan Garrison, twenty-eight years old, born in Boone, Iowa, and last known address was an apartment in Mesa. We've already been there. He moved out a month ago, no forwarding address."

"There's your expertise," I said. "It's a miracle he hasn't used plastic explosives or something worse."

"The apartment manager said he only had one visitor, an attractive blonde in her forties."

Lindsey perked up. "That's our hacker, I bet you."

I asked. "What does this twenty-eight-year-old man see in her?"

Lindsey said, "Maybe she's a cougar."

"A what?" This from Peralta. Lindsey explained the term for an older woman who sought out young men as lovers.

After he stopped blushing, he said the detectives showed the manager a photo array that included a couple of women who had been convicted of fraud involving computers. He couldn't pick her out.

"Which brings us to this," Peralta said, sliding a file toward Lindsey. "I want to know if anybody else is involved in this who worked for me."

The file held an inch-high stack of mug shots. She slid off the rubber band.

Peralta leaned in. "These are deputies and other Sheriff's Office employees who might have had regular contact with you in the Cybercrimes Bureau. Take your time."

She lifted each one, studied it, and then turned it facedown.

"The person who wrote that first note knew you close-up, Lindsey," he said.

"But didn't know that I was back in town."

"So now she's down here reminding everyone that she is back in town," I said sourly. Looking down and seeing the Glock 26 and two extra magazines in her purse was not reassuring enough.

She ignored my comment and continued looking, sometimes saying a name. "He was married. This one was gay. This guy was LDS. No passes but he did give me a Book of Mormon." Another mug shot. "This one was good at impersonating teenage girls in chat rooms." A second later. "Knuckle dragger. He liked me, but he was harmless."

The phone rang and the sheriff answered as he always did, saying his name as he was lifting the receiver to his face. On the other end, you might hear, "…alta." He listened for a minute, then said, "Get a BOLO out on this guy."

Dropping the receiver into the phone, he said, "Kathy Jarvis identified Garrison as the man who attacked her."

Lindsey slid the rubber band over the mug shots, dropped them into the file, and slid it back across Peralta's desk. "Nobody," she said. "What about county employees? People in IT?"

"I don't think I can access those," Peralta said.

"Get up," Lindsey said. "I can."

He complied and she took his place, occupying about half of his luxurious executive desk chair. She leaned back and grinned. "I could get used to this." She lowered her voice: "Mapstone, progress!?"

This time I made myself laugh. I was surprised that Peralta did, too.

She pulled over his keyboard and adjusted the screen. "I can't believe you're using Internet Explorer as your browser. No wonder the system is so vulnerable. But you can install Tor or something better later."

She said it as if we knew what she meant.

Twenty keystrokes later and she was in the county personnel files.

"Hold on," Peralta said. He walked behind her and pulled a book from his desk drawer. A Bible. "Stand, please."

She did so as I said, "Wait a damned minute…"

They both ignored me.

"Raise your right hand."

She did, while placing her left hand on the Bible.

"Under the emergency authority vested in me by the State of Arizona, I am swearing you in as a deputy sheriff." He administered the oath and she said, "I do."

From another drawer, he produced a deputy's star, already in a leather badge case, and handed it to her. "We'll get your identification made next. Then I'll fast-track your credentials through the Arizona Peace Officers and Training Board. As a former deputy sheriff with a perfect record, it won't be a problem."

It was a problem for me.

Lindsey avoided my eyes and went back to the computer.

I looked at Peralta. "Did anything strange happen to you at the fortieth anniversary event?"

"Strange how?"

I kept silent and made him think about it.

"Actually, a woman came on to me. She said she had a room at the hotel and invited me upstairs..." His shoulders sagged. "She was blond, attractive, mid-forties. It happened fast. Sharon swooped in, not that I would have done it anyway."

I told him that the same thing happened to Tom Goldstein.

His features brightened. "A cougar liked us old dudes." Then the scowl returned. "But for what purpose? Was she going to kill the one who agreed to go up to her room? How the hell does that fit your canon of Phoenix organized crime?"

"Neatly," I said. "She probably had cameras in the room. The idea would be blackmail, especially if it involved illicit sex with the Maricopa County Sheriff. Back in the day, some of the local bigs, including Harry Rosenzweig, were said to operate brothels. Among the customers were prominent businessmen, lawyers, and cops. They were photographed *in flagrante delicto*, and the evidence was used as leverage against them. Good thing Sharon was there."

He pointed a heavy index finger at me. "I never would have gone up there. We need a list of the attendees."

I told him I already had it. From my soft-sided briefcase, I produced the file. He grabbed it and ran through the page of names.

"It doesn't include guests," I said. Then an idea caught up with me. "Give me that."

I ran my finger down the names until I came to: Ophelia Pond, Cronkite News Service. I'd bet this was the blonde who came on to Peralta and Goldstein.

Amid my profanities, I reminded him that Ophelia was Hamlet's love interest and she drowned herself in a pond when he spurned her.

"I never did like Shakespeare," he muttered. "We've been played for fools."

I resisted the egghead temptation to tell him that in Shakespeare the fool often had one of the most important roles.

Lindsey said, "Now maybe we can turn it around." She swiveled the screen and showed a color photograph of a woman with shoulder-length golden hair, high cheekbones, blue eyes, and a wide smile set off by sensual lips.

"This woman worked in the county IT department when I was in the Cybercrimes Unit. She was very good, a troubleshooter. She knew way more than me. She would be forty-six now."

The photograph belied that. Like Lindsey, she looked more than ten years younger than her real age.

"She left the county two years ago, while I was in Washington, Lindsey said. "I only knew her by her first name, Elizabeth. But the record says her last name is Sleigh." She first said it like Santa's vehicle, but then: "If the 'e' is silent, we've got Sly."

We both watched Peralta as he studied the photo. "I think that could be her."

It wasn't a door-kicking breakthrough, but it was the best we had.

Chapter Twenty-five

At nine the next morning, I was at the construction site for the new Fry's supermarket as part of a mixed-use development on Block Twenty-Three. For years, the land had sat as a parking lot, but with the development boom set off by the downtown ASU campus, it was finally about to see life. A fence surrounded the site draped with colorful renderings of a flashy glass building. On the sidewalk was a plaque that read "Del E. Webb Construction Co. 1952," all that was left of the old J.C. Penney's.

I badged the construction supervisor and told him I wanted to see the bomb shelter I had read about in the newspaper. He immediately started complaining about the delays as archeologists exhumed the Hohokam artifacts that had been uncovered with the excavation. More remains of the advanced irrigation society. Eons from now, nobody would be excavating the Super Walmarts and shopping strips of our quote-unquote civilization. The construction guy's agitation brought me out of the reverie. He worried that I was there to cause another holdup. I assured him that I wasn't—I only wanted to see the bomb shelter.

I had already been on the phone to the head honcho of the Cronkite News Service. She told me that they hadn't written anything on the supermarket site or the fallout shelter. None of the reporters were named Iverson or Pond. She couldn't even recall a student with either last name during her five years at the journalism school. The call I had received was fake. But why? My suspicion immediately turned to Ryan Garrison and Elizabeth Sleigh. Something about Block Twenty-Three was connected to the Page murder.

We stamped down a dusty stairwell and the sunlight disappeared, replaced by strings of bare light bulbs. He explained that this was part of the J.C. Penney's that had been built here in the 1950s, with three subbasements running off an underground parking garage. Cars pulled in and went down a spiral ramp. From there, the shoppers could enter the store through an elevator. Parts of the subbasements were also used for storage.

We hit bottom, a concrete floor that was caked in what seemed like a quarter inch of dust. He led me through two thresholds where double doors had once hung, now gone. Then we were in a spacious room lined with dark green barrels and disintegrating cardboard boxes. They were marked with the circular CD civil defense logo and capital letters denoted them as SURVIVAL SUPPLIES FURNISHED BY THE OFFICE OF CIVIL DEFENSE. As I suspected, this was not a bomb shelter, per se, as in a space designed to ride out a nearby nuclear detonation. This was a fallout shelter, where lucky civilians could hunker down until the worst radioactivity from World War Three dissipated. That was the theory, at least. All the years I was growing up, buildings were marked with the yellow-and-black fallout shelter signs. In downtown Phoenix, at least one of the civil defense signs from the fifties hung around until a few years ago: red CD in a white triangle, surrounded by a blue circle, then a red background with "Shelter" and an arrow in white. The latter would be a real collector's item.

My eye went to the hulking bank of metal at the end of the room studded with individual doors. They were like the baggage lockers one used to find in airports, train stations, and bus depots before 9/11 and the fear of bombings caused their removal. These looked ancient and rusty.

The supervisor shrugged. "I don't know where that came from. My guess is it was in the store, when there was still a Penney's here, so people could stash their purchases. That way they wouldn't have to leave the premises and could go back and keep shopping. Your guess is as good as mine."

I tried several of the locker doors. The ones with keys were empty inside. Each had a slot for coins to buy time for storage.

"Have any people asked to come down here? Any reporters?" I said, the dust thick on my tongue.

He shook his head. "One of the TV stations shot a segment above ground about a week ago. That's it."

I took another five minutes of this impatient man's time as I stood in silence, trying to parse what it all meant. I could have called Peralta and asked for a bomb-sniffing dog. Maybe the two suspects had stashed a bomb in the bomb shelter. But it didn't feel likely. If they were going to set off an explosive, this place made no sense. It held no place in the history of Phoenix's underworld, either. Maybe Luc Iverson, whoever he was, was merely pulling my chain. Another misdirection.

I thanked the supervisor and headed back up to the sunlight.

The state archives were housed in a new building on Madison Street, a block from the railroad tracks and south of the State Capitol. It was definitely new Phoenix. Homely structure built on the cheap? Check. No shade? Check. The finely milled harvest of the rock-products industry spread out in front with a few ailing desert plants? Check. On the other hand, given our legislature, it was a miracle the place was funded at all.

I took the Prelude for the mile-and-a-half journey from downtown. The temperature was back above 110 degrees and this morning's *Republic* said we should expect an extended "heat emergency."

Lindsey and I didn't fight the night before. It's not as if I am some passive-aggressive Midwesterner and would take out my frustrations on her later. There didn't seem to be a point. She told me she understood that I didn't want her to get hurt. But, she said, I needed her help. I couldn't argue with that. I also knew that Lindsey now had skin in the game: Elizabeth Sleigh—Sly—had bested her this time. She wanted revenge. So did "Sly"—for the murder of Page, or for something else?

As Lindsey fell into the deep sleep caused from being out in the Phoenix heat, I got out of bed and found my hefty complete works of Shakespeare on one of the bookshelves that lined the stairway at the back of the living room. I brought it to bed, clipped on the book light, and began reading *Hamlet*. I made it as far as Act Two, Scene Two, the title character's famous Hecuba speech.

"What's Hecuba to him or he to Hecuba that he should weep for her?"

What's Buzz Page to "Sly" that she would kill for him?

Was it all a play within a play…

When I woke up this morning Lindsey was still asleep and the heavy Shakespeare volume was collapsed on my chest. I was no wiser for my late-night reading.

Now, one of the archivists led me to a private room where I found Malik Jones. The space contained chairs and a long table, and except for the cart of Hollinger boxes it was a decent replica of one of the Sheriff's Office's interrogation rooms.

"Chief Gillespie!"

He shouted it out without a smile and didn't stand. I pulled a chair and sat across from him. Despite the heat, he wore a smart gray suit with a starched white shirt and black tie, the knot insouciantly off-center.

"Mr. Jones," I said. "You know, I've read that James Baldwin didn't like that movie."

"Ah…" He gravely appraised me. "You've been reading your Baldwin. Well, I like the movie. Let me ask you this, Chief Gillespie, define the black American experience?"

Now I was aggravated enough that I spoke unfiltered. "That's sophistry and you know it. There's no single 'black American experience.' There are black Americans who have experiences every bit as varied as white Americans, Hispanic Americans."

After the longest pause, he gave me a wide smile. "I'm only messing with you, David. Don't take things so seriously. I'm surprised you didn't stop by before now."

"I'm patient, even if my boss isn't."

"Well, check this out." Piles of records were neatly stacked around him and he was taking notes on an iPad with a Zagg keyboard.

"I've spent two days going through trial transcripts.

Reid's first trial. And the retrial of Darren Howard after his conviction was overturned. The most interesting thing I've found so far is the lawyers."

I didn't say anything, so he continued.

"As you know, the master narrative has the martyred reporter, the journalists who worked to avenge his death, cops good and bad, the dog-track people, and the gangsters. Gangsters and cops and businessmen all mingled, especially at the bars. All three of the dudes convicted were part of this scene. The bars are where the plot was allegedly hatched. But here's the thing. There's another set of players that gets less attention: lawyers. And I don't mean prosecutors, although the County Attorney was a question mark. I've found a whole layer of lawyers who hung out with the other suspects, and at least a couple have a bearing on the Page killing."

"Consider me interested."

"Excellent. Here are two that really grabbed me. The first is Bobby Bell, given name Maurice, who had done some legal work for Ned Warren, the Godfather of Land Fraud in Arizona. And this brought him into Mark Reid's orbit, too. The master narrative, at least from the *Phoenix Project* reporters, has Reid confessing to Bobby Bell in a north Central bar that he bombed Page. Not only that, but he mentioned Darren Howard. Now we've got a conspiracy. Bell was scared shitless and went to the cops. That's known. What's less known is that the State of Arizona disbarred Bell within a year. Why?"

"Ethics?" I speculated. "You know how to tell if a lawyer's lying?"

"His lips are moving," Jones said. "Or her lips. My girlfriend just passed the bar, so I know 'em all. What do you call a hundred lawyers chained at the bottom of the ocean?

A good start. Know the difference between a catfish and a lawyer? One is a cold-blooded bottom feeder…and the other is a fish. But stay with me, Chief Gillespie. This Bell cat did the right thing."

"And was ruined."

"You've got it. Meanwhile, we have Norm Reardon. Now this guy is very interesting. He was connected to all the major figures in the case. Mob lawyer. Political fixer. Friends on the police force. He even went to North High School, like Reid, Kemperton, and Howard. When he was arrested, he got the best defense attorney in town and made a deal, total immunity, accessory after the fact, and no jail time. Total immunity! As far as I can tell, he didn't give the cops anything they didn't have from somewhere else. He implicated Darren Howard, as Bell had done. Why the hell wasn't Reardon disbarred?"

I knew some of this from the *Phoenix Project*, too. Reardon was a mysterious figure, perhaps at the periphery of the case, but maybe at its center. He even had his office a few blocks from our house, on Virginia Street.

I said, "Maybe he was the cleverer attorney."

Jones indulged me with three nods. "Or he was part of the real conspiracy that's hiding in these archives and he was owed."

"Owed?"

"Protected. Look, Reardon did major work for Warren starting back in the 1960s, when the New York mob sent Warren here. Much more than Bobby Bell. Reardon personally handled payoffs to politicians, to the state Land Commissioner. It went on for years. I read a report that people were defrauded of five-hundred-million dollars or more in the Warren era. This is serious money: It would be nearly two billion in today's dollars. And the morning of the bombing, Mark Reid stopped by Reardon's office. Years later, Reardon was called to testify in Howard's second trial."

I wondered if this meant the Mafia was actually behind the assassination, or maybe RaceCo., and old man Burke was not the headwaters of the conspiracy.

"I can't tell you that yet." Jones pointed at the Hollinger boxes. "But the wonderful thing about archives is when you find something misfiled. You said there were two levels of classified stuff beyond what I'm researching. I suspect this should be on one of those, probably the one sealed for fifty years. And yet, here it was, stuck in the middle of Box Fifteen."

He handed me a piece of paper, eight-and-a-half by eleven. At the top, Phoenix Police Intelligence Unit was printed in bold letters. Then typing: 6/2/78, Reardon wiretap, 1525 hours. It was the day of the bombing.

I read.

Caller: You son of a bitch. I heard about Buzz Page.

Reardon: Senator...

Caller: Don't say my name, you goddamned fool. The police probably have your fucking phone tapped.

Reardon: I pay the police. The line is clean.

Caller: Where the hell are you?

Reardon: I'm walking out on the patio. The phone has a long cord. Nobody can hear us.

Caller: So, it's true? Somebody planted a bomb in Page's car?

Reardon: Yes.

Caller: (Yelling) Goddamn it to hell! Is he dead?

Reardon: No. He's at St. Joe's. In bad shape, I hear.

Caller: Who did it?

Reardon: Reid.

Caller: Son of a bitch. I like Buzz Page. He's a good man. Nobody bombs the press. Do you have a goddamned idea what this is going to cause? This is the worst possible time for something like this.

Reardon: It had to be done.

Caller: "Had to be done." Listen to yourself.

(Pause)

Reardon: Page has the ledger.

Caller: (Inaudible)

Reardon: I don't know. All I do know is that Page has the ledger and if he gets the key to the entries, he'd blow the lid off Arizona. You understand that, right?

Caller: And I'm in there?

Reardon: You are, Senator. So are a lot of your friends. Don't worry. Everything's under control.

Caller: You call this under control? You've tried to murder a Phoenix Gazette reporter.

Reardon: He wasn't supposed to survive.

Caller: You goddamned idiots. I want to know who ordered this. Mark Reid wouldn't have done this on his own. He bailed out on the Navajo job. Was it our friend? Was it you?"

Reardon: (Inaudible).

Caller: That's not good enough. It was a stupid move, you son of a bitch.

Stupidest move of your life. If Page dies, it's murder and I'm not going down for it. I never would have let you people do this. Where's the ledger now?

(Pause)

Reardon: We don't know. My detective friend says it wasn't in Page's car. Nobody's found it yet.

Caller: Where the hell is Reid?

Reardon: On the way to Lake Havasu City with his lady friend. I chartered a plane and booked a hotel room so he'd be out of town. Gives him an alibi in case his name comes up in the investigation. He's got the fifty-eight-hundred we paid him. If he gets arrested, he knows there's a lot more money if he sticks to the story we discussed. Our friends put up a few mil. It's worth it."

Caller: You're too trusting. Reid isn't that bright.

Reardon: Unlike the law, his people don't give immunity. He knows that. I've already got a hitman lined up from Detroit to take him out if necess…

Caller: Shut the hell up. I don't want to know any of this.

Reardon: I'll call you when I know more.

Caller: (Yells) No! You will not god-damned call me for any reason. (Normal voice) I'll have someone check in with you in a couple of days. You'd better get your ass a good criminal lawyer.

Reardon: Calm down, Senator. It's all under control. (Pause) Senator? You there?

(Call ends)

I handed it back to him. It wasn't the same as discovering a lost diary of Abraham Lincoln, but it was pretty damned sweet. My heart was beating fast. He slipped it into a new file folder of its own and laid it aside. I didn't know whether it would be appropriate to take it as evidence or not. I decided not and we agreed on a plan. Malik Jones had earned his thousand dollars from the taxpayers.

He said, "That's got to be Goldwater on the phone tap."

"Seems that way," I said. "I've never heard of a ledger."

Jones clapped his hands. "Exactly. You told me Page was killed for something he was going to write, not for what he'd written. Let's say he had a ledger that showed payments, dates, amounts, and recipients, important people. That would sure as hell blow the lid off Arizona."

"It also calls Reid's confession into question. How much is really true?"

"I've been wondering. Reid's confession says he planted six sticks of dynamite and four magnets under Page's car. But the ATF report said it was only three sticks, maybe even two, and two magnets. And Mark Reid still avoided the death penalty."

Jones said, "What does he mean by this being the worst possible time?"

I thought about that and shrugged. I had to make a second try with Tom Goldstein. "So you said Reardon testified at Howard's second trial."

"He was supposed to. Howard's lawyers learned that Reardon had told a man at the La Costa resort that he set Howard up to take the fall."

"But the police had witnesses who saw Reid with Howard," I said.

"Reardon introduced Howard to Reid at the Ivanhoe that spring. Howard was a year ahead at North High and didn't remember him. But Howard didn't have anything to do with Page's death. Mark Reid lied to the police about that, too. Or that was what Darren Howard's lawyers argued."

I knew La Costa. It was north of San Diego, where I used to live, and it was so popular with the Mafia that its nickname was La Cosa Nostra.

I said, "Yet they convicted Howard again."

"Because when Reardon was called to the stand, all he would say was, 'I can't recall.' He was a heavy drinker like all of them. Probably worse. That's what the prosecution used to demolish his credibility. He was portrayed as a drunk who wasn't trustworthy. Maybe the years after the bombing had killed too many brain cells. Or..."

I finished the thought. "Or he was still afraid that he might be killed, too."

Chapter Twenty-six

I started the car and cranked up the air conditioning. I called Lindsey.

"I'm fine, Dave. Working."

"At home."

"Yes."

That made me hope that her stunt coming into headquarters was harmless. It indicated that nobody at the Sheriff's Office today was involved in the plot.

She said as much, asked what was new with me, and I filled her in.

"Stay safe," she said. Then my phone beeped. The readout said "Peralta."

"It's the Sheriff. I'd better take it."

We said we loved each other and I hit the accept button.

"Get your ass to Fountain Hills." He gave me an address. His voice was tense. "Now."

"What...?" But the line was already dead.

I drove east to Seventh Avenue, then caught the Papago Freeway inner loop through the tunnel under the deck park. It provided a few blocks of relief from the sun before emerging beyond Third Street. I took the lane to the Red Mountain Freeway and sped at eighty through east

Phoenix and into Tempe. Then the Pima Freeway swung north, Scottsdale to the west and the Pima-Maricopa Salt River Indian Community to the east, plenty of farms and casinos. I got off at Shea Boulevard in north Scottsdale and crawled in the traffic eastbound. If you want to see what old Shea, two lanes amid stunning empty desert, looked like in the early seventies, rent the movie *Electra Glide in Blue*.

Fountain Hills, a suburb at the northeast corner of the metropolitan area, was created in the seventies. McCulloch Company bulldozed one of the most beautiful virgin stands of saguaros in central Arizona to create a new town aimed at retirees. Nobody made a peep. Its centerpiece was alleged to be the world's tallest fountain. Houses and golf amid the foothills of the McDowell Mountains. Now it was attached to the cancerous sprawl of Phoenix and today the fountain was turned off.

I swung up Fountain Hills Boulevard and rolled into an older subdivision pod. Looking back toward town, Phoenix was nearly lost in a haze of air pollution. The worst ozone readings in the Valley were up here in the exclusive ZIP codes, not in benighted Maryvale or the historic districts. The address wasn't hard to find. Seven Sheriff's Department cruisers were parked on both sides of the street, along with unmarked units, a crime-scene van, and Peralta's distinctive SUV.

After finding a parking spot two blocks away, I made sure my badge was on my belt and walked. The house was older, low-slung, stucco that glared white in the midday sun, brown bricks framing windows and arches. Someone had put plenty of love in the front yard, which had a mini-botanical garden of native plants. I nodded to two uniformed deputies standing curbside. No bystanders needed control. If anyone was watching it was from behind their blinds. These two looked peaked, as my grandmother said. When I started up the concrete walk to the house, the smell hit me.

No words can describe the scent of rotting human flesh.

Peralta emerged from the front door, evidence gloves on his hands. I gloved up myself as he called me inside. Crime-scene made me sit at the entrance and slip hospital booties over my shoes.

In the living room, evidence technicians were hovering over a woman's body, short gray hair, facedown on a sectional sofa. Her hands were tied behind her back with some kind of fabric. Her head was propped toward the back on yellow and orange pillows.

"Throat cut," Peralta said. "But the blood didn't leak onto the carpet. Pillows channeled it. Before her throat was slit, she was beaten badly with a wine bottle." He indicated the full red bottle off to the side. Tastefully arranged shelves of Mexican Day of the Dead carvings, pottery, and books about the West and Indian tribes laughed at us. Nothing was out of place, no signs of a struggle.

My hands tingled. I didn't say a word, but I knew what was coming.

He led me down a hallway to the master bedroom. A man-shape in white linen pants and a colorful camp shirt was bloating on the king-sized bed. The bed was made. His head lolled off to the side, drained of blood but turning black, a ghastly rictus grin, eyes wide in terror. His throat was opened like a trench in a highway construction project, with darkening blood spread out to the bedclothes and spurting up onto the headboard and, behind that, spraying an Ansel Adams print on the wall. A tech was photographing it from every angle.

"His head was nearly cut off." Peralta's face was full of sangfroid while I was trying to suppress my gag reflex, breathing through my mouth. There was nothing you could do. Breathe through your nose and you'll want to vomit. Breathe through your mouth and pretty soon you'll be tasting the smell of death. Anything from masks and Vicks VapoRub in your nostrils to smoking cigars—the home remedies of cops and paramedics facing a "stinker"—ultimately failed.

I thought about the Western Front in the Great War a century before, where thousands of bodies rotted in No Man's Land shell holes and open terrain, or were buried in shelled trenches. Anecdotes told of soldiers becoming accustomed to having decomposing bodies in the trench walls. In one case, at least, a dead hand hanging out was shaken for good luck before the living went "over the top." Compared to that horror, this was another day at the office.

"Killers shut off the air conditioning before they left," he said. "The mailman called when the odor hit him coming up the driveway this morning. We estimate they've been here at least two days in a hot house."

"What's in the kitchen?" I asked.

"You know." His eyes were nearly black with rage. "A plate with most of a steak eaten, baked potato skin, a little creamed corn."

He pushed me back into the hall. "If you tell me this is canonical, I'm going to kick your ass all the way downtown."

"Start kicking." I met his angry stare. "This is how it went down with Gus Greenbaum and his wife in Palmcroft. Nineteen-fifty-eight. You know that. Who are they? Retired mob? Retired journalists?"

"Hardly," he said. "Meet Rusty Clevenger, the lead investigator on Page for the Attorney General's office. We should have had protection here. Goddamn it. Then there's this."

He handed me an evidence bag. Inside was a note:

> Sheriff Peralta and Deputy Mapstone:
> To die; to sleep, no more. SOLVE THE CASE.
> Sly

Consciousness of the stench went away for a few seconds. Another dead man with answers I needed.

I said, "What was Clevenger's reputation?"

"Sterling. Nobody had a bad word to say about him. I saw him at the fortieth-anniversary event."

"Files?"

Peralta broke out of his tough-guy expression, looking puzzled.

"Files!" I waved a helpless hand. "Have they checked to see if he had files here on the Page case? Diaries, office calendar, anything that could help us? Or was the house tossed and were things taken?"

"No evidence of a burglary. I doubt it about the other stuff. I'll check."

"How did he get in?"

Peralta said it looked like one of the Clevengers let the killer in. The alarm system was working but not armed. The panic button was never activated. To me, this opened some promising possibilities, that maybe the couple actually knew Ryan Garrison and didn't see him as a threat.

"Sounds like a reach to me." Peralta quietly cleared his throat. "We don't even know for sure it was Garrison. What if Sleigh did it herself?"

Young unis dutifully stepped aside. We walked out to the street and I huffed in gloriously polluted air that at least didn't smell like perdition.

Once we were out of their earshot, I continued: "You know better than that. It was Garrison. Nearly sawing off a man's head takes serious upper body strength. There's something else. Have someone get the Greenbaum murder book from Phoenix PD, the whole damned thing. Let's see what was held back from the newspapers or never leaked out. Things you couldn't find today on the Internet. If that murder was faithfully repeated here, with all the details, our boy might be something more than your average psycho."

He put his hands on his hips. "Anything else, Your Majesty?"

"That'll do for now." I did my best imitation of Lindsey's smile.

"Mapstone, I don't even know what they mean, 'solve the case.' How? What does that mean? Disclosing new information? Finding a suspect who's still alive and was never prosecuted?"

I shrugged and turned away.

"Where are you going?" he demanded.

"To check on Tom Goldstein."

Chapter Twenty-seven

My phone rang before I could open the broiling hot door latch.

"It's Tom Goldstein."

"I was thinking about you," I said, relieved to hear he was alive.

"Why?"

I thought about telling him the bad news right off, but hesitated. "I've been at the State Archives. Norm Reardon said that Page was killed because he had a ledger. What ledger?"

He sighed. "There are some things I didn't tell you. My memory isn't what it used to be. I'm sorry I gave you a hard time."

"It's not a problem."

"Yes, it is. Justice wasn't done in this case. Forty years go by, like a few days ago. The anniversary got me thinking about it all over. Then you got me thinking more. About the things that weren't settled. Things powerful people didn't want settled."

"Such as?"

"Come out here and let's talk again. I have something that might help. I kept it out of the case files when the

Attorney General took over. Didn't want them to 'lose' it. Thought it might come in handy someday." After a pause, his voice changed. He spoke slowly, almost dreamlike. "I haven't been to temple since I was a teenager. But the Talmud taught that the world needed thirty-six righteous men or it couldn't exist. I guess today, you'd say thirty-six people. Maybe you're one of them, Mapstone."

"I doubt that."

"The righteous ones wouldn't necessarily know they were. But without them, without those thirty-six..." He let the thought dangle. "When can you come?"

I said I'd be there in half an hour, less if the traffic allowed it.

"Watch yourself," he said. "I think I've been under surveillance. Your people?"

"No."

"Well, come on. And I have something you might find useful."

"In the meantime, be on guard," I said, and told him about the slaughter in Fountain Hills.

•●●●•

Twenty-five minutes later, I spun around to the double-wide on Nasty Ridge Trail. I went past doing normal speed and saw nothing but Goldstein's truck. The closest dwellings looked shut up tight against the weather. I hadn't seen another car since I left the freeway. In that sense, Black Canyon City resembled the classic desert towns before technology fooled us into our present hubris. Those towns appeared deserted on a summer day. Only a fool from back east would be driving through. Turning around, I came back, parked behind Goldstein's truck, and stepped out into the bludgeon of the heat.

From ten feet away I could see the door was ajar. The space was enough that I could see inside and, as I got closer, a pair of boots on the floor attached to legs covered in blue jeans. I drew my .45, flipped off the safety, and approached slowly with my finger along the gun's sleek housing, ready to move to the trigger at a second's notice.

"Tom!" I called. "Detective Goldstein!"

Nothing but the preternatural quiet of the desert.

The five rattlers were still slung over the railing as I took one step up, then positioned myself to the side of the door and got low. With my left hand, I slowly started to push it open.

The concussion was sharp and loud. Then I was deaf and an invisible hand was hurling me over the railing, into the air. The ground came up suddenly and hard.

Where do orphan socks go?

They finally got me. Reid, Mafia, RaceCo! Find Mark Reid.

First, breathing...I couldn't—and panic came quickly. Didn't know where I was, who I was. Couldn't breathe.

Then, like the tide coming in, a big breath filled my lungs. A sense memory took me back to grade school, to the first time I "had the air knocked out of me."

Overhead was the G-type main sequence star ninety-three million miles from this planet. It felt about a block away. My arms and legs were rubbery. For several minutes—I'm sure it was probably seconds—I wasn't even sure I could feel them. Needed to make sure I was in one piece. The likelihood of what had just happened began to form coherent thoughts.

Then I noticed the four-foot-long diamondback rattlesnake staring at me, fangs bared eight inches from my face. That brought me around in a hurry. It was only a second before I realized it was one of the dead trophies from Tom Goldstein's railing, but it was enough. I tossed the remains of the viper away with my left hand.

My right hand, my gun hand, was empty.

Then a man blotted out the sun.

I couldn't hear his words—my brain was awash with a symphony of tinnitus—but his lips were easy enough to read.

Looking for this?

Ryan Garrison stood over me twirling my semiauto with his finger. By now, my wits had returned sufficiently that I knew if he applied appropriate pressure to the trigger the gun would discharge.

My backup gun was strapped to my ankle. But between the near paralysis I felt from landing hard on the ground and the fact that he would shoot me even if I succeeded in making the reach, the .38 might as well have been ninety-three million miles away.

He squatted, leaned in, pressing my chest with his knee and putting the semiauto in my face. I felt his other hand behind my head. He lifted it until my neck hurt worse than it already did.

"Alas, poor David!" His voice was surprisingly pleasing, trained. "I knew him, Horatio, a fellow of infinite jest, of most excellent fancy."

I felt the barrel under my chin, pressing hard. I couldn't have moved my tongue to swallow even if I had dared. The skill of his moves made me think he had done this before.

"But, Horatio, he won't solve the case."

Here I'd like to tell you I was thinking of Lindsey, saying a prayer, musing *Think fast, wabbitt!*... But I was only in second by second, breath by breath mode, without even the crashing pilot's consolation of tasks to run through in an attempt to prevent the inevitable. His body position prevented me from moving my right arm or torso. I could bring my right knee up violently and try to get him off me, but...Oh, yes, the .45 caliber bullet that would pass through my jaw, sinuses, and brain if his finger applied pressure to the trigger. He was very strong. The back of my head throbbed from his grip.

He dropped my head and stepped away.

"He won't solve the case!" The pleasing light baritone went up an octave into the crazy scale.

A pickaxe slammed into my right side.

That's what it felt like.

Then a flash of movement in my peripheral vision and a second kick. Pain, lots of it, overriding almost every other sensory input and brain circuit.

I assumed a fetal position away from him but another blow didn't materialize.

"You're too old to be in this game!" That shriek came again. "But you don't have a choice! Solve the case! Or next time you're dead!"

I waited long moments as the wildfire of pain on my right side grew. I forced myself to listen. Nothing. Was he standing there, waiting to execute me?

The advantage of my new position was that it had naturally draped my right arm over my right leg and brought my ankle up.

In one move, I pulled the .38 and rolled, then came up on one knee, sweeping the revolver toward my target.

He was gone.

In the distance, I heard an engine gunning. The sound faded as I struggled up and staggered toward the double-wide. The door was blown twenty feet out onto the hood of Goldstein's pickup and all the windows were shattered, curtains catching the wind. Every breath I took set my side on fire again. It was a good thing I had been beside the entry, kneeling, when the explosion happened. But I also knew Garrison had customized the blast to hurt me, not kill me. Not this time.

Inside, it smelled vaguely like bananas. A cloud of smoke hovered like Phoenix smog. Tom Goldstein was on the floor, his face pointed up, eyes open. His throat had been expertly slit, ear to ear. Jets of blood on the carpet were drying rapidly in the fifteen percent humidity. Nevertheless, I felt for a pulse in his wrist, watched for chest rise—nothing.

A shotgun lay nearby, useless. I wondered how Garrison had gotten past that. A full-length twelve-gauge was not a particularly good close-quarters weapon. Still, do bring a gun to a knife fight, such had always been my motto. Garrison somehow got past a lifetime of police skills learned by Tom Goldstein, plus the scattergun. The young easily beating the old again? Now Garrison had my semiautomatic pistol.

The railroad layout was wrecked, the little police car resting a few inches from Goldstein's left hand. All the hours and years spent building this magnificent work of art and history, lost. Two sets of legs of the wooden benchwork had been sheared by the dynamite and the tabletop now sat at the angle of a sinking ship. Carefully crafted buildings were smashed, rail cars and locomotives, hundreds of objects, really—tiny mailboxes, street lights, palm trees, X-shaped railroad crossing signs, among them—strewn about. I can't say why, but this particularly offended me.

I started sobbing.

When I turned away, I saw it. Plastered against the Age of Exploration map was a sheet of laminated plastic. I pulled latex gloves from my pocket and peeled it off. A Post-it note was attached to one side, not visible at first glance: Mapstone scrawled in old-man script. The page was about four inches wide by eight inches long, about the size of an old railroad timetable. It was a grid with names in one column and sequential numbers in the other. I scanned it. Then I read it slowly. Each number corresponded to a name. It was a code key. My emotions steadied but my heart rate kept going like a race horse.

In the remains of Goldstein's kitchen, I found a large Ziploc bag and slid the sheet inside. I also found a Sharpie and wrote, "Evidence," marking the date, time, location, and signing it.

In the distance, I heard sirens.

Chapter Twenty-eight

"You're very lucky. No concussion or brain damage. You're dehydrated so we're running an IV to fix that. You have two cracked ribs from the kicks. Lucky there, too. Your spleen is fine, no internal bleeding, no punctured lung. How many times were you kicked?"

"Twice."

"It's a good thing. People watch these beat-downs on television, kicking someone in the side, stomping on them. They copy it, especially the gangs. They don't realize it will kill a person in real life."

The doctor was compact and efficient, a thirtysomething Latina. Under her lab coat, her blue scrubs showed a tiny spray of blood drops. I looked her in the eyes.

"I want to leave."

"Not yet," she said.

The paramedics had insisted on taking me to John C. Lincoln Hospital in north Phoenix. So I was lying in bed, feeling unmanned by my confrontation with Garrison. My clothes, shoes, and gun were gone, bagged up at the nurses' station, I assumed. But I insisted on keeping my evidence bag. It lay under my left side. X-rays were taken. So was an initial interview by Yavapai County detectives and an ATF agent. I didn't tell everything I knew.

"The ribs have to heal on their own. I'm going to give you a prescription for the pain," she said. "Do you have any questions, Deputy Mapstone?"

I felt very tired. From a dry mouth I said, "None you can answer."

•••••

When I woke up, they were all around me and for a moment I thought I was hallucinating—or dead.

Lindsey was holding my hand. Mike and Sharon Peralta were standing on opposite sides of the bed. Malik Jones was sitting in a chair on my left, still in his suit.

"He's awake," Sharon said.

I wasn't dead.

"I'm so glad you are all here." I spoke in my best French accent. "Now we will get to the bottom of this.

"Quit screwing around, Mapstone," Peralta said.

I continued, touching my right temple. "All the time Poirot was lying here, he was trying to use the little gray cells. Remembering being kicked and kicked by one of these thespians reciting *Hamlet*, thinking, *tant pis?*

"What?"

Sharon said, "It's French, roughly translated as 'the situation is regrettable but nothing can be done.'"

"Correct, *Madame*. But, no! I realize, how wrong Poirot has been. *Imbécile!* We had begun treating this as two cases. The 1978 bombing of Buzz Page. And the new murder of Rudy Jarvis, the assault on his mother, the jail break, and now... Now Rusty Clevenger from the Attorney General's office and Tom Goldstein, the lead homicide detective. It is murder most foul."

"Looks that way to me." Peralta folded his arms.

I lifted a finger, jiggling my IV line. "No, *mon ami*. It is one case. Only one. But why do our criminals want us to solve the Page murder? This perplexed Poirot. No more. We will now walk toward the truth. And each of us is involved in our way..."

"David." This from Sharon in her soothing professional voice, an indulgent smile.

"You, *Madame* Sharon, you were on the radio, no?"

Her smile fell. "Yes. That summer was the first year of my show. I was in grad school, raising the girls, hadn't finished my doctorate yet. But we needed money and I started working as a gofer at the old KOY. They liked my voice and they had late-night air to fill. So, we started an hour show called "Ask Sharon."

Still in the accent, I said, "And you talked about the Page bombing, no?"

"Actually, yes," she said. "I hadn't even remembered until now. The usual calls were about relationships and love, that sort of thing. But after the bombing people called in on that topic. We talked about the fear they felt, the..." She paused and gripped the rails of the bed. "Some callers wanted to know what I thought about the killers. I never tried to diagnose from a distance. But obviously, we were dealing with sociopaths."

"And the entire Valley heard this, no?"

"It was a very popular show," Sharon said. "I think you should rest."

"And that is all, *Madame* Sharon? Poirot doubts that."

Our eyes locked. She spoke slowly. "We didn't have a call screener then, so people called into the studio directly. I answered during the breaks, to get a sense of what they wanted to discuss, and put the best ones on hold. One night in August, I'm sure about the month, I got a call from a woman. She said the police had it all wrong. That Darren Howard was innocent."

"You never told me this," Peralta said.

She continued to look at me. "I didn't want to put Mike in a jam, so I kept it to myself. I told her she should go to the police. She said she was afraid to, that the mob owned the cops, and they'd kill her."

"*Bon*," I said. I shifted my gaze to Jones. "And here is Monsieur Jones, a doctoral student in history. But you are also a former Army officer."

"The sheriff and I were talking about how we had both served in the Seventy-Fifth Ranger Regiment," he said. "He in Vietnam, I commanded a company in Iraq."

"Like *Madame* Lindsey, you are too young to have direct involvement in the Page incident when it happened. But now you have unearthed, how do you put it, a bombshell. And in good time, Poirot will put the pieces together. But let me tell you this, *capitaine*: Your Army knowledge will also be needed if we're to snare this Garrison fellow."

I swiveled my head right, wincing in pain.

"*Madame* Lindsey, the expert hacker. You are part of this, too. *Mon amour*, this woman Elizabeth Sleigh has a, how do you say, thing about you. She respects your expertise, even fears it. We will make use of this, too. And Poirot? He was a student then, not yet at the Sheriff's Office. But he had an apartment at Thirty-Sixth Street and Campbell. His next-door neighbor was my age. Over time, he confided to Poirot that his father had worked for the Mafia in Chicago, then turned witness, and was killed by a car bomb. 'Page was warned,' he told me. 'They always warn you.' This man came home at night and always circled the block several times, looking for trouble. After the Page bombing, he was terrified."

Then I looked at Peralta, gently leveled my index finger at him, and dropped the accent.

"Which leaves you, *mon ami*."

He started to blow up—I knew the early warning signs—but suddenly stopped, as if the detonator had been removed from a nuclear device at the last second. He stood very still.

"You promised to reopen the case," I said. "But it goes deeper than that, doesn't it?"

"Mapstone, I was a nobody young deputy then."

"You were never a nobody, *mon ami*, so it's time to tell us what you've been concealing."

"Do you have a concussion?"

"No concussion."

He started gesticulating and speaking quickly. "This is neither here nor there. What happened in Black Canyon City today?"

"What happened to you in 1978?"

I watched the turbulence in his dark eyes. Then he said, "I was going to tell you. The sheriff offered to help on the Page investigation. He pulled out after he received a threat that his family would be killed if he did it. So, he dropped it."

"But there's more to the story, no?"

Peralta stared at me angrily, then at the floor. "I became the sheriff's driver that summer. There was no protective unit back then. He was a good man and he grew to trust me. He put me on the fast track. But I'm pretty sure that the reason he backed off the Page case went beyond the anonymous threat. He told me that 'people down on Seventeenth Avenue'—that's how he put it—wanted the whole thing to go away."

"Meaning the Capitol. The governor? Attorney General?"

"I don't know, Mapstone, and that's the truth. The Sheriff ordered me to take the file boxes to the incinerator. I took them to the trunk of my car."

Peralta walked over to the window and stared out. It was a full five minutes before he spoke again.

"When he left office, he pulled me aside and asked me if I had destroyed the Page files. I admitted that I hadn't. But he wasn't mad at me. He was pissed with how the case ended. It was a burr under his saddle until he died. He told me one day I'd be Sheriff and maybe I could make things right."

I said, "So your comments that night at the Claremont weren't off-the-cuff."

He shook his head. "The years went by. They were busy years, we did good work. And to tell you the truth, even a casual glance into those files made me realize what a snakes' nest they were. Then I was voted out of office and I kicked myself for never going after it. But back in again, I decided, after forty years, it was time."

I said, "Did the Sheriff know who threatened his family?"

"He was convinced it was the mob," Peralta said.

The room was a vacuum of silence amid the sounds of a busy hospital floor. Sharon looked at her husband, who scowled down, then back at me. Jones pensively rubbed his chin with his left hand. Lindsey slowly nodded.

I said, "Which brings us back to what my fussy Belgian friend was getting at a few minutes ago. It is one case. Everything is connected. And why do these two want us to solve it? When we discover that answer, we will know the truth. And I bet it begins…" I pulled out the Ziploc bag holding the laminated sheet. "…with this."

Chapter Twenty-nine

I was somewhere in central Phoenix, outside the historic districts, when the drugs began to take hold. It was only one bottle of Vicodin, no refills, but the pill I took didn't cause every breath to leave me in agony. The day was late and the sunset was a disappointment.

Back at JCL, when Peralta first saw the laminated sheet, he cleared the room and was about to chew me out for pilfering evidence from the scene. Then he studied it and a deep silence settled over his features.

"Do you realize what this means?" His voice was low, almost a whisper.

"That's a who's who of Phoenix in 1978," I said. "From politicians to gangsters. A name and a distinct three-digit code next to it. And 001 says F. Burke. As in, our friend Freeman Burke, Sr. For some reason Goldstein kept it instead of entering it into evidence. My guess is that it connects with the ledger that Buzz Page supposedly had when he was blown up. Maybe Mark Reid dangled this decoder as bait to get him to the Clarendon. Because if you put the two together, you'd have the story that would bring down the Phoenix power structure. Right into the Phoenix Forty"—the corporate elite—"the cops and important politicians."

Even at Goldstein's ruined double-wide, I had checked the list for Peralta's father, who was on the state Court of Appeals. Thank God, he wasn't there. But at least two judges who heard Page-related cases were.

"Christ, Mapstone." His tone was still uncharacteristically low, as if he feared ghosts from forty years ago might hear. He carefully slid the sheet back into the Ziploc, then produced a real plastic evidence bag, slid it in, and signed and dated it.

"What are you going to do?" I said.

"For now, it's going in my office safe. And the safe isn't connected to the goddamned Internet. Where do you think Goldstein got this?"

I shook my head. He had a chance to mention it in our first talk, but he didn't. Obviously, he had a change of heart and was going to give it to me. Then Ryan Garrison showed up. For all I knew, the concussion from the dynamite sent the sheet across the room and plastered it against the map. Fortunately, Garrison didn't see it.

Then I told him about the transcript Malik Jones had discovered in the state archives, mentioning a ledger. Peralta fell heavily into the bedside chair and shook his head.

"So what do you need, Hercule, smartass?"

I thought about that scene in the movie *The Matrix*, and I wanted to answer, *Guns. Lots of guns.*

But I said, "We need a court order to let Jones get into the next level of records."

"You'll have it in the morning," Peralta said. "And keep this guy on the payroll. He's good. As for you…"

"I'm going after Garrison and my goddamned gun."

He stood and his familiar authoritarian voice returned. "No, you're not. You're not going to freelance this because he got the better of you. There'll be a next time, but we'll do it right. As it stands, the shit's going to hit the fan."

"A jurisdictional goatfuck."

He almost—almost—smiled. "Yup. Thanks a bunch, Mapstone. You need to get back in the historical angle."

I was too sore to argue. A nurse came in and disconnected the IV, removing the line from the top of my hand. When he was gone, Peralta said, "Who does this, Mapstone?"

"Criminals."

"But I've never had a case where the criminals want this. Sure, you have the psycho killer who secretly wants to get caught. Maybe he even plays a game with the police. Publicity-seekers are common, too. And maybe this is an elaborate version of all that. Still..."

"Maybe they're batshit crazy," I said, playing devil's advocate.

"Could be. But Sharon says they're very high-functioning for batshit crazy. She bets it's some angle of revenge, right down to the plot of *Hamlet*. They think they can play us, force us to dig into the case again, maybe even dig up and hang the corpse of old man Burke, and then get away with it. Vanish. Or so they hope. That's what Sharon thinks."

"Nemesis," I said.

He cocked his head.

"Nemesis, as in the goddess of retributive justice. The trouble is, all the offspring of the victims either have alibis or are gone themselves. Unless they're paying Garrison and Sleigh to do this."

He shrugged and stood to leave. "Maybe it's something simple and we're overthinking it. You'd never do that, right? And by the way, Goldstein's murder isn't in the canon, right?"

"No," I admitted. "Unless you believe some of the

stories that 'Star' Johnson and Frenchy Navarre were part of a mob contract, which was never proved." I could see his eyes start to glaze. "Anyway, you're right. It's not canonical. They've gone off script."

"Script." He drew out the word, turning it over in his mind. "How does *Hamlet* end?"

"Everybody dies, pretty much."

He shook his head as he left the room.

On Cypress Street, Lindsey pulled into the carport and we went inside.

"Do you want to lie down?" she said. "Shower the desert off you? I'll help. I'll be very gentle."

I smiled but shook my head. "I'd rather sit up for now."

She brought me a grape popsicle to help me cool down. I slid it out of the wrapper and finished it in silence. Between us was the electricity of what happened that afternoon: I thought I was doing to die, never see her again.

She laid her hand on my arm. "I know you're angry over losing your gun. You can't blame yourself. Thank goodness you're not hurt worse."

I didn't answer, but went into the bedroom and discarded my shamefully empty holster. From the bedside table drawer I retrieved my four-inch Colt Python .357 magnum in its Galco Combat Master Belt holster and slid it on. It was heavy and reliable. Familiar as a lethal old shoe. I pulled out the revolver and opened it, made sure it was loaded, spun the cylinder, slid it back in. I added the two Speedloaders, six additional rounds each, and returned to the living room.

Lindsey saw the big Colt, put her arms around my neck, and gently kissed me.

"Please don't go all dark and be obsessed about Ryan Garrison. We'll get him."

"I'll get him," I said, "and he'll never get my firearm again. What about Sleigh?"

She sat and folded her hands. "I can't track her online, yet. My hacker bag of tricks is empty. I spent most of the day making sure the jail system was secure and nobody else could walk out. But I learned a few things. She left the county around the time I went to D.C. She works as a security consultant for a couple of tech outfits in Silicon Valley."

"So, we go there."

Her mouth curled into a smile.

"She's here. She has a condo in Ahwatukee Foothills. I guess she's part of the elite bunch that takes Southwest from Sky Harbor to San Jose every Monday morning, works in the tech sector, and then comes back later in the week."

I eased myself back into the chair and started to run my hand down my face. It stung sharply. I felt several small cuts I received from the fragments of Tom Goldstein's doorframe when the bomb went off.

"So, you're telling me Elizabeth Sleigh—"Sly"—is right here, in town, out in the open?"

Lindsey nodded.

"Why doesn't Peralta pick her up?"

"On what charge?" she said. "Ryan Garrison's landlord couldn't definitively pick her out of the photo array the detectives showed him. He lingered on her. Maybe it was her. But he couldn't be certain. I can't connect her to the computer virus, certainly not enough to convince a judge. Peralta isn't even sure he could get probable cause for a phone tap."

"You could hack her phone."

"I could," Lindsey said, "but it would be illegal. It

wouldn't be admissible. And, by the way, the cell phone they got from Garrison when they picked him up was a burner. It erased all its data when I tried to turn it on. As for Elizabeth, we have someone who knew me."

"Sexually harassed you."

"Well, she had a crush on me. She could be the hacker—she definitely has the skills. No connection to Buzz Page, as far as I can find. She did hit on Peralta at the anniversary event...."

"And Tom Goldstein, I bet. He described an attractive blonde."

"But that's not a crime."

"At least we could tail her," I said. "Garrison's got to make contact at some point."

"Peralta's already got surveillance in the works. Doing that subtly in the World's Largest Cul-de-Sac won't be easy."

"We sit and wait for the next person to be killed by these maniacs?"

"No," she said. "I have a plan."

She laid it out calmly and I listened.

Then we had a big fight. And no intense make-up sex afterwards.

Chapter Thirty

Suddenly, the media were very interested. The lead homicide detective in the Buzz Page case was murdered in a dynamite explosion, a copycat bomb of the one that killed the *Phoenix Gazette* reporter forty years before. And the AG's investigator murdered, too.

That's the way Peralta told it at a packed press conference Thursday morning at the Starship. Beside him were the bosses of the local ATF and FBI, the Phoenix Police Chief, and Yavapai County Sheriff. I was there, too, in my summer Haspel suit, starched French blue shirt, dark-blue rep tie, and aching ribs.

We held back the real cause of Tom Goldstein's death, as well as the copycat nature of the Clevenger killings, to weed out the kooks who would inevitably call in to confess. Ryan Garrison's booking photo was prominently displayed on a large screen behind the stage and also on handouts for the press. Armed and dangerous.

The *New York Times* sent a hotshot national reporter on a red-eye flight from the mothership. The *Times* reporter in Phoenix mostly wrote lightweight features, so she was over her head on this story. The *Washington Post* sent someone, too, as did the *LA Times*. Peralta took the

Post reporter to his office and leaked that Rudy Jarvis was Mark Reid's son. From "a law enforcement official who was not authorized to speak on the record." It was on the newspaper's website by two p.m. The headline read: "Forty Years After a Reporter's Murder, Phoenix Is On Edge Again." Later, he would tell the same thing to a *Republic* reporter, attributing it to him on the record, playing to the home crowd.

When the *Post* reporter left, I asked where we were with tracking down Ryan Garrison.

"'We' are nowhere!" Peralta shifted from his charming voice for the East Coast journalist to a harsh shout.

I went off, too. "Wait a goddamned minute—"

"No," he cut me off. "You're lucky I didn't take you off the case entirely. You were supposed to be doing research, being discreet. You know, circumspect. Instead, you had to go see Tom Goldstein. Twice! Have you considered you're responsible for his death?"

I had and dismissed it. Sly and Garrison were going to kill him anyway. He was *processing* his anger, as Sharon had taught me.

"Bullshit." Peralta waved me away with his big hand. "And so much for your theory that they were repeating the canon of Phoenix organized crime. Murdering a detective sure as hell wasn't canonical."

"We already had this conversation," I said. "Something made them go off script. For all we know, they bugged Goldstein's house and knew he was going to tell me something, give me the code key. Garrison might have had time to root around and find it, but I showed up. Or Garrison has a hit list and Goldstein was on it. We hadn't been making public progress on the Page case. Lindsey had to shut down their malware into the Sheriff's Office. They wanted to push us."

He wasn't done processing. "That's a good story but you can't prove any of it. And you lost your weapon. I'm doing you a favor by not suspending you and having the Professional Standards Bureau investigate you."

"You'd put the rat squad on me?"

He assumed his Buddha pose.

I put my head down so he couldn't see my eyes welling up. It was because I was mad, not weak. That's what I told myself. In the hospital, they had asked about my pain level: one being no pain and ten being the worst I had ever felt. Right that moment, I was about an eight. Underneath my French blue shirt, my right side looked like a maniac's abstract painting, and every inhalation brought a stabbing ache.

I said, "You need to do a press briefing every day."

"Why"

"Because these two are publicity junkies and we need to show progress so they don't kill somebody else."

He started to protest. What would he say? I promised that Jones and I would feed him tidbits from the archives that he could use to brief the media.

"Trust me."

He harrumphed.

We sat in silence for a long time before he started to talk about Garrison. Phoenix Police assigned half a dozen detectives to track him down. The investigators got his bank records, which didn't show anything unusual. His checking account balance was nine-hundred-twelve dollars.

A year before, he got a speeding ticket coming out of Ahwatukee, the district of Phoenix that sat on the other side of the South Mountains.

"Maybe visiting Elizabeth Sleigh?" I said.

"Maybe." He continued: Garrison had been working for a company that installed garage doors, and they showed Sleigh's picture to his co-workers—unfortunately none had seen her with him and he never talked about a girlfriend.

The man was universally described as hard-working and quiet. Yet he didn't have friends. Family back in Iowa claimed they hadn't heard from him in more than a month. The detectives were searching cellular companies for his phone—we could subpoena his calls and text messages. And they found the bars he was known to frequent in the East Valley, showed his photo, and staked them out. His Army records came, too, and showed the same anonymous good service. He was the perfect assassin.

I said, "What about neighbors at the apartment? Have they been interviewed?"

"It's happening."

"And Sleigh?"

"This morning the Deputy County Attorney found a friendly judge. I wanted advanced surveillance on Sleigh as a person of interest in the case. The judge didn't grant a phone or Internet tap—Sleigh has not so much as a moving violation on her record—but he did sign off on a tracker to be attached to her vehicle."

It gave us a better shot at finding Garrison. He had to make contact with her, if he hadn't already done so. For all we knew, he was hiding in her condo, had a secret way in and out.

"They could pay her a friendly visit, ask questions," I said.

"They could," he said, back in a calm voice. "Then she'd know we suspected her."

"Right. Forget I said that."

Peralta also told me he borrowed twenty police academy cadets to canvas the garages at Sky Harbor in search of her car. She wasn't home, so she was likely in Silicon Valley.

I said, "Did Lindsey talk to you?"

He nodded. "It sounds like she has a good plan."

My ribs burned. "How is this not entrapment?"

He spoke to me as if lecturing a rookie: It would only be entrapment if it caused a defendant to do something he or she wouldn't have done without the fraud. And the police were allowed to use trickery or lying. Blah, blah, blah.

I didn't let up. "It sounds like a very dangerous plan."

"I've green-lighted it. First chance we get."

"Do you remember what I told you?"

He shrugged his big shoulders. "That's why you're going along."

I started to protest when he stood and told me he had a meeting.

"Get back to your office and do your research. If I find you're off the reservation and trying to prove your manhood by taking Garrison alone, your ass is grass. And use the damned alarm system in your office. In the meantime..."

He handed me an envelope.

•●●●•

Malik Jones and I took the court order out to the State Archives that allowed us into the second level of classified documents about the Page case. With the radio saying it was 117 degrees, I noticed the white lettering on the large lighted plastic street signs at major intersections was starting to melt like wet paint. Inside, the officials seemed surprised by my request and sent for someone—the title wasn't exactly clear—who appeared, wizened and bespectacled with the strange bearing of an undertaker. He looked over the court document and checked my Sheriff's Office identification.

"Mr. Jones is a historian working with the Sheriff's Office," I added.

The archivist nodded, then went back to the legal document that allowed us here.

"Funniest thing." He raised his head and assessed us. "Nobody's been in these files for at least twenty years, when the last of the appeals was over and they were all placed with us. Suddenly in the last month…"

"What do you mean?" I said.

"You are the second in the past month." He laid out papers for us to sign, showing we had read the rules of access, etc. "I read the paper so I understand why you're here. But, oh, maybe late May, a lawyer came here, with a court order from Pinal County granting his access."

"Ah," Jones said, "that was Mr…" He tilted his hand slightly, as if searching for the name. I suppressed a smile.

"Barrington," the archivist volunteered. "Theodore Barrington."

"Of course," Jones said. "Ted told me he might spend a week."

"Oh, no." The archivist smiled. "He was in and out in only an hour. I think he knew what he was looking for. I have no idea what it was. Maybe you do."

After the man guided us to a secure reading room, he laid down a binder. "This gives abstracts on all the file collections, but with the budget cuts it might be incomplete. I assume you'll want to start with the D Files."

"Of course," Jones said.

When the man wheeled in the D Files, whatever they contained, and went away, I closed the door and leaned on the table. "You're good."

"Librarians and archivists can be lifesavers," he said. "You know that. Any idea who this Barrington cat is?"

I thought I had heard the name, but couldn't place it.

Jones began unpacking his tools: iPad, notepads, pencils.

"You know, Chief Gillespie," he said, "I feel kinda guilty taking the taxpayers' money for this. It would take years of archival work to get to the bottom of this. Robert Caro kind of research."

"I know. I told Peralta."

"And even that probably wouldn't show how it ties into your digital Bonnie and Clyde."

I laughed and winced from the pain in my side.

"How are you holding up?"

"Hanging in," I said. "It hurts like hell." Then for some reason, I went on: "I was blown about ten feet from the trailer door by the explosion. Then I was on the ground, trying to get my hearing back and see if I still had arms and legs, when Garrison was standing over me. Next he had me pinned and my gun under my jaw, reciting Shakespeare. It sounds so surreal. I thought I was dead. But I'd never felt so fucking helpless…"

Jones set aside his paperwork. "You felt like a bag of smashed asshole."

"That's a good way to put it."

He gently smiled. "You can't blame yourself."

"Peralta does."

"Maybe, but I doubt it. He did tell me his men in 'Nam nicknamed him Ironass."

"What did your men nickname you?"

"A story for another day."

I looked into the ceiling lights—that was a mistake, given the all-in aches of my entire body—and then carefully craned my neck to face Jones. "I've never lost control of a situation like that before, never had a suspect get me down, where he was in total control and all my training and experience wasn't worth a damn."

"And you were afraid."

I studied his eyes. "Yes."

It was very unlike me to be in confessional mode. Men don't have friends on the same basis as women. Men friends talk about sports or, I suppose today, video games. Consequence: I had few male friends after high school. Suddenly I was uncomfortable, as if I had told too much. "Shared" in the corporate lexicon of our age. On the other hand, we barely knew each other. Who better to confide in?

Jones studied my face for a long moment. "I was in the second vehicle of a convoy on a highway fifteen klicks outside of Baghdad. It was supposed to be a safe, cleared roadway. Sure. No such thing there. The lead Humvee hit an IED. The device was very well camouflaged and they ran right over it." He slowly shook his head. "I lost more two soldiers. They weren't the first and weren't the last. They were under my command and their deaths were on me."

"Not on the bad guys?"

"Over there you can't tell who the bad guys are. I tried really hard not to hate every civilian. I was afraid all the time we were outside the wire, but I could never let my soldiers see it. Only a fool isn't afraid. But writing letters to the wives and parents of those guys…toughest thing I ever had to do. But, yeah, I owned those deaths. Still do."

All I could do was listen.

"This Garrison fights like an insurgent," he said. "For what cause, I don't know...yet."

Jones was getting more comfortable with me.

I prayed there wouldn't be a police shooting of a person of color and send this relationship down the toilet.

My phone rang. Peralta.

"One of the cadets found Sleigh's car in the East Economy Garage and attached the tracking device under the fender," he announced. "A BMW M6. This is not a poor woman." It was also not the car captured on the video picking up Ryan Garrison outside the jail.

Then Peralta said his visitor was an attorney for the Freeman Burke, Sr., Family Foundation. "It was a very interesting conversation," he said. Interesting in that, although Peralta never mentioned Burke's name in the press conference, the news stories inevitably did. And the lawyer didn't like it. "He told me that's a red line that shouldn't be crossed."

"What did you tell him?"

"I said the investigation would lead where the investigation would lead. Hell, I've got a few years until the next election. I tried to be nice. You would have been proud of me."

"Speaking of lawyers, who is Theodore Barrington?"

"He's a white-shoe lawyer, corporate, water, real estate. Why?"

I told him and the line was silent for at least thirty seconds.

He said, "Curious."

"What?"

"Only that. And don't even think of contacting him, Mapstone."

"Where does he practice?"

"Phoenix."

"So why did he bring a court order from Pinal County?" I said. "Trying to fly under the radar?"

"Enough," Peralta said. "I need to think this through."

He hung up, as usual without a goodbye. Still, there was a sense of momentum.

On the case, at least. Lindsey and I exchanged heart and kisses emoticons via iPhones that day but, in my mind, nothing from last night had been settled.

Chapter Thirty-one

Saturday night the heat emergency continued. But we were rewarded with a glorious sunset in otherworldly colors, finally a funnel of shimmering copper and red in the west and lingering bands of pink all around. By nine p.m., though, it was still one-hundred-ten degrees as we pulled up to the hottest club in downtown Scottsdale. The parking attendant looked over our ancient Honda Prelude as if we had exited a turd. I slipped him a twenty and he was more amenable.

Despite the temperature, a long line was waiting on the sidewalk behind maroon velour ropes hanging from silver stanchions. Lindsey took aside a security guard, a black guy who looked twice my size and made of all muscle, and discreetly badged him. He opened the door and nodded for us to enter. The people standing outside wondered about us: VIPs.

Elizabeth Sleigh had entered the club fifteen minutes before. Two plainclothes deputies parked across the street had confirmed it on the radio. They were staying there as our backup, especially if Ryan Garrison showed up. Then things would get hairy. Then Lindsey's plan would go worse than sideways.

It was throwback night to the seventies, including a rotating mirrored ball over the dance floor. How appropriate to this case. Debbie Harry was singing "Heart of Glass" and the speakers were turned so high up that it felt as if the walls were pulsing in and out from the sonic impact. My eardrums, which had made it through the explosion at Tom Goldstein's trailer, might not survive many minutes of this. Bodies were all around us, ripped young men in T-shirts and jeans, heavily made-up young women with fake boobs and deep tans. This was the off-season, so I couldn't imagine how far above the fire marshal's capacity the place would hold in the winter.

I also wondered: Who were they? Did they work in call centers and behind the Nordstrom makeup counter during the day? Were they the Scottsdale crowd that couldn't make it in LA or New York City but here they were a deal? In a city with so many retirees seeking sunshine and golf, it was rare to see so many beautiful young people outside of the ASU campuses. I certainly didn't fit in. Too old for the game, as Garrison said. Underneath my white guayabera shirt was the Colt Python. Lindsey, in her little black dress and with her Ivory Soap girl skin, blue eyes, and dark hair, instantly stood out as the most beautiful woman in the room. She was older, too, even though in my mind's eye she remained the twenty-nine-year-old I first fell in love with.

It was cool, thank God. And dark. I scanned the faces for Garrison and Sleigh. Nothing.

We both had Bluetooth devices hanging from our ears. The plan was for our backup to be able to hear us and we could hear each other. The noise of the club made that impossible.

"We need to be seen," Lindsey said, grabbing my hand

and leading me to the dance floor. We disco-danced to the Bee Gees' "Boogie Child." I hated it then, and the intervening years had not changed my mind. Still, I made an effort, an improvised one-man foxtrot, not afraid to make a fool of myself amid all the lovely people doing their hip-hop kick-step-back steps around us. My pain level jacked up to around eight.

"You've got the moves, Dave!" Lindsey shouted it as she gyrated to the music. Our senses were bombarded by green and blue and silver lights.

Then, "Beth." KISS slowed things down. I pulled Lindsey close and slow-danced, taking the lead. Many fewer couples remained on the dance floor. Raised on rap, they didn't really know how to disco dance much less slow-dance. I actually was pretty good at that and I noticed a few admiring glances from the nearby couples. *Beth, what can I do?*

Suddenly, I saw the blond woman approach us. She walked around and tapped me on the shoulder.

"May I cut in?"

And then she was slowly twirling with Lindsey, her hand proprietarily set behind my wife's back. "Beth" played on, the timing of song title and encounter surreal. I stood and watched them dance. Lindsey caught my eye. Her message: *Let me take the lead here.*

When the song ended, the three of us walked to the bar.

"Lindsey, you're back!"

She nodded. "Elizabeth, this is my husband, David."

Her handshake was very firm and she held it an extra few seconds, looking me in the eyes. "I know all about the famous David Mapstone. But I didn't realize he could dance. I'm Elizabeth Sleigh." Sure enough, it was pronounced "Sly."

She looked about five-ten, busty, poured into a teal blue cocktail dress. Her wheat-colored hair was parted in the middle and swept back from a face with high cheekbones, translucent green eyes, and full lips in a cupid's bow. Screen-siren looks—she was much more attractive than her five-year-old county employee photo. If she had had work done here in Silicone Valley, it was of the highest quality. Maybe she merely had good DNA, like Lindsey. Luck of the draw. The light-show glittered off the diamond studs in her ears and the heart-shaped pendant hanging from a silver chain around her fine neck.

The women ordered sweet drinks off the extensive cocktail menu. I tried to convince the bartender to make me a martini. Just a martini, dry, one olive. No Beefeater? How about Bombay Sapphire? Yes.

I felt Sleigh's hand on my upper arm, pulling me close.

"You have a very talented wife, David."

"I know." Then I took a risk. "Are you with someone?"

"Not tonight." I felt her breath against my cheek. "So you're the man who's going to find out who really killed Buzz Page."

I gave a self-deprecating smile. *Keep talking, lady.*

She smiled back, released my arm, and let my implicit questions dangle unrescued in my mind. Maybe it was all a mistake and she was innocent. Nothing conclusively linked her to Garrison. Peralta said this was the woman who had invited him up to a room in the Clarendon at the anniversary event. Maybe he was wrong. Maybe. The drinks arrived and we clinked glasses.

"New friend and old friend," Sleigh said. "I've got to go to the ladies. Come with me, Lindsey."

I grabbed the side of her dress, but she brushed aside my hand and joined Sleigh.

"It's co-ed, you know," Sleigh said over her shoulder. "You can join us in a minute. There's a bar there, too."

I raised my glass and stayed at this bar. Most of me believed this was an intolerable risk. But Lindsey was the only one who might be able to bring Sleigh out. My research wasn't getting us anywhere. I had nearly gotten killed. For all my threat that I would stake Peralta in the desert if Lindsey were hurt, I very nearly got staked myself. We were in this dark tunnel of her plan. The DJ queued up "Disco Inferno" and a wave of humanity washed onto the dance floor. The remaining people at the bar, mostly men, were playing with their smartphones. I wondered if young people had sex today or they only stared at their screens.

In my Bluetooth, I heard Sleigh: "He's good looking."

"What about you?" Lindsey said. "Who's your…?"

Then the sound cut off and they disappeared.

I had to let it play out, at least for awhile. I let the gin burn my throat and scanned the room for Ryan Garrison. So many of the young men looked like him, cut in their T-shirts, short hair, about half with visible tattoos. They were sleeky handsome in a mass-production way, but callow-looking. None had the maturity and air of adult responsibility that distinguished Malik Jones. They were all Anglos, too. And none had a man-bun. Of course, if Ryan were smart he would have cut it off. A few of the men had the Civil War-style shaggy long beards that had made a comeback. How could they stand the heat? Maybe their short hair helped. When I lived in the Midwest, I heard that forty percent of a person's body heat was lost through the head. I never looked it up to see if it was true. I did start collecting fedoras. Lindsey thought they were sexy.

My watch hand moved with agonizing slowness. Three minutes. Five. Ten. Nothing on the Bluetooth. I strained to see the entrance to the restroom. The luxurious fixtures of the club were lost on me. K.C. and the Sunshine Band sang "Get Down Tonight."

"Are you picking anything up?" I spoke into the Bluetooth.

"Lots of bad music," a deputy outside said.

"Tell me about it."

I was missing something very important. Maybe many very importants. Nineteen-seventy-eight. Pretty girls stood in the median of streets selling flowers. High-school kids still cruised Central Avenue on Friday and Saturday nights. People ate at Helsing's, Hobo Joe's, and Googies in midcentury architectural gems. They went to bowling alleys and depended on land-line phones. Mark Reid was running Ned Warren's old crew of thugs. And Buzz Page was working on the most important story of his career. But something more was hiding in that fated year.

By now, I was starting to think the trip to the co-ed restroom was bullshit and Lindsey had been hustled out the back of the club into a van, now headed into the desert.

It was enough. I headed off into the direction that Sleigh took Lindsey, oozing through the crowd, then pushing people aside. A few profanities followed me.

I found a bouncer. "Where's the co-ed restroom?"

He nodded toward a wall, where I saw an opening. I kept the gun inside my shirt as I followed a gaggle of young women past the entry. The heavy door closed behind me and the music went away.

Inside was a spacious room, perfect low light, with sofas and a bar. They weren't hard to spot. Lindsey was in an embrace with Elizabeth Sleigh and they were kissing. Not a friendly peck. This was tongue-wrestling and Lindsey wasn't resisting. Passionate kisses. Lindsey's straight hair swayed like a waterfall. Sleigh's right hand was on my wife's fair inner thigh, moving up under her dress. People pretended not to notice. Nobody paid attention to me, so I withdrew and floated back to the bar where my orphan martini was waiting. I took a deep slug.

Do a little dance.

Make a little love.

I realize this is a fantasy of many men: to see their girlfriends or wives with another woman. I felt as if a baseball bat had been rammed into my stomach. I forced aside feelings of conflicting territoriality and arousal. Where the hell was Ryan Garrison?

Then I saw Lindsey and a minute later she was beside me. Her face was flushed.

"She wants me to go to Talking Stick and gamble. I took a pass."

I managed to ask what was next.

"We need to leave."

In the Prelude, I navigated through Old Town and south on Scottsdale Road, then made a right on Osborn. I instructed the unmarked unit to follow Sleigh to the lavish, twenty-four-hour Indian casino and then shut off the Bluetooth. Otherwise, neither of us spoke.

"Pull in here, now!" Her voice was husky and insistent.

I turned into the empty parking lot of the First Baptist Church.

"Over there."

I went to a corner and parked.

She grabbed me by my shirt. "Get over here and fuck me. Now."

At six-feet-two, I'd never had sex inside a car. Lindsey is five-feet-seven. Car coitus was for shorter people, or you needed a soccer-mom van. Once I had sex on the hood of a Pontiac Firebird, leaving dents in the metal, but that's another story. Now I did as told, leaving the car and the air conditioning running.

She was already out and pushed me into the passenger seat. I rolled it back as far as it would go. She climbed in, shut the door, undid my slacks, hiked up her dress, and pulled aside her soaking wet panties. I slid in with no problem, savoring her scent of arousal. She was already coming after the first thrust but rode me like her life depended on it. I gripped her hips and almost blurted out, *I'm taking my woman back!* Her pupils were fully dilated. Then she pulled me close, broken ribs be damned, her hair fell over my face, and her moans turned into a sharp scream. I came, too, and we stayed there, panting, making half-articulated sounds.

"Love you," she managed. But I wondered who she was thinking about as we were having sex.

I whispered, "I love you, too."

The next second she was sobbing. I held her close, wrapped my arms completely around her.

"I've got you," I said. "I'm not going to let you go."

I held her tight for a long time.

The tap on the window was sudden. A flashlight showed this old married couple. I was sure we were both dead.

Then I saw the dark-blue uniform of a Scottsdale Police officer.

"Get a room," she commanded.

I rolled down the window halfway. "We're going now."

•••••

We sailed into the Phoenix city limits and the darkness of Papago Park. Lindsey was driving now. It was easier for her to dismount and climb to the driver's seat. Safer, too. If I had opened the passenger's door back at the parking lot and the Scottsdale cop had gotten a look at the Python, unpleasant things might have transpired. McDowell Road lifted us westbound between the two buttes and then, as we floated downhill, the vast lights of the city spread out below us.

Half a mile later, we pulled in at Sonic and ordered a footlong chili-cheese Coney dog for me, a Chicago dog for Lindsey, and tater tots to share. I added a Diet Cherry Coke for me, a Sprite for her. One of the irritating gifts of the evening was "Beth" replaying over and over in my head. Bubblegum score, dumb lyrics, a band I had never cared for, and now sinister connotations. The songs from the drive-in's speaker didn't wash it away. The windows were up. I kept the engine running, doing my part to worsen climate change, anything for the precious air conditioning.

"So this woman is a hot-shit coder," I said. "How does she end up making forty grand a year working in county IT?"

"Not everybody gets to go to the computer science program at an elite school." This was a sensitive point for Lindsey and I regretted bringing it up. "I learned computers in the Air Force," she continued. "Some people have natural skills. Tech is a youth-oriented culture, though."

"She hasn't 'aged-out,' as you would say. But if she's such a good hacker, why can't she support herself with ransomware?" I was proud of myself for knowing this term of art.

"Those attacks don't always bring in much money," she said. "Companies and individuals wise up and refuse to pay. WannaCry hit something like two-hundred-thousand computers in one-hundred-fifty countries, but didn't make much. That grew out of stolen cyberweapons from NSA, by the way."

"Now that I know that, do you have to kill me?"

She smiled slightly. "Not yet. Keep doing what you did in the parking lot a few minutes ago. The attack did sow a lot of chaos. Anyway, having a legitimate job gives her a good cover. Or…"

"Or?"

"I don't know," she said. "Black-hat hackers can make money plenty of ways. They can steal login information and financial data from banking sites. They can sell malware. The Petya attack was much more effective as blackmail. Turn the loot into Bitcoin, Ethereum, or another virtual currency. Move it offshore. Make a killing. Work for North Korea or Russia."

"That's why we need white hats like you."

She smiled and finished the hotdog and a few tater tots. Then she popped open the glovebox and pulled out a pack of Marlboro Reds, her occasional antidote to extreme stress. She couldn't get her favorite Gauloises anymore. The window came down and she lit up, blowing a long blue plume out into the night. Across from us, several teenage Hispanic girls were sitting on the tables outside the door, drinking sodas, and laughing like this was the fanciest night out they could image.

"My point," she said, "is that maybe Elizabeth is innocent."

"Give me a break!" I toned myself down and continued. "She has too many things that connect her to this case."

"I know." After a pause. "She's very interested in you."

"What about you? For somebody who worked in county IT and you rarely saw, you two seemed pretty friendly." I didn't look at her. I kept eating the Coney and popping tater tots.

"She kissed me." It was a simple declaration. "I kissed her back."

"Okay, then." I didn't ask, *Do you want to be with this woman?*

"Don't be jealous, Dave. I was on the job. She did say she wanted to take me to Vegas some weekend."

I didn't know what to say. Our marriage hadn't been faithful on either side. But I had hoped we were past that. Anyway, a trip to Vegas with Elizabeth Sleigh would be fatal. She and her partner had already killed one cop. Lindsey knew this.

She said, "Here's the deal. Elizabeth told me how awful it was that the retired detective had his throat cut…"

I looked at her. "What?"

"Yes." She tapped some ash out the window. "And she said I had to be relieved that you weren't hurt when the bomb went off."

"What the hell?"

"Exactly. That information was never reported to the public."

"I can't believe she would be so careless."

Lindsey said she played her reaction cool, saying she couldn't bring herself to watch any of the coverage of the bombing on television or read the newspaper.

Then: "If she was being careless."

"What do you mean?" I said.

She turned her head to exhale the tobacco. "It's so hard to tell. Our suspects love to play games. She might be infatuated with me, but it doesn't mean she wouldn't try to play me…"

Play with you, Jealous David thought.

"She asked where I was working. I said I was a homemaker."

"Do you think she bought it?"

"Maybe. Either way, we know she is 'Sly,' she knows information on the Goldstein murder that only the killer would know, and she will lead us to Garrison. We still don't know her interest in the Page killing."

I washed down a Vicodin with the Diet Cherry Coke. "Could you get any information on Garrison?"

"I asked about a husband or boyfriend. She said she preferred her freedom, but she also liked younger men. Luke was her current 'project,' as she put it. He's a little crazy, but that's attractive. Her words."

A shiver ran up the back of my neck.

"As in Luc Iverson, the guy who called me asking about the bomb shelter, impersonating a student journalist. That was Garrison. Fuck me."

"I just did." She smoked in silence, then tossed the filter. "Wait a minute…"

She pulled out a pad and printed his name. I corrected her: He made a point of saying his first name was spelled L-u-c. She wrote that out and studied it.

How did he spell his last name?"

"He never did. I assumed I-v-e-r-s-o-n."

She scratched out the first two iterations and printed again.

"Maybe not. Well, what do you know? Check this out."

She showed me the name massed together with one

vertical line drawn two-thirds of the way through. It read:

LUCIFER | SON

I sat back and studied it, eating my slushy cherry ice.

"'Hell is empty and all the devils are here,'" I said. "But that's from the *Tempest*, not *Hamlet*."

Her phone let out a ding.

Lindsey studied the screen. "It's from her. 'I had fun with you, Lindsey. Can't wait until next time. Beth.' "

"I used to like that name," I said. Then I nearly dropped a ketchup-slathered tot on my shirt. "You gave her your phone number?"

"I gave her a phone number." She held up the iPhone. "This isn't mine. Peralta approved a purchase for me. Of course, she won't know."

She typed a line and I heard another sound, a swoosh.

"What did you write?"

"'Me, too.'" She lit another cigarette.

Chapter Thirty-two

On Monday morning, I arrived early at Temple Beth Israel for Tom Goldstein's memorial service. I was in uniform, a black band across my star and the Colt Python in the holster of my equipment belt. It was the LAPD black that Crisis Meltdown had switched to, discarding the historic Sheriff's Office tans-and-browns. Peralta had bigger problems than the uniform style. One of them would be if he saw me here, rather than holed up with the archives. Too bad. I owed Goldstein this much. Plus, I wanted to see who else might attend amid an overflow crowd of officers from different departments.

Located slightly north of downtown, the Spanish Mission-style building was home to the first permanent Jewish congregation in Phoenix. It had been sold in the late forties to a Chinese Baptist Church, which later became a Spanish-language congregation. It was restored in the 2000s and was officially the Cutler-Plotkin Jewish Heritage Center. Today, Phoenix Police vehicles surrounded it. One would expect that for a cop's funeral. They provided a barrier against a car bomb or other mischief from Ryan Garrison.

Afterwards, I spotted J.C. "Jack" Wesley. The retired

PPD detective had helped me before. Still tall and rugged, he looked younger than his seventy-plus years. I told him Lorie Pope had said he was involved in the Page case, along with Sergeant Tony Peterson. He was, he said, and Sergeant Peterson was "right over there." He steered me to a man of medium height, no hair. Introductions were made. They both wanted to know about Lorie.

"She was a sweetheart," Wesley said.

"Still is," I said, and then asked if they could set aside some time to talk to me about Page.

"How about now?" Wesley pointed toward Will Bruder's stunning Central Library Building, recently reopened from the damage the microburst did to the roof tiles, setting off the sprinkler system. We walked across the blazing expanse. Neither of the retired cops seemed bothered by the weather, while I was on the verge of wilting. Inside, we took the elevator up and found a table in a quiet, deserted section with a view of downtown out the enormous windows.

I only knew Peterson by reputation and was a little intimidated, but he quickly put me at ease and did most of the talking.

This entailed a good deal of background on the repeated attempts to bring down Ned Warren. Much of it was in the IRE reports, some wasn't, including the colorful anecdotes. These were primary sources, living history. I began making extensive notes as he spoke.

Peterson had joined the Intelligence Bureau to set up the first organized-crime unit, especially targeting white-collar offenses. Money came from a federal grant and the support from then-chief Larry Wetzel. Among the many asides, they told me Wetzel was the first supervisor on the scene of the 1958 massacre of uber mobster Gus Greenbaum and his wife.

"For my money, Wetzel was a cop's cop," Wesley said. "He was caught in the middle. But he supported us."

This was especially important when the unit began catching corrupt city officials, even sending some to prison, others to forced retirement. The larger Intel Bureau was a mixed bag, at best, with plenty of placeholders or worse.

"One sergeant was dropping all these Mafia names, and I thought, why weren't they putting any of them in jail?" Peterson said. "Something was not right with this unit."

Wesley said, "The FBI identified him as a member of the Albert and Joseph Tocco Mafia out of Chicago. He was forced to retire. Within a year, he was set up running a titty bar owned by the mob. Lots of cops went there."

Then we were back to Ned Warren. I forced myself to be patient and let the conversation flow to its own destinations. Case after case against Warren was brought to the County Attorney, but they went nowhere. The prosecutors tried to discredit the cases. They never made it to court. Grand juries were shut down. The prosecutors discredited Lonzo McCracken, the most incorruptible detective in the department.

Witnesses against Warren, often his front men in various land frauds, also had a habit of dying: heart attacks, car crashes. The most notorious was Ed Lazar, his accountant, who agreed to testify before the grand jury. It was February 1975 and he never showed up. Lazar was found dead in the stairwell of his office with five bullets in him. Chicago sent a violent message: too much talking going on. The assassin even dropped a few coins on Lazar's corpse.

McCracken finally confronted the County Attorney, who was willing to talk. He didn't realize McCracken was taping him. Peterson leaned in. "He goes, 'You've gotta understand, I don't make all the decisions. Harry

Rosenzweig says, I don't want that prosecuted. What can I do?'"

McCracken made a transcript of the conversation and went to Rosenzweig Jewelers, waiting at the bottom of the stairs to be summoned to Harry's sanctum. "He went up and gave Rosenzweig the transcript. Damn, that fucker could read fast."

The next day, the County Attorney was gone. And twenty-two counts of fraud were sitting on his successor's desk.

"Don Harris," Wesley said. "He was good with us. 'You can saddle up,' he said." They would prosecute Warren. The king was losing his grip. He tried to bribe the County Attorney investigators. It had always worked before. Warren gave money to a host of politicians, including the state Land Commissioner, through the sixties and into the seventies. Now it failed.

Peterson said, "We brought Ned in. Said, 'If you can help us, maybe we can help you.' I'll never forget. He shook his head and said, 'I'm going to have to decline.' He died in prison. But while he was in jail before and during the trial, he still tried to run what was left of his empire. His man on the outside was Mark Reid."

Wesley mentioned another detective. "Jim Kidd got Bobby Bell downtown and worked him. Bell had been one of Warren's many lawyers. I came in as the good guy. Bell was pleading, 'I don't want to go to jail.' So we rolled him. We had the string on him. He told us about a guy named Jack West, a developer who talked too much. Reid and Kemperton took him into the desert and he was never seen again."

"This was before Page?"

"Yes," Peterson said. "That should have been put in an

intel file. Those names should have been cross-indexed. But when Mark Reid's name came up because of Page, the files showed nothing. 'He's a nothing guy,' they said. 'There's no need to make a file.' You trust cops until later you realize you can't."

He closed his eyes for a few seconds. Then: "The day Page was bombed, I was in the office. Wetzel came and said some reporter got bombed. Get up there right away.' So I did. I reported in to the Chief and he told me to go to the hospital and make sure they don't finish him off. Homicide didn't have anything. But after Page's last words, I remembered that Bobby Bell had mentioned Reid. I told Kidd, to see if Bell comes through. Build a fire under his ass. Shake him up."

The memories sounded like they were from yesterday.

"On Sunday, I got a call from the front desk. Bell wants me to call him. He said he had something really good. So that evening, we met at the Googies at Thirty-second Street and Camelback. He didn't want to talk to Kidd, so I went with McCracken. Bell said he'd run into Mark Reid at Chez Nous the night before."

"So Reid was back from Lake Havasu City," I said.

"Correct. Bell said Reid told him he bombed the reporter. Reid said he got the dynamite from Stan Tanner's explosive locker. He bought the remote control from a toy store over in San Diego. He had a hit list. Buzz Page, Bruce Babbitt, who as AG wanted to go after Freeman Burke's liquor distributorship, and a third guy, King Alphonse. He had garlic all over him and had somehow antagonized Burke." Peterson leaned in again, as if the dead old man was listening. "It always comes back to Freeman Burke. He's the common denominator."

They took all this to Homicide and Reid was put under twenty-four-hour surveillance.

"One night, a few days later, Bell and Reid and their girlfriends—I think Bell's wife—went to Scottsdale. It looked like he was checking for a tail. He went through a parking lot of an apartment complex. But they never made us. The next day, we brought in Bell. 'Anything new?' 'No, no.' He almost fell out of his chair when we told him. His ass was grass."

That old cop saying again. My ass would be grass, probably Bermuda but maybe dichondra like we had in the front on Cypress, if Peralta knew I was carrying out this interview. Whatever.

Peterson said, "Bell goes, 'Okay, I may as well tell you. Darren Howard paid Reid fifty-eight-hundred dollars up front for the Page hit.'"

About this time, as Buzz Page was still alive if barely, Peterson was contacted by a *New York Times* reporter he'd worked with before. The national press was going to demand that Washington step in because the Phoenix Police had never solved a contract killing—a losing streak that went all the way back to the murder of Gus Greenbaum and before.

"I told him to hold their horses. We've got it solved and don't need the FBI fucking it up. He agreed, and the day Page died we picked up Mark Reid."

"What about Darren Howard, was he guilty?"

Peterson said, "Goldstein was convinced Howard had nothing to do with it." That was news to me, based on Goldstein's definitive statement in our first meeting. "The polygraph is inconclusive. The examiner asks, 'Does the number fifty-eight-hundred mean anything to you?' Howard says, 'I want to talk to my lawyer.'"

"Howard's problem," Wesley said, "was he got into Reid's orbit when he wanted in on this silver ingot scheme."

This was another ten-minute detour into Phoenix sleaze, but I didn't complain. "Howard saw a chance to make big bucks. Mark Reid saw an easy mark. My theory is that Reardon gave him the money to pass on to Reid. Howard didn't even know what it was for."

I paused from writing. "And that money might have originated with Freeman Burke?"

Peterson raised his eyebrows and his lips made a tight smile. "Draw a line."

I said, "Yet Bobby Bell did the right thing, under pressure, sure, but he's disbarred. And Norm Reardon kept on practicing law."

"I always felt bad for Bobby," Wesley said. "But Babbitt was determined to have him disbarred."

Peterson said an enduring question was why the state Attorney General's office gave Reardon blanket immunity. "This was a guy who said, 'But I don't know a thing about it.' Then why the immunity?" He shook his head in disgust. "To close the door on the street killers, to Freeman Burke, that's why. They had Reid, Kemperton, and Howard, and they were shutting the case down. Dumping our organized crime cases. Something strange is happening. Why wouldn't you want to solve a crime? The AG didn't want it investigated. Neither did the Governor. Remember, in 1978 Babbitt had moved from being AG to Governor after Raul Castro resigned to become an ambassador and Wes Bolin, the Secretary of State, died."

"But Babbitt was a target," I said.

"Who understands fucking lawyers?" Wesley said. "Hey, remember that sleaze Murray 'The Snake'?"

Peterson smiled grimly. "The attorneys, all professional courtesy and giveaways."

I was about to ask him what that meant, when he said, "Then there was the missing 851 file…"

"What was in it?" I asked.

"I heard it was stuff about Reid, RaceCo, and Freeman Burke," Wesley said. He told me he caught an analyst in the Intelligence Bureau sticking the three folders of the 851 file in his desk drawer. Wesley took them to a Captain, who looked at the contents. Peterson said the Captain claimed he turned it over to Internal Affairs. It was hard to keep up with all the names, ranks, and units.

"I didn't have confidence in any of them," Peterson said.

Wesley said, "I never saw what was in the files and the analyst has always contended that after we took the files from him there was a page missing. To this day, I do not know what that was about. I wasn't given the results of the IA investigation. Were you?"

Peterson shook his head. Then: "But this probably doesn't get you any closer to who killed Tom Goldstein, does it?"

"I'm not sure." I put my pen down. "What do you know about a ledger?"

Chapter Thirty-three

I got on the light rail at McDowell and rode to Central Station, then walked a block to Seamus McCaffrey's. Five minutes later, Malik Jones walked in. He had shed his suit coat but still looked natty in starched white shirt and thin black necktie.

"You're looking unusually storm trooper-ish." He slid into the booth across from me.

"I went to the memorial for Tom Goldstein."

He fished in the pocket of his slacks and slid something over. "This should be better."

I pinned the Black Lives Matter button above my right shirt pocket, above my name plate and opposite my badge.

He laughed. "Perfect."

The waitress took our order: a Rueben for me, a salad for him. I added a Harp, ice water back. It seemed sacrilegious to be in Seamus' and not have a beer. Jones raised an eyebrow and asked for a Guinness.

"There are lawyers and cops all around," I said.

"Point taken."

We quietly compared notes. I told him about the conversation with Peterson and Wesley, as well as Saturday night with Elizabeth Sleigh. I left out the mad makeout session between her and Lindsey.

"Maybe she's innocent," he said.

"Don't be naïve."

"Don't make me tell war stories about seemingly innocent civilians who had caches of AKs and explosives at home."

I held up my hands.

"My point," he continued, "is that you can't connect her to the computer hack, even if she has the skills. You can't connect her to Garrison. You told me yourself the people at his apartment couldn't be sure it was her."

Then I told him about Elizabeth revealing details of Tom Goldstein's murder that had been held back from the media.

"No shit."

"Real shit," I said.

"No chance an enterprising police reporter might have dug and found those things?"

"There are no enterprising police reporters anymore," I said. "An old girlfriend was one, but she's been gone for years."

"This is why you guys aren't worried about a reporter being blown up as part of this deal now." He sank into the hard back of the booth. It was nothing like the luxury of the banquettes at Durant's.

He said, "I'm learning that two kinds of people seek out the facts about the past for the truth, historians and detectives."

"And investigative reporters like Buzz Page. But there are fewer and fewer today."

"So bring in Elizabeth," he said. "'sweat her,' as they say on TV."

I said if we did that she'd know we were onto her. We might never get Garrison, who was the one who killed

Goldstein and probably Rudy Jarvis. Better to see if Lindsey could trap her.

"Makes sense." He nodded. "But we still have to watch for confirmation bias." Interpreting evidence to support our existing beliefs. "I've seen it sink many an undergraduate's paper."

I agreed and he told me his latest. The first box of files the archivist had shown him contained paperwork used by Rusty Clevenger.

"I found plenty of confirmation bias there, too," Jones said. "Reports from witness interviews, contents of search warrants, more wire-tap transcripts, all sorts of things. But they were all aimed at burying Reid, Kemperton, and Howard as deep as possible. There's plenty of tantalizing threads, about the mob and RaceCo, but they weren't followed up. At least as far as I can tell."

"They wanted the case closed," I said. "That was what my retired detectives thought."

"They were hot to disbar our Bell friend, if you know what I mean."

Bobby Bell. Scanning the room with my eyes, I figured he was wise to keep it low-key. Who knew which guy sitting at the bar or the next booth had a connection, even after four decades?

Jones said, "He only did a little legal work for Mark, in his 1975 divorce. The lawyer connected to Burke and the mob was the other one." Norm Reardon.

"I didn't even know Reid had been married."

"He lost custody of their little girl," Jones said. "The guy comes off as quite the upstanding citizen. Drunk on vodka, doing valium and Quaaludes. Several arrests for assault, but the victims had a bad habit of not wanting to press charges or testify."

I thought about the scumbag Mark Reid spreading his seed across the Valley to create children, when I couldn't succeed once with Lindsey. I barely noticed the arrival of our pints.

"Are you with me, David?"

I snapped to. "Yeah. Sorry." I lifted the Harp. "*Salud*."

"*Salud!*" After the first sip, Jones leaned in and whispered. "The Mafia is all over this. No way Reid wasn't a made man. But this connection wasn't pursued, even though Page said 'Mafia' in his dying words. He also said 'RaceCo.' I want to see where this goes, but I bet the cops back then didn't push it. Why?"

"Payoffs to the powerful," I said in a low voice. "Organized crime, white-collar crime, they were very profitable to 'respectable Arizona.' The reason Burke wanted to be on the Racing Commission was to oversee skimming money from the dog tracks. Remember, this is a guy who got the first liquor distributor's license after the end of Prohibition. He had a monopoly on the most coveted brands. Before that, he was selling illegal booze from Al Capone, who had a suite at the Westward Ho for when he was in town. In the late forties, Burke wanted to take over the mob's gambling wire, which Gus Greenbaum had set up here in the twenties. Greenbaum didn't like it, but the mob wanted Gus managing its casinos in Vegas. That was where the future was, at least as they saw it, even though illegal gambling continued in Phoenix for decades until the Indian casinos. Burke ran whorehouses, too."

Our food came and Jones shook his head.

"Something wrong?" the pretty server asked.

"No, no," he said. "You're great."

She walked away and his eyes appreciatively followed her. "More than great. Anyway, I'm seeing a whole other

Phoenix. I'm not sure I can go back to seeing that clean, sunny new place ever again."

"It was never that."

"So, answer this, David. Here's a man with land holdings all over the state, including north Scottsdale. He ends up owning a big ranch in Mexico, too. He's the richest man in the state. He's got the ear of the other power brokers. Why do this?"

When I had swallowed the first bite of the divine Rueben, I attempted a theory. "The man was remembered as a product of the frontier, and I guess he was. But in a lot of bad ways. He was a thug. Back in the thirties he ran a crew to beat up farm-labor organizers. He was already wealthy then. Why do that? Because you rule by intimidating most people, and letting the more powerful in on your action. The other thing, I've never known a rich person who thought he had enough."

"Buzz had already antagonized him by getting him kicked off the Racing Commission..."

"That's the 'frontier justice' theory of the crime," I said.

"And in June 1978, Buzz was apparently preparing to write the story that might hurt him even worse. Motive, means, opportunity. Do I have that right?"

I nodded. "Plus, plenty of willing allies, from mobsters to cops."

We ate in silence for several minutes, a loud babble of conversations enveloping us.

"I feel like we're chasing our tails," Jones said. "Too many suspects, too many leads, too many supporting players. It's getting discouraging. If we were researching this for a major book on Sunbelt crime and capitalism, with a sweet advance from a major publisher, it would be one thing. But people are dying again. You almost got killed. You white people are violent. Don't get me wrong. I like white folks as individuals. I even have white friends. But get 'em together in a group..." He shook his head. "Nothing I'm finding is pushing us closer to catching the bad guys."

"Me, neither."

"But you used to be an academic. San Diego State, University of Denver, Miami University. I checked you out."

That made me uncomfortable. My career as a scholar wasn't covered in glory.

He continued: "What would you tell a grad student facing this situation? Without the potential for death and all."

"Gives a whole new meaning to 'publish or perish.'" I allowed myself a laugh. Then I began to lay it out. Be conversant of the existing historiography. What are you bringing that's new? Make sure you know what your subject really is. Watch out for over-gathering of the same material, but do be on the lookout for new details and perspectives. Where are you going to place the lens to tell the story—close up, back a bit? What's the larger context? What's going on in the bigger world, the social reality? Be wary of rumors, legends, and frauds. Untangle the facts.

Jones gave a weary smile. "Hard labor makes royal roads."

"Jacques Barzun and Henry Graff," I said, naming the authors of a famous work for researchers. "That's the way I learned back in the stone age, when the card catalogue was my best friend. It made me stop and think. Now the Internet gives us too much, including plenty of nonsense."

Jones said, "If we had time to scan every document at the State Archives, these days we could use a computer to sort for names and connections. There's not time."

"No, there's not. I would also ask that student if he had confident command of his sources."

Jones shrugged. "And we don't."

We paid and walked out into the furnace. Five minutes later, we were in my office, continuing to bounce around ideas. Again, Jones seemed drawn to the fifth box, the one I hadn't yet sorted. And again he pulled out the key attached to a faded orange tag. The tag had black lettering: 103.

"Did you ever find out what this is?"

The connection didn't click—it clanked like heavy steel beams.

"Holy shit. Come with me."

Chapter Thirty-four

I paused at the little office refrigerator and retrieved two frozen bottles of water. I tossed one to Jones, who caught it on the fly.

"We're going to the Fry's construction site."

"Think you can hump that two blocks, soldier?" Jones shot me an amused smile.

"You'll be glad we have it," I said. I armed the alarm and shut and locked the door.

We went downstairs and cut through CityScape, then continued east on Washington Street, catching shade from the tall buildings.

At First Street, with the sun blasting us from directly overhead, Block Twenty-Three was busy with heavy equipment and dust. My heart fell into my stomach and I let out a string of profanities.

The same Anglo construction superintendent met us at the main gate. He didn't look happy.

"You again!" He wrapped his timber-hard arms across his chest. "The city approved our permit, so we're finally doing the site work. What now?"

"The lockers," I said. "The ones down in the fallout shelter."

"Gone," he said. "All that shit was hauled away yesterday."

"To where?"

"How would I know?" He turned his head. "Hey, Manny?"

A portly Hispanic man came up, wearing the same style of grimy white hardhat and safety vest with lime green stripes.

"Where'd they send that stuff from the bomb shelter?"

"Yucca Recycling, I think," Manny said, taking off his hat and wiping sweat from his brow.

"Where is that?" I demanded.

"I dunno," Manny said. "Wait a minute and I'll find out." He walked away.

"Are you going to shut us down?" The superintendent stomped a heavy boot in the dirt.

"No," I said. "But I need to find those lockers."

He relaxed, put his hands on his hips. "Good luck with that. I learned their story, you know."

I didn't know.

"They didn't come with the old Penney's," he said. "They were from Union Station, back when they had train service. When Amtrak pulled out in the nineties, the city brought them over here. By that time, the city owned the Penney's building and was using it for offices. Maybe they were going to use them for employee lockers. Who knows? But they let them sit down in the sub-basement with the fallout shelter supplies, probably forgot about 'em. Most had keys in the doors, but not all of 'em."

The pieces were together in my mind, finally, but had we run out of time? I could feel the pulse running under my temples.

The superintendent threw back his head and laughed.

"You know, some of the guys opened a box of survival crackers from the shelter supplies and tried 'em out. Tasted like cardboard."

Manny returned with a slip of paper and handed it to me. It showed an address down on Broadway Road.

"Thanks." I turned to Jones. "Are you up for another walk to get my Honda?"

He had his smartphone out. "Why don't we book Uber instead? I've got the app here."

It sounded like a better idea. While we waited, I pulled the .38 out of my ankle holster and handed it to him.

"You might need this."

He took it warily. "Chief Gillespie's going to trust a black man with a gun…"

"Oh, cut the crap, Mr. Jones."

He chuckled and slid it into his waistband in the small of his back.

In five minutes, a silver Prius pulled up. It might be a serial killer or a ride-service driver. We got in and told him where we wanted to go.

"You sure you want to go *there*?" he said.

I said we were sure.

The ride into south Phoenix reminded me of old cases, especially the one that led to the death of Lindsey's half-sister, Robin. My beautiful Robin, tough and knowing on the outside, very different inside for the few she let in. She let me in. My sin. Sure, I could justify it a dozen ways—I was sure Lindsey had left me—but that didn't cut it. The woman who shot Robin was to blame and in prison. Sure. *I was to blame*. All Lindsey asked of me was to keep her sister safe and I failed. I still questioned whether I did the best thing by having the woman arrested rather than executing her, which had been my initial plan. How could a righteous man be capable of all that? Nobody in the car spoke, a good thing.

The landscape was also a reminder of how the city leaders had spent decades clustering the dirtiest industries in these poor neighborhoods. When you looked at City Hall from this direction, with its spire, it looked as if the city was giving the finger to south Phoenix.

Broadway was named after an early landowner, not New York City's famous avenue. It was also one of the homeliest thoroughfares in a city full of ugly, so leave it to Phoenix to ceremonially give it the dual name of Martin Luther King, Jr., Boulevard. Between Sixteenth Street and Central, crossing west to Seventh Avenue, Broadway had once been part of the city's black community. The whites had the ugliest name possible for the area: niggertown. Now, it was still as poor but mostly Hispanic.

The address took us father west. We were slightly south of the dry channel of the Salt River now, the landscape marked by quarries, junk yards, impoverished subdivisions, and, in the distance, the Sierra Estrella. The mountains would have provided some visual relief if not for the thick black smoke boiling up from a fire in the riverbed, a few miles west. Tires, maybe. The sky overhead was cloudless but dirty white.

At Yucca Recycling, the driver pulled over and we stepped out on hard dirt at the entrance to a vast junk yard. It was surrounded by a stout wall topped by rusting concertina wire. Through the gate, crushed car bodies were stacked two stories tall and seemed to go on forever. Cranes with claws rose in the background. An ancient corrugated metal building stood a hundred yards back with a tilted sign promising auto parts.

When we stepped into the trailer office, the dark-skinned man with the push-broom moustache saw my uniform and his eyes widened with fear. It's not as if the Sheriff's Office had a good reputation in this part of town, not after Peralta's interloper played Border Patrol in the Hispanic precincts of the city.

I quickly said, "*No hay apuro! No somos la migra.*"

His jaw muscles relaxed and he slowly sat back down. I noticed Jones was taking a hit off the melting water bottle.

I explained why we were there: the junk that came in from the Fry's construction site downtown, especially the old bank of luggage lockers.

He shrugged and went through a stack of papers on an battered metal desk.

"It's a small job," he said in English. "The stuff might already be gone. But we can check. Don't you need a search warrant?"

"I can shut you down while we wait for one," I said. "Why would you want that to happen?"

He got my logic—there was probably a chop shop for stolen cars at work in this vast repository of consumer cast-offs—and he heaved himself up out of the chair.

We stepped out into the heat again and began walking down a path wide enough for big trucks, lined with stacked car bodies and misshapen, unidentifiable scrap. The superheated air was a soup of burning metallic and plastic smells. He explained the workings of the junk yard, draining fluids, pulling parts that could be resold, separating steel from other materials.

"Lots headed for China." He spread his arms to encompass this little pocket of the ten-thousand-mile supply chain. With the citrus groves and farms and even Motorola gone, it was good to know Phoenix could export something.

I was searching for the lockers, staring past the stacked,

crushed cars. Jones was different. He was scanning the tops of the heaps, as if an insurgent sniper would suddenly appear, moving loose and ready to crouch.

In a low voice, Jones said, "If Ryan Garrison was going to do us, this would be a good place for it."

"That's why I wanted you armed."

In ten minutes of wandering, we finally reached a small pile of miscellaneous junk. I made out the dark green fall-out shelter supply barrels. The lockers were missing.

"There!" Jones pointed into the maw of a crane.

"Get those down," I ordered. The man ran to the crane operator, yelled in Spanish, and the bucket descended, opening its clamshell jaws and spilling the bank of lockers on the ground. Amazingly, it was upright.

I walked to it quickly, looking for the right number.

"Here." Jones pointed to a door in the middle of the bank, about three feet high.

I inserted the key with difficulty, but it eventually went all the way in. For only the smallest moment, I hesitated. Not because I worried a bomb might go off—I didn't even consider that possibility until later. No, it was more the sense an archaeologist must have before stepping into a tomb. I turned the key, slowly so it wouldn't break. It smoothly shifted clockwise and the door fell off.

"I'll be damned," Jones said.

I pulled out a pair of latex gloves and slid them on. I gave my second pair to Jones.

Careful to make sure black widows hadn't nested there, I reached into the baggage locker and gently slid out the dark brown soft briefcase.

CWP were the initials on the outside.

Back in the air-conditioned trailer, we took over the desk. The dry desert air was kind to many things, including human bodies protected from the sun and coyotes. Leather was more vulnerable. One of the two straps had disintegrated above the gold brass buckle. The other side was intact but came apart when I tried to undo it. I opened the flap, and, again, alert to the possibility of a black widow's nest, leaned back as I raised the inside of the case. No spiders or scorpions.

I slid out a two-inch-thick ledger book, bound, with hard cardboard red covers. On the spine and front, it simply said RECORD in gold letters. The pages held four vertical lines. Each was filled with handwriting, entries with dates, a code, and an amount. The money ranged from one thousand to twenty thousand dollars. The dates began in January 1974 and ended in May 1978.

"Payoffs?" Jones said.

"Looks that way," I said. "Or money received. There are two columns tracking cash, one must be coming in, the other going out. Good bookkeeping is important in organized crime, too. Today's cartels have accounting departments."

"Zero-zero-one. Kemper Freeman." He ran a finger down the first sheet, showing 001 on about a quarter of the listings. "I suspect he's on almost every page."

I continued a quick flip-through, easy so as not to tear the pages, and it was true. He was getting more money than he was giving.

Jones pulled out a stack of business cards and set them on the desk. "Charles Page, staff reporter, *The Phoenix Gazette*. And this."

He next held up a spiral-bound reporter's notebook. Page's name was written on the outside. On the first page: Piero Scarpelli, with a line under it. Date: 5/30/78. Followed by dense notes. We could read this later.

"This was the basis of Page's big story," I said. "He was killed for what he was going to write. The police transcript you found, where the lawyer, Reardon, was telling Goldwater about the ledger. This is it. All Page needed was the key to the names."

"I bet Mark Reid dangled that to get Page to meet him," Jones said.

My iPhone was out, ready to call Peralta, when it rang. The readout said "Lindsey."

"We found the ledger!" I couldn't contain my enthusiasm.

"I need to see you, Dave." Her voice was both excited and grave. "Now."

"What's going on? Are you okay?"

"I'm safe, if that's what you mean. But I need you now."

Chapter Thirty-five

It took me half an hour to get back to Cypress Street, again taking Uber. I had much ambivalence about the so-called gig economy but in this situation I needed fast transportation and didn't want to hope Yellow Cab would come to one of the dodgier parts of south Phoenix. Good thing Jones had an account. Before leaving, I called Peralta and left Jones with the new evidence.

Lindsey opened the front door before I even stepped onto the curb. She kissed me, handed me a fruit popsicle to help me cool down, and led me by the hand into the study.

"Saturday night, in the co-ed lounge, Beth gave me her business card. I didn't think anything about it, dropped it into my purse."

That's because her hand was headed up your inner thigh and beyond, Jealous David thought.

"I took it out a minute before I called you."

She handed it to me.

On one side was the usual, name, address, phones, e-mail.

"Turn it over," Lindsey said.

Hand-written in blue ink were two words: HELP ME.

"What does that mean?" I felt the stupidity gushing out of my mouth as I said the words.

"It means we may have to reevaluate our suspects."

I paused in nursing the popsicle. "What? You think she's innocent?"

She nodded.

"What about 'coding like a girl' and all that," I said, too loud and too intense. "Are you sure you're not letting your emotions get the better of your judgment?"

Her eyes went from sea-blue to a near dark violet. "No." She said it quietly.

Calmly, I said, "From the start, these crimes have been marked by deception and misdirection. How do we know this isn't more of the same?"

"We don't," Lindsey said. "But this feels different. She has the phone number to the new iPhone, but she hasn't tried to insert any malware. Maybe I got her wrong. Maybe she's in trouble."

"She knew details of Tom Goldstein's murder that only the killer would know."

"But maybe the killer told her. She was trying to telegraph that to me Saturday night."

I let out an exasperated sigh. "What do we do?"

"I'm going to meet her tonight, at Durant's." She held up her right palm to deflect my inevitable protest. "I texted her. Said I wanted to see her again. She agreed. You can sit in the parking lot. I'll have my phone going so you can listen."

"Lindsey, they could snatch you right there, a gun in your ribs, walk out the front door or else."

"Carol and the staff are there. They know me. They wouldn't let anything happen."

I kept shaking my head. "I need to clear it with Peralta."

She stood and stomped away. "Whatever. I'm going tonight."

Halfway across the room, she stopped, turned, and came back, kneeling in front of me. She took my hands.

"Tell me about the ledger, History Shamus."

Chapter Thirty-six

At seven-thirty, I was sitting in the car at the far end of the Durant's parking lot. The restaurant faced Central Avenue, a coral-painted one-story right up on the sidewalk like in a real city, a lighted yellow sign above with the name on it, and a single door to the street with a D as the door handle. Walk in and you're in the bar and close to the restrooms. In the men's room, they put ice in the bowls of the urinals. But most people came in from the rear, using the large parking lot to the east of the building. They walked through the kitchen like made men.

Which was appropriate, because Jack Durant, the longtime proprietor, cultivated his ties to the mob from the restaurant's founding in 1950. That wasn't even his real name. The former James Earl Allen of Tellaco Plains, Tennessee, hopped a freight train to Arizona when he was a teenager, hung out in the little mining town of Miami before arriving in Phoenix. In that decade, the FBI named him one of the top ten most dangerous men in the state. He ran a cathouse on the side, or so went one of the many stories. His foul language was real and part of the legend, and so was his friendship with Gus Greenbaum and Johnny Stompanato, the famous bodyguard of LA crime boss

Mickey Cohen who was killed by Lana Turner's daughter, Cheryl. Jack also bragged that the Page bombing had been planned here, although testimony said the particulars were worked out at the Ivanhoe.

The owners after his death worked hard to downplay that unsavory past, but there was no getting past it, at least for old Phoenicians. Inside, the place was out of the fifties, too: red curving leatherette banquettes, red flocked wallpaper, white tablecloths, impeccably attired servers, and a long bar where the bartenders knew your name and what you drank. Steaks, chops, and crab cakes. Huge martinis, expertly mixed. It was a longtime hangout of politicians and the business elite. Lindsey and I loved it. This was much more of a foodie town than ever before, even showcasing "chef-driven" Mexican food. But nothing said old Phoenix like Durant's. "In my humble opinion, Durant's is the finest eating and drinking establishment in the world," went a quote by Jack Durant. It was also the last remaining piece of the swinging Midtown of the seventies, so an appropriate place for Lindsey to meet Elizabeth Sleigh—Beth.

I let her out by the Central sidewalk so no one in the parking lot would see us together. As I purred the car past the valet parking and farther into the lot, I heard the noise of the bar area on my earbuds, the bartender call her name. Then Sleigh's voice do the same.

"They're packed," she said. "I put in our name, but we can sit at the bar."

"That's fine," Lindsey said.

The reception was good.

I made a spin through the lot. It was nearly full. If anyone was sitting in a car, I didn't see him. Beth's ride was parked in the valet zone. I backed into the farthest spot that still gave me a straight-on view of the rear entrance. The downside was it would take me extra seconds to get inside. But the advantage was a view of the lot and the comings and goings. I shut the engine off and rolled down the windows. It was a full five minutes before I began sweating.

We were rogue. I thought about telling Peralta so we could have backup in the parking lot and inside the restaurant. But it would be too many people, too many things that could go wrong. It was only the two of us. Ask forgiveness instead of permission.

I adjusted my earbuds. The conversation was ordinary girl talk, after its fashion. They talked about the latest Apple products, whether the Microsoft Surface was any good, clothes, yoga, men. I imagined Beth's fingers discreetly climbing up inside Lindsey's miniskirt from the occasional sigh and giggle. Beth asked about the Page investigation. Lindsey, as we had rehearsed, gave her tidbits, including the fact that I had found the ledger of payoffs and collections from the old baggage locker once at Union Station, then at the fallout shelter downtown.

"You can't tell anyone." I heard Lindsey's voice.

"Of course not," said Beth.

The ledger. It was locked in Peralta's safe along with the code key. If I was expecting a ticker-tape parade, he quickly disabused me. It was a longshot that we could find fingerprints after forty years. The chain of custody for the evidence was nonexistent. I didn't buy it. This was a major breakthrough in the case: the backbone of Buzz Page's blockbuster. What he was going to write. What made him a target like never before.

I did some backgrounding on Piero Scarpelli, including a call to retired Detective Tony Peterson. "Shaky Pete"

Scarpelli was an alumnus of the Gambino crime family and did five years in Sing Sing for refusing to roll on his compadres in a protection-racket bust. He drifted to Chicago, then Phoenix, where he was a bagman and sometime enforcer of the Chicago Heights gang here. Specifically, he worked for "Papa Joe" Tocco. Papa Joe and his brother Al were major Phoenix gangland figures. Even though the Mafia proclaimed Phoenix open territory, where any made man could operate, the Toccos were probably first among equals. Narcotics, prostitution, gambling, murder.

What if Scarpelli got in a jam or wanted revenge and decided to roll, by giving the ledger to investigative reporter Charles Page? It's not as if he could trust the police or the county prosecutors.

Peralta acted as if he was not impressed. He'd never heard of Scarpelli. If he wanted out of the life, why not turn the ledger over to the FBI? I didn't have an easy answer there, except that he didn't want to testify as the price of getting into witness protection. Now, I thought about the instances of organized crime infiltrating the Bureau—maybe Shaky Pete thought or knew that was the situation at the Phoenix Field Office. Maybe he had amassed a stash of money that would allow him to flee the country. I found no mention of him after 1978. He was not in the IRE's *Phoenix Project*.

Whatever Peralta thought, this was gold. Looking at it just as history, Jones and I had found a primary source that could transform the way we understood the crime of 1978. One of the most important pieces of information was on the last page of the ledger, dated May 25, 1978. It was in the amount of fifty-eight-hundred dollars and given to 0143, Norm Reardon, the lawyer who got the total immunity deal. The mob, or Freeman Burke, paid for the hit. It wasn't Darren Howard, although Reardon might have used Howard as a gullible courier.

I imagined Buzz Page walking to his GTO, carrying the briefcase that held the ledger, stopping to talk to Senator Gutierrez, then driving to meet Mark Reid at the Clarendon. Except he made a stop at Union Station, where he went inside, maybe exchanged pleasantries with the station agent, then dropped coins in the baggage locker and slid the briefcase inside. Then, he went to meet Mark Reid, or so he thought.

At least Peralta had the briefcase and ledger, put them in his safe. I worried he might order me to hand them over to the evidence unit, where they might not be secure. Or even toss them out. Still, his lack of commitment made me do a slow burn that continued as I listened to Lindsey and Beth chat. There were periodic silences where I only heard the other voices at the bar.

About an hour later, I saw Lindsey step out of the kitchen and under the awning. I started the car and swung around to pick her up.

"That sounded like a waste of time," I said.

"Oh, no." Lindsey pulled out her Moleskine notebook and tapped it. "Let's go home."

Back on Cypress Street, I took Lindsey's notebook and settled in the big leather chair to examine it. It was two sets of handwriting. I recognized my wife's printing. Beth wrote in cursive, in blue. I tried to imagine their voices as I slowly read.

"Why did you write HELP on your business card?"

Beth wrote, "I'm being held hostage by Luc."

"How?"

"See my necklace? Explosive in the pendant. He's threatening to detonate it if I ask for help. If I try to take it off, it explodes, too. Something about undoing the clasp triggers it automatically."

"He's nearby?"

"Yes, probably in the parking lot. He followed me here."

Then she wrote, "NO! Don't text your husband. He'll set it off. He said it has a kill radius of a hundred yards. Even through walls."

"His real name isn't Luc."

"I know that now. I read the newspapers. He gave me the pendant as a gift. After I put it on, he told me about his killings. When I reacted, he said, 'Be careful. I'd hate to see that pretty head severed from that killer bod of yours.' I was terrified."

"How did he get out of jail?" Lindsey asked.

"I didn't even know he was in jail. That was before he gave me the pendant & he came and went, wasn't living with me. But he's very good with computers. He bragged about giving Sheriff Peralta a data stick that would allow him inside the Sheriff's Office system."

"He has someone helping him?"

"Yes, he must."

"Do you know who?"

"No."

"But you went to Silicon Valley last week. Couldn't you get help then?"

"Didn't really go," Beth scribbled. "Drove car to airport and took Lyft back home. Then went and got it at end of week, so I'd appear in normal routine. His orders. He moved in. Said I had to act normal. He'll let me go out some, but warned me that I'd never know when he was watching."

"Maybe he's faking you out?"

"Would you bet your life on that?"

I imagined Lindsey, sitting on a barstool, shaking her head.

Beth wrote again: "I was afraid if I went to the cops, I would be blamed for his crimes. Thank God I ran into you in Scottsdale."

Lindsey asked, "What is his story?"

"He claims his grand-uncle was railroaded on the Page murder. His going to prison broke up the family, trials took all their money and caused his mother to become an alcoholic & then kill herself. He wants revenge."

"On?"

"On Phoenix."

I let my finger rest on the page and thought about that. We hadn't done a complete family tree. Was Garrison related to Darren Howard, the most obvious character who was probably innocent?

Lindsey wrote, "You were there in Fountain Hills and Black Canyon City."

"Yes. I had no idea what he was going to do. He handcuffed me to steering wheel. I saw him kicking your husband in the dirt. There was nothing I could do. Afterwards, he told me what he did in detail. Also about bombing the man's car. It's awful."

Lindsey wrote, "How do I know you're telling the truth?"

"I am telling the truth. If you don't believe me, I'm screwed. When you were with the Sheriff's Office, I always felt there was a chemistry between us. Have you ever been with a woman before?"

"Yes."

Yeah, I knew that one. It was in the confessional letter that Lindsey wrote me when she came back from D.C. and never sent. I snuck it out of her suitcase and read it, then replaced it like a thief who accidentally broke into jail. The letter admitted several infidelities. We never discussed her time away, after the miscarriage of our baby and the doctors telling her she could never have children now, when I thought I had lost her, when Robin was living in the garage apartment and curled up in the bed beside me. And I let her stay, night after night. I pushed myself back: The important thing was that Lindsey had come home, that we did reconcile. Most people go their entire lives without this kind of simpatico connection with another human being. I had it. I read on in the notebook.

Lindsey persisted. "Did you go to the fortieth anniversary event for the bombing?"

"Yes. We went together under assumed names. I thought, edgy fun. He's a crime buff, risk taker. Didn't know what was coming. At first the crazy was edgy & sexy. Then it turned into this terror."

"What's with the *Hamlet* references?"

"He was in theater arts in high school. He played Hamlet. Don't have all the answers. He's crazy. Lindsey—I. Am. Desperate. Help me."

"How?"

"Don't know. Can the cops find a way to jam the signal? Maybe we can meet again, jam signal, they can catch him."

"Where are you staying?"

"My place."

"Where is that?"

Beth wrote out the address in Ahwatukee. Then

said,"He's going to kill again. When he killed those people in Fountain Hills, he wiped his bloody knife on my clothes. I'm very afraid. I'll testify about all this."

"Are you ever outside the radius of his device?"

"No. At least I don't know when. He won't let me go to Silicon Valley now. I've had to make an excuse & work remotely. Surprised he let me come out tonight, but he's obsessed with your husband & solving the crime."

"See what I can do," Lindsey wrote.

Beth ended the Moleskine dialogue with, "I am sincere about being attracted to you."

I closed the book and joined her in the bedroom, where we talked for an hour before calling the Sheriff.

Chapter Thirty-seven

Tuesday evening, we invited Malik Jones and his girlfriend over for drinks and dinner. Fresh sockeye salmon from A.J.'s cooked on the grill, Caprese salad with heirloom tomatoes and the last basil from Lindsey's garden, and asparagus. His girlfriend was in California so it would be the three of us.

All day, silence from the Starship. Peralta was in a high-command meeting with the multi-agency task force at Phoenix Police headquarters. They were discussing Lindsey's encounter with Beth Sleigh and next moves. Beth's condo was in an upper arm of Ahwatukee, the development on the far south end of Phoenix begun in the seventies. So much came back to that decade, didn't it? The cops and firefighters called it "All-White-Tukee," but although it was still predominantly Anglo, some of the older construction was showing its age, like similar places throughout the metropolitan area. Phoenix: building tomorrow's slums today. But it also had some very high-priced McMansions.

Beth lived in a newer condo near the boundary of South Mountain Park. Phoenix liked to brag that it was the largest municipal park in the world, but it was more of a desert preserve, very popular with hikers. I checked her address on Zillow: the front was dominated by a giant garage door. Then I looked at the building from Google Earth. It was on Fifth Avenue, but far south Fifth, as far from the same street that ran through Willo as from the earth to the moon. One way in, one way out. Ahwatukee was the same way. You could only drive in from the east, on Chandler Boulevard, Ray Road, or Pecos Road. Hence the nickname, World's Largest Cul-de-Sac. Any police operation there would be dangerous. Even surveillance was risky. Park a fake utility van out front and it was sure to draw suspicion. Better to get Beth out again and separate her from Garrison.

Jones arrived at six-thirty and I was bringing in drinks when I saw Peralta's SUV in front and him marching up the walk. I met him at the door.

"You're right in time for cocktails."

"We're going in," he said. "I want Lindsey to be there to call this woman out. You can come if you promise to stay out of the way."

"Wait a minute. Have you seen this property?"

"I have. It's going to be tough. But Garrison is a cop killer and the Phoenix Chief is adamant. She wants to take him tonight. Her jurisdiction. We're along for the show."

By this time, Lindsey and Jones were behind me, listening.

I put my hands on my hips. "The show, as you call it, sounds risky as hell. Are you willing to bet this woman's life on it?"

"They have a jammer," Peralta said. "Military grade. It will block the detonator signal. Used in Iraq and Afghanistan. Too bad Buzz Page didn't have one." He looked over my shoulder. "Maybe Captain Jones can check it out and see if it will do the job."

I looked at Jones. He shrugged. "I'm in this deep already. Why not?"

Peralta spun around. "Let's roll."

The three of us piled in the Prelude and followed Peralta's SUV south on Fifth Avenue, jogged east on McDowell, and sped onto the Papago Freeway doing eighty-five from the Third Street ramp. The sunset was a dud as we blended into the jetstream of taillights turning south, passing the west side of Sky Harbor. We crossed the dry Salt River and went by the tacky-imposing University of Phoenix headquarters, strangely unmoored from downtown, to turn east past a joyless landscape of tilt-up warehouses and offices. Then the Broadway Curve and heading straight south. I couldn't believe people made this drive twice a day or more. Lindsey briefed Jones on her meetings with Beth Sleigh and the explosive she said was on a chain around her neck.

As I took the Chandler Boulevard exit and entered Ahwatukee, Jones said, "They ought to do this at four a.m. It would be the best time to catch them unaware."

I agreed but doubted our advice would be welcomed by the badass SWAT people or Phoenix PD. The closer we got, other things troubled me, including the lay of the land and the sightlines.

Peralta took Desert Hills Parkway, a long loop that turned into south Fifth Avenue near Beth's condo. Two blocks before we reached the condo development entrance and beyond the Jehovah's Witnesses meeting hall, the street was blocked off by an array of police units: cars, SUVs, vans, the bomb squad, and an enormous command vehicle. In addition to numerous unis, more than a dozen SWAT officers mustered with helmets, body armor, and assault rifles. Coming this way, rather than turning right off Chandler Boulevard onto Fifth—and passing the condo development—was the less visible way to mass a force nearby.

So far, not so bad. But I knew from the satellite images that Beth's condo sat at the northeast corner of the project, the common driveway in front and, beyond a wall, desert leading to South Mountain Park behind. At two stories, it was possible the condo afforded Beth or Garrison a glimpse of this gathering of blue before the sun went down. The thin palo verde trees around Kingdom Hall offered scant concealment. And if Garrison saw it, the escape route was obvious. The one-way-in and one-way-out layout of Ahwatukee, along with the bafflement of curvilinear residential streets that went nowhere, made this unfriendly for a fugitive in a car. PPD probably already had Fifth and Chandler blocked. No, refuge lay overland—and with his military training and experience he would be a formidable opponent.

After parking and showing our badges, we caught up with Peralta and stepped inside the command vehicle. It was crowded. Officers were sitting at a bank of screens that showed the condo from three angles. High-ranking cops, including the SWAT commander, were sitting and standing where they could.

The Chief was in uniform. "Glad you could make it, Mike."

"Wouldn't miss it," he said.

Then she ran through the plan. Cameras were in place, embedded in two streetlights set by police technicians using a city transportation department bucket truck. One condo next door was empty. A cop impersonating a FedEx driver had contacted the other nearest neighbor three hours earlier and told them to quietly evacuate. Fifteen minutes ago, the police made calls to the other neighbors, telling them to remain inside, away from windows, and not use their phones. The assault team was briefed and ready to make "dynamic entry" if necessary. That piece of cop argot meant surprise, speed, dominating force. Snipers were in the foothills to the north. They confirmed visual sighting through the windows of two people in the condo, one male, one female. A helicopter was on the ground at the Chandler airport and could be here in minutes. She turned to Lindsey.

"Can you text Sleigh and get her outside so we have the best chance with the jammer?"

"Sure." Lindsey pulled out her phone. "I can try."

She typed and showed the text to the Chief, Peralta, and finally me:

Husband is out of town. I rented a room at Mission Palms in downtown Tempe. Can you come?

The chief nodded. "Send it."

I heard the telegraph beep from her phone. Behind me, a cop at a console spoke into his microphone. "Text is sent."

Peralta cleared his throat. "Malik Jones was a captain in Iraq. Can he be of any assistance with the jammer?"

The SWAT commander waited for a nod from the Chief. "Sure. The more expertise the better. Come with me."

The door opened and closed and they were gone.

We waited for a long ten minutes, only the muted sound of radio traffic, the tension in the comvan as palpable as static electricity.

Then the incoming text signal sounded.

Lindsey read:

I'm so sorry. Can't get away tonight. Want to do it soonest, though.

She typed again:

Sneak away for an hour. I won't tell. Hope you're not all talk.

Two seconds later came back:

Slammed. Next time, I promise, with words and actions.

She appended a hearts emoticon.

The Chief sighed. "It was worth a try, at least. So, we'll do it our way. Let me know when everyone is in position."

I said, "Garrison is armed and has explosives."

"We know." She looked at me as if I were a piece of lint to be brushed off her immaculate uniform.

"Don't you think it would be smarter to try this in a few hours? Early morning. When Garrison might be asleep?"

"I don't want to give him the time, *Deputy*, and..."

I interrupted, instantly realizing I was committing a male-privilege microaggression. I did it anyway, would have interrupted a man, too, said the same thing: "It's tactically *unsound*. With all due respect."

Every eye in the suddenly hushed comvan was on me, even the people charged with monitoring the screens. I avoided Lindsey's eyes.

The Chief's eyes narrowed and she was about to light into me when I felt Peralta's hand on my shoulder, pulling. "You might want to wait outside. They're going to need the room in here," he said quietly.

"Fine."

I was ten feet into the parking lot when I heard his voice. "Where the hell are you going?"

I walked back and stood close. "This is all wrong and you know it. People are going to die. Or he's going to slip away. Or both. If you don't need the fucking historian, I have things to do, places to go. I'm 'out of town,' remember Lindsey's text?"

His big head slowly moved side to side on a narrow axis. "Don't even think about it."

"Are you ordering me to stay here?"

He studied me for a long moment. Then he silently handed me a black police hand radio, turned, and went back inside.

I stalked to the Prelude and opened the door.

"David, where are you going?"

Jones jogged toward me from the SWAT formation.

"They don't need me," I said. "I'm going to take in the view."

"Want some company?"

"Sure."

Chapter Thirty-eight

From central Phoenix, the South Mountains look like a solid straight mass, brown or purple depending on the light, rising up to mark the edge of the Salt River Valley. In reality, they ran at an angle—northeast to southwest, with the latter being slightly farther south than the former. As a Boy Scout, especially, I had hiked them extensively, though never in the summer like today's iron men and women from the Midwest. Some of the hiking trails were carved by the Civilian Conservation Corps during the New Deal. I recalled many of the features: Telegraph Pass, Maricopa Peak, Piedmont Canyon, Two Peaks. Three distinct ranges made up the South Mountains, or that was what I remembered.

I returned the way we had come, but left the freeway quickly, taking the Baseline Road exit. After waiting for the extravagant multitasking of the traffic signal, I turned left and we drove west. This used to be a two-lane road, named after the Gila and Salt River baseline, or meridian, set in 1851 as the initial point of survey for the entire territory. Miles of the Japanese flower gardens used to spread out along both sides of Baseline—when I was a boy, we would come down every Saturday and buy cut flowers. You used to be able to look down the colorful sweep of fields to see groves, ranches, and finally the city and its mountain necklace against a pure blue sky as the land sloped to the river. I've decided "used to be" are the saddest words in my life with this city.

Of course, "used to be" also meant a city overrun with gangsters, where even a reporter was a target of murder. A city overrun with hucksters, ready to sell off the lovely flower gardens for quick profits and dross. Now the gangsters were cartels and gangs running drugs, an international big business, as well as occasional mischief from a resettled Mafioso. And the hucksters were selling a "Sun Corridor" from Prescott south to beyond Tucson, nevermind climate change bearing down.

The radio switched to the tactical channel snapped me to the moment, as we drove the wide avenue lined with the cheaply built apartment complexes and shopping strips that replaced the flower fields.

"Adam Team in place."

"Charlie Team in place."

"Stand by. We're placing a call to Elizabeth Sleigh, ordering her and anyone else inside to come outside."

I said, "What do you think of their jamming equipment?"

"They think very highly of themselves," Jones said. "I hope that's backed up with ability."

"So, you don't think much of it."

"It's an improved version of stuff we used in Iraq against IEDs." He sighed. "I'd give it a fifty-fifty chance."

At Central Avenue, with boxy off-the-shelf Circle K and KFC buildings, I turned south again.

"Where are we going?" Jones said.

"Into the park. I can let you out here and you can get a bus."

"I'll stay."

"Then take this." I pulled out my backup gun, the .38, and handed it across. He took it.

"You're going to set up an ambush."

"Probably a longshot."

"I'd say. Why do it?"

"If I were Garrison, this is where I'd go. Northwest, as far away from the cops and helicopter as possible. Either exit the far side of the park or get lucky and hijack a car."

We drove toward the blackness of the mountains. The television transmission towers blinked with red lights above. Inside the entrance to South Mountain Park, I badged a city ranger, who swung open a gate and let us in. I followed a narrow asphalt road southwest.

"What kind of music do you listen to, David?"

"Jazz."

"Ellington?"

"Of course. Basie. Stan Getz. Charlie Parker, Bill Evans, Monk, it's a long list."

Jones chuckled. "You're one out-of-step cat, David. How about Future? Kevin Gates? Rae Sremmurd?"

"Never heard of them. Check this out."

I slid in one of my mix tapes—the Prelude was so old it handled cassettes—and Bing Crosby and Louis Armstrong sang, "Now You Has Jazz."

He laughed with delight. "You're so savage, man. I have to develop some historian eccentricities, I guess."

"I highly recommend it."

At the fork, I swung left and started back to the east as the road climbed. I watched the odometer click over the mileage, then we made a sharp U around a outcropping near Telegraph Pass and I killed the car lights. Night fell on us.

"I hope to hell you remember this road, David."

"Me, too."

"That's reassuring."

The radio interrupted. "Front door is opening. Female is coming out."

I was doing about ten miles per hour now, trying to feel the road beneath the tires. Then it grew more visible.

"Oh, my God," Jones said. "Look at that. Wait, don't look."

From my peripheral vision, I could see the vast ocean of lights to the left that captivated my traveling companion. It only became more pronounced as we gained altitude.

"Phoenix is still beautiful at night," I said.

The radio squawked: "We have the female down on the driveway. Jammer appears to be working. Bomb squad moving in. Permission to make dynamic entry."

"Permission granted. Air support is three minutes out."

A second later: "Fuck! Got bit by a rattlesnake. Tac one. Need medical. Now!"

"Stand by. We'll send paramedics. Stay off this channel."

Jones and I were silent as the television towers loomed closer and then nearly overhead. I crept forward and laid out my plan. We would park the car at the Dobbins Overlook and hide in the desert. If Garrison came this way, he'd see the vehicle and try to steal it.

"How the hell are we going to avoid snakes?" he said.

"Stomp," I said. "They're as afraid of us as we are of them. They can feel the vibrations and will move out of the way. Don't reach under any bushes."

"So goddamned reassuring."

"Shit," I whispered. As I crept forward, I saw a four-door car was already parked at the overlook, facing toward the spectacular view. It was illuminated by the city and the blinking TV lights. The car was swaying. The windows were open, and in the backseat I could see a man's back moving rhythmically and a woman's legs and feet tight against him, meeting his thrusts. Car sex, short people. They shouldn't be here but they were.

"Stay here. I'm going to run them out."

"House is clear," the radio said. "No one is inside."

I quickly turned the volume down low.

"Repeat?" An agitated voice, probably from the comvan.

"No one else here. The male suspect is gone. Beginning search. Seal the perimeter."

Another voice cut in: "Wait…stand by…we have a booby-trapped rear door. Hand grenade. There may be other explosives. All teams clear the residence."

I notched the Prelude into park, opened the door, and stepped out onto the road. I was fifty feet away. The temp had fallen into the nineties and a breeze was blowing from the west.

Easy steps, long strides. I closed half the distance. Up here, it was preternaturally quiet.

Then a shadow emerged from the blackness to the east. A running figure. Then walking. Amazingly, he didn't see me or, in the distance, the Prelude. He was lasered on this car, his escape pod. He made a wide semicircle around the vehicle, checking it out. I could hear the woman moaning loudly. Then his back was to me and he came up to the driver's side rear door and flung it open.

"Get the fuck out now! Otherwise, I'll kill you! I'm taking this car!"

I knew that voice: Ryan Garrison.

Imagining the treacherous climb he had to make, over peaks and through canyons in the dark, I was amazed he had gotten here so fast.

By that time, I was ten feet away, undetected, the Colt Python in my right hand. I side-shimmied so my aiming point would be toward the city, not into the car.

"What the fuck are you waiting for?" he screamed. "Give me your keys and get the fuck out!"

A man's voice, shaky, said, "Chill, dude. We gotta put on clothes. You can have the car."

I slipped into a combat shooting stance and spoke in a conversational voice.

"Freeze, Garrison. It's all over."

Everything slowed down.

My body temperature felt as if it fell ten degrees.

He turned to face me, what I wanted. He was dressed all in black, with a black backpack, and black camo face paint. My .45 semiautomatic was at an angle downward.

"Deputy Sheriff! Put down your weapon slowly and lie on the pavement!"

Now the legal niceties were out of the way.

"You people get out on the passenger side and lie on the ground. Do it now!"

Garrison hesitated, started to turn.

"Don't move, Ryan. I don't want to kill you. Put the gun down slowly."

He didn't. "Mapstone. You didn't solve the case. To be or not to be?"

I shouted, "Drop your weapon! Drop your weapon!"

But he didn't. He took two steps toward me and raised it in a sudden motion.

I let out a slow breath and my finger actuated the world-class mechanism of the Python.

Boom!

Boom!

Fire spat out of the barrel and the sound echoed against

the mountainside. I hit him twice in the chest and the force of impact blew him backwards into the open door and onto the pavement.

I stayed put, keeping him in the gunsights.

"Get the hell out of that car!" The couple looked frozen inside.

I stepped toward Garrison.

Then the pair began climbing out the passenger side. They were both nude. It distracted me for precious seconds.

Suddenly Garrison popped up standing straight, the .45 aimed between my eyes.

Body armor.

I sighted his head and was about to fire when I heard a sharp explosion to my right rear. Garrison's face snapped backwards and a wide jet of blood, brains, and bone fragments sprayed from the back of his skull.

Jones.

"Move away! Move away!" I used my left hand to wave the couple back as I got to Garrison. I used my shoe to slide away the semi-auto, went through the pro-forma of checking for a pulse. I pressed on his chest. Sure enough, he had a ballistic vest. Then a light pat-down, where I felt what seemed like two hand grenades. A bad experience with Los Zetas had made me know what they felt like.

I whispered, "Not to be, asshole," and holstered the big revolver. Then loudly, "Everybody move far away! He's got grenades!"

The man and woman, barely put together, just stood there. The woman was filming me on her smartphone.

"I said, move away!"

After they finally began walking, I turned and saw Jones, five feet behind me. He was looking at the backup gun in his hand. Then he heaved it over the low rock wall and off the side of the mountain. When he turned around and faced me, even in the backlight of the city beyond, I could see the blood in his eyes.

He came at me so fast, I barely had time to assume a T-position—left foot facing forward, right foot behind at a forty-five degree angle. It kept me standing, barely, when he slammed his fist into my chest.

Pain level: nine. I swear I could feel broken ribs grinding against each other.

"You!" He grabbed me at the upper arms, pushing me against the trunk of the car. "You did this! You shot a black man! That's not Garrison!"

I brought up my arms, my hands laced together with enough force to break his grip. Clutching his shirt, I pulled him to the body and ran my fingers across the face paint, showed it to him and stood up.

"Doesn't matter!" He had me in his hard grasp again. I gripped him back, all my anger and terror from the shooting now firing adrenaline into my system, and we fought for traction. "You didn't try to deescalate! You killed! It's what you do! Anything to protect your white privilege, your unearned white privilege! You fucking cops killing people to preserve white supremacy!"

"Stop that grad-school jargon shit," I shouted back. "You don't even believe it! That's slovenly thinking and that's not you."

His eyes lost their angry focus on me.

"You assholes stop filming! *Now!*" Jones called across the car in an Army captain's voice.

"You saved my life." I pushed away from the car, he pushed back toward it. We were both sweating rivers. "I did everything to not have to shoot Garrison. We may never know the truth now. Would you be happier if I'd let him kill me?"

"Maybe fucking so! You're so entitled! So fucking un-woke, you don't even know it!"

"Then you should have let him do it. But you didn't."

A hard shove, but I wouldn't budge or let go.

His hot breath came against my face. "Do you know how many people hate me simply because I'm black?"

"No. I don't know what it's like to be black."

He gripped me tighter. "I watched you pump two rounds into that man, cool as an icicle. You like it. You set this up."

"Training kicks in." I dug my fingers into his upper arms. "You were a combat infantryman. You know that."

"But I didn't *like* it. You do! How many people have you shot, David? How many?"

"Too many. What about you, Captain Jones?"

He whispered, "Too many. Goddamn you. I only wanted…" His voice choked and he looked down. "… only wanted away from the violence. But it'll never happen. Not in this white supremacist country."

I steadied my voice. "We must learn to live together as brothers or we will all perish together as fools."

His head came up, eyes ablaze. "Don't you dare quote Dr. King! You have no right, no right!"

"I have every right! I have an obligation! He spoke of universal truths to all people!"

By this time, we were hanging on each other like exhausted boxers.

We broke our holds simultaneously. Jones started walking down the road into the darkness. I let him go. I put the car-copulaters, a good-looking pair of Anglos in their twenties, in the Prelude, a safe distance away, and retrieved the keys. I thought about confiscating their cell phones, but decided that would cause more trouble than it was worth. Then I used the police radio to call it in. Below us, Phoenix had never looked so magnificent.

Chapter Thirty-nine

The next two weeks tumbled past with me on administrative leave, which was normal for an officer-involved shooting. It put Peralta in a dilemma, because the move typically meant shifting the Deputy off his or her "pre-incident assignment." Did that mean my archival work on the Buzz Page bombing? Or simply the running down of Ryan Garrison? He compromised by moving me to a cubicle at the Starship, where I was ordered to run through hundreds of tips and leads that had poured in after he announced the reopening of the case.

My armory shrank. The Colt Python was taken, as well as the .38 Airweight used by Jones. My fancy Springfield Armory XD taken by Garrison was evidence. I was left with the M1911 .45 caliber semiautomatic pistol that my father carried as a Mustang pilot in World War II and Korea. The weapon was in mint condition and regularly cleaned and oiled.

I had three sessions with a department-approved shrink, an older man with a gray ponytail and an office at Twenty-fourth Street and Camelback. With a sweeping view of the Phoenix Mountain Preserve, the Arizona Biltmore, and the Wrigley Mansion, he put me through the expected paces. Talking about my feelings. How was I sleeping? Was I receiving support from my "peer officers," higher ranks, and family members? Did I feel stigmatized or guilty? Did I want to participate in a group discussion with other officers who had been involved in shootings? The folkways of law enforcement had collided with the culture of therapy and human resources.

I tried to play well with others.

When Sharon Peralta visited on Cypress Street, I was different.

"Do you feel any regrets about shooting him?" she asked.

"Are you asking as my friend or as a shrink sent to spy by your husband?"

"Your friend." She wasn't insulted. We had a long tradition of banter.

I said, "Then the answer is, none in the least."

"I don't believe that." Her tone was measured.

She waited me out.

"Look, Sharon, I didn't want the man dead. He aimed a gun at me and would have fired. He refused repeated commands to drop the weapon." After another pause. "The last time Lindsey and I went to church, the minister talked about how every individual is precious in the eyes of the Lord. I think about that often. But I couldn't let Ryan Garrison kill an innocent civilian or me. I feel as bad for Malik, who decided to step in. I'm convinced it wasn't necessary. But maybe he saved my life."

"You have to understand that both of them potentially suffered from post-traumatic stress disorder," she said. "It's common with soldiers and Marines, especially those with multiple deployments."

"And when Jones shot Garrison, it brought it all back to him."

"Very possibly."

"What about Garrison? It couldn't have all been PTSD."

"No," she said. "Maybe it was simple revenge for what he saw as a wrong. Or maybe he was trying to rewrite his past."

I didn't quite understand that last point, but I was talked out and didn't ask.

The morning after the shooting, as per policy, I gave a formal statement to two detectives from the Professional Standards Bureau. I got about three hours of sleep, Lindsey spooning me for comfort. They were younger men, blond and impossibly clean-cut East Valley residents, very different from the old-school rat squad dicks. They were so nice, but persistent. I bet they were Latter-day Saints and wouldn't have been surprised if they asked me if I knew Jesus and handed me a Book of Mormon. I wondered if they were holdovers from the Melton years.

I caught a break, thanks to a white lie. Peralta said he sent me to the Dobbins Overlook to give me something to do but get me out of the way. I agreed that was how it happened. I caught another break, thanks to the couple in the car that filmed the event. It backed me up in every specific, especially identifying myself as a Deputy Sheriff and repeatedly ordering Garrison to drop his weapon. It also quickly appeared on 12News and then went viral on the Internet. Someone had edited the aftermath to make it appear Malik Jones and I were in a supportive, brotherly embrace. His face was blurred out, too.

Still, the Saints ran me repeatedly through the timeline. My timeline was forty years ago. But I kept answering consistently about the night of the shooting. The idea was to catch me in any lie or misstep in procedures. I stuck to the only story to tell. Three separate interviews, totaling seven hours, me trying not to get rattled or appear as a suspect, which was how my badged traducers treated me. But so nice. They lingered on why I didn't take the kill shot when Garrison suddenly stood. I said I was momentarily distracted, concerned for the safety of the two civilians, but I still could have made the head shot. Malik Jones beat me to it. Before that, I fired twice into the mass of Garrison's body, per regulations, and he went down. I had no indication he was wearing a ballistic vest that could absorb the .357 Magnum hollow points. Replaying the events of Tuesday night to myself, I figured I had at best a twenty percent chance of killing him before he got me. It wasn't unprecedented for a cop and a criminal to shoot each other simultaneously.

Jones' statement coincided with mine, although we didn't speak. He could have burned me, claimed I was the white privilege killer he called me that night, but he apparently didn't. Surprisingly, the Saints didn't dwell on the filmed confrontation with Jones. He was a civilian upset from shooting someone. He also asked that his name not be released and Peralta agreed. But he got plenty of coverage in the media as the anonymous hero who saved a Deputy's life and stopped a cop-killer. I called the State Archives. He hadn't been there since the Tuesday of what the Sheriff's Office relentlessly called "the incident." Of everything that happened, his anger toward me hurt the most.

By Friday, the Vicodin ran out. No refills. Lindsey bought a container of Mentholatum—the outside, at least, hepped up for the twenty-first century. But I was convinced that inside it was the smelly old go-to ointment used by my grandmother. The idea of liniments turned into a long-running joke in our loopy, coming-down-off-a-crisis mood. We chased each other around the house threatening to apply the goop.

That was also the day I had a review-board hearing before three Sheriff's Office Captains. Everyone, even me, was in uniform. Not until halfway through the questioning did I realize I still had the Black Lives Matter button pinned on. I left it. If they noticed, nobody said anything. I was the historian, the oddball, not even a real Deputy in the minds of many. Once again, I ran through what happened. After another week of waiting, increasingly wondering if I might lose my badge or even be prosecuted for homicide, I was cleared to return to normal duty. All my guns were returned and the pistol that belonged to the father I never knew went back in its padded wooden case.

Lindsey and I took in a Diamondbacks game and the team won. While she scored the game, I continued to marvel at the way Garrison evaded the SWAT perimeter and snipers—with the help of a rattler biting one of them—and hiked in the dark through the South Mountains to the overlook. I had dreams of snakes on me and Garrison taking aim, and when I pulled the trigger the bullet exited my barrel in slow-motion and dropped on the pavement after traveling a few inches. I didn't tell the shrink, who had to sign off on my "fitness for duty" evaluation. He did and Peralta accepted it.

Lindsey told me about the investigation into Garrison. His backpack contained an Alienware 17 R3 laptop, "one of the best hacker computers," she said. On it was the malicious software program that had been inserted into the Sheriff's Office system, as well as many files on the

Page investigation, especially articles from the *Republic*, *New Times*, and bloggers obsessed with the crime. My Page timeline was there. So were names and addresses for Tom Goldstein, Rusty Clevenger, and, unsettlingly, my accurate address and the one for Malik Jones. The pack also carried an electronic detonator, several sticks of dynamite, C4 plastic explosives. A paperback volume of *Hamlet* was heavily underlined. The same with a second-hand *Phoenix Project*. In addition to the two hand grenades on his belt, he had a folding combat knife whose serrations were consistent with the wounds inflicted on Goldstein and the Clevengers. Finally, his smartphone. Lindsey carefully hacked it, and it contained the original threat text sent to Peralta, as well as the one to Rudy Jarvis.

Detectives found that Garrison's grand-uncle was indeed Darren Howard. His sister, who lived in Oregon, confirmed the damage the case had inflicted on the family, including their mother's alcoholism and suicide.

As far as Phoenix PD was concerned, the case was closed. A cop-killer had gotten what he deserved.

The necklace around Beth's neck was a genuine explosive. It took the bomb squad an hour to disarm and remove it, while she lay facedown on the driveway. She wasn't arrested, but she was interrogated five times by Phoenix cops and Sheriff's detectives during the two weeks I was on leave. Beth stuck to her story: The younger man who started as an edgy fling turned into a kidnapper. They kicked her loose and the County Attorney declined to file charges. She gave teary interviews to the media about her ordeal.

I asked Lindsey if she had spoken to her.

"I did," she said. "I spent an hour with her in an interview room. At first, she was angry, said I'd betrayed her.

She calmed down when I told her I was trying to get her out of the condo and away from Garrison…"

"And soon she was holding your hands and telling you she loved you."

Lindsey's fair skin flushed a deep red.

I felt cold and shaky. After a long silence, my dry mouth managed, "Do you want to be with her, Lindsey?"

"Of course not."

"Keep our marriage and have her on the side?"

"No. You're letting your fears or your voyeuristic fantasies get the better of what you know is real. You and me, we're together. That's real."

I hoped so. But I pressed.

"Are you telling me the truth?"

"Yes!"

"Are you telling yourself the truth?"

"Yes. But aren't you attracted to her, Dave?"

"She's very beautiful, very magnetic. Can I have her on the side?

"No fucking way. But if it gives you any consolation, she's attracted to you, too."

I absorbed that.

"She said you are 'sexually weaponized.' I took that as a compliment. Especially because I bet you think the same about her."

It sounded more like a term out of academia. I said, "But you believe her."

She said that she did.

"And you don't," she said.

I shook my head. "I don't trust her. Misdirection, concealment, these have been the features of this case from the beginning. Maybe Garrison did the whole thing and framed her, right down to using her last name on the notes to Peralta. On the other hand, maybe she took an impressionable, traumatized young veteran with a vague grudge, made him fall for her, and turned him into a weapon. They saw the cops massing and she sent him out through the mountains. She told him when the heat was off they'd meet up, and she packed that laptop and smartphone to set him up perfectly. It's all too neat."

She looked in her lap a long time. "As you would say, my History Shamus, it's impossible to prove a hypothetical. Only his fingerprints were on the laptop and the phone. Sometimes there are tales of black and white."

"What about 'coding like a girl'?"

"I was wrong."

I tried to keep my frustration in check. We were both fragile, me coming close to death and her coming close to losing me with a .45 round to the head. Closed-coffin service and underground furniture.

"We still don't know who picked up Garrison outside the jail," I said. "That's the loose end. Odds are, it was Beth."

"She said Garrison had a friend from high school, a big Samoan she met a couple of times."

"Name?"

"He went by T, that's all. We've run it through NCIC for aliases and nicknames. No luck on his phone."

"All we need is for them to have met up at the Ivanhoe, in a smoky barroom filled with gangsters and bad seventies music."

She shot me an evil grin. "And liniment."

Chapter Forty

Most of my cubicle time was wasted. Four decades later, the Page case still generated an enormous amount of speculation and conspiracy theories. I spent an hour that I would never get back on the phone with a lawyer who claimed he was the prosecutor who put Ned Warren away. It was a good story and maybe even true. But he mostly wanted to settle scores, make sure I knew he didn't get the credit he deserved. He offered nothing on Mark Reid or the bombing.

Two envelopes with no return addresses interested me.

One contained a fresh photograph of a battered mailbox. On it was a street number on Colter and, below that on an ancient nameplate, FREEMAN BURKE. I couldn't avoid a chill.

The second envelope held a Xerox copy of a field interview card. These were the three-by-five cards officers would fill out when they interviewed a suspicious subject but didn't have grounds for arrests. I wondered if they were even used now. This one chilled me, too.

I took both back to my courthouse office.

Monday morning, I called Detective Kate Vare at PPD.

"Good morning, sharpshooter," she said cheerfully.

"We all should take along an armed civilian to save our asses when confronted with an armed felon. Whatever it takes, Mapstone. I'm glad you took down the asshole. As many times as I wanted you to lose your badge, I'm glad the shooting board cleared you."

"I see you haven't changed."

"You're tone policing, Mapstone."

"What?"

"Tone policing. Being from academia, I'm surprised you don't know about it. You're trying to invalidate my argument by attacking me."

"Are you done?"

"Oh, I could go on. But how may the real police department help our friends at the county?"

"Do you have FI cards on file from the seventies?"

She laughed, a rare and unpleasant sound coming from her.

"Are you shitting me? There would have been thousands of them. Those were probably all purged twenty years ago. Why?"

I told her. The copied FI card that someone had mailed showed the date May 29, 1978, 2120 hours, at Two-Zero Street and Colter, subject sitting in his vehicle, name Mark W. Reid, valid Arizona driver's license, no wants or warrants. The officer's name and badge number were blacked out.

I heard her take in a sharp breath. "Are you yanking my chain, Mapstone?"

"No. This was five days before Buzz Page was bombed. And twenty minutes after nine p.m. Reid was parked outside Freeman Burke's house. The officer wrote, 'Subject states he is visiting Freeman Burke and went to the house after the officer concluded the interview. The officer observed the door open and the subject went inside without incident.'"

I told her what we had found about the Page case, especially the briefcase and ledger, and the key to the ledger that Tom Goldstein had kept.

"Well done," she said. "Let me see what I can find out. I'll be in touch."

•●●●•

Monsoon season had begun, when moisture from the Sea of Cortez formed into storms that moved north over the wettest desert on Earth. When I was growing up, the monsoons meant scary lightning and thunder, rain, and some dust storms. As the city spread out, the weather changed. By the late seventies, the storms often didn't come into the city, kept at bay by the expanding concrete. We often had to watch the majestic thunderheads and lightning at a distance. Then, in recent years, it had changed again: Sometimes the storms came in and turned violent. I had read it had something to do with the collision of the cool fronts with the urban heat island, especially the concrete expanse of Sky Harbor International Airport. The result was microbursts. A few years ago, one flattened the utility poles on Third Avenue and ripped part of the roof off a lovely bungalow a block away on Holly Street. Television and social media showed images of apocalyptic brown tsunamis rolling in, calling them haboobs after the phenomenon in the Sahara. These weren't new, and older natives called them dust storms. The vicious microbursts were.

By the time I got to Colter Street, the temperature was only around a hundred, with higher humidity that the newcomers could complain about. In the southeast, I saw clouds start gathering. But here the sun was out and the area was a magical leftover of old Phoenix: narrow streets, shade and citrus trees, oleander hedges, even a few stretches where the city's manic program of installing sidewalks, curbs, and gutters hadn't reached. Birdsong filled the air. I felt as if I were back in 1978, wondered what it would be like if I could go back in time. But only if I knew what I do now. Except for Lindsey, I would have made so many different decisions.

And there it was: the most ordinary mailbox on a two-by-two, curved top. An address number was painted in fading white paint. And Freeman Burke's name was on an aging plate, all in capital letters. Atop the mailbox was a wrought-iron figure of cattle and horses. It was exactly as in the photo. I parked where Mark Reid was FI'd, under the shadc of an expansive ficus tree.

Beyond the mailbox was a driveway bracketed by trees and oleanders. No gate. I walked up toward a rather ordinary low-slung house. If this was once the home of the richest man in Arizona, he lived relatively simply. The grounds were sumptuous, however—manicured lawn, flower beds overflowing even with the heat emergency, neatly trimmed green hedges, Indian hawthorn still festooned with purple blossoms, and, framing the property, two-story oleanders. Mature trees enveloped me. The temperature dropped at least ten degrees.

"Whatcha doin?"

The voice startled me from behind. I turned to find an old cowboy. That was my first impression, at least. He looked about seventy, weathered face, and slicked-back hair the color of henna. A Western shirt, neat blue jeans, and boots completed the look.

I showed him my star and identification, introduced myself.

"I'm the caretaker," he said in an Okie twang that was once more common here. He smiled without showing his teeth. On closer examination, his complexion had a yellow tint and everything about him seemed caved in.

"Who are you the caretaker for?"

"The Burkes, of course. Didn't you see the mailbox?" He put his hands on his hips and looked me over.

"Do they still live here?"

"Oh, my, no. Not since Mr. Freeman passed. The grandchildren are scattered to the winds." He made a gesture with both hands as if he were shooing birds away.

I asked if he lived in the house.

"Oh, no. I have the caretaker's house in back."

"Must be lonely."

"Not at all," he said. There were the comings and goings of the yard crew and the housekeepers, plus he had his cat and books.

"May I look inside?" I nodded toward the house.

"I'd like to help you, Deputy, but nobody but family can go in. They insist that it be kept exactly the way it was when Mr. Freeman passed, you understand."

Now I really wanted inside.

"Did you know him?"

"Oh, my, yes. He gave me my first job, cowboying on his ranches, here and the big one down in Sonora. He was a good man."

He repeated that odd, not-really-here smile and I smiled back.

"But you ended up here at the house?"

"That was later. I did a lot of his business, you see."

I tried, and saw him as a younger man forty years ago, potentially a dangerous one.

"I'm investigating the Charles Page murder from 1978," I said.

He kept smiling and shook his head. "You people won't let it go, will ya? Mr. Freeman won a libel suit against those big-britches out-of-town reporters. He was a self-made man, treated everybody fair, did so much good for this state, gave a lot of men their start."

"Men like Darren Howard."

His smile drooped. "Felt bad for Mr. Darren. I don't think for a minute he did what they said. They put him in prison to get revenge on Mr. Freeman, plain as that."

"Who is they?"

He spread his arms to encompass the world. "Babbitt, Harris, Clevenger, that Jew Phoenix cop, and then Bob Corbin and Grant Woods when they became Attorneys General. And the outsiders, the Easterners. Somebody had to pay for that reporter getting blown up and they couldn't get Mr. Freeman because he was innocent. So, they took poor Mr. Darren."

The caretaker spoke with more authority than a simple-minded cowpoke.

"What's your name besides the caretaker?"

"I'm the caretaker," he repeated and gave me a spooky look that might have unnerved me if I didn't have my lightweight semiautomatic on my belt.

"Did you know Mark Reid?"

"Can't say that I did."

"Can't say or won't say?"

The smile returned.

"You have a nice day, Deputy."

After a long moment, I walked slowly back to the street. He followed me, whistling an unrecognizable tune, smelling of Old Spice. I imagined the children in the neighborhood being frightened of him. I imagined him kidnapping them and burying them behind the house. The whistling continued until we were at the hood of the Prelude. Then I turned on him.

"Now that we're out in a city street, I'll see your driver's license."

His voice turned hard. "You'll see no such thing, sonny."

I stepped into a T position. "I'll see it when you take it out of your wallet, or I'll get it myself when you're down in the dirt wearing handcuffs."

"You have no right..."

"I have every right. You might be the caretaker or you might be a burglar."

His eyes narrowed. They were the same henna color as his dyed hair. He reached behind him.

"Do it slowly."

He simmered but handed me the license.

"Put your hands on the hood."

When he complied, I did a quick pat-down. No guns. "You have anything in your pockets that's going to stick me?"

"I've got a pocket knife."

I slipped out a heavy folding Buck knife and put it on the hood, out of reach.

He suddenly lurched forward and let out a whimper, but like a pro he kept his hands on the hood.

"You alright, sir?"

He rose up slowly. "Fine, goddamn you. Get this over with."

The license went with Paul Rossi, this address, valid. He was eighty years old. I pulled out my phone, typed his DOB and Social Security number on a note and called in to records. After a brief wait, I gave my name and badge number, then requested wants and warrants on Rossi, Paul D. He came back clean.

I gave the license back. "Thanks for your cooperation, sir."

He scooped up the Buck knife, pocketed it, and walked to the driveway. There he turned to give me a look of cold hatred before disappearing beyond the foliage.

The car was wonderfully cool, thanks to the shade. I climbed in and dialed Lindsey.

When she answered, I started heavy breathing.

"You again! You'd better not let my husband find out."

"Are you busy?"

"Nope. Finishing the forensic report on Garrison's computer. I'm bored."

"Then maybe you'd look somebody up for me." I gave her Paul Rossi's name and identifiers.

Chapter Forty-one

At five p.m., I was about ready to shut down at the courthouse and go home when the phone rang. It was Vare.

"You owe me big-time, sharpshooter." Her voice was snarky but excited.

"You found the FI card?"

"It was on microfiche. The card is real. Holy shit, Mapstone. This connects Mark Reid to Freeman Burke! It changes the entire case."

"Who was the officer who wrote it?"

"James McNally, retired as a Sergeant in 2004, died the next year."

"So, he didn't mail the copy."

"Not unless the Postal Service reaches beyond the grave, and I'd hate to see the postage for that."

I had never heard Kate Vare make a joke. After an obligatory laugh, I asked her why he hadn't pointed out the field interview after the Page bombing?

"I've been thinking about that. He would have been a rookie, so he might have been afraid to bring it up, worried that he might somehow get in trouble. Or he did, but his info went to one of the mobbed-up detectives or detective-analysts in the old Intelligence Squad. Maybe his contact ended up in that stolen file."

"The 851 file."

"Exactly. But I pulled his jacket and found family information. I'll shoot you an e-mail with it. Maybe one of them found the FI card copy that McNally made and mailed it to you."

"Thanks."

"Oh, you're not done thanking me yet. When I hear about shit like this, it makes me crazy. When you hear that I finally snapped and went on a shooting spree at headquarters, it'll be something like this."

I waited.

She let out a long sigh. "A few minutes ago, found a message from May, contact from a civilian wishing to speak to a detective about the Page case. It got flushed into the bureaucratic toilet and finally floated to the surface. The caller was Rudy Jarvis."

"Jarvis contacted PPD?"

"Did you fucking hear me? Yes!"

I held the phone away from my ear.

"Did anyone call him back?"

"No. And nobody put it together with his murder, either. As I say, I want to kill somebody."

I let it settle into my brain. Mark Reid's illegitimate son calling the cops a month before he was sent the threatening text that put him on the road to his death.

Kate spoke again, in a calmer voice. "We have a backlog of twenty-four-thousand cold-case murders here, classified as ones with no fresh leads in a year. Phoenix is one of America's capitals of unsolved murders. And you picked the biggest one of all time. Get these bastards, Mapstone. Burn them to the fucking ground."

Chapter Forty-two

The next day, Tuesday, a fire erupted in the High Country. It was arson, not a monsoon lightning strike, and the blaze had already consumed nine thousand acres of tinder-dry ponderosa pines and ten houses. It was the biggest fire in the state. Last year, four-hundred thousand acres of Arizona's forests and grasslands burned—more than the size of the entire city of Phoenix.

At the courthouse, I saw from halfway down the hall that my office door was open. It was possible that a break-in had happened, more likely that I would find Peralta sitting behind my desk.

And there he was. I shut the door.

"I was afraid you'd come in with that hand cannon of yours," he said.

"It's back in storage now that I have my little .45 back." I settled into one of the vintage straight-back wooden chairs in front of the desk.

"So now maybe you'll tell me why you braced a man who's the caretaker of the Burke home?"

"All the new evidence I've given you and that's why you're here? Give me a damned break."

His voice was calm. "Why are you so defensive, Mapstone?"

"Now you're tone policing."

His big jaw dropped.

"That's a thing," I continued. "Look it up."

I had to wait while he produced his smartphone and typed. Lindsey had taught him how to use Google.

"Actually," he said, "I can't tone police. It says here that tone policing is another way to protect privilege, which you have as a white, straight male. You are tone policing me as a Hispanic."

"You went to Harvard and you're my boss."

"Doesn't matter."

I started to get heated. "I have never criticized you for being Hispanic."

"Ah, now you're 'virtue posturing.' It's a thing. Look it up."

He was inordinately proud of himself. "I told you that you're a walking microaggression. They'd eat you alive on campus, or in a place like San Francisco or Seattle. Good thing you're here."

"And you're going to tell the audience at your next speech in the suburbs about tone policing and their white privilege, right?"

He gave a pre-eruption volcano laugh. "I like my job too much, Mapstone."

"Well, stay in your safe space and listen. I braced him because he refused to break out his ID. He could have been a burglar. As it turns out, he was more."

He folded his hands. "I'm listening."

"Paul Rossi, aka 'Paulie the Silencer' for his weapon accessory of choice. A soldier in the Mafia's Chicago Heights crew. Known associates include Pappa Joe Tocco and Al Tocco. He did five years in Joliet for assault before coming to Phoenix. Suspected in ten homicides of mob witnesses, never convicted. He dresses like a cowboy now but I suspect the closest thing he ever came to a cow was eating a steak. He was a retired hitman and now he's Burke's caretaker."

"Where did you get this?"

"Lindsey. Remember, the intel had it that a hitman was in town that summer of seventy-eight to do Reid? I suspect it was if Reid didn't stick to his story. But Mark was a good made man, did his time, and Paulie stayed on, working for Burke."

Peralta's pursed lips opened. "Well, tone police this, asshole. The bottom of your chair hurts because half of my ass is gone. Half of my ass is gone because I spent an hour being threatened by the Burke family lawyer. Harassment. Trespassing. A civil suit against you personally."

"And who is this mammal?"

"Ted Barrington."

Shock and anger competed for my attention. My feet felt very heavy against the hardwood floor.

"You son of a bitch," I finally began. "This is the same Barrington who snuck a court order through Pinal County to get into the Buzz Page archives. Why didn't you tell me?"

He sighed. "You're digging into very sensitive territory, Mapstone. Plenty of powerful people still don't want the Page murder connected to Freeman Burke, Sr."

"What happened to 'let the chips fall where they may'?"

He leaned on his elbows, a yellow Hermès tie wrinkling against the desk.

"You got the guy who killed three people and sent the threats. Why not declare victory and go home?"

I nervously rubbed my right ear, a stress eccentricity that came out of nowhere. "I don't believe this. We've got new evidence that doesn't merely put the Page assassination on Freeman Burke's doorstep. It kicks down the door, goes inside, and slaps the murderous old man in the face."

"He's dead, David. They're all dead. This can only bring pain to Page's family."

Peralta hardly ever called me by my first name. When he did, it was in moments of tremendous stress. I plowed ahead anyway.

"Your wife would say this will bring them closure. I don't believe in that. Never happened with my losses. But it sure as hell would bring them justice. This is one of the most heinous crimes in American history and the bastards got away with it. Killing a journalist is a direct attack on the public. The ledger shows Burke receiving and giving money to the Chicago mob. And by the way, the existence of the ledger is validated by the phone-tap transcript that Jones found when Goldwater called Norm Reardon. Reardon, Burke's main lawyer, got fifty-eight-hundred dollars and paid Mark Reid. Darren Howard was set up to take the fall."

Peralta started to speak but I held up my hand.

"It gets better. I have an FI card placing Reid at Burke's house a few days before the bombing."

He blinked fast as the revelation processed. "Why? If Reardon is acting as an intermediary."

I'd wondered about that myself. "My best guess was that old man Burke wanted to check Reid out, see if he was up to the job. He must have known that Shaky Pete Scarpelli had given the ledger to Buzz Page. And if Page broke the code, if that got in the newspapers, it was all over for Freeman Burke and half of his buddies in the Phoenix elite. Burke had to prevent that, so he selected Ned Warren's enforcer Mark Reid. But he wanted to see him in person. Reid had chickened out on the bombing on the Rez, remember. Maybe give him special instructions, too. We now have the evidence for an entirely new theory of the case, and the twisted thing is that we have Ryan Garrison to thank. He pushed us to solve the case. He put out the bread crumbs that led to the bomb shelter and Page's briefcase. How he knew about it, we'll never know. But it wouldn't mean squat if he brought it forward on his own. It had to be us who found it and cleared Darren Howard forty years later."

The Sheriff heard me out. He leaned back, smoothed the expensive tie, and laced his fingers behind his head.

"You think I should call a press conference and lay all this out."

I nodded, then walked over to study the white board.

His big head followed me like a monitor lizard. "And what are you going to do? Stand beside me grinning as the shit hits the fan?"

"I may," I said. "But there's more work to be done. We don't know what's hidden in the deepest classification of the records at the State Archives."

"It might take the Legislature to declassify them early."

"So? They're your buddies. You have favors. Call them in. See how many people want to stand behind Burke when all this comes out."

He looked as if I had dropped an anvil on him.

Then I told him about the call Rudy Jarvis made to the Phoenix Police a few weeks before he was killed.

Chapter Forty-three

Without further orders from Peralta, I drove to the State Archives. My first goal was to find what Ted Barrington had sought when he visited in May. Also, I wanted to page through the index book and get a sense of what the files held, considering I was on my own now. It would be gold to find anything on Paul Rossi or Shaky Pete Scarpelli.

At the tinted door, I saw a shadow coming from the inside and waited. When it opened, I saw Malik Jones.

"Chief Gillespie," he said in a sunny voice. "Come right in. You look overheated."

I stepped into the blessed air conditioning of the lobby. Jones was wearing a taupe summer suit, with a slim fit he could pull off, and a solid dark blue tie. I had fashion envy, wished I had worn my old Brooks Brothers seersucker today.

"Are you still pissed at me?"

"As I recall, you were pissed at me. But the answer is no."

"I was," he said.

"And now?"

He folded his arms. "Let me ask you something, David. Do you think you're a racist?"

The question didn't surprise me and I had no studied response, so, as usual and often to my regret, I just started talking. "If by racist, you mean that I think whites are superior, that I support keeping other ethnic groups from equality, that I'm only judging you by the color or your skin, no. I'm not a racist. I try hard as hell not to be. What about you?"

"You don't even get to ask that, David. There's your privilege showing again."

"So, it's all on me." I shrugged and felt such hopelessness. My voice was toneless and low. "We're so polarized right now. I don't have the answers and nobody would listen to me if I did. We all have prejudice. The question is whether we act on it. I try not to, and that includes my actions as a law enforcement officer. Am I prejudiced against people who don't read books, deny science, spread lies as 'news'—you bet."

"It's your country, David. You have the power."

"Right. I'm the same as the white supremacist who burns a black church or the oligarch who moves jobs to China. Bullshit. We have racism in our society. Things are so much better than they used to be. I thought we were making real progress until recently. Are we a uniquely evil racist society among nations in the world? You're too good a historian to believe that."

He raised an eyebrow. "Continue."

"But something evil's loose in the land, no question. I saw it here first, when my friend was voted down as Sheriff only because he was Mexican-American. All I know is if we're going to be separated in our tribes, if we're not going to strive to be *e pluribus unum*, if we don't also value each other as individuals...then it's all over." I had said way too much.

He dropped his arms and shook his head. "I don't think you're a racist, although on campus you'd be accused of having internalized racism. I do think you have your blind spots."

I thought: *I'm glad I passed your fucking purity test.* Instead, I crossed my arms.

He said, "Now, bring me up to speed."

We sat on a sofa in the lobby and I briefed him on what I had found since the shooting.

He buried his head in his hands. When he looked up, "I can't believe Peralta wants to walk away from this. Add the ledger and the key and we've revised the entire history of the Page murder. This is like finding something new in the JFK assassination."

"I'm sure somebody in the government would want to bury that, too. What have you been up to? I called and the archivist said you hadn't been here."

"I haven't been in the Page files. I needed a break. So, I wandered around until I found the Freeman and Eleanor Burke Papers."

"What?"

"Donated to the archives upon his death in 1990. Eleven Hollinger boxes on the second floor."

I let out a long breath. "Hiding in plain sight."

"That's the beauty of research. There's a bunch of nothing, or so I thought. Documents on his cattle, land, and liquor businesses. Transactions and financial stuff, taxes. It must have been a very big deal to get the liquor distribution monopoly after the end of Prohibition. There's warm correspondence between him and Samuel Bronfman, the guy who owned Seagram's in Canada and made it an international empire."

Jones opened his iPad and looked through notes.

"Letters to and from politicians. He called them by their first names. They called him 'Mr. Burke.' This guy would fit right in with today's reactionaries, only the Red Menace was at the top of his agenda. He also wrote to support certain water-rights issues, ones that benefited his land. You know his attorney was a young William Rehnquist? I read through a vanity biography he commissioned in 1975. He owned so much of what became north Scottsdale that the land alone would have made him a billionaire."

"What about Buzz Page?"

"Interesting that you should ask. He had several files of clippings, some the stories that Page wrote about him that cost him the Racing Commission seat, and others about the bombing. Among these are several While You Were Out slips with Page's name and number, from his secretary, I assume. Unclear whether Burke and Page ever spoke or Burke dodged him. I'm surprised whoever curated these papers before donating them didn't remove this."

Of course, the papers would have been sanitized. "Diaries?"

He paused and smiled. "No. But I did find calendars."

I sat forward.

"Decades of spiral-bound calendars up there. Very simple, not Franklin Planner kind of stuff. Meetings, trips, birthday and anniversary reminders, most in a neat female hand. Yes, there's 1978. I took pictures of three months of pages before the bombing and three months after. Better to ask for forgiveness than permission."

He handed me the iPad and I scanned the entries.

On May 29th, the female hand wrote two names in blue for nine-thirty p.m. The first said "Reardon" and the second was completely scratched over in black ink. It had to be Mark Reid.

"If the cops got a search warrant, they wouldn't see the killer's name," I said.

"And Reardon being there, with attorney-client privilege, would give Burke an alibi, right?"

I nodded, disappointed.

"So, what next, Chief Gillespie? How do we shake more things loose?"

The idea was instantly there.

"It's risky, but it might work. Want to take a drive?"

He stood. "Sure. But let's take my ride. No offense to your vintage Honda Prelude, but every time I see it I'm afraid it will give up the ghost at the worst possible time."

Outside, he clicked a fob to unlock a new silver Accord, two-door. I grabbed something from the Prelude, climbed in his passenger seat, and gave him directions.

He pulled up under the tree on Colter Street, marveling at the shade and me being obliged to tell him that much of Phoenix used to look like this. Then he saw the mailbox.

"Holy shit! Is that real?"

"It is, indeed."

Rossi met us halfway down the driveway. His eyes widened in surprise, and if I didn't know better, terror. He quickly recovered.

He drawled, "Mr. Freeman wouldn't want a nigger on the property."

"What the fuck did you say?" The word punched me in the gut and I coiled my fists.

I felt Jones' hand on my arm, firm.

"Now suh, don't you pay no mind to Mapstone here," Jones said, assuming a convincing Southern accent. "He's a guilty white liberal so he don't get it. Why, we call each other that and don't even get me goin' about the words in those rap songs. I could call Mapstone 'my nigga,' term of endearment, if I felt endeared to him."

"See!" Rossi nodded approvingly. "Your friend gets it. But I'm gonna make one phone call to Ted Barrington and you're gonna be busted down to jail duty, the prisoners throwing shit on you from their cells."

Based on his time in Joliet, I'm sure he spoke from experience.

I said, "Actually, I'm here to apologize. Barrington insisted on it and he's right. I was serious when I said you might have been a burglar. But we got off on the wrong foot. I'm sorry."

Rossi studied me suspiciously, then his face went slack. He straightened his posture and puffed out his chest. He had won. He started to turn and walk back but stopped.

"All right then," he said. "Apology accepted. C'mon back here."

We followed him on cobblestones around the rambler brick ranch house, one I badly wanted to get inside and toss. Out back was an enormous swimming pool, shaped like a clamshell. He indicated we should sit in the expensive outdoor furniture under a thatched veranda. A large gas grill, old but perfectly maintained, sat off to the side. This appeared the very opposite of a haunted house. He had a resort all to himself.

He rubbed his face with both hands. "Like I said, family won't allow any outsiders in the house. But I think this'll be awright. Truth be told, don't get many visitors anymore. The Burke grandkids never come. I'm surprised they haven't sold the property, but glad they let me stay."

I eased down in the cushion and said in a friendly

voice, "I know who you are, so you don't have to do the Okie bit."

He smiled wide, still not showing any teeth. It was the strangest smile I had ever seen.

"I been doin' this so long, I don't think I could stop."

"You've come a long way from Chicago," I said.

He nodded.

"Were you working for Papa Joe or Freeman Burke?"

"Both," he offered without hesitation. "And it was Buddy, by the way."

When I looked confused, he continued. "*Buddy* Tocco. His friends called him that. Papa Joe's was the name of his pizza place on Thirty-Second Street. Totally legit. But Papa Joe sounds more like a scary mob name."

"Like 'Paulie the Silencer'?"

His body tensed for a millisecond, then the smiling-clown mouth opened. "Oh, you read too much *New Times* garbage, Mapstone. After I came here, I was never convicted of so much as a parkin' ticket." Chicago and Tulsa competed in his intonations.

"The truth of the matter," he said, "was that Al Tocco sent me here to help his brother with legitimate business. Then I went on loan to Freeman Burke and ended up working for him and then the family."

"As muscle?"

"Do I look like muscle, boy?" He tilted his head to Jones.

"No, suh."

I leaned in. "Forty years ago, I can see it. Word was the Outfit dispatched a hitman to kill Mark Reid if he didn't stick to his story. You were a hitman. Reid must have had a lot he could tell."

Rossi shook his head. "There's plenty of 'word was' after that reporter was killed. Trouble is, most of it isn't true."

I asked what was true.

"It's as simple as it sounds. Reid, too big for his britches, that simple-minded Dick Kemperton, and whoever paid for it. My guess, it was RaceCo, but it's only a guess. Young Joey Cameron…" He turned to Jones. "…Joey's family owned RaceCo and he was supposed to take it over when his father retired. Trouble was, Joey was a hothead, and he was convinced Charles Page was schtupping his girlfriend. I can't say whether that was true one way or the other, but Joey was crazy enough to pay for the bombing. And Page had written plenty about the dog tracks."

He sighed, bony shoulders pistoning beneath the Western shirt, and put a hand on his left side, pushing, his face wincing. "Mr. Darren ended up taking the fall. They needed a scapegoat and RaceCo had better lawyers. Funny how that works. That's the truth. I know your sheriff loves publicity but there's nothing new to be found."

I watched the pool for a moment. A breeze rippled the top.

"What I don't get is why Mark Reid was parked outside this property on the night of May 29th, 1978, and then seen walking inside the house."

Paulie the Silencer tried to control every muscle in his body but it didn't work. His left eye nervously ticked twice.

"More *New Times*?"

"No, actually a field interview card that a Phoenix Police officer filled out that night when he found Reid parked in front."

His eye pinched again. "I want some ice tea. Mapstone?"

"No. thanks."

He looked at Jones.

"I'd be very appreciative, suh! Thank you, suh."

Rossi disappeared inside the house. I quietly said, "What happened to Sidney Poitier?"

"Go with the flow, David. We're a long way from an antifa protest."

"Hope he doesn't poison your ass."

Rossi returned with two glasses and sat across from us. Once again, Jones thanked him.

He turned to face Jones. "So, what's your story, young man? You're too polite to be the law."

I thought you'd never ask.

"It's the way I was raised, sir," Jones said in a more normal voice. "The Golden Rule. Treat your elders with respect."

"My God, what a breath of fresh air. That's how I was raised, too. My neighborhood was tough. You either became a cop, or you went on the other side. But we treated adults with respect."

I was waiting for him to launch into the made-man code of honor bullshit, but he wanted to know more about Jones. He placed his right elbow on the top of his thigh, raised his hand and set his head on it, as Jones gave an elevator speech about his time in the Army, coming here to work on his doctorate because his parents were here and getting older. His doctoral thesis on crime and race in old Phoenix.

"Doctorate!" Rossi's henna eyes twinkled. "I appreciate a learned man. My mother, God rest her soul, wanted me to stay in school, and I should have. She wanted me to become a priest, if you can believe it. Do you know my grand-nephew is a professor of urban studies at Northwestern University? I'm proud as hell of him. But Al Tocco took me under his wing. He was only a few years older than me. Died in prison. Anyway, he gave me a different kind of education."

I wondered how many people paid with their lives for that learning.

"I'll tell you this," he said. "I always got along with the blacks in Chicago and here. But the black criminals weren't into heavy stuff in Phoenix. Robbery was mostly their thing. City cops assigned investigation of robberies by race."

"Really." Jones sounded interested and maybe he was.

Rossi adjusted his body again and warmed to the topic. "Crime and race. Sounds like an interesting topic. There've always been a few low-level black gangsters in Phoenix. I heard that Hodges of Hodges Barbecue ran a wire service out of his restaurant back in maybe the fifties and sixties. Gambling, you know. Oh, Freddy McWilliams. He was a safe-cracker, who always left a signature! He'd take a shit in front of the safe before leaving the scene of the crime. John Sabari was the biggest drug dealer in the black part of town, but he was white, Italian. As I recall, he married Freddy's sister, and he and Freddy started working together. But Sabari grew up south of Buckeye. Woulda been hard for outsiders to break that world."

Jones nodded at appropriate moments, told him this was helpful. Rossi stared across the pool at the shadows under the oleanders.

"Mr. Freeman was different from me. He hated blacks, Mexes—Japs, especially. He wasn't a bad man but he was a product of his times. This was a peaceful place in those days. For the most part. Every now and then, not so much. But nothing like now, with the cartels. They adopted a lot of the Italian business models, but they have no code, no honor. If a made man played by the rules, he could do very well here and avoid the wars back east."

Jones said, "And if he didn't?"

"There were a lot of concrete foundations being poured."

"Or he ended up in a stairwell, like the accountant." I tossed this in, trying to get a rise. Was Rossi playing us?

He didn't bite.

"Never knew who killed Lazar." He shook his head. "Obviously somebody who worked for Ned Warren, keep him from testifying."

I bet he never knew.

"How did the Outfit get along with Mr. Freeman?" Jones asked, using his best innocent inquiring historian's voice.

"I would say…I didn't catch your name."

"Jones. Malik Jones."

"Well, Mr. Jones, Freeman Burke wanted to be the godfather of Phoenix. Only the Mafia, if it existed, because remember J. Edgar himself said it didn't, refused to allow one."

"But after the Apalachin meeting of 1957, Hoover couldn't deny it," Jones said.

Rossi smiled. "You know some gangland history, Mr. Jones. I'm impressed. Yeah, that was at Joe the Barber's house. A hundred Mafiosi. No denying that. Hoover still wanted to chase commies more."

I steered the conversation back to the seventies.

Rossi rubbed his chin. "How did they get along? I would say, uneasy. Mr. Freeman ran some gambling and prostitution going way back, paid off cops and politicians. He was tight with Harry Rosenzweig, so that was that. When he was a young man, he was the Capone organization's point man for liquor here during Prohibition and then he went legit with the distribution company afterwards. So, he had local power and friends in Chicago. This is the truth, Mapstone. Mr. Freeman had the juice and the money, so even if he was involved in the reporter's death, he was never going to see the inside of a jail."

Rossi leaned back slowly, as if the movement hurt.

"Now, Mr. Freeman was an ambitious man. Comes with the bootstrapping, I guess. The Wild West. He tried to muscle Greenbaum out of control of the gambling wire in the forties and got his way. This was way before my time. By the time I got here, my job was…what would you call it?"

Assassin, I thought.

"Liaison?" Jones prompted.

"Exactly, Mr. Jones. I kept Buddy informed on Mr. Freeman's doings. I'd like to think I kept things smooth."

I said, "What did Mr. Freeman think of reporters?"

"Hated 'em!" Rossi said. "He was a very wealthy man by the time I knew him. People were envious. The newspapers wrote about him, especially Charles Page. He was obsessed with Mr. Freeman, cost him the Racing Commission."

I was about to go in for the gut punch but Jones spoke first.

"Mr. Rossi, I heard Page was obsessed himself, with some kind of ledger."

The involuntary tick bit him bad this time and his color turned ashen. For a full minute, we listened to the song birds.

"Never heard that one." Quick shakes of the head. He drank from the glass of ice tea. Major *tell*.

"Wonder what was in that ledger?" I asked Jones.

"Nobody knows. This is great tea, better than what my mother makes, and that's saying something."

Rossi recovered enough to give his puzzled-sinister smile.

"Why, thank you Mr. Jones."

Jones said, "I ran across some police files on a man named Pete Scarpelli. Know where I could find him?"

"Shaky Pete," Rossi said. "I haven't heard that name

in years. He left for points unknown. My guess is he ratted out his bosses in New York and went into witness protection. I met him a few times at the bars back in the day." He swung to me. "Look, if Mark Reid was here that night, I never saw him. Can't recall I was even here. But why would a lowlife like Reid come here?"

A thought tap-tap-tapped its way into my head. Reid had to tell a story that made the conspiracy all about him, Kemperton, and Howard. He wasn't only threatened with death if he deviated. The mob probably promised him money, too. So far, so good, as far as his organized-crime masters were concerned. But he also had to tell the truth that Buzz Page was killed about something he was *going* to write, not something he had written. Otherwise, suspicion would be all over Freeman Burke, who had serious motive over losing his chance to skim the dog tracks from his seat on the state Racing Commission. That Page *had written*. And that little blurt of truth didn't matter unless the cops knew about the ledger, which was the basis of a story that would win Page a Pulitzer and kick the rocks over in Phoenix showing some very prominent bugs. Finally, we had the ledger.

"Mr. Jones, bear this in mind," Rossi said, "if the mob had killed Charles Page, he would have been warned first. They all were, even Greenbaum repeatedly. Especially Gus. He made 'em lots of money in Vegas. But he couldn't kick the horse addiction or stealing more than his share. The reporter might have been warned more than once, and not only with a phone call. Something that would really get his attention. But I don't think that ever happened. So, I go back to crazy Joey Cameron. Didn't Page say 'RaceCo' when they were pulling him from the car?"

I looked Rossi straight on. "He also said 'Mafia.'"

The Chicago cowpoke didn't take the bait. He said, "Americans love mobsters. Look at *Goodfellas* and any gangster movie. But the government nearly destroyed the old organized crime families with RICO. The fathers didn't want their kids going into the family business. Not many happy endings in the underworld. One of the worst things that happened was John Gotti, Sr. You never wanted to be flamboyant. You wanted to be in the shadows and make money. The world changed, too. Gambling became legal all over the country. Liquor, too. The people who used to go to the Mafia for money can get loans at the bank. Supply and demand, gentlemen. The demand went away. Folks moved out of the old neighborhoods into the suburbs, too. Italians who could once only make money in the mob became accepted in regular society. They have the same opportunities as anybody. So, business dried up and the life lost its allure."

He stared past us for several moments, lost in the past. "I'll tell you this, when I was a made guy I felt such freedom. I do miss that. But being a caretaker for the Burkes is a lot safer."

I pushed again. "So, it's gone in Phoenix?"

"Far as I know," Rossi said. "The kids all went legit. New York, Philly, and Chicago, that's another matter. But the cops are way more sophisticated now. It's not worth it. If I was starting over, I wouldn't be a priest. Maybe computers."

I set aside a fleeting suspicion—what if Rossi was behind the Garrison rampage? What if he did know computers? It was too far sideways to make sense.

"Well, hypothetically," I said, "would a reporter have been warned? I thought that was a courtesy for a made man?"

Rossi's dark red eyes tracked between me and Jones, back to me. "Hypothetically, I guess it depended. The code was, don't kill reporters or cops. Bad for business."

"But if the mob felt such a threat from a reporter, would they have warned him? Hypothetically?"

After a long pause, he shrugged. "I'm an old man. Never thought I'd make it this long when I was young and stupid."

I left Rossi my card, in case he remembered anything else.

"I won't," he said.

Later, sitting in Jones' Accord, I said, "Did you get it?"

He pulled the slim tape recorder from his suitcoat pocket and clicked it off. He rewound and I heard the conversation.

Jones smiled. "Yes, suh."

Chapter Forty-four

Warnings.

Signs.

Omens.

Years ago, I had a lover who wasn't who she claimed to be. Her name was Gretchen. In the end, when I discovered the deception, I was pretty sure she was a murderer. To her, the killing was justified. And I let her go, even though murder is never right, never justified. Ever since, with greater or lesser degrees of anxiety, I have wondered when she would come back. But, as Mark Twain said, history doesn't repeat itself, but sometimes it rhymes.

Gretchen floated in and out of my head as we drove back, playing and replaying the tape, unpacking the truth, lies, and in-betweens of what Paul Rossi had told us from underneath Freeman Burke, Sr.'s, veranda. Arizona was a state where clandestine taping was legal so long as one of the parties to the conversation—Jones, in this case—consented. Whether it was admissible evidence was doubtful, but we were working for history now as much as for the law. Clouds were boiling up from the northeast and the southeast. A storm might come in tonight.

We both talked.

I filled in first. His romanticizing of the Mafia was misleading and incorrect. Plenty of innocent people died at their "honorable" hands: shop owners who failed to pay protection money, gamblers and loan-takers who got in over their heads, potential witnesses, and made men who tried to leave the life.

But I kept thinking about my next-door neighbor at Thirty-sixth and Campbell streets. "Page was warned," he said. "They always warn you." Having lost his father to a Mafia bomb, he would know. And yet, we hadn't found any evidence about Page being warned.

I was pretty sure Rossi was slinging lies when he said Joey Cameron was behind the bombing. His father was in the ledger, faithfully handing over skimmings to bagman Pete Scarpelli. RaceCo was a target of Page's previous reporting, yet it wouldn't benefit from his death. Indeed, heat from the Attorney General and the investigative reporters came down on it hard.

In my mind, it came back to Freeman Burke *and* the mob, more so now that we had Burke in the ledger and Mark Reid FI'd outside Burke's house a few days before the bombing.

"Page didn't name Burke in his last words," Jones said.

I nodded as the wide, bland expanse of Twenty-fourth Street rushed past. How much can you get out after your body is shattered and your brain has been compressed in a way never intended by nature?

Jones said Rossi's reaction to the ledger was interesting. Reardon knew Buzz Page had it. That meant the mob and Freeman Burke knew, as well. He said, "Maybe he's afraid we have it. I'd love to know how Tom Goldstein got that key and why he didn't do something about it."

"It's possible he didn't know about the ledger," I said.

"Probable, even. He might have speculated but couldn't turn it into evidence. Plus, everything we keep finding indicates that the powerful wanted the investigation wrapped up and buried. But Goldstein knew it was important, so he kept it."

"Waiting for you to walk in the door." Jones made a right on Washington and pointed us toward the skyscrapers.

"Or us," I said, and told him the story of thirty-six righteous men required by the Lord to keep the Earth from destruction. "Maybe you're the righteous man."

"You sound like my grandmother. She talked about the Lord telling Abraham that he would spare Sodom and Gomorrah if just fifty righteous people lived there. Abraham bargained Him down to ten. But there was only Lot, and we know the rest."

"Maybe Lot's wife was the first historian."

Jones was silent for a long time. Finally, he talked about the tension between the Mafia and Freeman Burke that Rossi laid out. Could they have been at odds about how to handle Buzz Page? Maybe one or the other wanted to do a break-in and steal the ledger back rather than kill him? Did they disagree about the risk the ledger posed—Page didn't have the key, after all. So who made the decision to assassinate Page, and that he was such a threat that he had to be killed? On the other hand, we will never know some of the most important things about the reporter's investigation: what was in his head.

"We're only playing hunches now," Jones said.

I asked him what else we could do. We weren't going to get three years to go through the case files in the archives meticulously—at least not on the county's dime. I had a few loose threads but otherwise we needed to force Peralta's hand.

By the time we reached the parking lot of the State Archives, Jones was determined to dive back into the Page boxes. I went to the Prelude and hoped his malediction toward it didn't come true anytime soon.

•••••

In the car, I called Lorie Pope and brought her up to date.

The pause was so long I thought I had lost the connection. Then: "Oh, my God, David! You've cracked it! Darren Howard's offspring coming back for frontier justice! That's so Phoenix freak-show gothic. All he needed was to be selling some real-estate hustle, too." In my briefing, I left out the part where I shot Ryan Garrison. She continued: "I never knew about a ledger. And I don't care what your old mobster says, I think it was Burke who ordered the hit."

"Tell me how an investigative reporter would work on something like this?"

She walked me through it. First, corroborate the material, make sure it was authentic. With the source being mob bagman Pete Scarpelli, this was a sure thing. Scarpelli probably also told Page about some details of the transactions, such as where the money came from—illegal gambling, narcotics, prostitution, protection, you name it, and where it went, including bribes to useful politicians. Then talk to friendly sources, such as cops and ex-cons. At this point if not before, editors would be brought in and planning would commence about how to handle the story. The newspaper's lawyers would be consulted for libel or other legal issues. Finally, with the story nearly ready to publish, would come the hostile interviews with people such as Freeman Burke and Papa Joe Tocco.

"The trouble is that Page didn't have the key that identified the people in the book," I said.

"I know," she said. "He would have been digging for that. Based on what you found, the Mafia and RaceCo, and Burke would have known he had the ledger. Page was a marked man."

"Did he know it?"

"He might not have cared. For one thing, he was parked out at the Legislature as part of the legal settlement with RaceCo over his earlier reporting. One story was potentially libelous. Truth isn't necessarily a defense in a libel trial. What I'm getting at is that Front Page might have avoided telling his bosses he was working on this until he had it airtight. He might have been cultivating this Scarpelli for months before getting the ledger, or it might have fallen into his lap. Any info on what happened to Scarpelli?"

None, I told her. If he went into witness protection, the feds would never tell us. Based on Lindsey's research, he virtually disappeared. Or they caught up with him and, in Rossi's telling, was one of the bodies entombed in a tract-house foundation.

"Was Page warned?" I asked.

"You mean by the bad guys? Not that I know of. Wait…"

So I did. When she spoke again, her voice was agitated.

"Six months before Page was killed, his girlfriend died in an auto accident. Fuck! How could I have missed this?"

"Tell me more."

"Cindy Hodges. Page was very sweet on her. She was driving eastbound on McDowell at the intersection with Grand and Nineteenth Avenue, where the railroad tracks cross…"

I knew the place. It was north of the mouth of the old Santa Fe Railway Mobest Yard, now Burlington Northern Santa Fe.

"It was after sundown and there were no crossing gates. A southbound freight train came through and she pulled right in front of it. The train wasn't going very fast, but it was a train. And she was driving one of those deadly Ford Pintos. The train hit it and dragged it, the gas tank caught fire. Cindy and her daughter, three years old I think, were both killed."

"Witnesses?"

"Only the train crew. The warning signals were working properly. The engineer thought Cindy's car might have been pushed into the grade crossing, maybe by a pickup truck with its lights off. But he couldn't be sure, he was pretty broken up about the whole thing, and nobody else saw it. The cops chalked it up to distracted driving."

"How did Page react?"

"I heard he was devastated, but he threw himself even more into his work." After a pause: "I know what you're thinking. Was this aimed at Cindy's boyfriend? I don't know. But what you've uncovered so far is amazing, David. It makes me wish I were a reporter again, although there are only a handful of newspapers left that would even go after this story. Peralta's got your back on this, right?"

Now it was my turn to waste the digital air with silence.

"David?"

"I'm here." But I had the vision of the map on Goldstein's wall.

Here be monsters.

Chapter Forty-five

That night, we were lashed with dust, wind, and rain. Lindsey and I sat curled up together in the living room and watched out the big arched picture window as the brown cloud blew through, wind swayed the trees, and a rain bomblet soaked the lawn. The lightning shot straight down or spidered across the sky, breaking into tributaries stunningly bright against the darkness. She flinched slightly when the thunder pounded down, giving me an excuse to hold her closer. This night, the storms were more normal—in Midtown, at least. In the morning, I learned that a real rain bomb—one of climate change's gifts—flooded parts of Mesa and Tempe, while winds left thousands without power. The local news didn't mention how climate change was altering these timeless weather patterns.

It couldn't avoid the fire up north, which had doubled in size and was nowhere near being contained. Smoke jumpers were deployed from around the West. Gretchen had been a smoke jumper. The ferocity of the fires was climate-change, too, the forests so dry from prolonged drought and vulnerable from the bark beetle. No writing about that, of course. It might upset the car dealers and sprawl homebuilders who were advertisers. But the newspaper said the smoke was drifting toward Phoenix. I already could tell. Lindsey was coughing, saying she felt it in her chest.

By ten that morning, the two of us were in the southern neighborhoods of Scottsdale. It was far in every way from the new money, plastic surgery, and golf that were now synonymous with the suburb's name. It sucked every piece of life out of the city that it could, but it still wasn't even a poor man's South Beach or Beverly Hills.

Instead, these were tract houses built in the late fifties and early sixties, when the American middle class was headed toward its zenith. When Scottsdale was still a little town, not too far removed from its farming roots—its namesake, former Army chaplain Winfield Scott introduced citrus trees to the Valley—and downtown was a cheesy but endearing combination of "the West's Most Western Town" and a real town, with local shops like Lutes' Pharmacy and places like that Baptist church where Lindsey and I cavorted on a night that seemed years ago.

We were near Coronado High School, where my first real girlfriend Julie graduated. Like so many, her father worked for Motorola. Coronado was a grand mid-century modernist creation of the famous Phoenix architect Ralph Haver. Famous among the little tribe of local history buffs, at least. Torn down now, of course, replaced by the dead prison design of Arizona schools, the deep-water irrigation campus shorn of its trees and grass. This was "south Scottsdale" now, the solid middle-income area turning Hispanic and uneven, some houses still beautiful, others fading. Coronado, once one of the top high schools in the nation, was now considered a distressed "inner city" school as Scottsdale's center shifted far to the north. Revival was happening at the old Los Arcos Mall, which had been leveled and turned into an ASU innovation outpost called Skysong. Like everything in Phoenix, it was basically a real-estate play. The newspaper said it was a big success, which made me suspicious.

The address we sought was on Seventy-second Place a little south of Oak Street. Oak was the continuation of Encanto Boulevard east of Central. Otherwise, the street grid was pretty much the same as Willo, with Almeria, Coronado, Granada, Palm Lane, Holly, Monte Vista, and Cypress. A number of years ago, a man killed his family nearby and for good measure blew up his house. He was still on the lam.

This was another Haver design, with the distinctive long pitched roof and wide windows facing the street, very different from the bland ranch where Kathy Jarvis lived. Haver delivered panache, even for buyers of average means. Some of the nearby homes had succumbed to gravel and rocks but this one sported a lovely, well-maintained lawn with a hefty healthy palm in front and mature shade trees in the back. The grass was still puddled from the rain last night. The place was pleasant but nowhere near as fancy as the redone Haver next door, expensively restored and landscaped, with a leafy deck added above the carport. It certainly didn't fit with Rudy Jarvis' Ferrari, but maybe he knew the architectural treasure he owned.

A little boy, maybe four, answered the door. Lindsey bent down and asked his name and soon they were engaged in a lively conversation. My love would have made a wonderful mother. A few moments after an adult voice told us she was coming, a thirtysomething woman emerged into the living room. She was willowy, with a conventionally pretty face and light brown hair, pulled back in a ponytail. Emily Jarvis was Rudy's widow and her fine features were caved in by grief.

She saw our badges and invited us inside, saying over her shoulder, "I have talked to so many cops this last month, I can't imagine what else I can tell you. Let me get him settled down." She led the little boy off to another room amid laughing, shrieks, and reassurances. He didn't understand the fullness of his loss yet.

She returned to the toy-scattered living room, sitting across from us in a rigid posture.

"You people caught the man who killed my husband, right?"

"We did. He's dead."

"So it's over, thank God."

We didn't say anything.

"I'm not going to say I'm sorry," she said. "He was a monster. What would make a person do that to an innocent man?"

I asked her to tell us about Rudy. He was four years older. They were married in 2010. Rudy made a good living as a pool contractor, doing custom homes. He never had trouble with the law. He was the teenager who didn't do ecstasy, didn't go to hookups, didn't follow his best friend in boosting cars, a pastime that landed the friend in prison. Rudy went to Coronado and this had been his parents' house. They lived modestly, saving for their son's college. The Ferrari had been his birthday indulgence. "I would much rather the car be his midlife crisis than leaving me for some blond cheerleader type." Her voice caught.

"Had he been followed or contacted by anyone suspicious?" I asked.

She looked down and to the left, the classic *tell*. "No," she said. "I didn't even know he had received that threatening text until you people told me. Oh, my God, I wish he had. I wish we could have talked it out and decided what to do. We always talked things out, made big decisions together. But he didn't. He thought he was protecting me."

I said, "Would you mind if I went in the kitchen and got a glass of water?"

"Of course not. Glasses are in the first cabinet to the right of the dishwasher. Want me to get it?"

"I can manage," I said. "Excuse me for a sec."

I went into the nearby kitchen. Out the arcadia door was a shady pool surrounded by a fence. A mongrel dog watched me silently from the other side of the glass. I took my time, pulling out a tumbler, using the icemaker, and pressing the cold-water button on the door of the refrigerator. I was about three-quarters through my miracle from the Salt River Project when I heard a loud cry from the living room, followed by heaving rounds of sobs. Lindsey had played good cop to tragic perfection.

When I went back in, Emily Jarvis was in Lindsey's arms. It took at least ten minutes to put her back together. I sat silently and waited. Luckily, a box of Kleenex was on the table.

Her face was deepened into a landscape of unbearable heartache. *Closure*, my ass. With Lindsey's arm around her, she rocked forward and back, talking haltingly.

"Rudy was a good, good man. You need to know this. We had the spats every married couple does. But he never hit me, never cheated. He doted on Henry. He didn't know who his father was until he was eighteen. Kathy debated with herself whether to tell him at all. He said I was the only other person he ever told, told me when we got serious. That was how much he loved me."

A car went by outside, taking the curve too fast. Then she continued.

"About a month before he was killed, a man came to the door. He was very well dressed, gave us his card. A lawyer. Sat where you are now." She nodded at me. "He said that Rudy was about to come into a large sum of money. It had been held in trust for Mark Reid's children and would be dispersed on the fortieth anniversary of the reporter's death. He needed proof of Rudy's identification, his birth certificate, and a DNA sample."

"What did Rudy do?"

"He threw him out. I'd never seen him so angry. He called it blood money and said the man could go to hell."

More crying. Then: "You have to understand. This lawyer told us we couldn't speak about this or we would face severe legal liability. That's exactly how he put it. I thought Rudy might have overreacted, considering how powerful this man seemed. You see, we were working-class kids who had built something together. We didn't want Henry to have the struggles and worries we did. I didn't want some lawsuit to take all that away." She blew her nose in a working-class way. "After…after my husband was murdered, I was afraid to mention it. Who could I trust? Now I guess I have to trust you."

Lindsey said, "Do you have the man's card?"

"Of course." She reached for her purse and handed it to Lindsey. She reached it over to me.

I read: Theodore Barrington, Esq., Attorney at Law. Partner. Boyce, Hiatt, and Elliott P.C.

Outside, two men in suits were waiting on the sidewalk. They were in cheap suits with the unfortunately contemporary features: flat-front slacks and too-short coats. Both were Anglos in their thirties, matching wraparound sunglasses, and bulked up with brush cuts and nasty expressions. My insides tightened as one approached me, closing ten feet rapidly. I thought: mob.

"You're wanted," he said and poked me hard in the sternum. He poked again, harder.

I sensed Lindsey taking a step behind me. My heartbeat slowed. I said pleasantly, "Guess what, genius? You just assaulted a Deputy Sheriff."

I grabbed the offending finger and bent it backwards until I heard bone snap. He screamed. I stepped close, put my right foot behind his left calf and pushed. He went down hard and sprawled out onto the wet grass. Like many weight-room guys, he lacked balance and nimbleness in a streetfight.

His partner started to reach inside his jacket.

"Gun!" I shouted.

"Don't even think about it." Lindsey had her Glock out, aimed at his head.

He held his hands up, while his buddy froze despite continuing to whimper.

"Quiet," I said, producing my .45. "You're lucky I didn't break the other four fingers."

"Is everything okay?" It was Emily's timorous voice behind us.

"Mommy, the lady has a gun!" Henry shouted with a combination of wonder and curiosity.

Without turning away, Lindsey commanded, "Get inside. Call the police. Stay down on the floor and away from the windows."

The door whooshed shut.

"We're DPS! DPS!" This from the standing wraparound.

"Keep your hands up and get on your knees," Lindsey said, taking a step closer but still out of his reach.

"The grass is wet!"

"I'm not going to ask twice," she said.

When he was down, she told him to produce his credentials. "Ah, ah, ah," she said. "Use your left hand. And do it slowly."

He awkwardly reached into his suit, opening a leather badge case with the seven-point star of the state Department of Public Safety. It was a much better-looking badge than our six-point star or Phoenix's big shield copy of the LAPD badge. But cartel members or other bad guys—and girls—could easily procure them. I said as much.

"We're real," he said. "We're on the Governor's Protective Detail. He wants to see you."

The first Scottsdale Police cruiser came roaring down the street from Oak, so I took a minute to process that. Then I holstered my gun and produced my badge, holding it high so the cop didn't get itchy and open fire on all of us.

Chapter Forty-six

Thirty minutes later, Lindsey and I got in the Prelude and headed south on Scottsdale Road, both quiet in our thoughts.

For me, it was the growing realization that the more we shook this poisoned tree, the more serpents fell out. Kate Vare said Rudy Jarvis tried to reach the police, but his message was lost in the bureaucracy. Now, having talked to his wife, it was clear Jarvis wanted to tell them he had been contacted by Ted Barrington, telling him he was about to inherit money from his father. I wished he had heard the lawyer out. Why now, after forty years, was Mark Reid's son about to receive a large amount of money? Barrington kept showing up like a bad case of the clap: Carrying a court order allowing him into the sealed records. Warning Peralta about reopening the case. Then complaining about me bracing Paul Rossi. What was Barrington's stake in all of this? It was more than protecting the reputation of Freeman Burke, Sr., deceased.

I thought about Buzz Page's girlfriend, Cindy. Her death was suspicious, to use an understatement. How did Page react? Did he go to the cops? I thought about my own reaction. I wouldn't back off the story, no way.

I would want revenge, the same way I did when Lindsey was shot, when Robin was killed.

"Dave." Lindsey's voice was calm. "Did you have to break his finger?"

"I didn't know who he was. Why didn't he identify himself?"

"I don't know."

We were at least rid of the two gubernatorial bodyguards. They were off to the hospital.

"You're very angry, you know that." Her voice wasn't accusing.

I agreed that I was.

After a moment: "I'm sick of the lies. Almost everybody seems to want to keep this case buried, even after all these years. Why? So, yes, I'm angry."

She put her hand on my thigh.

At the wide sunblasted intersection of Scottsdale Road and the Red Mountain Freeway—"the 202"; only I seemed to use their names—the In-N-Out Burger stood temptingly on the other side.

"God, that looks good," she said.

"Screw it." I shifted lanes, drove under the freeway, and we stopped for lunch. The Governor could wait. Lindsey only liked her fries when they were hot. Fortunately, in this weather, the dashboard provided a heat lamp to keep them that way.

●●●●●

I called Malik Jones on the way. He told me of a few finds. For example, the first search warrant executed on Mark Reid's place after his arrest found a small notebook, a log of Buzz Page's comings and goings. Reid was following him for two weeks before the bombing, including the day of the attack. He noted the stop at Union Station. Did Reid notice that Page went in with a briefcase and came out without it? The notebook didn't say.

I gave him a quick update from our end, promising more after the meeting with the Governor.

"Governor?" he said. "Watch yourself, Chief Gillespie, I have a bad feeling about this. Most days I have the strong conviction that you and I are the only ones who actually want to solve this mystery."

I agreed.

He kept me on the phone. "Go back to the movie." It took a few gear-slips for me to realize he was talking about *In the Heat of the Night*. "In the end, the killing was partly about the big factory the northerner wanted to bring to town. About the diner owner who robbed the victim to get abortion money for his girlfriend and accidentally killed him. Nothing was what it seemed. It wasn't only about the little Southern town and its grudges. It was about big money and the future. Think about that, Chief Gillespie."

The Executive Office Tower was built in the mid-seventies directly behind the charming territorial capitol building with its copper dome. The result was to put a tan brutalist shaft in the spot most designed to maximize its offensiveness. I set my architectural grievance aside as we walked in and presented ourselves to the front desk. They asked for our weapons. I even handed over my backup gun.

Almost immediately, a young woman in a smart gray

suit and disappointing flats came into the lobby to greet us. With her was Peralta, wearing a severe expression.

He grabbed my arm and pulled me in.

He whispered, "You broke a state trooper's finger."

"I would have done worse," I said. "Here's the thing. New information. Your buddy Barrington showed up at Rudy Jarvis' house before he was killed, promising him money."

I watched his curiosity and sense of political duty duel, five seconds, ten.

His grip tightened to painful. "The Governor is waiting."

"What's this about? I smell something…"

"Hear the man out. Keep your mouth shut. Follow my lead."

I was about to say more but stopped. After all these years, I was still a little afraid of him.

He released me. The young aide's frozen smile had never changed. She led us to an elevator and we went to the ninth floor, as high as you could go.

"Please put your phones on silent," she instructed.

The Governor was shorter than me. Score one for Dave. He was also younger than me. Lose points. It says something when Governors are now younger than me, and nothing good. Introductions were made. When he noticed Lindsey and I had the same last name, he paused and smiled.

"We're married," she said.

"Neat!" came his response. He was one of the businessmen-turned-politicians favored by the Republican Party, with a helmet of dark hair, and a navy suit and red tie. He guided us to a low sitting area adjacent to his desk. The heavy coffee table was full of picture books, copies of *Arizona Highways*, and, suspiciously, my two books. His office was decorated with flags, photographs, awards, and Indian art. It was less impressive than Peralta's suite at the Starship except for the view—downtown Phoenix through big windows.

"I want to say, it's an honor to meet you, Dr. Mapstone."

"David is fine, Governor," I said, forcing a pleasant face. "I'm not a physician, dentist, or veterinarian."

"Or a chiropractor," Lindsey added.

He laughed. "Well, whatever you want, David. You performed a very brave act in taking down that cop killer and solving this crime. There's nothing worse than a bomber, the anonymity and randomness of it. Terrible." He shook his head.

I suddenly remembered: according to *New Times*, his father was a police officer in Dayton but dad's in-laws were part of an infamous Ohio organized crime family. I wondered if he spoke from some personal experience before he changed his last name, moved West, became an entrepreneur, and cultivated a Norman Rockwell image. At least in my part of blue Phoenix, plenty of people disagreed with his politics but nobody thought he was mobbed up. Now, with my hoodlum radar on high, I didn't know what to expect.

He kept talking. "To recognize your bravery, I've signed this proclamation on behalf of the people of Arizona." He nodded to the aide and she handed me a framed document with several "Where As" paragraphs.

"Thank you, Governor. It was a team effort. I wouldn't be here without Malik Jones."

"And I plan to honor him, too." He shifted his posture to face Peralta.

"So, it's over, right Mike?"

Peralta cleared his throat. "No, sir. We've discovered important new evidence in the Page case."

The answer sat there like a steaming pile of manure.

"Such as?"

"Such as Darren Howard was innocent. He was framed. And it's very likely the murder was ordered by Freeman Burke."

The Governor had been sitting on the edge of the sofa. Now he sat back and unbuttoned his jacket. His expression was pained.

"Why are you doing this, Mike?"

"It's my job, sir."

He nodded and smiled sadly, spreading his arms on the sofa back.

"We both have jobs, Sheriff. We answer to the voters. We're both practical men."

I tensed but felt Lindsey surreptitiously dig her thumb into the side of my leg. *Stay cool, Dave.*

He continued. "Nobody really knows what happened forty years ago. No one can know. Not me. Not you. All the main participants are dead, including Darren Howard. If you open this can of worms, who knows what might happen? I can see the state facing a wrongful prosecution lawsuit by Howard's family. Yes, this bomber was related to him. But he was also a combat veteran and could garner public sympathy as suffering from post-traumatic stress disorder. Then throw in your contention that Howard was victimized by this state…"

"It's not a contention, Governor," Peralta said. "We have hard evidence. This is why my detectives, people like Mapstone, work on cold cases. And a man having his name cleared is no small thing."

"You really believe this?"

"I do."

He hunched forward and cupped his hands. Tension wafted across the room like the air conditioning.

He raised his head, speaking to each of us in turn. "I don't need to tell you that Arizona was one of the hardest-hit states by the Great Recession. Coming back has been tough. But good things are happening. With my low-tax, light-regulation policies, we're taking jobs from California. We're the place to invest. We're seeing a high-tech renaissance…"

He continued but I silently poked holes in the campaign speech. California was keeping and expanding its high-end job base, Arizona was still a back-office and warehouse operation, low taxes helped make a crisis in the public schools, with the worst working conditions for teachers in the country.

"…Dredging all this up again can only hurt out national image," he said.

Lindsey pushed hard with her thumb again and in the nick of time. I didn't say what occurred to me: This is exactly the conversation the bigs had forty years ago when they made a commitment to bury this case instead of pursuing it to the dark headwaters. Jones nailed it. The year before the Page bombing, President Carter had indicated he would cancel the Central Arizona Project, the grand enterprise to bring Colorado River water to Phoenix and Tucson. Without it, the astronomical growth that followed would have been impossible. The big profits for the real-estate industry, too. That was it. As Phoenix was thrust in the national spotlight by the assassination of a reporter, newspapers across the country telling about the mob and corruption tolerated in our sunny state, the CAP hung in the balance. The leaders had to show they successfully prosecuted the crime and "cleaned up" the state. I felt sick. In hindsight, without the CAP, most of my Eden would still be here and four million more people wouldn't.

"I can't let that happen," the Governor announced. "And I'm sure you'll agree on reflection. I've spoken to the Attorney General, and he agrees. We're going to revoke your access to the sealed case files. And I expect you to turn over your new work within a week so it can be properly handled."

Buried.

He stood and we left without handshakes. I was at the threshold of the office suite when I heard his voice.

"David, don't forget your proclamation." He held out the frame.

"You keep it, Governor," I said. "So it can be properly handled."

When I was downstairs, Peralta stomped ahead without looking back at us. I didn't chase after him. Pulling out my phone, I unmuted it and saw a message. It was a call from Paul Rossi.

Chapter Forty-seven

It was full dark when I pulled up in front of the Burke property. The location dropped the temperature by ten degrees, allowing me to turn off the engine and roll down the window. I only had to wait five minutes before a big SUV parked behind me. I got out as a burly member of Peralta's protective detail opened the back door and the Sheriff stepped out.

"We're not supposed to be here." His dark eyes blazed at me. "*You're* not supposed to be here. Barrington warned you."

I leaned against the Honda and attempted nonchalance. "We were invited here tonight. And what is it with you and Barrington? Does he have a photograph of you fucking a goat?"

The doorman-Deputy stifled a laugh but went gravestone stiff when Peralta shot him a look.

"Barrington's firm is involved in the federal case against the department," he said. "You know, what that turd Crisis Meltdown left for me to live with. He can make plenty of trouble."

"And he's the mouthpiece for the Burke family."

"That, too."

"But you said this is a white-shoe firm. Who handled old-man Burke's dirty legal business?"

"Norm Reardon," he said. "But you already know that. Anyway, you were told to stay away after you barged your way in here."

"I've been back and talked to Rossi again..."

"I can't believe you. It's a wonder we're not in court facing..."

"Shut up and listen."

Surprisingly, he did. I told him about my second visit and how Rossi admitted me to the estate, opened up a bit, how I left my card and he called today, saying he wanted to talk more.

"Well," he said, "let's go."

"Leave the goon squad here."

He waved Deputy Burly back into the SUV. Then the old mailbox caught his eye. In the ambient light, he walked to it, running his fingers across the letters FREEMAN BURKE, as if to make sure it was real.

It was. We headed up the driveway, around the house, and to the pool. Landscape lights gave a magical cast to the palm trees and hedges, the pool was lighted, a broad turquoise expanse—it took me back to old Phoenix, circa 1978. Lightning was flashing in the velvet black southeast sky. The poolside overhang was softly lit with strings of small overhead bulbs. Paul Rossi was small in a wicker armchair, tucked into a robe, bony legs and ankles sticking out. His face looked gaunt, his eyes sunken. Maybe it was the shadows.

"Hello, David. I didn't realize you'd bring your boss."

Peralta stood there like a redwood.

"You and I met before, Sheriff. Years ago, you were a Detective on an organized crime task force and you questioned me."

"I don't recall," Peralta said.

"Probably as well," Rossi said. "One of my talents was that people never remembered me. And I never sang. Where's Mr. Jones?"

"He's working." Before they throw us out of the State Archives.

"That's too bad. I wish he were here tonight."

He beckoned us to sit and we did. He said one of the benefits of being the Burke caretaker was using the pool. When he was younger, he'd swim laps every day. Now he came out at night and floated around, sat here, and watched the monsoon storms come in. Then his voice changed.

"David, you asked me if I got lonely here and I said I didn't. That was true for a long time. You know, I had a dog, lived to be eighteen, that's long for a dog. Just a mutt, but she was the sweetest thing you could imagine. Showed up as a little puppy. I named her Ginger. She was the best companion, never judged me. One day, I don't know why, she went across the street. Coming back, she was hit by a car. It broke her back. By the time I got there, the car was long gone. Didn't have the courtesy to stay and help. Lot of times, a dog gets badly injured it has the instinct to bite you. Not her. I picked her up and she licked me, rubbed her muzzle against my hand. Nothing could be done. Had to put her down."

I said I was sorry.

"Me, too. At the vet, he showed me how some of her back toes were gone. Shorn off. She'd done it dragging herself across that asphalt. I wondered why. And I realized, she was trying to get home. In that pain and terror, all she could think of was to get back here, get home, to me, and everything would be all right." He was quiet a long time. "God, I miss that fucking dog."

Then: "That's when the dreams started. The faces. Every night. I couldn't stop it. Went to the doctor and got pills. They didn't stop the dreams."

"Who were the dreams about?" I asked.

"The people I killed."

Peralta jumped in. "You don't have to talk to us."

"I know my Miranda rights, Sheriff. I can recite 'em by heart. Anything I say can be used against me in court. I have a right to an attorney. If I can't afford one, blah, blah, blah. God, I miss that dog." Now the old cowpoke was sounding pure Chicago.

"I whacked twelve people for Albert," he said. "Witnesses, mostly. One who robbed a protected liquor store and shot the owner. I was fine with it then, never gave it a second thought. Until the dog died. In my dreams, I see their faces at the exact moment they knew. They *knew*. It was over. Paulie was there, the hand of fate, and they were done. And every goddamned one of 'em, every face, only wanted to get home. Same as Ginger." He let out a long breath. "I'm so tired of those dreams."

"Maybe if you gave us names and dates," Peralta said, "it would give the families some closure."

That word again.

"Maybe," Rossi said. "Whatever you want."

"Did you murder anyone here?" The Law West of the Mazatzal Divide was interested in case closure in his jurisdiction.

"No." Rossi pulled the robe tight. "You know, I went to confession today at St. Thomas the Apostle. First time since I was seventeen. They say confession is good for the soul. Do you believe that?"

Peralta gave a non-committal grunt. Criminals lie. They manipulate. I was afraid Peralta would run out of patience and shut Rossi down. But he sat still.

"Can't say it made me feel better," Rossi said. "The church has changed a lot since I was a kid. Maybe I did it for my mother. She hated it when I went to work for the Outfit, said I was ruining my life. Before I left Chicago and came out here, she begged me to stop." With the lightning sketching the thunderheads behind him, he continued slowly. "She told me I had to repent, that she'd had a dream where someday I would be visited by two avenging angels, one white and one black. When that happened, she said, it would be my last chance." He sighed. "I forgot all about that until you and Mr. Jones showed up here."

The wind picked up and Paulie the Silencer finally sang.

In November 1976, Rossi arrived and did odd jobs for Buddy Tocco, including overseeing various rackets, from vending machines to heroin, and picking up the skimmed money from Greyhound Park earmarked for the Outfit. Rossi was glad to be out of the hitman role. Only occasionally did he have to pistol-whip a recalcitrant pimp, bar manager, or loan customer. He met Mark Reid for the first time at the track, where he not only bet and took his dates but owned dogs. Rossi wasn't impressed, even though Reid worked for Ned Warren. "He wanted to be a made man but I didn't trust him." Rossi carried cash from lawyer Norm Reardon to Buddy, too, origins unknown.

1977: Buddy assigned Rossi as go-between with Freeman Burke. He liked the old man, with his hardness and austerity, "like the Marlboro Man only he drove a Cadillac." The tensions between the richest man in Arizona and the mob went back decades, to when Burke wanted to take over Gus Greenbaum's gambling wire. But the Outfit needed Burke for his political connections and the share of earnings from Burke's liquor distributorship. Burke was stubborn and always wanted more. Throw in the dog track owner RaceCo., where the Outfit had its tentacles, too, and things got even more complicated. The Toccos needed Rossi to finesse things, keep the peace.

This was the year when Rossi first became aware of Charles "Buzz" Page, the *Phoenix Gazette* reporter. As the biggest contributor to Raul Castro's successful campaign to become Arizona Governor, Freeman Burke wanted to be appointed to the state Racing Commission. Castro obliged, probably not realizing the old man wanted to use the perch to expand his influence over the dog tracks. Influence meant more of the skim, the track proceeds before they were officially accounted for. It was going behind the Outfit's back, or at least that's how they saw it. Page solved the problem by writing several articles about Burke's unsavory side, forcing him to resign. Rossi read other Page stories in a thick file Buddy Tocco kept, where the reporter had exposed Warren's land frauds and the rising Mafia presence in Phoenix.

"I never met the man but I was impressed." Rossi kept his hands rested at his sides. So much for the stereotype of the gesticulating Italian. "He was easily as good as the best mob reporters in Chicago. But Freeman hated him. Freeman was a good hater."

Rossi's wife left him that year, taking his son and daughter back to Chicago. "It was my fault," he said. "There was so much pussy then. The sex in this town was unbelievable. I didn't look like I do now. And I was a soldier, a real made guy, in the Life with money and cocaine, and the women found it irresistible." Among his duties were managing fuck pads for top Arizona politicians and businessmen. Rossi even had his own fuck pad.

In late 1977, Pete Scarpelli disappeared. Scarpelli was

the Outfit's most important bag man in Phoenix. He was responsible for bribing the top Phoenix politicians, businessmen, and cops. The most favored also received no-interest loans from the Outfit, large sums, sometimes so big they came out of the Teamsters' Central States Pension Fund, which was a piggybank for the mob. He usually delivered Freeman Burke's cut of money from the rackets he shared with Chicago: untaxed revenue from whorehouses, bars and the taxicab company Burke secretly owned, drugs, protection money for two dozen businesses, gambling, and, of course, the dog tracks. It was a big flare for the Toccos because they knew Scarpelli maintained a record of each delivery in a ledger. The ledger used codes to identify each party, but Scarpelli probably also had the key. Rossi did a black-bag job and searched Scarpelli's apartment. All his clothes were gone and the ledger wasn't there. Nobody had whacked or kidnapped him. The best guess was that he had ratted them out to the feds and gone into witness protection. "Everybody was paranoid," Rossi said. "Buddy ordered some serious questioning of Pete's friends and his ex. They didn't know."

1978: In February one of the detective-analysts in the Intelligence Bureau at Phoenix PD told Buddy that Buzz Page had the ledger and was asking the cops about it. But did he have the key? Nobody knew. Rossi did another break-in, at Page's place—no ledger. But based on his questions to the cops there was a real danger he would figure out the payments and write about them. "We called him. Warned him," Rossi said."

"What about his girlfriend?" I asked.

He shook his head. "We had guys following her so she'd notice, try to scare her."

"Push her into a train?"

"That wasn't supposed to happen. One of our guys, a crazy Mex, came up fast behind her, spooked her, and she drove right into the front of the engine. They were the only two cars at the crossing, her and him, so he got the hell out of there."

Freeman Burke was enraged when he found out about the missing ledger. He was prominently featured among the entries. And his anger grew when it became clear that his old nemesis Buzz Page probably had the record. Page was quietly interviewing people, but word got back.

"Burke wanted the reporter dead."

I asked what happened next.

"Buddy refused to do it. A lot of the old rackets were dying anyway. We were finding new places to invest, legitimate land deals and savings and loans. It was the future, but Freeman was living in the past."

Peralta said, "But Page was killed."

"Freeman did it on his own. I tried to talk him out of it. You don't clip a reporter. But he wasn't that kind of man, not once his mind was made up. He already had a grudge against Page over the Racing Commission. The ledger was the last straw." Rossi paused and watched the sky, the lightning drawing closer, the wind rippling the top of the pool. He tilted forward, grimaced and messaged his middle with his left hand.

"To tell you the truth, I was a little under the old man's spell by this time. I was supposed to be Buddy's spy, but I felt my loyalty torn. Freeman Burke had, what would you say? Charisma."

With the help of Norm Reardon, Burke enlisted Mark Reid to kill the reporter. He wanted it to look like a mob hit, and Reardon said Reid was good with car bombs. Reid got his tag-along buddy Dick Kemperton to push the detonator. "Kemperton was stupid," Rossi said. And Reardon asked Darren Howard to handle the payment to Reid. "Didn't tell Howard for what, but that it was a favor to Freeman. Howard worshipped Freeman Burke, felt he owed him for giving him his start in business. So you had your three conspirators." He shrugged. "It was a damned fool thing." Still, even Buzz Page was convinced that either the Mafia or RaceCo was to blame.

"Mark Reid was here, at this house." Peralta said.

"Oh, yeah," Rossi said. "Freeman wanted to size him up, see if he could pull it off. I was afraid he'd fuck it up, but he put on a good front. Turns out, I was right. He didn't use enough dynamite, placed it wrong under the car. If he would'a done it right, we wouldn't be sitting here right now, would we?"

"But there was still the problem of the ledger," I said.

"The ledger, the goddamned ledger…" Rossi muttered. "We figured it'd get blown up in his car. But our friends on the force told us it wasn't there."

Peralta said, "Tom Goldstein?"

"Oh, God no," Rossi said. "That Jewboy was one of the clean ones. Tony Peterson, Lonzo McCracken, Oscar Long, Cal Lash, J.C. Wesley. They were the untouchables. But we had plenty who were touchable. And we never found the ledger or the key. Or Pete, for that matter. If he would have gone to the local FBI, we would have known. See, we had an agent there in our pocket, gambling and drug problem. If Pete would have gone to the Bureau, we would have killed him. But he went to the reporter. Buddy was so fucking mad, and pissed at me personally for letting the bombing happen. I warned him that Freeman was going to do it but he didn't believe it. I'm lucky he didn't take me to an abandoned mine shaft and put a bullet in my head. But he didn't. I think one reason was that Albert had pity on me. In fact, the decision went all the way up to Joe Batters in Chitown."

"Tony Accardo," I said. "Aka "Joe Batters," aka "Big Tuna." The Outfit boss."

"Very good, David. You know your Mafia history. I think what finally saved me was that it didn't look like a Mafia bombing. Even the feds could see that. So, I got to live. But I lost my privileges, which meant my income streams. Eventually I went to work fulltime for Freeman, then the family, after he passed. It was a good thing. Took a long time to burn those years out of me."

He stopped and appraised us. "But something tells me that David and Mr. Jones found the ledger."

"And the key," Peralta said.

The wide clown smile appeared on his face for the first time that night and he laughed until his middle hurt so much he bent forward and moaned. That was the first time I saw the glint of silver between his robe and the side of the wicker chair, within reach of his right hand. I slowly slid out my .45 and kept it out of sight.

Rossi said, "You know they'll never let you make any of that public. The Burke family won't allow it. They were big contributors to the Governor and Attorney General. If you do have the key, you know how many powerful people were dirty. Some of 'em are still alive. The dead ones' families won't let you sully their beloved reputations, either."

"You're wrong," Peralta said. "It's all coming out."

For the first time since our audience with the Governor, I felt better. Or I would have, if Paulie the Silencer wasn't concealing something at his side that looked like a gun.

"Good luck," he said. "I hope you do it."

I said, "Why did Burke think he could get away with it, that Reid wouldn't roll on him?"

"Money," Rossi said. "Simple as that. It was a perfect crime, when you think about it. The plan was for Page to be blown up, end of story. When that didn't happen, and Reid's initial alibi of being at Lake Havasu City fell apart—Reardon worked hard to get him out of town, but he came back and blabbed. Anyway, what made it perfect was you had Reid, Kemperton, and Howard. A conspiracy. All Reid had to do was stick to the story that Howard was the mastermind who hired him. If he did that, Freeman would set aside a million dollars for when he got out of prison…"

"But he was going to the gas chamber," I said.

"That was never going to happen, David. Freeman had too much money, too many favors. Reid got a deal, went to prison, did his time, stuck to his story. It helped that Freeman made Reid believe that the Outfit had sanctioned the hit and would kill him if he told the truth."

More things were clarifying in my head. I wished I could indulge in putting them together. Instead, I needed to focus on a tactical solution to an old man who was armed.

Peralta said, "It wasn't perfect. The murder brought down investigative reporters from around the country. It spawned forty years of conspiracy theories. And the case was never closed."

"All true, Sheriff. So, it was good enough. Freeman Burke died in his bed. Don't you get it? The most powerful people in the state wanted an excuse to bury it, and Reid's story gave them that. They could prove Arizona was clean, justice had been served. Otherwise, no Central Arizona Project, no continued growth, a lot of worthless desert real estate."

Jones was right.

"I have a lot of questions," Peralta said.

"I know you do," Rossi said. "But those are the only answers I have. There's things about this mess that will never be resolved."

Peralta raised his Glock and pointed it at Rossi's middle.

"Then maybe you'll tell me what's sitting beside your right hand?"

"This." Rossi slowly held out a nickel-plated .38 Chief's Special. Only five rounds but enough to kill. He held it with his index finger in the trigger guard.

I told him to put the gun down. He didn't.

"I've got pancreatic cancer," he said. "You know the survival rate? About seven percent. And mine is advanced. I'm not going to end up in some stinking nursing home, covered with my shit, in constant pain so bad I can't even remember the beautiful women I could have by snapping my fingers in a Midtown bar. Fuck that. I gave my confessions today. Now it's up to you and God."

I had my .45 on him, too. "Put it down, Paul. No suicide by cop tonight."

He stared in his lap and then, in one quick move, palmed the gun and placed it against his right temple.

"Don't," I said. "The Lord is merciful."

He said, "The Lord is just," and pulled the trigger.

The result was instantaneous and unarguable. I looked at Peralta. He shrugged and holstered his weapon. I shut off the tape recorder in my pocket.

The storm was closing in, whipping the palm fronds, and swaying the oleanders. It began to rain, hard drops, first a few, then a downpour, hammering the top of the pool like gunshots. I knew we had a long night ahead, but right that moment I only wanted to be home, with Lindsey. I had to settle for a text.

Chapter Forty-eight

In the Old West, the Sheriff stepped into the street to face-down the outlaws. In the New West of Phoenix, the Sheriff stepped in front of the television cameras to facedown the Arizona establishment. Thanks to Lindsey, he was armed with PowerPoint.

Malik Jones and I stood beside him on stage at the Starship as Peralta said we had new evidence in the murder of *Phoenix Gazette* reporter Charles Page. A new theory of the case. We would offer new details, including things withheld from defense attorneys in the original trials. Jones and I took it from there.

It was two weeks after our meeting with the Governor. Although Peralta was prepared to have the County Attorney get a temporary restraining order to allow Jones continued access to the Page files in the State Archives, it never came to that. He revealed to me that during our time as private investigators, he had done more than favors for the politicians who ruled the state. He had collected copious amounts of dirt: kickbacks and bribes from private prisons and charter schools, under-the-table money from developers who wanted water waivers to build where there was no water, the sexual indiscretions on the part of the most moralizing legislators. The intelligence swept up the Governor himself and Ted Barrington. Peralta had turned himself into a modern-day J. Edgar Hoover. They backed off.

Now, we laid it out. The mob ledger given to Buzz Page. All he needed was the key to write the most important story of his career, how organized crime had penetrated the city's power structure and members of the police force. We had the key and we named names. Chief among them was Freeman Burke, Sr. Not only did we have Paul Rossi's pre-suicide, first-hand account, but Jones had found a receipt. It was from Norm Reardon, received from Burke one week before the bombing, totaling fifty-eight-hundred dollars. "For services to be rendered."

Burke knew he was in the ledger and Page was to be killed for something he was going to write, not as "frontier justice" for what he had written. He ordered the hit to prevent Page from writing about his illegal payments detailed in Pete Scarpelli's neat, diligent handwriting. Mark Reid was at Burke's house, to be vetted and receive final instructions. The reporter's last words were only partly correct. Mark Reid, yes. But neither RaceCo nor the Mafia were to blame this time. The Outfit told Burke not to do it. When he did, they were blindsided. So was Senator Barry Goldwater, although he was also in the ledger.

"If we knew this at the time," Peralta chimed in, "Freeman Burke would be facing a murder charge. Several people in the ledger would be under investigation for tax fraud and conspiracy."

I saw Kate Vare sitting among the reporters. She smiled at me. I had burned the place down sufficiently. Tony Peterson and Jack Wesley were there, too, nodding in satisfaction as we ran through the highpoints.

There was no question that Darren Howard was framed, an innocent if gullible man. There was a conspiracy, but not the one put forward by prosecutors. It was much larger and more monstrous than even the conspiracy theorists imagined.

We were lawyered up. Despite Ted Barrington's threats, it was impossible to slander a dead man, much less one who had for decades been loudly suspected for ordering the hit.

Some things might never be known: What was in the stolen Phoenix Police 851 files, how Tom Goldstein found the code key to the ledger and why he kept it after he retired, the full story of the state taking over the case and burying it as quickly as possible, despite all the holes and unanswered questions.

Other details had come clear. The baggage lockers at Union Station, for example. We tracked down the last living station agent, who confirmed that Page often stopped by and used a locker, for which he paid a monthly fee, made conversation. The locker bank was removed later in June 1978—train travel had declined so badly—and hauled off to J.C. Penney downtown. No, they didn't check the contents. What was the point? The man didn't make the connection to Buzz Page until our conversation. He cried. The locker key was blown a hundred yards away from Page's car and was missed by the police evidence sweep. A hotel worker found it that evening and called his friend, a Sheriff's Deputy. That would explain how it ended up in Peralta's file boxes. At the time, it wasn't clear to the previous Sheriff that it was even connected to the crime, but best to save it. Thank goodness, he did.

After a half hour of questions, it was over. Aides distributed a bound fifty-two-page white paper, glossy cover with the Sheriff's Office Star, on what we had found, including an Excel spreadsheet Lindsey had compiled on the ledger. Burke alone had received almost a million dollars in tax-free gangster money. Within an hour, it was the top national news story. The press was dying, but it wasn't dead yet.

"Are you saying the Page case is solved?" a young *Arizona Republic* reporter asked.

"Yes," Peralta said. "I'm sorry it took forty years."

I walked with Peralta back to his office, his bear-like arm around my shoulder. Lindsey followed us. Jones was gone.

"Did you ever doubt me?"

"No," I lied.

"So, I'll leave you to your cold cases. We need to keep clearing them. But take the day off. Homemade Mexican food at our place soon." He turned to Lindsey. "Thank you, beautiful. And I remember: Don't ever piss off Lindsey."

She flashed an angelic smile. "Correct."

He gave me a rare, rough *abrazo*. Lindsey got a more natural hug, disappearing momentarily within his large frame. "It's a good day for law enforcement, kids."

He went inside his office suite, we walked the other way.

Zora Neale Hurston said, "There are years that ask questions and there are years that answer." This was a year that finally answered.

• • ● • •

Afterward, Lindsey and I walked out of the Starship and found Malik Jones standing in front of the bronze *They Served Well* sculpture, studying the expression on the horse's face. The sky above was brown with smoke from the wildfire, which kept growing. But two men standing downtown in crisp suits, starched shirts, shined shoes, and stylish ties. We looked *good.*

"Press conference went well," I said.

"Did you have to call it a white paper?" His expression was grim. Then it morphed into a wide smile. "You did it, David. Congratulations."

"We did it." I risked patting him on the shoulder. He gripped my arm in friendship.

I was emboldened. "You know, you ought to propose a different thesis. Write about this case in the context of power and politics in the emerging Sunbelt. You uncovered new sources, new information and insights. It would be a best seller."

He smiled. "Too white, too, male, too cispatriarchial."

"It doesn't have to be," Lindsey said. "You have the beginnings, not the final product. I bet there are plenty of stories of women, minorities, marginalized people."

Jones crossed his arms. "Maybe."

"Think about it. You didn't seem too jazzed about your original topic."

He shimmied left and right. "Now you has jazz, jazz, jazz? Any other free career advice you want to dispense?"

"As a matter of fact, yes," I said. "Finish your doctorate, publish, get academia out of your system. I think I know you well enough to say you won't like it, especially today. Intellect, wit, and savoir faire, plus a commitment to the truth. That's you. A West Point graduate. In an environment where other-thinking people are not welcome. You're a walking microaggression, whatever your skin pigmentation."

He chuckled in a rich baritone. "I've worried about that."

"Well, I'm not going to be here forever. You should go through the academy, become a deputy, take over as the Sheriff's Office historian someday."

"I like it," Lindsey said. "Dave and I can ride off into the sunset."

"Whoa!" He struck a hands-up-don't-shoot pose. "Next you're going to give me the speech about changing the system from the inside."

"Yes, actually."

He lowered his hands. "I don't think so, Chief Gillespie. This is the scene where you take me to the depot, we part as friends, and I get on the train headed north. You say, 'Virgil, you take care, you hear?'"

"Okay," I said. "You take care, Malik, you hear? But think about what I said."

We shook hands. I almost—almost—saw his eyes tear up. We had a great run. I would miss him.

"You two be good," he said. "And watch out for those lawyers. Gillespie and Tibbs never had to deal with them. I'm going to marry one but she's the rare exception to the rule."

I was about to congratulate him and renew that invitation for us all to have dinner at Cypress Street, but suddenly I felt a funny jolt.

I said, "Did you tell me that Norm Reardon did some legal work for Mark Reid?"

In the firehose of information coming at us, I had forgotten.

"Not Reardon," he said. "Bobby Bell. He represented him in his 1975 divorce. Reid lost custody of his daughter."

"Daughter." Lindsey almost growled the word. "He had two children. Rudy Jarvis and the daughter."

I remembered when Jones said we needed to go backward and forward—back into the Page case and ahead now to protect potential targets of Ryan Garrison. But there was another forward. The story didn't end with the convictions of the trio. It continued. Mark Reid was paroled in 1996 and died in 2004. We never investigated those years. We never accounted for a daughter who might have made contact and gotten to know her father.

Lindsey said, "What's the daughter's name?"

Jones shrugged.

Her drop-dead blue eyes darkened to lapis. "The daughter will inherit all Reid's money. That means she had every motive to kill her half-brother. Or manipulate someone else to do it." She took my hand. "I want to go home."

Chapter Forty-nine

Lindsey's iPhone rang at exactly nine that night. She let it go through three rings before she answered.

"Hello, Beth."

"Hi, babe. Have you got me on the speaker phone? Hello, David."

Lindsey held up her hand.

"It's only me. You must have a scratchy connection. I texted you hours ago."

"I'm not in town," she said. "But you know that, don't you?"

"I do."

We sent a marked unit to check Beth Sleigh's condo in Ahwatukee. It was unoccupied and had a "sold" sign out front.

"I'm out of the country, in fact. Don't bother trying to trace the call or find a location. You're not as good as me."

Through the speaker, I heard some wind in the background.

"Probably not." Lindsey was typing, bringing up multiple windows on her Mac. "Why would you worry about that? You were cleared."

"Because you have a suspicious husband, and he's probably finally figured out that I'm Mark Reid's daughter, and that might lead to all sorts of harassment by the Sheriff's Office."

"Actually, I figured it out," she said. "It would have been good to know earlier."

"Did I hurt your feelings, babe? Sorry, genuinely. I actually thought about asking you to come with me. Together we might have been world-beaters. But you're shackled to your older man. And you have that good girl character flaw, from growing up where you had to be the adult in a chaotic household."

"Tell me about your growing up, Beth?"

"My parents divorced when I was very little. My mother remarried, a nice man, much nicer than my evil mom, and he adopted me. I took his last name. This was in Southern California. It was an all-American upbringing, only we were broke most of the time."

"But you were curious about your real father."

"Yes. My mother refused to discuss it. When I was eighteen, I paid a private detective to find my birth certificate and my biological father. That was when I learned he was the infamous Phoenix bomber."

"And that intrigued you."

"You know me, some. Yes. I visited him. These kinds of reunions can go one way or the other. No guarantees. But we hit it off. He was nice to me. I saw myself in him, in the good parts of him. I don't expect you or your judgmental husband to understand. When he was released from prison, I saw him regularly. He lived a quiet life, working in an auto-body shop. Nobody knew who he was."

"Did he talk about his crime?"

"No, and I didn't ask him. He paid his debt to society, as they say."

Lindsey let the connection hang for a few seconds.

Beth finally asked, "Are you there, babe?"

"I am," she said. "But you must have resented him. You grew up poor, never got to go to college, ended up working in County IT fixing computers."

"It all worked out," Beth said, again through a gust a wind. "I resented my mother. She always ran down my stepfather, sabotaged him. It kept us one step removed from white trash. But I learned how to use my looks to open doors for my natural skills. Like you."

It was a world-class mind fucking. Lindsey appeared unperturbed.

She said, "And you knew some big money was coming your way from Mark Reid?"

"What if I did? All I knew was that a million dollars had been given my father by a wealthy patron in Phoenix, a legal gift with taxes paid. It was put in a trust with a San Francisco wealth-management firm, which invested it quite well, especially in technology stocks like Microsoft and then Google and Amazon."

"No strings?"

"I wouldn't receive the trust until forty years after the reporter bombing, and unless Darren Howard was officially cleared of being part of the conspiracy."

I sat down. My feet felt numb. Lindsey typed slowly, clicked the trackpad.

"That's pretty specific, Lindsey said, "considering your father never talked about the crime."

Beth said, "I learned about this last year from a Phoenix lawyer named Barrington. He said my father wanted me to be well off, but at an age where I wouldn't do the stupid things he did. My father also felt bad for Darren Howard, who was innocent. And I know where your lovely mind is headed. You suspect that I used my feminine wiles to lure poor Ryan Garrison into a scheme to pressure the authorities to reopen the case, clear Howard's, name Freeman Burke as the mastermind. That's so sexist and shallow, babe."

Lindsey sat back. "So, it was happenstance?"

"It was. I met him at the fortieth anniversary event at the Clarendon. Do I prefer well-endowed and sexually proficient younger men? Do they find me attractive? Guilty as charged. Did I cause Ryan's crime spree? No."

I scribbled on a pad: They met earlier, witnesses placed someone who looked like Beth at Ryan's apartment. Neither was on the guest list. Snuck in? Why trying to seduce older cops there, including Peralta? Impersonating Cronkite journalism student/faculty? Ophelia Pond.

"I don't recall seeing you on the guest list," Lindsey said. "Who was this Ophelia Pond?"

"What, babe? You cut out."

Bullshit, Lindsey mouthed to me. She repeated the question.

Beth laughed. And said nothing.

"I have a couple of older cops who said you came onto them, the Sheriff, too," Lindsey said. "That doesn't sound like a cougar. Maybe you were going to try the soft entrapment. And if that didn't work, then Ryan could be manipulated or turned loose for the hard stuff."

"You have a very vivid imagination, babe."

"How else could you get your money, Beth? Howard had to be *officially* cleared. So, the threatening text to the Sheriff that couldn't be traced. The very advanced malware delivered for him to plug into the department's computer system. It allowed Garrison to break out of jail. Very few people have the skills to do this, especially with such panache. Not Ryan, whatever stuff you put on his laptop. Then there was the storage locker. The only people who knew about that were Buzz Page and Mark Reid, who followed him. And he told you about it, that it might contain valuable evidence if it was still around. My guess is Ryan Garrison was in love with you and would have done anything for you. And you used that right to the end. You sent him out into the mountains that night, promising him you'd be together and have all this money. Meanwhile, you'd stay and play victim, moxie your way out of it. Your best hope was Ryan would be killed."

One-thousand-one, one-thousand-two, one-thousand-three.

"You ought to write mystery novels." Her tone dropped an octave and had none of its usual flirtatiousness. Then, back to normal. "I spent hours being interrogated by the police. I was cleared, the victim of a kidnapper, a monster."

"Why did this monster have it in for Rudy Jarvis?"

"Too bad you can't ask him. He never told me. He was obsessed with this case."

"And Shakespeare."

She laughed. "The time is out of joint. O, cursed spite. That I was ever born to set it right. Nay…"

"But only you knew that Rudy was your half-brother and stood to inherit from your father's trust, too. If he were alive. Rudy only told his wife of his parentage. His mother told no one. Either your father or Ted Barrington told you that you'd have to share. Beth doesn't like to share."

"You're talking crazy, Lindsey. I've always wanted to see justice done. Are you off your meds?"

"I don't take meds. How much?"

Beth paused. Then: "Thanks to wise investment, the trust was worth eighty-three-million dollars. It hit an offshore account in my name yesterday.

Yesterday? That seemed odd, considering the press conference announcing our findings was today. Unless…

"Look," Beth said, "if I wanted to be rich, I could be a black-hat hacker. They'd never catch me…"

"Yeah, I thought about that," Lindsey said. "I wondered about it. Why would she do this, hurt and kill these innocent people, when she could make as much selling her computer knowledge?"

"And what's your theory, babe?"

"Bad character, *babe*."

Suddenly, the full screen of the MacBook was a live shot of Beth, standing on a ferry crossing a body of water, broad daylight, framed by a wall of skyscrapers. Hong Kong, Victoria Harbor, fifteen hours ahead. It was *tomorrow* there.

"What the fuck?" Beth yelled.

"Hi, Beth," Lindsey said. "Say hi, Dave."

I leaned in and put my arm around Lindsey. "Hi, Beth."

"So fucking what?" she said. "You're better than I thought. You can't prove a thing."

"Are you on your way to do a Snowden?" Lindsey said. "Nah. Not even a pretense of nobility from our 'Sly.' You're going to sell your skills to the highest bidder. Pyongyang's very cold."

"You're not so smart, bitch." She spat the words at the phone.

"Smart enough."

I was distracted from Beth's fine, if rattled, features and the spectacular scenery behind her by a keening sound. It took a few seconds for me to see the police boat speeding toward the ferry with siren going. It hove into clearer view and I saw Chinese characters above all-caps English POLICE.

"You can't do this, Lindsey. I'm an American citizen."

Lindsey looked at her increasingly distraught expression.

"Do you hear me, Lindsey??" Her head was twitching between the smartphone screen and what was happening behind her. That lovely blond hair blew in the breeze. Four Hong Kong police officers in light-blue shirts, dark slacks, and peaked caps quick-stepped onto the deck and moved toward her. Onlookers gawked.

"You make too many assumptions, *babe*," Lindsey said. "Like, assuming your passport is still valid. I learned a few things at the NSA."

"You wouldn't!" She screamed as two cops seized her. The phone screen tilted as she fought to keep the connection.

"Get your hands off me! I'm an American citizen! Lindsey! No! Don't leave me alone here! I love you."

"You wouldn't know love." Lindsey gently closed the laptop.

She looked at me. "I do."

Paying My Debts

This is a work of fiction. As with all the David Mapstone Mysteries, it is informed by real events in Phoenix history. Blame me for any errors, inconsistencies, and deliberate changes in names, procedures, descriptions, or timing.

I am especially indebted to David R. Foster, Virginia Foster, Cal Lash, Oscar Long, Dave Wagner, and the late Jack August, Jr., whose death too young is a calamity for the study of Arizona history. They were patient with my questions, always illuminating in their answers. We all owe the remaining investigative reporters in America, who in real life put everything on the line, trying to keep truth alive.

The Poisoned Pen Press is a national treasure. My editor Barbara Peters is rightly considered the finest working in the mystery field. I've been most fortunate to have her guidance through most of my novels. I'm also grateful to Robert Rosenwald, president of the Poisoned Pen Press, and an excellent staff.

My biggest thanks go to readers, librarians, and independent bookshop owners. You are an author's dream come true.